Love Notes

From Bestselling Author

STACI HART

Cover design by **Quirky Bird**

Photography by **Perrywinkle Photography**

Editing by **Jovana Shirley, Unforeseen Editing**

Book design by **Inkstain Design Studio**

To those who have survived the storm:
Here's to finding sunshine
after the rain.

Happiness, not in another place but this place...
not for another hour, but this hour.

WALT WHITMAN

Love

Notes

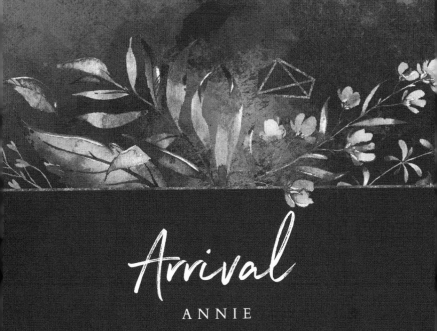

Arrival

ANNIE

The first thing I recognized was the Chrysler Building.

I think I noticed it because of how it shone, the sunlight setting it ablaze like a silver beacon in the midst of a maze of steel and glass. There was nothing else I could compare it to, certainly not anything I'd seen in Texas, and the truth was that I hadn't been anywhere else.

I reached for my little instant camera, adjusting the settings before aiming it at the city and clicking the button. It spat out the familiar white-framed photo, black in the center where the memory would appear.

Meg's mouth hung open, her eager ten-year-old eyes as big and wide as ping-pong balls as they bounced across the horizon.

"Whoa," she breathed. "It's so … *big*. It takes up the whole sky."

My face was close enough to the window to feel my breath against my cheek when it rebounded off the glass, my own eyes as big as Meg's as they did their best to drink in everything I saw like I'd been thirsty my whole life.

"How many square miles is it?" Meg asked.

"Let me look."

I reached for my phone, glancing at Mama. She was less impressed than Meg and me, the normally invisible lines between her brows and the corners of her mouth pronounced. For her, it was a homecoming, one that was as unwanted and unwelcome as it was absolutely necessary.

My older sister, Elle's, expression was unreadable, her hands on the steering wheel and gaze in front of her as she drove us toward the Lincoln Tunnel. The only betrayal of her sadness was reflected in the rearview mirror, buried in the depths of her eyes.

I pulled up Wikipedia and read through the city's statistics. "Manhattan itself is twenty-two square miles, and one-point-six million people live there."

"*Whoa,*" she said again, her breath fogging up the window. "How big is San Antonio?"

A quick search and a brain-crushing second later, I said, "Four hundred sixty square miles and one-point-four million people."

"No way." Her eyes were still on the horizon. "There aren't any trees."

"Probably only in Central Park."

She frowned. "Can I climb them?"

I offered a smile, but it was sad. "I don't know, kiddo. We'll find out."

Meg sat back in her seat and unfurled her map of Manhattan, marked with a red marker at places of her interest and blocking of sections of the city for a purpose unknown to me. She dug her old calculator out of her backpack and, lost in thought, began punching out numbers and jotting down notes in the corner of her map over the Bronx.

There wasn't much to see in Boerne, my little hometown just

outside of San Antonio in the hot Texas Hill Country. It was beautiful in the way wild country was—with scrubby mesquite trees, rolling grasses the color of a sun-faded paper bag, and forests of oak with pine-lined spring rivers. The area boasted the only hills to speak of in the entire state. Those hills were rocky and craggy, the definition of untamed land, making it easy to think back a hundred years, two hundred years, and imagine what it was like to live on the frontier.

But when you lived your whole life in a place like that—one untouched by time, one that never changed, even when you did, even when you lost the things you held most dear—it sometimes didn't feel like *enough*. You could feel your insignificance in that sort of place.

I was reminded of the time my family drove down to Galveston to go to the beach. I'd stood at the shore and dipped my hands in the gritty, silty sand, letting it slip through my fingers as I considered how small I was. I realized my life was just a single heartbeat in the life of the universe.

The world was infinite, and I was not.

You see, my heart was full of holes.

The one I'd been born with destined me to a life indoors with my family, my books, and my music to keep me happy. It stopped me from running barefoot through the fields behind our house, like Meg. It prevented me from tubing down the river with the kids my age. It restricted me to a life of physical inactivity, so I put everything I could into occupying my heart and soul and mind instead.

The hole in my heart where my father used to be wasn't so easy to accept. People kept telling me I would survive his death just as I survived my physical condition—with patience and acceptance and that ever-marching time. Part of me believed them.

The rest of me knew better.

My only comfort was a vow I'd made from a pew in the tiny church somewhere far behind me; I would honor my father's life by living mine.

I thought I'd been doing just that. I'd read thousands of books. I'd spent even more time with my fingers on ivory piano keys. I'd visited every spot on the globe through Meg's voracious explorations with thanks to National Geographic and the internet. But as we drove into New York City, I realized I hadn't seen or done anything at all.

That would all change soon enough. I was eager and ardent, armed with a list of firsts to check off, diligently jotted in the notebook in my back pocket where it had been since Daddy died.

Through the tunnel we went, under the Hudson, into the city. Meg and I were the only ones who spoke; the car had otherwise gone silent since the city came into view. She busied me with questions I could only answer with the help of the internet.

When was the Lincoln Tunnel built? 1934. *How did they build it?* With enough difficulty that the lead engineer died of a heart attack at forty-one. *What kind of metal is on top of the Chrysler Building?* Non-rusting stainless steel.

And on and on.

Unlike the silent front seats, I was happy to fill the air with something, anything to separate us from the truth of our feelings, which followed us like a balloon nearly out of helium, hovering too close to the ground to be joyful.

It took us an hour to get to the Upper East Side where my uncle lived, passing so many people, so many streets, so many buildings that the magnitude of the city set my mind spinning. Through Central Park we went, looping around Madison to Fifth Avenue, the park on one side and beautiful old buildings on the other.

My heart skipped and skittered as Elle pulled to a stop in front of the building where we'd live now that we had no home.

A doorman in a forest-green suit that matched the building's awning smiled amiably, moving to open Elle's door and mine at the same time.

"Hello, ladies. Might you be the Daschles?"

"Yes," I said with a smile as I took his offered hand and stepped onto the curb.

"Oh, good. Mrs. Jennings has been anxiously awaiting you. I think she's called down a dozen times."

I laughed.

"This hour." He winked and snapped to attention, following Elle around the car to the trunk. "Name's George," he said, touching the bill of his hat with two fingers. "Oh, let me get that, Miss Daschle."

"Thank you." Elle stepped back as he unfurled Mama's wheelchair.

Meg slid out of the seat and into my side, her lips together and hands twined, her eagerness gone so completely, it was as if it had never existed.

George unloaded our suitcases as Elle helped Mama into her chair, but when he closed the trunk and I caught sight of Mama's face, I found it touched with pride and pain and a smile that didn't reach her eyes.

He rolled all four of the suitcases to the door with the four of us in his wake. The elaborate foyer of the building was a landscape of marble and mirror and soft lights and glass fixtures, like a palace out of a fairy tale, lavish and rich and utterly alien.

When we were in the elevator, George asked about the drive and what we'd seen. Elle dutifully answered him, but the rest of us were turned so inward, we weren't listening. But when the elevator doors opened, we found ourselves in a tornado of chaos.

The door in the entryway to the penthouse swung open, and half a dozen barking dogs bounded out, tails wagging and tongues lolling. Behind them was our aunt Susan, her cheeks high and flushed, hands clasped at her breasts. None of her attention was paid to the dogs as they jumped and licked and barked in a chorus.

Meg knelt and threw her arms around a golden retriever's neck, her smile wide and eyes shining. A little Maltese hopping around my feet was too sweet for words. I had to pick him up and let him lick my face.

The comfort and joy I felt was immediate, second only to the hug our effervescent aunt gave me.

"Oh, I've just been waiting for you all day. I've nearly driven myself mad. I think I fluffed the couch pillows a thousand times," she cooed as she rocked me, holding me against her soft body.

I felt like a child, warm and protected and right and good, and I found I couldn't stop smiling or shake the feeling that I might also burst into tears.

She leaned back, proudly looking me over before moving to my sisters. We were still half in the elevator, though Elle had managed to push Mama into the entryway.

Susan greeted Mama last, kneeling in front of her with her eyes full of tears and a smile on her face.

"Oh, Emily," she said, holding Mama's hands in hers.

"Hello, Susan." The words trembled. So did my heart.

"I'm sorry. I'm just so sorry."

Mama didn't answer, just looked down at their hands; her chin flexed as she nodded.

"Well," Susan said as she stood, not dwelling, not pressing, "I am so happy to see you, I can barely stand it. Come, come in. Let me show you around." She ushered us in, the dogs running around our feet like a rolling ocean of fur.

George put our suitcases inside, and with the tip of his hat, he left.

"John!" Susan called. "John, they're here!"

My uncle walked in, tall and handsome with hair the color of graphite. His hands rested casually in his slacks pockets, and the smile on his face merrily crinkled his eyes. "Oh, I heard. I'm sure the whole building heard," he said on a chuckle, stopping in front of us to look us over. "It's only been a few weeks since the funeral, but it feels like ages." He turned to Mama, kneeling like his wife had.

"Thank you so much for this, John," Mama said.

"Please," he offered gently, "I've been trying to help for years. I'm just glad you finally accepted."

We had no choice, Mama's eyes said.

He squeezed her hand and stood. "We've been hard at work getting your rooms ready. And by *we*, I mean Susan."

Susan laughed at that. "It's true. My children are all grown and gone, and I find myself so very *bored*. Redecorating was a welcome distraction, and now, I'll have your company to occupy me." She pulled Meg into her side and smiled conspiratorially. "And I'll have someone to eat cookie dough and ice cream with. Mr. Jennings hates sweets; can you imagine? I'm convinced he's not human."

Meg smiled back, though her lips were together, her spirit muted.

We followed Aunt Susan through the massive house, through rooms that felt rich without being overbearing or stuffy. The living room with its tall windows and grand molding, framing views of Central Park below. The library with every wall packed to the ceiling, which was so high, a ladder on a rail was necessary to reach the top shelf. A large room that seemed to have no purpose other than to house the grand piano. My heart *ba-dumped* at the sight of it, my fingers itching to brush the cool ivory keys, my ears perking with imaginings of the rich sound they would make.

But Susan didn't stop, just chattered on, sweeping us through the house. We met the cook and the maid, who both had friendly faces that wore warm smiles, though they said nothing. It was impossible to; Susan filled the air in her genial way, in the way you felt compelled to be silent and attend without frustration, as it seemed to come from her very heart.

The bedrooms were on the other side of the house, she explained

7

as I tried to grasp how a home of this beauty and magnitude existed at the top of a towering building.

Our rooms lined a hallway that dead-ended, marking the end of the eternal space.

Susan had repurposed and redecorated all the rooms with each of us in mind. Her cheeks rosy and face alight, she told us of the details and watched our expressions for our approval. And approval there was.

Meg bounded into her room, her excitement found at last and bubbling out of her. A four-poster stood in the middle of the space with a beautiful old world map hanging over the head of the bed. One wall was lined with bookshelves, which seemed to be geared toward exploration, stacked with almanacs and National Geographic books, encyclopedias and atlases, books of discovery and adventure and mysteries of the world. Curios dotted the room—antique globes, ships in bottles, compasses, and more. In the corner near the window stood a small table topped with a huge Victorian goldfish bowl with fat, goggle-eyed fish swimming inside.

"Fish!" Meg gasped as she ran over to peer inside. "Have you named them?"

Susan laughed. "That honor is all yours, my dear." She motioned us on.

Elle's room was lovely—simple and practical and classic—with crisp white sheets and pillows and blankets in creams and grays of various textures—linen and velvet and silk—which gave the room a depth the inattentive eye might miss.

And my room… well, it was, for lack of a better word, perfect.

The ceilings in all the rooms were high—fourteen feet or more, if I had to guess—and in this room with its dove-gray walls against snowy white trim, they seemed even taller. The curtains pooled on the ground, the bedskirt made of chiffon whispered against the rug, and the bed itself was tall and piled high with decadent pillows. The quilt looked to be made of layers of lace, like a petticoat. A wardrobe against the wall was painted with a quiet branch, dotted with broad leaves and magnolia flowers with a little wren on one jutting crook.

But the best part was the antique piano.

I rushed over to the spinet, breathless as I opened it and laid my fingers on the keys, my heart thumping and hands tingling. It was too beautiful, too generous, too much. And I was overwhelmed with feeling—with my losses and pain and hope and gratitude. Tears fell, unashamed and unabashed, as I turned to my aunt.

"Thank you," I said on a whisper, the two simple words not nearly enough.

"No thanks required," she said, holding back tears of her own. "It will be nice to have music in our house again. And I know it seems silly to have two pianos in the house, but this way, you can play all you like without having to endure anyone's company but your own." She took a steadying breath and clasped her hands. "Come, Emily. Yours is last."

They left me alone in my new room, and I made no motion to follow them, too entranced, too surprised to leave. Instead, I sat on the gray velvet piano bench facing into the room, my eyes roaming every corner, every detail. Over the shelves stacked with books of poetry, across the gilded mirrors and framed book illustrations of fairy tales.

She had very aptly looked into my heart and soul and fashioned a room that spoke directly to me. It was sorcery or magic, and as deeply as I felt *right* in that room, resistance slipped over me.

Because this wasn't a fairy tale, and nothing in this room was mine.

I felt my losses so acutely in that moment that it set my heart galloping like a pony missing a leg, staggering and clumsy. Everything I had known was gone, and it would never be reclaimed. I was in a room I didn't know in a home that wasn't mine, relying solely on the kindness and generosity of strangers to care for those who meant the most to me in the world.

As perfect as the room and the welcome were, in that moment, it felt like a lie, like a faerie trick. A gilded cage. There was no way out and nowhere to go.

I heard my father, saw his face, felt the whisper of his breath against my ear when I closed my eyes.

Don't look back, Annie. That's a sure-fire way to end up tripping on what's in front of you.

I swiped at my tears, spinning around on the piano bench when I heard Susan making her way back down the hallway, pushing Mama in her wheelchair. They didn't stop, thankfully. I laid my fingers on the keys again, this time to play.

My heart opened up when the first resonating note struck, my sadness and loss slipping out of that thumping muscle and through my veins, into my fingers. Mendelssohn filled the room, the deep and slow melancholy leaving me with every note—notes that I knew by heart and memory—leaving me with every tear. And when my trembling fingers rested, the last note hanging in the air, I was lighter than before.

Music was the conduit for the abundance of feeling I had been blessed and cursed with. For my heart not only contained holes, but was too big for its own good.

I closed the lid and stood, making my way toward the sound of my aunt's voice.

Susan was sitting at the head of the table in the dining room with the Maltese in her lap and Mama and Elle on either side of her, each with a steaming mug in front of them. The table looked like a smile with a missing tooth where Mama sat, the chair gone to leave a gap for her wheelchair. She still hadn't gotten used to it. Her hands were blistered from trying to navigate on her own, her body and soul smaller than they'd been before. And when I took the seat next to her, her eyes begged me to save her from pretending, from the false smile and small talk.

I reached for her hand in the hopes that she could read my intention to do just that.

"And tonight," Susan said happily as she stroked the half-asleep dog, "John's associate and his wife—the Ferrars—are coming by for dinner. We just couldn't wait for Frank to meet you, though I must say," she leaned in, lowering her voice, "Fanny is insufferable. The woman wouldn't know happiness if it crawled in her lap and purred." She laughed pleasantly at herself.

I found myself smiling simply because Susan was so agreeable despite the fact that we were travel-worn and rumpled and in no state or mood to entertain.

Mama squeezed my fingers as if she'd been thinking the same thing, but Elle, with her ever-present smile of platitude and concession, said, "We'll be glad to meet them."

Susan smiled, pleased. "Wonderful!" Her plump fingers ran through the dog's cottony fur. "So, what would you girls like to do now that you're here? Anything in particular you'd like to see?"

"Only everything," I said on a laugh, my smile spreading.

Susan's chuckle was an echo of mine. "Yes, only that."

Feeling momentarily brave, I added, "I think I'd like to find a job."

It was one of the items on my list of things I'd never done, and I was determined to check them off once we made it to New York. Thus, *now*.

Mama's face grew stern. "Annie, we've talked about this."

If it was at the top of *my* list, you could be sure it was at the tippy-top of *Mama's* list of *nevers*.

I rolled my eyes. "It's not like I'm asking to run the New York

City Marathon, Mama. There have to be a million jobs in the city that don't require cardio."

She huffed. "You have to be the only teenager I've ever known who *wants* to work."

"I'm eighteen. I'm not a baby."

"Eighteen is still a teenager."

"Eighteen is when *most* people are moving out," I said a little louder and sharper than I'd meant to. So I took a breath. "I'm just saying, it would be nice to have a little independence."

"You worked at the library last summer," she volleyed.

"I *volunteered*. It's not the same, and you know it."

Susan brightened up, her spine straightening. "Oh! You know, there's a bookstore just straight across the park from here, near Columbia. A good friend of mine's son owns it. I hear it's quite the spot for people your age. It's called Wasted Words, and it's a bookstore that's a *bar*! Can you imagine?"

My eyes widened. "Yes. Yes, I can."

"It's just a ten-minute drive from here."

I frowned. "How long is the walk?"

She tottered her head back and forth. "Oh, maybe twenty minutes."

I sagged in my chair when Mama gave me a look.

"Too far to walk every day," she said with some finality.

And it was the truth. I couldn't walk more than a couple of blocks before ending up winded and colorless and drenched in sweat.

But Susan, my newfound savior, waved a hand. "We have a driver who can take her if she really wants to work there."

"See, Mama?" I gestured to Susan, as if there was no way Mama could possibly argue, my hope flapping proudly at the top of my flagpole.

If only.

She sighed with a note of impatience. "We'll talk about it later," she said, which meant, *Absolutely not, and I'll tell you why when Susan's out of earshot.*

"How about you, Elle?" Susan asked.

Elle blinked at her for a moment. "I ... I don't really know. I'd like to get a job too, but I'm not exactly sure where to start."

"What kind of work do you think you'd like?"

"Well, since I graduated, I worked at a small insurance company in Boerne, mostly as a secretary."

"Did you enjoy it?"

Elle nodded. "I suppose so. I liked the order of it, the organization of dates and calls and files. It felt ... safe. Is that silly?" she asked, laughing as if it were.

I laughed myself. "Safe because it's boring. The Petersons were lucky to find *anyone* who could sit in that musty old office every day and file papers."

"Well, I liked it," she said. "There's something comforting about routine and rules and repetition."

Susan chuckled and reached for her hand. "Comfort of habit. Yes, I quite know what you mean." She brightened up again. "You know, I'd bet John could place you at one of the magazines. They're always looking for good executive assistants, and it sounds like you might just be perfect for the job."

Elle flushed, her lips parting in surprise as she stammered, "Oh ... ah, I'm not ... I don't believe I'm experienced enough to work at that level. Really. I think the Petersons' phone rang five times a week, max."

I snickered. "And three of those were from Gigi Blanchard to gossip with Mrs. Peterson."

But Susan wouldn't have it. "I'm not worried about you at all. Anyone who enjoys secretarial work would be welcomed; I'm certain of it. I'll talk with John."

"Really, you don't have to do that," Elle insisted, the color in her cheeks deepening another shade.

"I don't mind at all!" Susan said, oblivious to Elle's discomfort. "We're happy to help however we can, including your place here. For years and years, John has wanted to do something, anything to help you. It just wasn't right—the way your parents turned you out, Emily. None of us have ever forgiven them for that."

Mama stiffened next to me, her back straight and that false smile on her lips. "It was a long time ago."

"But hardly forgotten," Susan said, not unkindly.

She was so forward—too forward for me in that moment of exhaustion. The family I knew was small, only the nucleus of my sisters and parents, and opening that business up to Susan felt like an intrusion even though she was family too.

So much change, so quickly.

I turned to Mama, eager to escape. "How are you feeling?"

Relief filled her face up, softening it. "I could use a little nap, I think."

I stood. "I'll help you. Excuse us, Aunt Susan," I added.

"Of course!" she said with a smile. "Dinner is at seven. Just let me know if you need anything at all."

"We will."

"And you'll stay and chat with me, won't you, Elle?" she asked eagerly.

"I'd love to," she answered with a polite smile as I rolled Mama away.

When we were out of earshot, Mama said, "We're horrible, cruel women for leaving Elle in there."

I chuckled. "Elle would sacrifice herself for your welfare any day of the week."

She sighed at that. "This…this is almost too much."

My throat tightened, and I swallowed to open it back up as I turned into her room. "I know."

I pushed her to the bed and turned it down before bending. She hooked her arm around my neck, bracing herself on the mattress top to hitch herself up with my help, dragging her limp legs behind her.

I tucked them under the covers as she watched with shining eyes.

Everyone said we looked alike—the same unruly blonde hair, the same slender frame, the same green eyes—but it was our smiles that I always thought made us look so much alike. We had the same shine—or we had before my father died.

I imagined her in a bed like this, in a room like this, long ago—before she had fallen in love and left New York behind. I imagined her rich and cosmopolitan, like a ghost twin of the simple, unfussy, easygoing woman I knew, the woman now dimmed and dulled by loss.

"I hate this, Annie. I hate everything about it." Her words were as shaky as my breath.

I sat on the edge of the bed, taking her hands in mine. "Me, too, Mama. It's…" I paused, thinking. "It's too confusing, too conflicting. It's a relief to have help, to be in such a beautiful home with such beautiful things, but everything has changed. This isn't home."

"It is now. We have nowhere else to go." Her tears fell freely, her fingers squeezing mine, her sadness making her look young and vulnerable and small, propped up in that big bed, surrounded by pillows.

"I know that too. And I know we'll find a way through it all."

"One foot in front of the other, as your daddy would say."

My gaze dropped to our hands, catching on her simple gold wedding band. "I wish he were here," I said barely above a whisper.

"So do I."

Neither of us spoke for a moment, chasing our thoughts through the maze of our minds.

When Daddy died, there hadn't been enough money tied up in the house, not enough invested in Social Security, not enough shelled away in retirement. He was too young, and in his youth, he thought he had more time.

We all had.

Now, Mama needed full-time care, and Meg was still so young, years and years from being on her own. I had no job, no means to support myself, never mind Mama and Meg too, which was another reason I wanted so badly to find something, anything that could help ease that burden. We didn't have the means to survive on our own. All we had left was each other.

I only wished that were enough.

A knock came from behind us, and we looked to the sound. Elle seemed both exasperated and relieved as she stepped in and closed the door.

"Well, I've gotten us off the hook for dinner," she said quietly as she sat on the other side of Mama's bed. "I convinced Aunt Susan that you needed rest and that we could all use a minute to settle in before entertaining. Put that way, she agreed and rescheduled for next week."

I shook my head, frustrated and edging on agitated. My flair for drama and saying exactly what I felt won over my ability to be reasonable. "I know she means well, but we've been driving for days. How could she not understand we'd be exhausted?"

Elle sighed. "Honestly, you should have seen her when I offered a little perspective. She was embarrassed and apologetic and…" She sighed again. "She felt like a fool."

The thought quieted my anger, replacing it with guilt. "This… this is so…" My throat squeezed closed.

Elle reached for my hand. "I know. And Susan and John have saved us in a way. They've protected us from an uncertain fate, given us the chance to live well, for no other reason than kindness. Look around; look at what Susan has done just to make us feel at home and welcome."

A shuffling came from under the bed, and Meg's head and shoulders emerged from under the bedskirt with a National Geographic book in front of her, split open to a spread about octopuses.

"My room is one of the best things to ever happen to me," she said matter-of-factly. "I like Aunt Susan. She gives good hugs and smells like flowers."

We all chuckled, and Elle stood, moving to Mama's suitcase to flip it on its side and unzip it. "I know it's hard, but it could be so much harder."

Mama nodded, but she still looked defeated and deflated.

"How are you, Mama?" I asked gently.

Her green eyes met mine. "I don't know how to feel. Mostly, I think I'm numb. Like part of my brain is driving my body, giving the absolute minimum to consider participation, while the rest of me has retreated somewhere deep inside. Because when I reach in and think or feel, it's too much. Too much—" The words were cut off by a sob that she swallowed, but her tears fell, unconfined.

Those tears drew my own from the well that I realized would never run dry. "We're gonna be okay," I said, wanting to believe it.

"I hope so," she whispered, trying to smile.

"We will," Elle added from the other side of the bed. "We'll survive. If Daddy were here, he wouldn't let us give up. He'd tell us to find joy every day, to hang on to each other, to turn our faces to the sun and warm ourselves with hope. So that's what we should do."

And we all knew she was right, though not a single one of our faces said we believed we could do it.

We'd try anyway.

Elle smiled, a comforting expression that coaxed a smile from my own lips, small as it might be. "I think a good night's sleep in a real bed in a real room will do us all good. Annie will be spreading her sunshine again soon enough, and Meg will tell us the wonders of the deep ocean. And Mama will smile and laugh like she used to, and we'll all love each other."

"Well, I *have* been reading about anglerfish," Meg said from the floor after a pause. "Did you know they can eat fish twice their size?"

I laughed. "You have something in common; you can eat a pizza twice your size."

"Dare me to try!"

I winked. "*Double dog* dare."

Her face brightened as she scrambled to her feet. "Oh, man, *now* I'm asking Aunt Susan if we can have pizza for dinner."

"I'm sure she has something planned, baby," Mama chided.

But Meg shrugged, grinning. "I'll tell her I'll name a fish after her." And with that, she bounded out of the room.

I looked from Mama, whose smile finally touched her eyes—not deep down, but enough—to Elle, who watched us with a veil of love and pride that covered her own sadness.

As for me, I found Elle's words to be true, simply by her having spoken them. And my heart lifted, that sagging balloon rising, warmed by the sun and reaching for the forgotten clouds.

Mittens

ANNIE

E lle was right; a good night's sleep and a hot shower had done wonders for my disposition. The luxurious sheets and pillows helped this endeavor.

Each night got easier, and each day brought with it a little more happiness. And over the course of the following week, I found a glimmer of hope that this could someday be home.

This morning, I woke like a princess in a Disney movie, fresh as a daisy and smiling like the world was full of possibilities. Because it was.

Mama had agreed to let me get a job.

It was likely due to my incessant pestering, bolstered by Susan's and Elle's support. Susan had been insistent in my favor and oblivious to Mama's distress. Elle, ever the voice of reason and sense, had noted that I needed a job, something to do, and really, there was no reason to refuse besides Mama's worry over my health.

I'd almost done jumping jacks to prove just how fine I was, but I hadn't wanted to push my luck.

Of course, *fine* was a relative term.

From the time I had been born, I'd been sickly, subjecting my parents to the pain and stress of having a child with a heart defect. I was diagnosed with a rare defect called Ebstein's anomaly, noted by a deformed valve—pulmonary stenosis, which obstructed blood as it attempted to leave my heart—and an atrial septal defect—the fancy name for the hole between the chambers of my heart. I had an arrhythmia, too—you know, because all that other mess wasn't quite enough for the universe to bestow upon me.

The result was a busted up jalopy of a heart, sputtering exhaust as it clanked and clacked around in my rib cage.

My first open-heart surgery was at three weeks old when they put in a temporary shunt. I tried to remember that fact when Mama was overprotective. I would imagine her lying in a hospital bed, her brand-new baby whisked away and put in an incubator so that she could breathe. I would picture Mama in the NICU, staring into that plastic box at her newborn whose skin was a terrifying shade of blue, her tiny body full of tubes and wires, her chest stapled up after being cracked open like a melon.

That usually worked to temper me.

My second open-heart surgery was at six months old, this time for a permanent shunt. At two, the shunt was no longer enough to keep my blood pressure and flow regulated. And so my third open-heart surgery was scheduled for the final phase in rigging my heart up in an effort to get me to my teenage years when the muscle would be fully grown, and then I could have surgery to fix it once and for all.

All of that, my mother had endured. She endured the fear and anxiety of having a child so sick. She endured my strict diet and inability to walk or run or play like a normal child. And all of that endurance had made her overprotective. As frustrating as it was and as angry as it sometimes made me, I couldn't blame her.

It had been traumatic for her, and I forced myself to remember that. It was easy to forget. I didn't know any different. She knew too much.

Nevertheless, it seemed we had worn her down by showing her the merits of my liberation—under the solemn promise that I'd be careful and mindful and safe.

So when I woke, it was with a smile on my face and arms stretched over my head. The winter morning sunshine filtered in through the curtains, and I greeted the day with hope and optimism and giddy, good cheer.

A job!

I found myself grinning as I reached for my little notebook on the nightstand. It was a hardback the color of a marigold with fine golden strands woven into the canvas and a shimmering satin ribbon resting between the pages where my list began.

My angled, looping handwriting smiled back at me.

LIVING OUT LOUD—or Things Annie Daschle Has Never Done and Is Ready to Do Already

1) Get a job. A real job with a paycheck and coworkers and maybe even benefits.

2) See falling snow.

3) Make a snowman.

4) Have a picnic in Central Park.

5) Get a tattoo.

6) Meet a boy,

7) Who will take me on a real date,

8) And kiss me.

9) *And maybe be my boyfriend.

I stopped scanning there. There were pages and pages of things listed—everything from, *Get drunk*, to, *Play piano onstage*. Some of them were specific to New York, and some of them were just specific—like, *Use very own money to purchase something completely unnecessary simply because it makes me happy.*

But that item on the top, that very first one—that one, I might cross off in a matter of hours.

It was enough to make me giggle there in the silence of the room, snapping the notebook closed and pressing it to my chest just over where my heart *tha-dumped* in a syncopated rhythm that felt like a cha-cha bongo.

Because for a moment, my pain was behind me in the coolness of my shadow and the whole world was spread out in front of me like a feast of possibility.

And I would take a taste of everything I could.

GREG

I never saw Annie Daschle coming.

I meant that in the most literal sense. Her small body slammed into my much larger one with enough force to send her reeling backward. The crates in my hand clattered to the ground, abandoned in favor of reaching for her.

I caught her by the wrist and pulled, righting her a little too suddenly. She tottered back into me—though softer this time. She landed in the circle of my arms, looking up at me with eyes the color of a green glass bottle, lit up from the inside with sunshine.

It was maybe only a heartbeat, a breath, but it felt like that second stretched out in a long thread between us.

She laughed, her cheeks high as she leaned away. The chilly air cut between us the second she stepped back, leaving me colder than the moment before.

"God, I'm sorry," she said in a lilting Southern accent. "Are you all right?"

I smiled. "I could ask you the same thing."

She brushed her wild blonde hair back from her face with a mittened hand the color of pink lemonade. Not a glove. *Mittens*, like a kid would wear. On anyone else, I would have considered it ridiculous. On her, it was adorable.

"I'm just fine, thanks to you. If you hadn't caught me, I'd have gone tail over teacups." She laughed again; the sound set a smile on my face. "Do you work here?"

We had collided just inside the doors to Wasted Words, the bookstore-slash-bar where I'd worked for the last year and a half.

"Almost every day. Anything I can help you with?"

Her smile widened. "Why, yes, there is. I've come to see if you're hiring."

The answer: no.

So like any good, honest employee, I said, "As a matter of fact, we are."

She lit up like the Fourth of July and began pulling off her mittens, which complemented her bright yellow peacoat and made her look a little bit like an adorable popsicle. "Oh, that's *great*. What are you looking for?"

"What kind of work are you interested in?" I asked, gesturing to a booth next to the bar.

Her face fell just a touch as she slid into the bench seat. "Well, I used to volunteer at the library back home, so I have plenty of experience with cataloging books and that sort of thing. And I'm pretty sure I could get the hang of a cash register, if you need a checkout girl. Really, I could learn just about anything," she added hopefully.

I'd unknowingly boxed her in, my hand resting on the back of the booth and my body blocking any exit she might have, as if I could pen her in and make her stay. At the realization, I stepped back.

"Let me go grab you an application."

"Thanks," she said. "Oh, what's the manager's name?"

I smirked and offered my hand. "Greg Brandon. Nice to meet you."

Her big eyes widened in surprise as she took my hand. "Annie Daschle. Nice to meet you, too."

Her hand was warm in mine, her fingers long for such a small girl, just a wisp. I wondered absently how old she was before letting her go.

"Be right back. Can I get you anything to drink?"

She unwound her pink scarf. "Water would be fine, if it's no trouble."

"None at all. Coming right up."

I turned and walked away, grinning like a fool as I made my way behind the bar, first pouring her a glass of water, then fishing around under the bar register for the folder of applications.

Technically, I *was* a manager, just not a *hiring* manager. I ran the bar, not the store itself. That was Cam's job—on top of running me. But I had a feeling I'd be able to secure her a spot doing pretty much whatever she wanted. I found myself already rearranging the schedule and concocting a plan to convince Cam.

I stopped for a moment to consider what had gotten into me. I'd never taken an interest in new hires before, but for some unknown reason, I felt compelled to help her.

I wasn't quite sure what it was that had struck me. She was just a girl, probably younger than I figured, maybe even as young as twenty. But there was something about her, something small and vulnerable, like finding a stray puppy or a floppy-eared, big-eyed bunny that needed a home. Something that made me feel the urge to protect her, to button up her coat and make sure she didn't lose a mitten or her hat. At the same time, she seemed perfectly self-sufficient with a sunny, optimistic look to her that spoke of a girl who would walk home in the rain or dip her hands into a bag of grain to feel every seed.

Living in New York my whole life, the concept was as foreign as it was fascinating.

I brushed my thoughts aside and took her the application and water, setting it on a coaster. She caught a glimpse of it as I set the glass on top, immediately moving it to read the coaster aloud.

"*No love, my love, that thou mayst true love call— / All mine was thine before thou hadst this more.*" She beamed. "Shakespeare, Sonnet 40." She recited the rest from memory, "*Then if for my love thou my love receivest, / I cannot blame thee for thou love usest; / But yet be blamed if thou this self deceivest / By wilful taste of what thyself refusest.* I love the sonnets."

"I can see that." I chuckled. "They barely read like English, but hearing it…I think I actually understood it that time."

She blushed, just the slightest tinge of dusky rose in her cheeks. "It's always better spoken. *All mine was thine before thou hadst this more,*" she said with depth and passion. "She loved him before he took her love, and she's begging him not to hurt her for the sacrifice. It's about the power one holds over another who gives their love. It's beautiful. Are all the coasters the same?"

"Cam, one of my bosses, loves finding quotes for these things." I grabbed a stack off the back of an adjacent booth and tossed them on the table.

Let other pens dwell on guilt and misery. —*Jane Austen*
Always laugh when you can. It is cheap medicine. —*Lord Byron*
And your very flesh shall be a great poem. —*Walt Whitman*

Annie looked them over with her big eyes and wide, smiling lips. "Would it be pathetic to beg for a job?"

"You wouldn't be the first. Let's start with you filling that out for me." I nodded to the application.

She straightened up seriously, a little embarrassed. "Yes, of course."

"Just come get me when you're through, and we'll chat."

She nodded, but I caught a glimpse of her nerves; she was an open book, her pages fluttering from one emotion to the next with an easy whisper.

I walked over to the empty crates, still sprawled across the entry, and picked them up. I carried them out to the sidewalk where my beer delivery guy was waiting, nose in his clipboard. We exchanged a few words, but I wasn't really paying attention; my mind was turned back to the girl sitting in the booth with pink mittens in her lap.

Her head was down, attention on her application. The tip of her tongue poked comically out of the corner of her lips. And I kept on walking until I was behind the bar, busying myself with anything I could think of, which wasn't much. We hadn't been open for long enough that morning to *actually* have anything to do.

I was in the middle of pretending to do inventory when she set her pen down. I was so aware of her, I sensed the motion rather than saw it.

I smiled and made my way back over, sliding into the bench across from her.

She beamed and pushed the paper in my direction. "Here you go. All done."

I glanced down the sheet, taking in the details. Her name and address—

Surprise jolted through me that she lived on Fifth and 94th, the Upper East—the Upper Crust. That surprise turned to downright shock when I noted her birthday.

She was eighteen.

Fresh out of high school.

With no job experience.

I looked up at her then, her face full of hope, laced with fear and longing, touched by a shadow of desperation. And there were only two things to do.

I packed away any notion that I might ever be able to be with her and asked, "When can you start?"

ANNIE

"I got the job!"

Everyone in the living room smiled—even Mama, a smile that was real and genuine even if it was a little scared—and Elle and Susan stood to congratulate me with hugs and kisses on the cheek.

"The bookstore is amazing," I said as I pulled off my mittens and coat. "It's huge, full of romance novels and comic books, and the bar is a coffee shop too. The ceilings are a mile high with all the pipes and everything exposed, and the floor is brushed concrete with swoops that make it look like the pages of books. Oh! *And* they have coasters with literary quotes, and they do these singles' nights where they try to hook the comic-book boys up with the romance girls," I rambled. "I mean, what an idea. Books and booze and baristas. Genius. But I'm such a klutz. I tripped right into the manager and would have fallen if he hadn't caught me. I can't believe he still hired me!"

"Ooh, a boy!" Meg teased, waggling her eyebrows.

I rolled my eyes and ruffled her sandy-brown hair, ignoring the rush of adrenaline I had at the thought of Greg—tall, handsome Greg with the nice smile and striking blue-green eyes who was *way* too old for me. "Psh, he's my boss, and he's *old*. He's got to be almost *thirty*."

Mama let out a noise somewhere between a laugh and a snuffle. "Practically ancient. Was it his cane or his bifocals that gave him away?"

"Ha, ha," I sang. "They want me to start *tomorrow*! I can't even believe it." My cheeks so high from smiling, they ached a little. I barely noticed.

"A real job. I'll be working the cash register at the coolest bookstore I've ever seen." I sighed and dropped into an oversized armchair.

Mama watched me, her face full of pride and trepidation. "I knew you'd get it. They'd have been crazy not to hire you."

"Thank you, Mama, for giving me your blessing."

She let out a sigh of her own, and it was anything but dreamy. "It was time. And this sounds like a nice *sitting* job, one without too much physical effort on your part. Did you tell them? About your heart?"

"I didn't think explaining Ebstein's anomaly to my new manager during an interview would get me any points, so no, Mama, I didn't mention it. But I will, if I need to."

"*When* you need to," she corrected.

I looked to Aunt Susan, who had been quiet for the longest stretch I'd ever witnessed. "What have y'all been doing all day?"

She smiled, her eyes meeting mine for only a moment before turning back to the embroidery in her hands. "Oh, not much. Meg has been informing us of the wonders of Egypt."

Meg lit up. "Did you know King Tut died because he was inbred, *not* in a chariot race like his sarcophagus said?"

My brows rose.

Susan laughed. "We've had nothing to do and spent the day rolling around in the luxury. Congratulations again, Annie. I'm so glad to see you're feeling better. I know moving here hasn't been easy for any of you, and I'm sorry if I've made it any worse than it had to be with my constant blather." She paused, considering her words. "I'm one of those odd people who laughs when bad things happen—my children never found it amusing when they skinned their knees—and I tend to cover up my sadness with humor and happiness, sometimes when it's not appropriate."

Guilt slipped into my heart. "Aunt Susan, your cheer has been one of the best things about coming here."

Her cheeks were pink and merry, but her eyes were sad. "I'm glad. And we're glad you're here." She moved her embroidery to the small table next to her. "Emily has been telling me all day about how lovely your piano playing is, but I haven't had the courage to ask you to play. Do you think you might like to? I would so love to hear."

And I smiled, partly at the thought of Susan not having courage for something and partly out of sheer pleasure at the prospect of playing for an audience. "Of course."

When I hopped up, my heart jigged dangerously in my chest. Black spots danced in my vision, my breath shallow and thin. Elle was on her feet, catching me as I teetered, staggering forward.

"Are you all right?" she asked, her concern weighing her voice.

"Yeah, I...I just stood up too fast; that's all," I answered with what I hoped was a comforting, believable expression on my face.

But I held on to her arm as we walked through the double French doors to the grand piano.

I took a seat at the piano bench and opened the lid, the toothy smile of the keys comforting, calming my heart, bringing my breath back to a steady rhythm.

"What do you want to hear? Mozart?" I made a snobbish face, my back ramrod straight as my fingers drummed the bouncing opening to Piano Sonata No. 11. "Tchaikovsky?" I banged out the dramatic ending of *Swan Lake*. "Maybe a little light Beethoven?" I *dum-dum-dum-dummmmed* the dark opening bars of Symphony No. 5.

Meg rolled her eyes so hard, I couldn't see her irises. "Boring classical. Play Elton John!"

I laughed, my fingers finding the keys without looking, plinking the ivory to the ragtime rhythm of the bouncing saloon opening of "Honky Cat." I sang—it was impossible not to sing along to it— roistering about the city lights and my redneck ways and just how good the change would do me.

Meg sang along, and everyone joined in but Elle, who was convinced she couldn't sing (this was a lie; I had heard her on occasion when she thought no one was listening, and her voice was quite lovely). But she swayed. She swayed and she smiled, her eyes twinkling like Mama's.

I made a big show as I broke it all the way down with the rolling, wild ending. And when I finally gave it up for good, they cheered.

I laughed and curtsied invisible skirts as they shouted *Brava* and *Encore!*

Aunt Susan was smiling so wide, I could almost count her molars. "Annie, that was *wonderful*!"

"Why, thank you." I bowed deeply this time with the sweep of my arm. "I'm here all week. Try the prime rib!"

"Do another!" Meg bounced. "Do Bowie!"

So I did. I played "Oh! You Pretty Things" and The Beatles' "Rocky Raccoon" with a little "Killer Queen" for good measure before I finally called it.

They clapped, and I stood for a final bow.

We chatted as we turned for the door to the room, but Mama touched my arm.

"May I talk to you?" she asked, her voice low.

Everyone kept walking out, not having heard her.

"Of course, Mama."

We moved to the armchairs where I sat, and she pulled up next to me, her face drawn.

"What's the matter?" I asked.

She shook her head. "Nothing's wrong; that's the thing I'm trying to keep in mind. Ever since you were born, I've been afraid. In fact, I can barely remember what it's like *not* to be afraid, and I can't recall what it's like not to feel guilty. You've missed so much, and it's my fault."

I reached for her hand. "Mama, I—"

"No, no. Let me finish. You see, every aspect of my job as your mother falls under one of three cardinal rules: to love you, to protect you, and to respect you. Sometimes, to do one, I have to betray another. In my effort to protect you, I haven't respected what you want. Baby, I'm happy you've found a job. I want for you to find independence and a life outside of me, outside of *us*. But I'm scared, too, and fear is a beast not easily slain. Sometimes, it's not even a beast you can look in the eye."

"I know," I whispered, squeezing her hand.

Her gaze dropped to the carpet and through it. "It doesn't make it any easier that I'm not myself. I don't even know what that means anymore—*myself*. Who I was is gone, and I'm left a stranger to myself. I wake up every day with a glimmer of who I used to be hanging on to the edge of my mind like a dream, and I live the rest of my day chasing that vision. But it's impossible to catch, and that impossibility is almost more crippling than my ruined legs." She took a deep breath and let it out slow. "Being here is easier though, isn't it? When every little thing is different, it feels like a fresh start. If we were back home, I don't know how any of us would get out of bed in the morning."

"I'm glad for the distraction, and I'm grateful you're all right with my working."

"Well, you're an adult, as hard as that is to believe."

I snorted a laugh. "I don't feel like an adult at all. Six months ago, I was taking chemistry finals and getting ready to graduate from high school. And the second I had that diploma in my hand, I crossed the threshold into adulthood with no idea what I was doing."

"Well, let me give you a hint, Annie." Mama leaned in, her smile small and conspiratorial. "None of us knows what we're doing. Nine out of ten people you ever meet are faking it."

The thought was comforting.

"I really am happy for you," she said. "Just bear with me if I occasionally lose my mind."

I moved to hug her, hooking my chin over her shoulder, her glossy blonde hair against my cheek and her arms around me.

"Thank you, Mama."

"I love you. No matter what, no matter where, no matter how, I love you."

I sniffled and stood.

"Well," she started, hands on her wheels, "I think I'll go see after lunch. You coming?"

"I think I'll head to my room for a bit."

She nodded and backed up her chair, turning it toward the door. "Let me know if you want a plate made up."

"I will," I said, and we parted ways in the hallway.

Once in my room with the door solidly closed, I let out a sigh that felt like it aged me. The afternoon sun cut into the room in a wedge, diffused by the sheer curtain. The wooden princess set my father had made stood in its beam on the desk, the sunshine gleaming off the shiny varnish of each piece.

He'd made it for me when Mama was pregnant, carving each piece with the same gentle hands and love he later gave me. The castle was made of blocks that fit together, and he carved little figures to live there—a princess and knight, a king and queen, a dragon and cave. They were the only things I'd packed besides clothes and the stuffed animal I'd slept with since I was in a crib. The rest of our possessions wouldn't get to us for a while, but this, I didn't want to be without.

I picked up the princess, running my thumb over her wavy hair and the details of her dress, imagining my father with a half-carved block of wood in his hand and his face scrunched in concentration. I'd seen that look a thousand times in my life; one of my greatest fears was that I'd forget the sight.

I sat on the edge of my bed, the princess in my palm, but my mind turned and looked back down the broken road I'd traveled in the last month.

No matter how much I'd thought about it, it still felt like a dream. The ringing of the phone. My sister's voice carrying the words that would forever change me. The smell of the hospital, stringent and sterile. The sight of Mama, unconscious in the hospital bed.

They'd been on their way home from our family's store where Daddy sold the furniture and art he made. The man who hit them had dropped his phone, speeding and swerving when he reached for it.

Daddy died on impact. His truck was left a snarling twist of metal.

I didn't even know how Mama had survived; every day, I woke with gratitude that she had.

She had been confined to her hospital bed, unable to attend his funeral. I was of little use, and we had no other family; our paternal grandparents had passed on, and our New York family were strangers to us. So Elle handled every detail with stoic grace while the rest of us unraveled, hour to hour, minute to minute. I spent those days at Mama's side in the hospital, Meg with Elle where it was easier. When the doctors determined the extent of the damage to her spinal cord, things moved quickly. Because there was no therapy to speak of, no recovery to plan. Only the transition into the reality of her life and her loss.

Every day for two weeks, a nurse would spend a few hours at the house, teaching us how to care for Mama, teaching her how to care for herself. We had to learn to transfer her in and out of her wheelchair, how to turn her every few hours when she was confined to the bed, how to look out for signs of sores. And those were the easy tasks.

There were so many more that stole bits of her dignity, and there was no easing into it, no little by little. It happened all at once with staggering suddenness. It was in the emptying of her ostomy bag—or worse, the changing of her ostomy bag. Her inability to shower on her own or cook for herself. She could reach nothing, couldn't see the stovetop from her wheelchair. She needed constant care, and we had no way to help her but with our own hands.

It was Uncle John who convinced her to come to New York. They had come for the funeral, and John spent several long afternoons in the hospital with Mama with one mission: persuade her to accept his help. He had the room for all of us, the funds to eradicate the medical bills and pay for nurses, and the desire to do something.

Her acceptance, as much as she hated it, was the best thing that could have happened to us. Because John had saved us from an uncertain future. We were indebted to him in a way we could never repay.

He'd given us hope when hope was lost.

And now, everything had changed, and it was going to be everything we needed, everything *I* needed, everything my father would have wanted, and everything that would patch up those perilous holes in my heart. Because even though they'd never mend on their own, I could endure them and honor him by living every second with every single part of me.

So I would.

I would live out loud.

Sweet & Salty

GREG

The pavement rolled beneath the wheels of my skateboard the next morning, my hands buried in my coat pockets and beanie pulled down over my ears, while I did my best not to think about Annie.

I'd tried to forget about her all yesterday afternoon when that yellow coat and pink hat crossed my mind, unbidden. And at home with my family last night when I'd replayed her running into me and stopping my universe for a breath. And this morning when I'd worried a little too long about what I'd wear today.

I'd settled on a black-and-white-plaid button-down, cuffed three-quarters to leave my tattooed forearms on display. I wouldn't admit that with a gun to my temple, but it was the truth.

Don't get me wrong; it wasn't like I'd been obsessing about her or anything. I hadn't thought of her *much*. But, out of nowhere, she would invade my mind like cigarette smoke. I'd wave thoughts of her away with a dour twist of my lips, all while jonesing for just one drag.

You're just attracted to her. That's normal, I told myself as my sneaker hit the pavement, propelling me on.

She was cute and innocent, *different* from New York girls. But she couldn't even drink, for Christ's sake. Not for nearly *three years*.

She was practically jailbait, which meant she was off-limits. This probably made things worse—the knowledge that I couldn't have her.

But it wasn't that simple. Nothing ever was.

The fact was that we were at completely different places in our lives; she was figuring out who she was, who she would become, and I had done that ten years ago. She was experiencing life for the first time; everything was speeding up for her while I found myself slowing down.

It would never work, and that was the heart of the matter. Nothing about pursuing her made sense.

But I thought of that moment when she'd fallen into me, and I'd looked into the depths of her eyes, felt her body pressed against me. And, if the last twenty-four hours were any proof, I knew she wouldn't be so easy to forget. The knowledge that it was chemical, that it had no depth or roots, didn't matter. Something in me recognized something in her, and that was that.

Hoping it would blow over was probably futile. I'd do my best to ignore it all the same.

The last few years had largely been spent devoted to my family. When lupus had finally confined my mother to her bed, my siblings and I'd moved home to help out. And when she died, we couldn't bear to leave our father. He needed our help—not only with his loss, but with the crushing weight of medical bills.

I'd tried to date, but the result was a long string of failures. I did the dating-app thing long enough to figure out that people were really strange. The only date that actually worked out was with Rose, one of the owners of the bookstore. We ended up going out a few times—until she admitted that she was still in love with her ex.

I'd sworn off dating websites after that.

More recently, my failed dating experience was thanks to a pack of well-meaning, meddlesome friends and family.

My family was one culprit. My sister brought home her friends from Columbia all the time, parading them in front of me like show ponies. The fact that they were all so close to my baby sister in age was a negative, the nature of which seemed to be lost on her.

Work was the other source of badgering, and Cam was the lead offender.

Matchmaking was a quirk of hers, a hobby fueled by compulsion and good intentions. She'd tried to set me up with at least two-dozen girls since we started working together, and none of them worked out, much to her frustration. In fact, she once went so far that we'd made her swear she'd stop.

It was a lie we all pretended to believe.

She wasn't the only one though. My two head bartenders, Harrison and Beau, loved to bring in girlfriends of chicks they were seeing. Even Rose had been working on me, introducing me to a tattoo artist who worked with her boyfriend. Once, she'd even had her roommate, Lily, bring me a ballerina she danced with at the New York City Ballet.

I was everyone's favorite project, probably because I wasn't interested in participating. I put my energy into my family and my job, and both areas thrived. It was my source of happiness. And even though I wanted to meet someone, it needed to be on my own terms. It would happen—and not by enduring a hundred uncomfortable setups.

I was resolved to hold out for something *more*. I didn't even really know what that meant and was—probably naively—banking on the hope that I'd know it when I saw it or that it'd hit me like a Mack truck—something undeniable, unavoidable, and potentially fatal.

Kinda like the feeling I'd gotten when I met Annie. Who I couldn't date. At least not for a minimum of five years, which would put her in the vicinity of a reasonable age.

I found myself frowning as I hopped the curb in front of Wasted Words and stopped at the door, propping my longboard against the building as I dug my keys out of my pocket and unlocked it.

The closed bookstore was weirdly still, like an alter ego of its open counterpart, especially compared to the nights when the place was jam-packed with people and chatter and laughter. I headed to the bar just as Cam came out from the back.

She was a tiny little thing with dark hair and big glasses, wearing a T-shirt illustrated with Phoenix from X-Men, jeans, a worn-out pair of Chucks, and a smile.

"Morning, Gregory."

"Morning, Cameron."

She hopped up onto a barstool as I packed my gear in the cubbies under the bar. "Rose told me about your unauthorized new hire," she joked with one dark eyebrow arched. "What's up with that?"

I shrugged and turned to the register computer to clock in, avoiding her eyes. "You guys were busy."

"I mean, you could have at least *asked* Rose."

"She would have said no."

Cam bobbled her head. "Maybe, maybe not. So, are you gonna tell me the story? This is the first time you've ever expressed interest in new hires who aren't working the bar." She leaned in, watching me like a chess board.

I sighed and rested my palms on the counter in front of her, hoping I had my face in check. Because if Cam caught a whiff of my interest in Annie, I'd be doomed.

"I dunno, Cam. Just a gut feeling, I guess. She seemed like she needed a job, and she got a thousand times too excited about your coaster quotes. I got the feeling she would fit in great. I figured you and Rose would be all right with it. I mean, it *is* okay, isn't it?"

She smiled, but she was still watching me a little too closely for comfort. "You like her."

I rolled my eyes. "Not this again. We've agreed you aren't allowed to set me up anymore."

"Oh, I don't think I'll need to do much setting up at all. That's why you hired her, isn't it?" she asked, eager as a Jack Russell terrier.

"*No*. I told you why, and I meant it. Honestly, wait until you meet her. You'll get it."

Her eyes darted to the door, and her smile widened. "Well, speak of the devil."

I turned as Cam hopped off her stool. Annie stood outside the glass doors, looking unsure of herself, bottom lip pinned between her teeth as she knocked, and by the look on her face, it wasn't the first time. We hadn't heard her over The Ramones playing over the speakers.

She smiled when she saw Cam, her worry gone, replaced with sunshiny happiness.

I found myself smiling, my heartbeat speeding up just enough to notice.

In other words, I was fucked, and in the moment, I didn't even have the good sense to realize it.

They were chatting as they approached and walked past the bar. Cam gave me an I-told-you-so look, and Annie raised one pink mittened hand in a wave.

She barely spared me a glance.

I tried not to consider the horrifying possibility that I might be invisible to her.

While I didn't consider it, I kept myself busy setting up the bar, carting ice from the back and rubber mats from dish while Cam showed Annie around.

A few minutes later, Ruby flagged me from the sidewalk outside, and I trotted around the bar to let her in, her fire-engine red bob peeking out from her black beanie and her dark eyes smiling.

"Heya, Greg-o."

"Hey, Ruby. I think you're training a new hire today." I nodded over to Cam and Annie behind the register counter.

"Aw, she's adorable," Ruby cooed. "So, does this mean I'm finally getting promoted to cocktail?"

I winked at her. "I'll see what I can do."

"*Yes!*" she whisper-hissed and fist-pumped. "Mama needs a new leather jacket."

We split up—Ruby for the back, me for the bar—but I realized I had finished setting up. So, I grabbed my laptop, poured myself a cup of coffee, and slipped into a booth to work on the bar schedule.

It really wasn't a bad idea to move Ruby up to cocktail; she could work in both the store and the bar for a while until she got her footing, and it would free up hours for Annie. Done and done. And as I looked over the schedule, it'd be easy to double Ruby in.

Harrison showed up to take over the bar just as it was time to open the doors. His smile was crooked, and his blond hair looked like he'd both just rolled out of bed and messed with it in the mirror for half an hour.

I headed to the liquor cage in the back to work on inventory— for real this time—setting up my phone to play music. The first half of my shift was spent locked up with cases of beers and shelves of rum and tequila. The only interruption was Cam, who popped in to tell me that I was right—Annie would fit in great—and that she knew I liked Annie.

She skipped away with the know-it-all pride of a nosy kid sister before I could argue. Not like it would have done any good. Once Cam saw an opportunity for hooking somebody up, she wouldn't quit. It was part of her charm just as much as it was my personal curse.

Around lunchtime, I emerged from the fluorescent cave to gather up lunch orders for delivery. But what I found at the bar had me slamming on my brakes so hard, my sneakers almost squealed.

Harrison was leaning on the bar with a sideways smile on his face, and his eyes were locked on his prey, just like I'd seen him do a thousand times.

Except this time, it was Annie.

She was laughing at something he'd said, but her body language told me she didn't realize he was interested in her, which was crazy to me. I could see it from across the room.

I stormed over, schooling my face as I approached.

They looked over, and Harrison's expression told me I'd done a piss-poor job.

I ignored him. "Hey, guys. I'm ordering sandwiches from Jonesie's. You hungry?"

"Starved," Harrison said. "Get me a Philly, extra onions."

I smiled as I made a note in my phone, hoping it would give him dumpster breath. "How about you, Annie?"

Her face quirked in thought. "Hmm. I've never been there before."

"Annie just moved here," Harrison offered enthusiastically.

"I heard," I said flatly, turning back to Annie. "It's pretty standard in the way of sandwich shops. But their Monte Cristo is the stuff dreams are made of."

Her eyes lit up. "I've always wanted to try one of those."

"You've never had a Monte Cristo?" I shook my head. "Man, you're missing out."

"You know what it is? The idea of putting jelly on meat. I just couldn't ever bring myself to do it. It's like mixing peanut butter and banana or bacon and syrup. Something about mixing sweet and salty frays the fabric of my universe."

I laughed. "I'll tell you what. How about I order something else? And if you don't like the Monte, we'll switch."

"Deal. Meatball or Reuben?" She asked the question as if the answer would determine my future.

I didn't even hesitate. "Either. You just named my second and third favorites."

Her smile said I'd answered correctly. "Meatball it is, extra cheese."

Ruby called her name, and she turned.

"Ask Ruby what she wants, would you?" I called after.

"You've got it," she answered over her shoulder.

I watched her for a second too long, turning to find Harrison still gazing after her.

"A pretty little thing like that, mowing down a sloppy meatball sub with extra cheese? Fucking dream girl."

My jaw flexed. "She's eighteen."

The shock and disappointment on his face made him look like he'd just dropped his lollipop. "Aw, *man*. That *sucks*." He dragged the last word out, and I found I could relate.

Upside: he'd been effectively scared off.

When our sandwiches walked through the door an hour later, Harrison and I were too busy for both of us to take a break, so we agreed I'd eat first and then take over for him. I waved Annie over, meeting her at a booth just behind where I'd interviewed her.

"I'm starving," she said as she slid in.

When her eyes met mine, they were alight, bright and green as Emerald City, her pupil ringed with a brilliant burst of gold like sun rays.

"Well, don't let me keep you waiting," I said, turning my gaze to my hands so I wouldn't get lost in fascination. I handed her sandwich over and took a seat across from her.

Annie unwrapped it with enthusiasm, her tongue darting out to wet her bottom lip and eyes bugging when she saw the massive deep-fried sandwich covered in powdered sugar.

"Oh my God, that looks incredible," she said, reaching for her bag with her eyes still on the sandwich.

I angled closer and lowered my voice. "Wait until you taste it."

Her eyes met mine for a split second of amusement before shifting to her hands, which held a pink Polaroid camera. She turned the sandwich forty-five degrees and took a picture, the flash blinding. A little undeveloped photo slowly ejected from the slot in the top.

I watched her, smirking.

When she met my eyes again, she looked a little sheepish. "Sorry, I know it's weird. My dad gave me this old camera when I was little, and I was obsessed with taking pictures of everything. And it just kinda...stuck. I have about a million tiny photo albums; I especially like to document my firsts."

"I like it. I feel like I forget everything. Here," I said, extending my hand. "Let me take one of you eating it."

She brightened, handing it over before turning back to her sandwich. She picked up the gigantic thing and turned it in her hands, opening her mouth but closing it again with a discouraged look on her face. "How in the world am I supposed to eat this?" she asked.

"One bite at a time." I held up the camera.

She laughed before taking a deep breath, opening her mouth comically wide. And by God, she took the best bite she could, which was something to be proud of. I snapped just as she got it in her mouth, and when she set it down, a little half-moon was missing from the sandwich. Her mouth bulged, and powdered sugar dusted the tip of her nose and chin, but she didn't seem to notice or care, not even when I snapped another photo.

Her lids fluttered closed. "Oh my God," she whispered reverently around the bite. "How have I lived my whole life without this?"

A chuckle rumbled through me. "I honestly don't know."

"Mmm." She swallowed and took another magnificent bite. "Mmm," she hummed again with enthusiasm. "*Dish ish sho good.*"

"You've got a little something right here." I wiggled my finger at my nose.

Annie set her sandwich down and picked up a napkin, swiping at her nose. "Did I get it?"

"Almost. Here." I grabbed my own napkin, and with delicate care that sprang from somewhere deep in my chest, I brushed it against the tip of her nose, then her chin. "There you go."

She laughed. "This sandwich might be too big for my face."

I unwrapped my sub, too amused to be appropriate or healthy.

"I have a confession to make. I'm totally not supposed to eat any of this. I'm destined for a life of chicken and broccoli, but I sneak every chance I get. Don't tell my mom."

"Your secret's safe with me."

"I have this thing about trying things I've never done before," she said. "Back home was … I don't know. Safe and quiet and small. My *world* was small, but now I'm here, and here is just so *big*. I want to take advantage of that, you know?"

"I do," was all I said before I picked up half of mine and took a bite, echoing her moan with my much deeper one. "Goddamn, that's good."

"Wanna split?" she asked hopefully.

"Absolutely."

She dropped her half on the paper and dusted off her hands, swapping our halves. "It's not as weird as I thought. The sweet and salty. Like, it still freaks me out if I think about it, so I'm just not gonna think about it."

"Does it make your world feel a little edgier? Jelly on meat. Next stop, street drugs."

That earned me a laugh that made me feel far too proud of myself.

"I wonder why they call it a Monte Cristo," she said, looking at the layers of ham and Gruyére and jam exposed by her bite.

"Because it tastes like revenge."

She let out a single *Ha!* "Sweet, sweet revenge. And to answer your question, yes, I really do feel like a bonafide risk-taker. Not that they didn't have Monte Cristos in Boerne."

My brow quirked. "Bernie? Like…Bernie Sanders?" It was the only Bernie I could think of on the fly.

"No, B-o-e-r-n-e. It's named after a German poet. Six square miles of Texas Hill Country just outside San Antonio, population eleven thousand."

I blinked at her. "I think there are eleven thousand people within ten blocks of here."

"I know." She smiled and took another bite that would have been rude if she wasn't so goddamn cute.

"I can't even imagine living somewhere so small. You've gotta feel claustrophobic here with all these people. Do you miss it?"

Her face fell just a touch as she swallowed. "Not really. I feel like maybe I should, or maybe it's just too soon to miss it. I've only been here a week after all."

"Why'd you move to New York?" I asked innocently, but judging by her reaction, it wasn't a question that had an easy answer.

She stilled, almost shrinking before my eyes as she resituated her sandwich, eyes on her hands. "My father died."

I lowered my sandwich, stunned. "I'm sorry," I said softly, knowing intimately how poorly those words explained the core of my feelings while conversely encompassing everything I could possibly say or feel.

Annie tried to smile and almost succeeded. "He wasn't even sick. That's the hardest part, I think. If he'd been sick or old, if we'd had any idea it was coming, it might have been easier. I keep telling myself that at least." She took a breath. "It was a car accident. Mama survived, but she lost use of her legs."

"Jesus," I whispered under my breath, my mouth dry as bone.

"My uncle—her brother—lives here and offered to help us out while we try to…I don't know. Figure out how to go on, I guess."

"But it doesn't feel like there's a way to move on, not really. Does it?"

She shook her head. "Most of the time, it feels like wearing a plastic mask over the truth my feelings. Or wrong, like I shouldn't even consider my own happiness or try to move on. But then I remind myself that it's what he would have wanted. In fact, I think he would have insisted on it."

"I understand how you feel," I said, my voice quiet. "My mom died a few years ago."

Her eyes met mine, wide and shining with understanding and connection. "Greg…I'm so sorry. I know that doesn't mean anything—"

"It does. There's no real consolation to give, only the offer of acknowledgment."

She nodded. "That's exactly it. I'd rather that than, *Just give it time*, or, *It'll get easier*. Because I know it won't. It's a wound that will never heal, no matter how much time passes. I'll just find ways to live with the pain."

"Years have passed, and I still sometimes forget she's gone," I said, half talking to myself, though I knew she understood. "The holidays are the worst."

Tears sprang in her shining eyes out of nowhere. "Daddy died just before Christmas."

Her hand rested on the table, and I didn't think, just reached for it, hoping she could feel that I understood as best I could.

She nodded again like she'd heard me, her throat working as she swallowed. "It's never going to be okay, that holiday. It used to be my favorite. The magic, the lights, the love, the food. And now…now, it's only going to remind me of what I lost."

"Do you have any siblings? Because that's what got me through—being there for them, with them and my dad."

"I have two sisters—one older, one younger. They're all I have left, besides my loss." She drew a breath. "It's just so hard to grasp how quickly everything changed, everything I'd ever known, all in the span of a moment. A stoplight. A phone call. A sentence. And now, I'm here. But I can hear him in my mind and in my heart, telling me not to waste the chance I've been given moping around." She laughed, her nose a little stuffy. Then, she smiled. "So, I'll listen to him like I've been taught."

I smiled back. "I bet he'd have approved of that."

"I hope so."

She moved her hand out from under mine to pick up her sandwich again, and I reached for my own.

The moment passed.

But the connection didn't.

ANNIE

Greg and I finished lunch—courtesy of the pocket money Susan had been keeping me stocked with—and as I stuffed the last bite of the meatball sub in my mouth, I found I felt lighter than I had in some time. I'd shared my grief with someone who understood, someone who could shoulder it.

Grief was strange that way. It was a constant companion, one my family saw and felt and understood *too* well; we could share that grief, but sharing sometimes made it harder. Because my loss was heavy, and they had their own weight to bear. I felt compelled to keep my grief to myself so I wouldn't weigh anyone else down more than they already were.

But Greg understood. He'd been through it too, in his own way. And the sense of connection, forged by sharing an experience so profound to both of us, was so strong and alluring, I yielded to the heady desire for more.

He was telling me a story about his younger sister, who was three years older than me, his face alight with love for her, and I listened, amused and enchanted.

His smile was bright and handsome, his jaw square and strong, the line sharpened by his dark scruff. Finger ruts cut through the top of his long hair, the sides neatly trimmed, the effect a contrast of clean and casually chaotic. And his eyes were the most stunning mixture of blue and green, the color deep and dark and rich as velvet. I tried not to stare at the tattoos on his forearms that rested on the table between us—I hadn't seen a lot of tatted up guys in Boerne—and I wondered what their stories were, thought about how tall he was, how broad his shoulders were under his well-fitted shirt that hugged the curves of what appeared to be quite substantial biceps.

Really, Greg was gorgeous. Gorgeous and funny and clever.

And he'd graduated high school when I was in the second grade.

It was just too weird to even consider—although I had in some detail—even if he *were* interested in me, which he absolutely wasn't.

No way would a guy like Greg be interested in a kid from Nowhere, Texas, who had never been kissed.

For years, I had considered ad nauseam why I had never been kissed, had never had a boyfriend, hadn't even entertained the idea of any of the guys I knew.

One reason was that I'd known the vast majority of the two hundred kids in my class since we were in kindergarten. When you grew up knowing everyone's business, it was hard to see anyone in a new light. I watched some boys go from pigtail-pulling bullies to pigskin-throwing jocks. Some went from country boys in plaid pearl snaps to drama boys with enviable eyeliner skills. Everyone wanted to reinvent themselves, but we all saw each other as we had in Mrs. Clary's first-grade class. I was sure they only saw me as the sick girl with eyes too big for her face, the girl who always had a book in her lap and laughed a little too loudly. And even though new kids occasionally moved in—Boerne was becoming an up-and-coming spot for new families—they were quickly absorbed into one of the defined social cliques.

But even beyond that, no one had caught my eye. There were three boys in my grade called Bubba, and although their names had nothing in common with their intelligence—one was our valedictorian—I couldn't see myself with a Bubba. Although, trust me when I say that if you'd heard their real names, you'd understand the appeal of the nickname. No one read. Instead, they threw keggers in their parents' pastures, tubed in the springs, camped at Canyon Lake. They hung out at Whataburger or Sonic, spiking their Route 44 Cherry Limeades with cheap vodka.

I'd be lying if I said I hadn't wanted to go too. But the truth was that I couldn't have walked the distance into the pastures, and I couldn't have run for it if the cops came (they always did). I couldn't have tubed in the springs because, if I had fallen in, I might not have been able to fight the current. I couldn't have camped; I wouldn't have been able to set up my tent or swim in the lake or go on any hikes. And I didn't drink—mostly because it was bad for me, but also because the idea intimidated me.

Oh, I'd been asked to go on those outings a few times—not many, but a few—but once you refused so many times, people would quit asking. And a few boys had tried to pursue me, but I always declined. As nice as it might have been to have a date to homecoming and get a big, jingly, ridiculous mum to wear, I didn't want to say yes until I felt that *yes* all the way through me, down to my toes.

None of the boys in Boerne made me feel anything down to my toes.

So I'd read books, and I spent my recesses, lunches, and homecomings with my best friend, Jill, until she moved away the summer before senior year. And then…well, she moved on.

Luckily, Elle was my other best friend.

Greg stayed to chat with me until Harrison started flicking coasters at him from the bar like tiny frisbees.

I quit eating when I was stuffed, which was just as Harrison approached.

"You're not gonna leave me here to eat all alone, are you?" he asked with puppy-dog eyes.

I chuckled, sliding out of the booth as he slid in. "I wouldn't, but I'll never get through training if I take an hour for lunch."

"It'd be time well spent. Just saying."

"I don't doubt that for a second. See ya later, Harrison," I said over my shoulder as I made my way back to Ruby at the register.

She was handing a bag of books across the counter. "Here you go. Read *Fables* first, and if you don't love it, come back here so I can tell you why you're wrong."

I laughed, a single, surprised burst of sound. The guy with the bag in his hand blushed, his ruddy cheeks splotchy and smile shy, lips closed over his braces.

"Thanks, Ruby," he muttered before hightailing it out of the bookstore like his pants were on fire.

"Man, that's the best part of this job," she said with a shake of her head. "How was lunch?"

"Greg was right; that sandwich blew my mind." I made an explosion sound with my mouth.

She laughed. "Man, Harrison is practically tripping all over himself to get you to notice him."

I frowned. "What?"

Ruby nodded behind me, and I turned to catch him watching us, smiling with a wad of sandwich in his cheek. He jerked his chin in acknowledgment.

I laughed. "Oh, he's just being...I don't know. Funny."

With one eyebrow up, she said, "Funny?"

"Well, yeah. He was trying to make me laugh."

"Guys like Harrison try to make you laugh so they can get your phone number."

My face quirked. "No."

"Yes," she said on a laugh. "Anyway, Cam wanted you to head to the back. She's got some more paperwork for you to fill out."

"All right. Thanks for your help today, Ruby."

"No problem. You're a real natural. It takes *a lot* of skill to manage these babies," she joked, stroking the plastic buttons.

I chuckled and headed to the office I'd become acquainted with earlier that day. Cam was sitting at her desk, laptop open in front of her.

"Hey, Annie. Come on in. You can sit at Rose's desk." She motioned to the empty desk butted up against the back of hers. "Let me grab some forms for you—taxes, that sort of thing."

She rummaged around in a file cabinet at her side, retrieving one paper at a time until there was a stack on the table. A minute later, she handed them over with a pen. "Here you go."

I scanned the one on top and got to work.

"So, how are you liking it so far?"

I looked up, smiling. "It's the best first job I've ever had."

She laughed. "Make any new friends?"

I thought there might be a question under her question, but there was no way of knowing what it was. "Ruby is so much fun. She even made stocking books interesting by riding the cart like a chariot."

"She's crashed three since we opened."

I giggled, imagining it. "Harrison's so funny. Oh, I met Marshall too, but I don't think he likes me. He keeps calling me New Girl. Like, he said, 'Hey, bring me some bags, New Girl,' all sour-like."

"Don't take it personal; that's just his face."

I laughed. "Well, that makes me feel a little better."

"He's not a bad guy, just an arrogant one who knows far too much about comic books to be considered normal. How about Greg? I saw you guys eating together."

"Greg and I just had the best lunch. He's so easy to talk to."

"Isn't he?" she asked with a smile that might be a little wily.

"He really is. We had a deal; I'd never had a Monte Cristo before, so we ended up splitting one of those and a meatball sub."

"Ooh, good choice. From Jonesie's?"

I nodded. "So good."

"Greg's worked here since we opened, and he runs the bar better than I could. I'm more the bookish, sensitive type," she joked. "I've actually been trying to get him set up for years. I've been known to... well, *meddle* is probably the nicest term for it. It's why I spend so much time organizing our mixers. I've sorta been banned from any matchmaking."

"That bad, huh?" I asked with a brow up and a sideways smile to match.

"Oh, trust me, it was *bad*. But I've learned my lesson. Mostly. So, do you have a boyfriend?"

I laughed.

"I told you, *mostly*." She shrugged.

"No boyfriend. I'm new in town."

"Fresh meat," she said, rubbing her hands together. "I remember when I first moved here from Iowa. It's a shock, huh?"

I conspiratorially leaned in. "It's crazy, Cam. There are so many things to see, so many buildings and bodies, and it smells... different.

Like metal and people and cars and possibility, all mixed up and packed into the spaces between buildings."

"I know what you mean. I was so overwhelmed, I thought I might bust. But it gets better. Easier. More fun." Cam turned to her laptop. "Speaking of fun, how often do you want to work?"

"Every day you'll have me."

"I like your enthusiasm, Annie," she said with a smirk. "Tell me you sing. I really need a better karaoke buddy than Rose. She only sings if she's tanked."

I laughed. "I love to sing, and I will karaoke with you any day of the week as long as you can find a place that will let me in underage."

"Duh, *here*. Tomorrow night and every Tuesday."

"Seriously, put me down for every day on the schedule, would you?"

"Karaoke is nothing. You should see our costume parties. We have one coming up where you come as half of your favorite historical couple."

I pointed at her computer screen. "Right, so put me down for working all the days that end in *Y*."

She snickered. "Done, starting with karaoke tomorrow night. But not to work—to sing."

My smile could have lit of Fifth. "Deal."

Cam typed away on her keyboard, amused. "How about thirty hours a week, and you can come hang out with us on the rest of your days off?"

"I accept."

She chuckled.

"Really, Cam, thank you. This is…I think this is just what I needed and at just the right time."

"Well then, I sure am glad you ran into Greg yesterday and asked for a job."

"So am I," I said, and meant it.

Come Sail Away

GREG

The bar was packed with smiling faces that night, and the karaoke mic had been well met with talent. We had yet to have the quintessential slurred rendition of Johnny Cash's "Ring of Fire" and instead had been graced with a version of "Single Ladies" that had the crowd's jaws on the ground. We'd also been given a few gems of the '80s hair-band variety, and a duet performed "Push It," complete with all of Salt-N-Pepa's dance moves from the video.

And those were just the highlights.

Beau and Harrison were behind the bar with me, and Bayleigh was working service, making drinks for the cocktail servers and bar-backing, which meant ensuring we were stocked with glasses and enough ice to keep the drinks coming.

I hadn't stopped moving but for a couple of times—when Annie walked in, waving at me over the crowd, when she swung by the bar to say hi a little bit after, and when she stepped to the microphone.

She seemed to favor '80s music, singing "Just What I Needed" by The Cars with Cam. The second song, "You Make My Dreams" by Hall & Oates, had me smiling and dancing a little with Bayleigh and Beau behind the bar. Beau went full Molly Ringwald and did the little kick-dance thing she had done in *The Breakfast Club*. But, when she stepped up onto the stage and the opening to "Head Over Heels" by Tears For Fears started, I stepped off to the side, abandoning the bar without even realizing I'd done it.

She closed her eyes, cupping the microphone in her hands, her shoulders swaying as she sang with a velvety voice about how she wanted to be with me alone, about being lost in admiration, begging me not to take her heart or break it or throw it away.

During the *na-na-nah* part, she had the crowd going, her arm waving over her head in time to the music until everyone else was doing it too, the whole bar singing along, even tone-deaf me.

I didn't know how she had done it, how the second she'd picked up the microphone, she *became* music. She sang like every song meant something to her, sang so deeply that she could have written the words herself. She felt it, felt it through every bit of her, and transcribed that feeling to us through her breath and her lips. And her feeling was so natural, so alluring that we all joined in with the hope that we could feel it too.

The crowd roared when she finished, and behind the bar, we were clapping and whistling and whooping our appreciation.

Annie waved and hooked the microphone back on the stand. When she wound her way through the crowd to the bar, I made sure to put myself where she landed, which was at the end near Bayleigh and out of the way of the crowd.

Harrison and Beau took over, covering me without a word spoken. After a couple of years of working together, we were a well-oiled machine of efficiency in the square feet of space behind that bar.

She brushed her hair out of her face, beaming and energized. "Hey!" she called.

"You are a woman of many talents," I said, trying not to beam back with quite a bit of difficulty.

A blush colored her cheeks. "Thanks. Mostly I just sing in my shower. Karaoke is my exception."

I laughed. "Something to drink?"

"Oh, that would be great. Water, please."

I reached for a glass and dumped a scoop of ice into it. "So, '80s music, huh?"

"I know. I was barely even born in the '90s, but my mom *loves* '80s music. I grew up to Journey and The Police and INXS and Eurythmics. Daddy was more into classic rock. So I didn't listen to a lot of pop music as a tween. Total freak, I know," she said on a chuckle.

"Please, don't ever apologize for not listening to Miley Cyrus."

She full-on laughed at that and took the water once it was poured and offered, downing half of it in a series of pulls. On a sigh, she set the glass down. "How about you? Are you gonna sing?"

"And bust a hundred people's eardrums? Probably not."

"Aw, come on." She leaned on the bartop, smiling. "There has to be a song you love to sing. Everyone sings in the shower when they think nobody's listening. And if they don't, they should."

I snickered and rested my forearms on the bar across from her. "I'm tone-deaf."

She rolled her eyes, but her smile grew even wider. "So? It's not about how you sound; it's about how you *feel*. I know you have at least one song. You sing it…" She tapped her chin in thought. "Ah, you sing it in the kitchen while you're making pancakes. Or in the car when you're driving—wait, you don't have cars here. Hmm…when you're getting ready to go out with your friends, you sing it into your brush in front of your mirror."

She looked so sure of herself, I had to laugh.

"In the shower," I corrected, my cheeks warming a little. "I sing it in the shower. Or I used to."

Annie bounced, satisfied at her rightness. "What song?"

"Styx, 'Come Sail Away.'"

A lovely, happy laugh burst out of her. "Power ballads! 'Total Eclipse of the Heart' is my go-to; it's Mama's favorite. Come on, we have to sing yours."

"Not on your life, kid."

Her smile shifted to a pout in a heartbeat. I wasn't sure if it was for the refusal or for calling her kid.

"Have you ever done karaoke?"

"Never. Tone-deaf, remember? You wouldn't even be able to tell what song I was singing."

"I'll back you up. Come on! Just once in your life, you have to sing your favorite song with a microphone in your hand."

I gave her a look.

She started to sing "Never Gonna Give You Up" by Rick Astley.

I didn't waver.

She switched to "I'll Be There for You," shimmying around with a corny look on her face.

I fought to keep my lips flat.

When she launched into the hook of "Please, Please, Please Let Me Get What I Want" by The Smiths, I gave up, laughing.

"All right, you win."

She clapped, her green eyes twinkling. "I'm going to go tell Cam! And don't worry; I've got your back—promise. Be right back!"

She turned to go and ran smack into a guy, who grabbed her, chuckling.

"Whoa, you okay?" he asked.

I watched through narrowed eyes.

"God, I'm sorry," she said. "I'm such a klutz."

"A klutz who can sing like an angel."

I involuntarily rolled my eyes at him, not that he was paying any attention to me.

She laughed, totally unaware that he was looking at her like she was an ice cream cone he'd like to treat exactly like an ice cream cone.

"You come here often?"

"I work here, so…yeah." Another laugh.

"I'm here every Tuesday. Tell me I'll see you again here."

She shrugged and stepped around him. "Probably! Nice to meet you!"

Annie bounded off, and the mystery douche and I watched her go.

No clue. She didn't have a single clue. And I wished it hadn't left me relieved, but it had.

I wondered briefly how many guys she'd inadvertently blown off. Which, naturally, made me wonder what kind of man would get through to her. He'd have to be clear about his intentions and obvious. Persistent. Because subtlety didn't seem to be something she responded to. I got the impression that Annie took everything at face value, accepting what was simply by what it appeared to be.

The thought sent a flash of unfounded worry through me.

I shook my head when I remembered that she'd just left to set up a circumstance wherein I would be singing in front of a crowd. At least, if I had to endure the horror of singing in front of people, I would be doing it with someone like Annie. Because I had a feeling that she didn't do anything in her life without some measure of fun and happiness, and I knew from experience that her brand of fun and happiness were contagious.

Jett, the manager of our extensive romance department, who had hair out of a fashion ad and a smile out of a toothpaste commercial, stepped up to the bar where Annie had been and extended his hand for a bro-clap. I obliged.

"What's up, man?" I asked.

"Nothing much. Good night, huh? Man, the new girl can *sing*."

I smiled. "She's something else."

"Yeah, she is. Harrison said he was going to make a move on her before he found out she's only eighteen." He shook his head. "Brutal."

"Trust me, I know."

His expression shifted into assessment, then realization. "Ah. You too?"

I made a half-assed *psh* noise. "Please. I like her, but she's barely out of high school. We're just friends."

Jett didn't say anything, but one dark eyebrow rose.

Annie pushed back through the crowd, breathless and grinning. "She's got us all set up! Come on!"

Cam's voice came through the speakers announcing us, and Annie hurried me out from behind the bar, all while Jett watched, laughing so hard, his hand was pressed to his stomach.

I shrugged at him, which only made him laugh harder.

The second Cam thrust a microphone in my hand, I regretted every decision I'd made to bring me to that point in my life.

The opening piano riff began to play, and I held that mic with a sweaty fist as I looked over the expectant faces of the bar patrons and my coworkers, who had incidentally halted all work and were watching with unbridled anticipation.

Worse: they were listening.

But then Annie took my hand, looking up at me with big, encouraging eyes and a smile that made me feel like I could climb mountains.

And with my magic feather in my hand, I sang.

I sang with timid discord at first, but Annie was unabashed, nurturing my courage. But she didn't sing to the crowd. She sang to me. And then it was like it was just her and me.

We air-guitared—I had logged hundreds of air-guitar hours in my youth, and I had to say I was *really* convincing—and we got a little psychedelic during the bridge. The crowd sang through the end with us, and we were all sailing away to our futures together.

When the song was finally over and the crowd clapped and cheered, Annie bounded into my arms, saying with her lips near my ear, "See? It's about how you feel. I hope you feel good, Greg."

And I did, better than I would ever be allowed to admit.

Hearts On Fire

ANNIE

"Who's that one?" I asked, pointing to the extra-fat goldfish in Meg's tank as his tail worked a little too fast to keep him afloat.

"That's Titus. And that one in the back is Athena. This one in the grass is Bruce Wayne because he's a loner, and that one is Giggles because it looks like it's smiling. See?"

I did see and laughed.

"That's the one I named after Aunt Susan."

"I love that."

"So," Meg said, "how was *Greg*?" She stretched his name into three syllables, fluttering her lashes.

"He's *fine*, thank you. We sang at karaoke last night. He'd never done it; can you believe it?"

"That's so sad," she said as she sat at the foot of her bed where Balthazar, the golden retriever, had taken up residence.

"I know! Oh, and he convinced me to eat a Monte Cristo."

Her mouth popped open. "He got you to abandon the sweet-and-salty rule? Are you sure he's not your boyfriend?"

I made a face. "Since when are you so into boys? Do *you* have a boyfriend?"

She shrugged and ran her hand down Balthazar's shaggy back. "Maybe."

It was my turn to gape. "Well, go on and tell me."

"His name is Jake. He brings me a brownie every day, and he always picks me for his team in recess, no matter what we're playing. We're reading *The Hobbit* together."

I shook my head, smiling. "That's some serious reading for the fourth grade."

"It's kind of hard, but I've got a dictionary on my phone. And Jake and I talk about it, so that makes it easier."

"I still can't believe Mama let Susan get you a phone."

"It was the only way they'd let me walk to school by myself," she said. "Anyway, is sweet-and-salty Greg your boyfriend or what?"

"I don't know where you get these ideas," I said. "I shouldn't have even told you his name."

"Why shouldn't I know the name of your future husband?"

"He's not my boyfriend. He's my friend. He's way too old to be my boyfriend. He's almost too old to be Elle's boyfriend. It would be…weird. Like if Jake were twenty."

She paled. "Ew."

"And anyway, why am I defending myself to a ten-year-old?"

"Because I'm adorable and persistent."

"That is certainly true—and too smart for your own good," I said on a laugh. "I'm going to go rest for a little before this dinner tonight. Hopefully, it's not too weird."

Meg's eyes lit up. "Aunt Susan said earlier—she didn't know I was sitting behind the couch—that Fanny's name is appropriate because she's a complete a-s-s." She snickered.

"Well then, dinner should be interesting."

I ruffled her hair and made my way to my room with about an hour to spare before the Ferrars arrived. I didn't have much to do in the way of freshening my exterior, but my interior reveled in the solitude for a little while. First, I dug through the piano bench in my room and the wealth of sheet music stored there. I was too happy for Rachmaninoff or Brahms but found a book of Haydn pieces and smiled, flipping to Sonata No. 59.

It was romantic and beautiful and happy, and my fingers played the cool keys with gladness, high off the day, holding my face just above the surface of the water, ignoring what lay beneath. For now, the sun warmed my cheeks, and I would enjoy it until I was pulled under again.

A quarter to seven, the dogs took up their barking, thundering toward the door. I closed the piano lid and left my room, moving toward the sound of voices, my sisters and Mama joining me in the hallway.

The dogs wouldn't allow passage for everyone from the entryway beyond the door, though Susan was shooing and nudging and asking John for help. Behind her was a man who looked unyielding though not unpleasant, more apathetic than stern. He stretched over the dogs and Susan to shake hands with my uncle, who was smiling, seemingly unaware of the obstruction his wife's dogs had created.

Behind Mr. Ferrars was a proud and pinched woman, her face hard angles and her eyes shrewd. She wore a smile that looked more like a scar than an expression, strict and humorless, her back as straight as a razor and her sharp chin lifted so that it seemed she *had* to look down her nose at you.

The dogs finally unjammed the doorway. Mrs. Ferrars eyed them with a level of disgust, masked ineptly by that cruel smile of hers. And as she moved out of the way, I caught sight of a third member of their party and wondered where in the world he had come from.

He was tall and dark, his face kind and smile quiet with eyes that sparked intelligently under his brow. I determined his age to be far too old for me, but when I looked over at Elle, a smile of my own graced my lips as I noted he wouldn't at all be too old for *her*. And by the way she was looking at him, I thought she might have figured the same.

Introductions went around. Mr. Ferrars had a handshake like a cowboy, strong and curt, while Mrs. Ferrars's handshake reminded me of a dead fish, cold and floppy and inanimate.

"And this," Susan said proudly, "is Ward Ferrars, their son."

My jaw would have popped open and hit the ground if I hadn't had it affixed into a smile. He shook hands with everyone in greeting, all while I dissected his appearance, trying to figure out how *they* had produced *him*. But I could see it, if I looked closely. His eyes were the color and shape of his mother's though with a merriment I doubted hers had ever possessed. He was a similar height and build as his father, and on closer inspection, I could see in the lines of his nose and jaw where the two men were virtually genetic copies, separated only by age.

I also noted that he greeted Elle last and lingered for a second too long.

This was maybe the highlight of the whole ordeal. My sister had had exactly one boyfriend, years ago. And the thought of her with someone so *dashing*—it really was the only word I could think to describe him—was enough to set my imagination skipping into the future to name their children for them (Marianne Margaret Ferrars for the girl and Fredrick Fitzwilliam Ferrars for the boy, respectively. Fitz for short.)

We were led into the living room for a drink before dinner, Uncle John and Mr. Ferrars—Frank—sojourning to the cocktail tray to pour scotch with Ward trailing behind them, leaving the women to sit in the living room.

"Emily and the girls have been New Yorkers for only a week—" Susan started jovially, but Fanny cut her off.

"Yes, we were supposed to have dinner ages ago to celebrate," she said coolly, eyeing Mama. "I trust you've been able to…adjust."

Color smudged Mama's cheeks, her head held high. "Yes, thank you," was all she said, not bothering to explain herself.

"Good. I can't understand why you all didn't fly. Three days in a car seems…excessive."

I opened my mouth to give her something to consider, but she kept talking. "You were the one in the car accident, yes?"

My eyes narrowed at her intrusive lack of manners. "No, the wheelchair is just a prop," I popped, not even realizing I'd said it until it left my mouth.

I put on a smile, as if it had been a joke.

Fanny laughed, the sound tight and awkward. "Yes, well, I'm sorry for the loss of your husband. It must have been a shock to lose him so suddenly and at such a young age."

Mama looked like a storm in a bottle. "Yes, it was."

"And then to have to take charity from family?" She shook her head and said with an unbelievable air of condescension, "You're *very* fortunate to have such a generous brother."

Susan wasn't smiling anymore. "It's not really about generosity as much as it's about right and wrong. Having the Daschles here has been nothing but a pleasure and a joy." The words rose and fell with cheery inflection and a warning edge.

Fanny smiled, lips together and curling at the corners. "Of course."

"I think we could all use a drink. John!" Susan called over her shoulder a little too loudly. "Would you mind pouring us wine?"

He nodded.

"Good. That will be good," she said as she settled back in.

The conversation momentarily lulled, something that never happened in Susan's company. Mine either, but my quick tongue was too shocked to even gather up a response. This was probably a good thing. I doubted anything I had to say would be in any way acceptable.

The men joined us a moment later with wine for everyone but me and Meg, carrying the conversation back into familiar territory. Uncle John was happily in his element at his friend's side, and when Susan looked up at him, her face touched in adoration and joy, I understood why she put up with Fanny; it made John happy.

Good manners are made of small sacrifices.

With that reminder, I resolved to keep my mouth shut.

A half hour later, I realized this might actually be impossible, though keeping my mouth *full* helped.

Fanny was sure to remark on dinner with an unwelcome abundance of deprecating compliments. The meal was *quaint*, she remarked, barely touching her steak which she noted was *gamy*, smiling while she cut off delicate slivers to slip past her thin lips. The wine was *very stout*, she was sure to say, and from a vineyard she hadn't heard of, though she was *certain* she was familiar with *all* the good wineries in La Rioja.

All the while, I chewed my steak—which was delicious by the way and was one of the best meals I'd had in several years, Monte Cristo included—doing my very best to keep quiet.

Susan kept Fanny on the safest of topics, steering her around with the mastery of a lion tamer. That probably gave Fanny too much credit. As much as she *wanted* to be majestic, she was more like a cold, slick python. No, not even that. She wasn't quiet or clever enough to be a snake. Maybe a rabid poodle, coiffed with a ridiculous haircut meant to make her look fancy. Because it was painfully clear that Fanny thought she was fancy. But it was hard to take her seriously when she was foaming at the mouth.

My only respite from Fanny was watching Elle and Ward.

It was almost imperceptible—the stolen glances, the inclination to look at each other when they laughed. I hoped beyond hope that something would come of it.

John and Frank took over the conversation, reminiscing about their college days and running the *Valentin Fabre* magazine empire.

The history of the magazine was largely unknown to me; we never spoke of this part of the family, and it wasn't until I was a teenager that I'd ever even known the broad-stroke details of that side of my family. I listened, enraptured.

"My grandfather was the son of French aristocrats, a family that immigrated to New York a generation before. He grew up in Manhattan at the turn of the century. Harvard Medical wasn't for him; what he adored was marketing. When he got his first job as an advertising executive for *Ladies' Weekly,* he turned it around and enjoyed doing it so much, he bought his first magazine—*Nouvelle*— with the help of his parents' fortune. And when he built that one up, he bought another. Then another. Twenty years in, he owned fifteen magazines, each of them still thriving today.

"My mother—your grandmother," he said with a nod in our direction, "was his only child, and he groomed her to take over for him when he retired. It was where she met your grandfather."

Mama sat silently, eating with her eyes down.

Meg launched into a string of questions, and everyone laughed.

"Too many questions for a full plate," Elle said gently, redirecting the conversation to something safer, for Mama's sake. "It must be very exciting, working in the magazine business," she said to no one in particular.

"It's long work and a great deal of stress," John said, "but it helps to run it all with people I enjoy so much."

Frank held up his glass, tipping it first to John, then to Ward. "Hear, hear."

Fanny spoke while they were occupied drinking "It's the *legacy* that I find so exciting. Having something to pass on, like Frank will pass on to Ward."

Susan's face betrayed her annoyance, but Fanny was too self-absorbed to notice. Neither of my cousins had gone into the magazine business, and the dig was heard all too clearly.

"Ward is our shining star," she continued, beaming. It was the first genuine emotion I'd seen from her other than general discontent or condescension. "He's currently the associate publisher at *Nouvelle.* We have *grand* plans for him, don't we, Frank?"

"Hmm? Oh, yes," Frank answered absently.

Ward gave Elle an apologetic look as Fanny rattled on.

"He's just simply amazing at it. They say they've never seen anyone quite like him, and I'd have to agree. Wouldn't you?" she asked no one as she speared a green bean, which she insisted on calling *haricot verts,* and forked it into her horrible mouth.

"Do you enjoy it?" Elle asked him once Fanny's mouth was full.

Ward watched her with a light of surprise in his eyes, as if no one had ever asked him that so directly. "It … keeps me busy," was his answer. "And what do you do?"

Elle blushed at that, looking down at her fork as she rolled a green bean away from her. "Oh, I—"

Susan brightened up and interrupted, as she so often did. "Oh! I nearly forgot! John, Elle was a secretary in Boerne; do you think we could place her at one of the magazines? I think she'd be quite an addition to your staff."

John nodded thoughtfully. "Yes, of course. I'm sure we have something you could do, if you'd like."

"Exactly what kind of secretarial work did you do in *Boerne*?"

Fanny asked with her eyes on her fork, which politely stabbed another green bean. She glanced at Elle as she lifted her fork.

Elle's hands fell to her lap, and I imagined she was twisting her fingers under the table, her voice gone a little soft. "I worked for a small insurance agency."

Fanny hummed. "How charming. But I wouldn't want you to *overextend* yourself, dear. The magazine is *very* busy. Things move quickly, and if you're not prepared, I fear you'd be swept away." She laughed—at least, I thought it was a laugh—an odd, successive intake of air, followed by a sound of mild amusement.

I set my fork down with a clank and glared, breaking my vow of silence. "Elle happens to be one of the most organized, composed women I have ever had the pleasure of knowing. She works tirelessly and thanklessly just for the sake of a job well done, and I honestly can't think of a better person to nominate to handle such a *busy* environment."

Fanny glared back at me.

"Thank you," Elle started quietly, "but—"

"I was only stating the nature of the competitive, high-level work, so your sister could make a wise decision," Fanny said, her eyes like fiery laser beams.

In that moment, I didn't have a single wonder as to how she managed to steamroll her entire family.

Fortunately, I wasn't part of her family.

"Oh, I think we all understood you quite well."

Her mouth popped open in furious shock at that, but Susan laughed, a big, happy sound that I sensed was orchestrated.

"Maybe we could all use another glass of wine—Annie included."

Elle was still staring down at her hands, and I endeavored to keep the spotlight on me.

"I'd love one," I sang cheerily.

Mama didn't think it was funny.

Frank chose the moment to speak up. "Elle, we'd love to have you at one of the magazines." He completely ignored Fanny when her head swiveled on her neck to gape at him. "I've never known Susan to recommend anyone who wasn't exactly what we needed. In fact, Ward just lost his executive assistant. Think you could come in Monday and take a look around? See if it interests you?"

"You can't actually be serious!" Fanny hissed half under her breath as if we weren't all sitting right there.

Frank looked at her like she was crazy. "Of course I'm serious. It's not your concern, Francis."

Her face somehow soured even more, but she shut up.

"Good!" Susan said.

No one asked Elle what she wanted, and I watched her, wishing she would meet my eyes so I could comfort her, but she was refolding her napkin with the focus of a Tibetan monk.

"So," Susan started, "I don't know if you all know, but Annie is quite the pianist. She played for us and was *brilliant*. I must say, she blew me away and down Fifth!"

Everyone looked at me with interest, and I smiled, fully prepared to tap-dance until Elle felt more like participating.

"Annie, you have to play for us. John! John, tell her how much you'd like to hear her!"

He chuckled and smiled at me. "Would you do us the honor?"

"Of course," I answered.

Susan clapped her hands together and held them. "Oh, *wonderful*! I think we're all quite through with dinner. Come, come, we'll take dessert and coffee in the music room."

We all stood, except Mama. Everyone's eyes drifted to her for a simultaneous millisecond before shifting away. Regardless of the brevity, Mama saw it.

I motioned for Meg to take the wheelchair and hung back for Elle, taking her hand. In the shuffle, we'd been left in the back of the pack.

"That was awful," I whispered. "Are you okay?"

Before she could answer, her gaze shifted to look past me. I followed her eyeline to find Ward.

He merged with us, his handsome face apologetic. "I'm sorry about my mother. I'd like to say she's not always so…"

"Rude? Condescending? Snobbish?" I offered.

Elle pinched my arm. "*Annie!*"

But Ward laughed. "All of those things are true, and I'm sorry for each one." He paused, his eyes moving to Elle. "But mostly, I'm sorry that no one asked you if *you* wanted to work at the magazine."

I nearly sighed with thanks that someone else had noticed, keeping my thoughts to myself with some difficulty.

Elle didn't answer right away. "I…I do want to find a job, and I *did* enjoy working as a secretary, very much. But…"

He waited for her to speak as we neared the music room where Susan was already arranging chairs and ushering everyone around. And on observing his patience and thoughtfulness, I decided I liked him very much.

"I have the same fears as your mother," she finally said. "I don't know if I can do the job well."

"They say there's only one way to find out," he suggested with his lips turned up in a quiet smile. "If you'd be willing to try, I'd be willing to help. No strings; if you're overwhelmed or unhappy, you can go without any hard feelings. What do you say?"

She brightened and blushed all at once. "I…I'd like that very much."

At her answer, his smile opened up. "Monday morning then, at eight."

She nodded, smiling back. "Thank you."

"The pleasure's all mine," he said with a slight bow, stepping away when his mother called his name, motioning for him to come sit by her.

When Elle glanced at me, we both nearly broke out into a fit of giggles, our hands squeezing together once before I split off to head to the piano.

"What would y'all like to hear?" I asked as I sat.

Meg opened her mouth, but Elle whispered in her ear. Meg closed it again, looking none too pleased with having to keep quiet.

"Play something from *Songs Without Words*," Mama said, her expression and tone encouraging.

I smiled at her. "I know just the thing, if it pleases y'all."

Everyone nodded, except Fanny—hateful bitch that she was. But I couldn't be bothered with her, not when I began to play Opus 19, No. 1. My right hand danced across the keys as my left played the slow melody, the gentle wave of the music rising and falling, the motion swaying my heart, swaying my body gently. I felt the music with an unfathomable depth, in a language I couldn't verbalize, couldn't translate in any way other than through my fingers on the keys.

And when my fingers stilled and I turned to look at the people in the chairs at my side, I found some level of their understanding on their faces, even Fanny, who looked almost soft. Mama's cheeks were shining with tears, and Meg was tucked into Elle's side, their faces rapt. Aunt Susan's arm was hooked in her husband's, their fingers wound together, tears clinging to the edge of her lids.

"Should I play a little Billy Joel to lighten the mood?" I joked through my own tight chest.

A chuckle rolled through them.

"How about this?" I asked and launched into another Mendelssohn, a bouncing, lilting piece that seemed to lift everyone's spirits. After that was Beethoven and a little Chopin.

And then I was ready for cake, which everyone else had already eaten.

When I stood, they rose with me, speaking at once.

Uncle John looked at me like his gears were turning in his brain but said nothing more than, "Congratulations," did nothing more than smile and offer me a hug.

The hubbub died down, and when Mama mentioned she was tired, she and I excused ourselves, our evening was blissfully over.

We said goodnight to the Ferrars, leaving them with Susan and John for after dinner drinks.

Mama's silent room felt like a sanctuary.

"Are you all right?" I asked after a moment as I slipped her nightgown over her head.

She sighed, threading her arms through the openings. "Yes, I'm all right."

"That woman is horrible. I can't believe Susan tolerates being in the same room as her, never mind inviting her into her home."

"He's John's oldest friend, and they came up together, worked together all these years."

"Did you know him?" I asked tentatively. "Before?"

She nodded, reaching for me when I bent to lift her. "Yes, we were all friends. Susan, too."

I paused, considering my question. "Why didn't you take John's help? When your parents disinherited you, why didn't you accept his offer?"

She didn't say anything for a moment. I hoisted her up to sit on the edge of the bed, reaching for her legs, the limp, useless things like exclamation points on her losses.

"It was easier to disappear, to lose myself in my life with your daddy in Texas, to pretend like everything before didn't exist. Looking back only hurt me, and we didn't need money. We had the store; Daddy had his workshop. We had you girls. We had each other." The words trailed off, rough and pained. "It was just easier to cut ties than live half in two worlds. I chose one world—*his* world."

My hands trembled as I pulled up her covers, my heart thumping and aching and sore. "But John could have helped. My medical bills, college for Elle, piano lessons, the mortgage. You and Daddy worked so hard just to make ends meet. It could have been easier."

"We were happy, and we did just fine on our own. But the truth is that it wasn't just my pride that kept me from taking the money. If I'd taken a penny from John, our parents would have punished him for the betrayal. We were still young, John still new in the company. They would have taken it all away, stripped him down and turned him out. Our parents…they're rigid and proud, and they never go back on their word. It's not in their nature. Fanny is right; we really are very lucky to have John and Susan. I only wish we hadn't needed them like we do."

I laid my hand on hers. "It's gonna be okay, Mama."

"I want to believe that, baby. I do. I just don't know how to convince myself it's true." She pulled in a long breath and let it out in a sigh. "So I try to remember that you girls have chances here you never would have had back home. Especially you." She clutched my fingers and looked into my eyes. "Life is full of contradictions. I want you to be happy, but I want you to be safe, too. I want you to be self-sufficient, but thinking of you on your own scares me. You see? It's not simple. Life never is, even if it looks simple from the top down."

I nodded, unable to speak.

"But we have an opportunity here, now, and even though it's scary and strange, it's wonderful, too. Fanny aside."

I smiled a little at that. "She really is a miserable cow."

"She is. But I have a bad feeling she's not going anywhere. We'll just have to endure her, and we will, just like we've endured everything else." She cupped my cheek. "I love you, Annie."

"I love you too, Mama."

She let me go, her face soft and pretty and sad. "I'm gonna read for a little bit before bed."

"Let me know if you need anything, all right?"

"I will. Night, baby."

"Night," I said as I left her room in search of Elle.

I found her in her room, turning down her bed.

"Hey," she said with a smile. "Mama okay?"

"Sorta. She's trying to be at least." I climbed into her bed, and she shook her head, smiling at me. "Are they gone?"

"No, they're still out there. Meg and I didn't stay long." She slipped in next to me so we lay facing each other. "Well, it was an eventful night."

I snorted a laugh. "If by *eventful* you mean unbearable, I completely agree."

"It wasn't *all* bad. You played for us, which was the highlight of my night."

"Only because Fanny shut up for a whole thirty minutes."

She chuckled at that.

"And anyway, you mean to tell me that *Ward* wasn't the highlight of your night?"

A flush crept into her pretty cheeks. "Annie, don't be silly."

"You like him!" I crowed. "I knew it the second you said hello. I think he likes you too."

"I don't even know him. We only exchanged a few sentences."

"Why should it take more than that? I think, when you find your *someone*, it happens the second you see them. Like getting struck by lightning or hit by a bus."

"So falling in love is a lot like dying, right?"

I rolled my eyes. "You know what I mean. That moment when you meet him and time stops and the sun shines on you and the angels sing the hallelujah chorus."

"I think two people need *time* to feel affection for each other. You've got to get to know each other, learn what kind of fabric the other is made of, what they love and what they don't, what they believe and what they want out of life."

"I think to love is to burn, and I want to set my heart on fire. Like Tristan and Isolde or Romeo and Juliet."

She snickered. "All of those people died."

"But it's in *how* they died," I insisted. "They couldn't live without each other."

"And Romeo and Juliet were teenagers," she noted.

"Romeo and Juliet were fictional—and not the point."

"Right, the point is that you think Ward and I should jump into a volcano together."

I shrugged my free shoulder. "I mean, if the spirit moves you."

"He might be my boss come Monday morning."

"So use the opportunity to *get to know him* so you can maybe, possibly decide if you think he's *amiable* or *affable* or *perfectly fine* or some other dull thing."

She laughed softly and let it go without even trying, whereas I would have liked to argue until the sun came up. "I might have a job, and you've already gotten one. Meg loves her school, and Mama seems to be doing better. Things are looking up. I mean, think about it, Annie. You've got a *real job*."

"I know! What is my life? I live in New York in a fancy penthouse with a cook and a maid, and I got a job at a bookstore. This has to be a dream."

"We have a lot to be thankful for," she said quietly, her smile fading.

Mine slipped away too. "We really do. It's easier to see now that we're here. If we were back home…"

"I'm glad we're not."

"Me too. There was nothing left for us there. And here, we've been afforded so much. You've got a job too, if you want it. I mean, not just any job—a job at *Nouvelle*. It's got to be one of the most famous fashion magazines in history, next to *Bazaar* and *Vogue*."

"It's madness," she said with wonder. "We'll see if I can actually do it."

"You can. I know you can."

"Look at us, a couple of independent women," she joked.

"Daddy would have been proud," I said softly and took her hand.

She smiled and said, "Yes, he would have."

And that almost made the pain a little easier to bear.

The List

ANNIE

I'd never been afraid of hospitals.

I knew people had this thing about them because, unless they were having a baby, most people would only go there when something bad happened. It was associated with anxiety, even for happy occasions like having a child—*What if something goes wrong? What if the baby is sick? What if there are complications?*—but worse than that, it was associated with death.

People went to hospitals when they were going to die. And even the people who *weren't* dying were afraid the doctors would find something to change that.

But I'd never been afraid. Because those hospitals would save me if something went wrong.

Being born with a congenital heart defect was scary, but I wasn't scared. I could have been afraid, could have made myself even sicker from worrying, but I had faith. I believed the doctors who had treated me over the course of my life were as magical as fairies or wizards, but instead of using spells or magic dust, they used science.

I wasn't even afraid of needles. I'd watch, wide-eyed, as the needle disappeared into my skin, watch my blood fill up the syringe, or feel the chill of fluids as they rushed up my arm, freezing me from the inside.

It just never bothered me, not the machines or the sterile smell or the needles or the hospital itself.

That was, until my new doctor walked through the door the next day.

It was something in his face that set my heart skipping, something in the tightness at the corners of his mouth and the almost invisible crease between his brows.

He took a seat on his rolling stool and began to type at the computer.

Mama took my hand.

"I'm sorry to have kept you here all day, but I'm glad you were able to stay for the MRI and results. After seeing your echocardiogram, I really wanted to get a better look and compare them to your scans done six months ago." He turned the computer screen to face us, displaying two scans illuminated in blue-black and gray. "This is your heart six months ago, which matches the scans from six months before that almost identically. This," he used his closed pen to draw a circle around my heart in the new scan, "is from today. Your tricuspid valve—the leaky one—is allowing too much blood into the right atrium, dilating it, and in turn shrinking the right ventricle. Notice the difference in size. It's slight for now, but it's very likely it will continue to expand. I think it's time we talk about surgery."

My palms were damp, my breath short.

"Has anything changed since your last scans, Annie? Are you still taking your medication regularly?"

"Yes, of course, but…my father died last month, and we

moved here."

He frowned, concerned. "That's a lot of change at once. I'm very sorry for your loss."

"Thank you," I said quietly.

"Have you felt any different? Noticed any new symptoms?"

I considered it, my brows drawing together when I realized the truth. "Not new, but more frequent."

Mama looked up at me from her chair. "Annie, you didn't tell me."

I tried to smile, squeezing her hand. "I didn't realize. Mostly, I've felt fine, just little bursts of dizziness or shortness of breath. And my arrhythmia has been a bit more…vocal than usual."

Dr. Mason's frown deepened. "Annie, I want to see you immediately if you have any increase in symptoms or frequency. Without scanning you, your symptoms are the only way we know if something has changed, and your condition could escalate very quickly, too quickly for you to be able to act."

I nodded dutifully.

"Truth be told, if I had been your physician all along, we would have done the surgery before now. My recommendation is to correct your valve using the cone procedure and repair the hole while we're in there." He grabbed a model of a heart off the counter and held it up in display, using his pen as a pointer again. "Your tricuspid valve is in the wrong spot. It's here," he pointed, "instead of here. In this procedure, we'll separate this part of the valve from the wall of the heart, rotate, and reattach it."

"Is there any reason not to do the surgery, Doctor?" Mama asked.

"Not one." He set the model down and turned to me again, hands clasped in his lap. "And while I don't see any reason to panic, I would like to schedule the surgery as soon as we can get the authorization from your insurance."

Mama's fingers were clammy in mine. "And how long will that take?"

"A couple of weeks, surgery scheduled a week or two after that. The mortality rate of the surgery is less than one percent, but it's still open-heart surgery. The recovery will be long, so I'd like for you to plan for that. But, otherwise, it's the gold-standard procedure for this condition, and our department at Columbia has a lot of experience with it. My colleague—the surgeon who will perform the procedure—has done more than just about any doctor in our field and was a pioneer in the research." He said it all without saying anything truly comforting or scary, just with that distant, clinical tone that lends nothing but facts.

It was time. I'd known it was coming for years, knew that surgery wasn't just possible but probable, not *if* but *when*. I should have had it at sixteen, but my old cardiologist seemed to think everything was fine, that we had plenty of time.

Regardless of knowing it was coming, I was shaken.

Mama looked afraid. The doctor looked professionally expectant. And so, I squeezed Mama's hand and smiled as my heart skipped against my ribs.

"Let's do it."

We spent the next hour filling out paperwork for the insurance company in near silence. It wasn't until we were in the backseat of the black Mercedes, which Susan had insisted drive us, when Mama took my hand again.

"I'm scared," she said, the sound so small.

"I know. But we knew this was coming, Mama. And, when it's all said and done, I'll be healthier than ever. No more taking a thousand pills every day or checking my hands for oxygen depletion. No more dizziness. My heart will beat as steady as a metronome. It's gonna be good. Don't worry."

She nodded. "I'm less worried about that than I am about your health in the meantime. I think … I think you should quit your job."

I backed away from her, meeting her shining eyes. "No, Mama. No. This is the first job I've had—*ever*. I'm making friends. I'm living, finally living. Dr. Mason told me what I could and couldn't do, and he gave me permission to work. I promise, if anything changes, anything at all, if I get worse, I'll quit. But please, please don't make me leave when I've only just started. Please." My voice broke as my throat closed around the words, tears springing too quickly to stop.

"What if something happens? Do they even know? Would they know what to do?" She shook her head. "Annie, this is dangerous, and I can't… I can't lose you too." Her face bent, yielding to her pain, a sob puffing out of her as she looked down at her hands.

"Mama," I said softly, my own tears sliding down my face, "you're not going to lose me. I promise. We've already set everything in motion. We'll talk to Aunt Susan about recovery and how we'll get through it. I'll talk to work about what's happening and about taking a break." I brushed away the thought that they might not even want to keep me on staff once they found out. "The doctor said if he was worried, he would have admitted me right away. Please, *please* don't worry."

She shook her head, trying to gain composure.

"Let me go talk to work and see, okay? Will you let me at least do that? And we can talk after that, when we've had some time to think through it all."

She nodded, and I wrapped her in my arms as she cried. And I watched out the front window of the car, my own thoughts and fears and wants tumbling through my head like a rockslide.

GREG

The day had gone by without much incident. The store was busy, which kept me busy, but I found myself worrying about Annie.

I'd answered the phone when she called that morning to let us know that she was at the hospital, getting scans after her doctor's appointment and that everything was fine, but she would miss her shift. She asked if she could come by to talk to me when she was finished. To which, of course, I answered yes.

I should have been gone an hour ago, and I could have left. Annie could talk to Cam; it didn't have to be *me*. But I'd found myself unable to go, not until I saw with my own eyes that she was all right. So I clocked out and sat at a booth, armed with a beer and my laptop to kill time, working on the schedule, which was ridiculous in and of itself. I was two weeks ahead.

I also placed all my liquor orders and cataloged the rest of the inventory, and frankly, I was out of shit to do.

None of that mattered when Annie walked in.

Her skin was pale, but her cheeks were bitten from the cold, those pink mittens on her hands and a matching sweater hat with a pom-pom on her head. But her face didn't quite look cheery, the dark smudges under her eyes ominous.

"Hey," she said as she approached, pulling her mittens off. "Mind if I sit?"

"Of course not," I answered, closing my laptop. "Everything okay?"

"Yes. Sorta." She sighed. "I don't actually know."

Annie added her hat to the pile of knit accessories in her lap and folded her hands on the table, her eyes searching mine for a long moment, a moment I waited through in the hopes that she'd have the space to say what she needed.

"I should have told you something before you hired me, but I didn't think it would end up being a big deal. I mean, I've dealt with this my *entire* life, and it chooses now to make a statement." She chuffed and shook her head.

"It's all right," I said, not understanding. "You can tell me."

"I…" She took a deep breath. "I have a heart condition."

A cold tingle spread down to my fingertips. "Are you all right?"

"I am, and it's not as scary as it sounds. I was born with a heart defect; one of my valves is wonky, and there's a hole in my heart." She said it so simply, as if she were making a note of the weather, but the shock I felt made my own heart skip a beat.

"How… how does that work? A hole in your heart? Does it… does it leak? Like… into you?" I stammered, trying to grasp how it was even possible.

Annie smiled. "No, the hole is *in* my heart, between the chambers. I mean, I've always had it, but… well, I saw my doctor today, and he wants to do a surgery that will fix my valve and the hole." Her smile slipped away, her eyes dropping to her fidgeting hands. "It'll happen in a few weeks, and I'll be gone for a month or so. So, I don't know… I'm not sure if you guys will still even want me."

I sat for a moment in silence, trying to process what she'd said. "Is it safe for you to work?"

"I asked the doctor, and he said it was fine. My mom… well, she's worried. I think she'll come around, but she's scared."

"What about you? Are you scared?"

She took a breath, and I thought she might say no, but something in her face shifted.

"A little bit, yeah. My whole life, I've known this surgery would happen, but the timing sucks. This job is the best thing that's happened to me in what feels like forever. I don't want to lose it, but I don't want to waste your time either."

I nodded. "If you want to stay, I have a feeling we can work something out. Why don't you let me talk to Cam?"

Her face brightened with hope. "Would you do that? I mean, it might put her on the spot less if it came from you."

"I think so too. Yeah, I'll talk to her for you."

Relief washed over her, and she hopped out of the booth to launch herself into me, her arms around my neck, her lips at my ear.

"Thank you," she whispered, two little words so full of appreciation that they broke my heart.

I laid a tentative hand on her back, wishing I could stand up and really hug her. But instead, I let her go and leaned away.

She took the cue and stepped back, beaming. "You're the best, Greg. I am so glad we're friends."

Friends. Whoopee, I thought.

But I said, "Me too."

She slid back into the booth. "Did I interrupt you? What are you working on?"

"Just the schedule. Nothing that can't wait." I waved a hand at my laptop. "You know, we just got a new root beer in, and I've got some vanilla ice cream in the freezer. Want a float?"

"Oh, that sounds like *exactly* the thing to turn my day around."

I scooted out of the seat. "Be back in two shakes."

She just smiled up at me and began unbuttoning her coat.

I snagged a couple of chilled mugs from behind the bar and made my way back to the freezer.

I could have let her talk to Cam. I should have let her fight her own battles, but I had a feeling that I could ensure Cam wouldn't say no, that she wouldn't turn Annie out—the girl with the hole in her heart, the girl who had just gotten her first job in the big city. The girl who wanted to *live*, and Cam might have said no. And Annie wouldn't argue. She would hang her head and drag her feet out of here, and I would never see her again.

I wasn't quite ready to let any of that happen. So I'd fight that battle for her.

Worst case, I'd tell Cam I had a crush on Annie, and she'd let Annie stay on that merit alone.

Out I went again and to the bar, which was starting to pick up, where I grabbed a couple of root beers, twisting the tops off with a satisfying hiss. And, supplies in hand, I headed back to the table where Annie was bent over a notebook.

"What's that?" I asked as I set the mugs and bottles down.

She snapped it closed. "Nothing."

One of my brows rose with the corner of my lips. "The look on your face says it's definitely not *nothing*. Let me guess … a list of conquests?"

She snorted a laugh at that. "Hardly."

I nodded my appreciation. "A hit list?"

"Nope."

"Hmm. A list of donut shops?"

"No, although I might like to get my hands on one of those. Do you have one?"

I ignored the deflection. "Come on, what is it? I won't judge."

A flush crept up her pale neck, but she was smiling. "Wouldn't you like to know?"

"Yes, yes, I really would like to know," I joked. "Bad poetry? Band names? Baby names? Puppy names?"

She laughed. "It's a secret, and you'll never know." She folded her arms across her chest. "Guess all you want."

I frowned. "Aw, come on, Annie. I've got root beer floats, and I'm campaigning our boss on your behalf. Is it really embarrassing?" I asked, leaning forward with a smirk on my face. "A list of future husbands? Tell me I'm on that list."

I tried to ignore the genuine hilarity she expressed at that, my pride wounded.

"That list doesn't exist."

"But if it did …"

"You wouldn't be on it because you're my boss and my friend, and you're old enough to be my uncle."

I narrowed my eyes in jest, but I really was pissed. "Fine, if you're not going to tell me, I'll find out myself."

My hand snapped out like a cobra and snagged that little yellow notebook off the table, and she watched my hand in slow motion, stunned, her mouth hanging open.

"Oh my God, Greg!" She jumped out of the booth, stretching up on her tiptoes to reach for it as I held it well out of her reach.

"Now, what do we have here? God, I hope it's bad poetry. I'm gonna read it to the whole bar," I mused as I opened it to the page where the ribbon bookmark lay.

"Greg, *gimme it*," she whined, hanging on my arm in an attempt to lower it.

"*Living Out Loud—or Things Annie Daschle Has Never Done and Is Ready to Do Already.*" I laughed, trying to concentrate as she hung her weight in the hook of my elbow.

"Dammit, Greg, I'm serious!"

Way in the back of my mind, I knew she was, but I kept going.

"One, get a job—crossed off. See snow—you've never seen snow?"

"Nope, that's the big secret! You win! Now, give it back!"

I laughed. "Make a snowman. I think you'll be able to manage that." I scanned down the list, looking for something juicy, and when I found it, my smile fell. "You've never had a boyfriend?" I asked quietly.

She went still. "It's on the list, isn't it?"

I looked down at her. She'd stopped fighting and was just standing there like a deer in a floodlight.

I glanced back at the list. "And you've never been on a date? And you've never—" My head swiveled around again to face her.

"Oh God," she moaned, letting me go so she could drop her head into her hands.

I looked back at the list and then back at her. "Are you serious? You've never been kissed?"

She dropped her hands, her face crimson. "I've been kissed!"

My brows rose.

"Just not since the second grade."

I didn't know what came over me in that long moment that I watched her, something deep and fierce and elemental, something that made me want to go back in time and change her past myself. Worse, it gave me flashes of visions of helping her cross that particular first off her list. I imagined the sweetness of her lips, the wonder she would feel, mused over being the man who would make her feel it.

But I shook the thought away and turned back to her book, fixing a smile on my face.

"Well, I'm pretty sure you'll have no trouble checking off the vast majority of this stuff. Some of it is doable sooner than later—kissing aside. Like this one: *Eat hot dogs on the steps of The Met.* That's an easy one. Just make sure you go to Phyllis's cart and not Enrique's. I don't trust his meat selection. *Learning to ride a bike* is a good one; you can rent bikes all over and walk them into Central Park. You're not supposed to ride anywhere but the bike paths, but I think you could sneak a good session in, if you're careful. Do it on the grass, that way, it's better if you fall. *Get a tattoo.* I've got ins at a great shop. I can get you an appointment, if you want."

Annie watched me, her embarrassment shifting into bubbling excitement.

I frowned. "What?"

"Greg, you've gotta help me. I mean, not with the kissing thing, of course," she added hastily, her eyes catching mine. A rush of heat shot through me. "I don't know anybody here who can help me figure this stuff out."

"You sure you don't want help with the kissing thing?" I said with a coolness I didn't feel—my insides were on fire. "I might know a guy."

She laughed and swatted at my arm. "I'm serious!"

So am I.

"Really," she continued, "I bet you could show me the perfect place for a picnic in the park, and I bet you could tell me where to get the best pizza or help me figure out what Broadway show to go to."

I drew a breath and let it out slow, considering. It was a bad idea—that much, I knew as well as I knew my name and our age difference. But I wanted to. I wanted to so bad, I almost said yes and ignored the rational voice in my brain, which happened to be yelling at me to run for cover.

"I dunno, Annie. I work a whole lot, and—"

She looked up at me, so small and pretty, her eyes opening wide, pupils dilating, lips in the sweetest pout I'd ever seen. "Greg, please? It would mean so much to me."

And it was completely out of my power to say anything but yes.

She squealed when the word passed my lips, jumping up and down and then into my arms. "*Thankyouthankyouthankyou.*" But then she sagged against me and breathed a word. "*Whoa.*"

I hung on to her, my arms tightening, and when I stood all the way up, I took her with me, her feet dangling. "You okay?"

"Yeah…yeah. I'm sorry."

"Don't be sorry," I said gently and set her in the booth, my hands lingering on her arms just under her shoulders. "Let me get you a glass of water."

She stayed me with a hand on my arm. "No, I'm okay. I'm okay. Come here and sit with me. You promised me a float, and I don't want to have to call the manager over."

I chuckled, still searching her face for signs of distress. The flush in her cheeks had washed away, leaving her skin and lips pale but smiling, and I gave her the concession, knowing she was embarrassed.

"All right," I said as I slid in next to her, reaching for a bottle of root beer. "Now, let's have a look at this list."

Go On & Jump

GREG

I wish I could have asked myself why I was riding up Fifth that day toward The Met or how I'd gotten myself into the mess I was most certainly about to step in, but I couldn't. I knew exactly how it had happened and when. And I knew what a bad idea it was. Maybe not the extent, but I knew I was setting myself up for heartbreak.

And somehow, I couldn't have stopped myself if I'd tried. Which I hadn't.

We'd spent the rest of that evening in front of our root beer floats and Annie's list, mapping out a day to cross a solid portion of things off—the easy stuff at least. For the next three days, we'd kept planning until Annie had an actual itinerary. Color-coded.

As suspected, it had required virtually no effort to convince Cam to let Annie stay, allowing her a hiatus when she had surgery and an invitation to come back to work when she was ready. And Annie's mom had agreed to let her keep working, as long as we let her sit down whenever she needed.

It didn't seem they were able to refuse Annie any more than I was, though I had been fully prepared to fight Cam tooth and nail to secure Annie's job. I wanted to protect her, save her.

Because she's like a little sister, I told myself for the thousandth time, the steps of The Met in view. *You only want to help her out because she's young and innocent, and she asked you with that puppy-dog look on her face.*

And because you want to kiss her, another voice in my head said.

Shut up, I shot back, hooking my back foot under the board, jumping with my front leg to shove the board around in a one-eighty. The wheels hit the ground with a punctuating *clack* that made me feel a little better.

When I looked up, I spotted Annie sitting on the steps with her big eyes sweeping across everything—the buildings stretching up around her, the people walking by, the fountain, the street, the cars, the hot-dog stands and back around in a circle again. It was warmer than it had been, and she'd traded in her peacoat for an Army-green military coat over a sweater the color of dusky sunshine. A sliver of her ankles showed, her jeans cuffed and worn, white sneakers turned into each other.

She caught sight of me and waved exuberantly, drawing a smile from me and quieting my nerves, though not before one final shock of warning zipped through me.

I jumped off the back of the board, popping it up with my back foot to grab it just under the trucks. Annie clapped as she walked to me, smiling.

"Man, that was cool. You just jumped off that thing and caught it in one motion. I would have been flat on my face," she said with a laugh.

I smirked, feeling way more badass than I should for something as stupid as stopping. "With years of practice, you too can jump off a skateboard without getting road burn." I pulled off my backpack and laid it down, pack up, to strap my board into the buckles. "I'm not late, am I?"

"No, I'm just early. I was so excited, I woke up at six in the morning like a crazy person." She chuffed a laugh.

I hitched on my backpack. "You hungry?"

"Starved. I've been sitting here, smelling those hot dogs, for twenty minutes."

"That's some serious willpower."

"What can I say? I'm determined. Plus, I couldn't possibly eat one without you."

"Good. I need a picture of your face the first time you eat a real dog. Come on," I said, starting off in the direction of Phyllis's stand. "Know what you want?"

She shook her head. "How do you like yours?"

"Chili and cheese, nice and simple."

"Well, I have a lot of faith in your sandwich choices, so I think I'll have what you're having."

I laughed as we approached the counter and ordered jumbo dogs from Phyllis herself, who incidentally had no idea who I was. And with dogs and a couple of water bottles in hand, we headed back to the steps.

Annie's eyes were locked on the dog, her tongue slipping out to wet her lips as she sat down. "I'm salivating."

"Wait, where's your camera?" I asked, setting my dogs down before taking off my backpack.

"Oh! Here." She rummaged around in her bag, extending the instant camera once she had it in hand.

"All right, open wide."

Annie laughed, and I snapped a photo—it was too real of a moment not to.

She made a face. "I wasn't ready."

I shrugged. "That's the danger of handing me the camera." I slipped the photo into my back pocket and raised the camera again. "Go for it."

And she did. I snapped it just as her eyes closed, her face softening with pleasure.

I set the camera next to her—she already had chili all over her hands—and took a seat next to her, reaching for my hot dogs, my mouth watering once it was in hand.

When I took a bite, a soft moan rumbled through me. "There is nothin' like this in the whole world."

"There really isn't," she agreed. "I had a hot dog at a baseball game once, but it had nothing on this. Like, *this* is what I imagined *that* would taste like, but it was just a cheap imitation." She took another bite, humming her appreciation again.

"My brother and I used to come here all the time. We'd come to the park to skate and eat at Phyllis's cart for lunch."

"Huh. I didn't realize she'd been here since the Clinton administration."

"Hyuck, hyuck, baby. Laugh it up," I teased. "Not my fault you weren't even alive when Kurt Cobain was."

She gave me a look. "And what were you? Seven?"

"Five," I corrected.

She laughed. "And who got you into Nirvana at the ripe old age of five? Aren't you the oldest?"

"My dad loves grunge. I knew all the words to Alice in Chains' 'Rooster' by the time I was ten, and my younger brother, Tim, and I used to have air-guitar competitions. He preferred Soundgarden."

"Please, tell me you got that on tape," she said, still smiling.

"Our little sister, Sarah, was the camera girl."

Annie laughed. "My older sister, Elle, would have been the camera girl in our family band. She's...well, she's shy and quiet, and she would much rather let me have the attention than to have it thrust on her. We're polar opposites, which is why we're so close, I think. She complements me, tempers me, and I complement her. My little sister, Meg, is a lot like me though, maybe even *more* gregarious. She would have taken home all the air-guitar medals."

"Maybe we should set up a concert."

Her smile widened. "Maybe we should. I can't wait for you to meet Meg. She has a knack for remembering almost everything she reads, which mostly consists of National Geographic books, and wants to be an archaeologist." She took a bite of her dog.

"How about you? What do you want to do?"

She thought while she chewed and swallowed. "Something in music. I'd love to play piano professionally, but there aren't a lot of jobs for concert pianists, if I was even good enough to get hired."

"Why don't you try?"

Annie thought for a second, rearranging her hot dog in her hands. "You have to get a degree in music and need credentials to apply. I don't have either. And my grades in high school were good, but…I don't know. It just didn't seem possible to leave home. Maybe once I have my surgery, I'll feel better about taking the leap."

"After hearing you sing, I'm not at all surprised to learn you want to do something with music. I say go on and jump."

She smiled. "One thing Mama and Daddy always saved for were my piano lessons. I think Daddy must have had a deal with my piano teacher, Mrs. Schlitzer. She always seemed to get his best work."

I must have looked confused because she added, "He was a carpenter. They owned a shop on Main Street, packed with furniture and these little statues he used to whittle. He was always whittling something." She laughed. "I swear, he never went anywhere without a block of wood and his pocket knife. And he could carve anything. He used to make me unicorns and ponies and princesses and knights. I still have them, but they're not all here yet. The rest of our stuff is supposed to get here next week."

"My dad worked with his hands too, but nothing so cool as a carpenter," I said. "He was a plumber before his arthritis got bad. When my mom died, he just … he sort of fell apart. We had all moved back home to help out, but after that, we couldn't leave him."

Annie's hands cradled her mostly eaten hot dog in her lap as she watched me with earnest eyes. "How did she die, if you don't mind me asking?"

"Lupus. It was long and cruel. And Pop couldn't afford the medical bills, even after their insurance. Their savings disappeared right along with his ability to grip a wrench."

"I'm sorry, Greg."

I forced a smile. "It's all right. I didn't really have anything else going on. I have no passion that I can monetize. I figured out somewhere around sixteen that I was never going to be a pro skateboarder. I have a bachelor's degree, but I don't want to sit in some cube all day, pushing paper. I mean, maybe I will someday, but for now, I'm happy enough. And I make good money running the bar—really good money, considering. We're taking care of Pop, and I'd never admit it to my brother and sister, but I actually like living with all of them. There's something safe about it. That's one place in the world I know I can go and will be loved without condition. Plus, they get it, you know? We've all felt the same loss, and some days, it feels like they're the only people who will ever understand."

"I know what you mean," she said gently. "I feel the same way about my family."

"When did you start playing piano?" I asked, anxious to change the subject. I polished off my first dog and moved on to the second.

"When I was six. They said I was a natural, but I think they were just trying to fluff me up. More than anything, I just loved it. It was almost like another language, one made of feelings." She chuckled to herself. "I know how stupid that sounds, but that's how it feels. Oh!" she started, reaching into her bag. "That reminds me; I've got the drawing for my tattoo. My sister did it for me. Mama isn't happy about me getting a tattoo, but she didn't put up much of a fight, just made a fuss about me taking antibiotics."

"Antibiotics?"

She sighed. "A heart thing. I'm more prone to infections. I have to take them before going to the dentist too. Ah! Here it is."

When her hand reappeared, it was holding a thick sheet of watercolor paper. As she angled it toward me, I saw a drawing of a music staff, but rather than notes, the lines bounced in jagged spikes, like heartbeats on tempo.

"Do you like it?" she asked with uncertainty.

"I … I love it. Where are you going to put it?"

"I was thinking here." She turned to display her back and reached over her shoulder to tap between her shoulder blades.

"It's gonna be perfect," I said a little too softly and took a bite to stop myself from saying more. It cleared a third of the dog.

When she turned again, the sunbursts in her green eyes flaring with joy. "Oh, good. I feel like such a poser. I have no idea what I'm doing."

"I think you're doing great."

She blushed. "Thanks."

"So what's next on the itinerary?" I asked, working on polishing off lunch.

"Let's see." Annie swapped the illustration for her schedule of the day. "We're renting a bike, and you have been tasked with teaching me something I should have learned when I was six."

I laughed around my last bite and dusted off my hands. "Yeah, how did that happen—or *not* happen?"

"I dunno. I think Mama was worried about my heart, and I have a suspicion she banned Daddy from teaching me."

I frowned.

"If it makes you feel better, he didn't teach my sisters either. Out of solidarity, I guess."

"Are you sure it's okay for your heart?" I asked for maybe the fifteenth time over the last few days.

"Yes, I'm sure. And I'm sure all the walking will be fine, as long as you don't mind me needing to stop to rest."

"I don't mind."

"You say that now," she said lightly, "but let me know how you feel after we've hit every bench in Central Park."

"Well, lucky for me, I've got great company. You scared? About the bike?"

"A little," she admitted.

"The good news is, once you learn, you're apparently set for life."

And with a laugh, she stood, hands in her pockets and sun on her face, blonde hair caught in the wind and her cheeks alight with untarnished joy.

The moment made an impression on me that wasn't likely to be forgotten.

We chatted as we walked down Fifth to the bike rental station and unlocked one of the blue bicycles. And a little while and one park bench later, we were walking through the park in search of a grassy stretch off the beaten path.

We found what we had been looking for—a space lined with trees, somewhat shielded from the rolling, open knoll by boulders jutting up out of the grass.

"This looks good," I said, lowering the kickstand before taking off my backpack.

She pulled off her bag, looking nervously at the bike as she took a seat in the grass. A thin sheen of sweat glistened on her cheeks and forehead, her face a little pale.

"You sure you're okay?" I asked, eyeing her.

She smiled—her favorite way to answer. "It looks worse than it is. Promise."

I frowned. "Really, maybe the bike is too much. Maybe we can do this after your surgery."

"Greg, I'm fine. Come sit by me for a minute."

I kept my arguments to myself and sat next to her.

"The cool air feels so nice," she said, gathering up her hair and pulling it over one shoulder, exposing her neck.

"When they fix your heart, will you still feel like this?"

"No. I should be able to do anything physical I want within a few weeks of the surgery."

My brows drew together. "Really? After open-heart surgery?"

"Really. It's not like a heart transplant or anything. The hardest part of my recovery will be the incision and the fusing of my sternum back together."

A shudder tickled its way down my spine at the thought of a bone saw opening her rib cage. "What all will they do to your heart?"

"Close the hole, repair my valve. I've had open-heart surgery before, but I was too little to remember anything about it. The scar is the only proof that it happened. Well, that and my mother's stories. But this shouldn't be too hard on the muscle itself, just some sutures when it's all said and done. My body will work a lot more efficiently once the surgery is complete—like, *immediately*. I just have to get through the whole split-ribs thing," she said with a little smirk. "All right, I feel better. Are you ready?"

She looked better. Her cheeks and lips were tinged with color, and the waxy quality her skin had taken on was gone.

"Ready when you are."

We got to our feet, and I stepped to the bike to lower the seat. Once it was down, I waved her over.

"Come here and see if this works."

She climbed on cautiously, her feet on the ground and her hands gripping the handlebars. The seat was probably too low, but I figured it'd be better for her center of gravity—plus she could stop herself easier if she tipped.

"Okay," I started, one hand on the back seat and my other on the handlebar next to her hand, "I'm gonna hang on and hold you steady while you pedal."

She shot me a worried glance. "And if I fall?"

"You get up and try again."

She laughed, not looking convinced.

"Don't worry; you're not going to hurt yourself on the grass, but I'm not going to let you fall. I've got you, okay?"

With a deep breath, she nodded once. "Okay."

"All right. Put your feet on the pedals." My grip tightened when the balance was all on me. "Ready?"

"Ready," she echoed with determination.

"Now, pedal."

She did, moving us both forward, the bike only wobbling a little bit under her.

"Good, let's go to that tree. Just keep it slow like this."

Her tongue poked out of her lips, her hands white-knuckled on the handlebars until she got to the tree. And when she smiled, it was with more confidence.

"I did it!"

I laughed. "You did. Come on, let's go back. Ready?"

She nodded, and we took off again. This time, she wobbled a little less, speeding up until I had to trot next to her to keep up.

When we stopped at our backpacks, she cheered. "Again!"

"All right," I said on a chuckle. "I'm just gonna hang on to the back this time. And ... *go*."

I did just that, my hands on the back of the seat, the handlebars swerving a little but nothing she couldn't correct. And then I let go.

She didn't notice, wholly focused on staying upright, and I kept jogging, pulling up beside her. When she glanced over, I held my hands up in the air and wiggled my fingers.

Her face opened up with joy, and a whoop passed her lips—just before she swerved into me.

A string of expletives hissed out of me as I tried to grab her, but it was too late. She tumbled into me, bike and all, taking us down to the cold grass.

Annie was lying on top of me, her hair tossed across her face. The ground was cold and damp under me, and the handlebar of the bike was jammed into my ribs, but I barely even noticed. Not with Annie sprawled out across my body, her green eyes sparkling and her laughter ringing in my ears.

My own laughter met hers like an old friend.

"Are you okay?" I asked, sweeping her hair out of her face to tuck it behind her ear.

She flushed but made no move to pull away from me. "I'm fine. Are *you* okay?"

"I'll live."

We watched each other for a moment through the rise and fall of my chest, the movement carrying her like a rocking ship. And then she giggled again, climbing off me before reaching for the bike.

It was then that I began to fully comprehend the depth of the trouble I'd found myself in.

A few more rounds had her riding on her own, and we practiced starting and stopping without falling. Within fifteen minutes, she'd graduated to the walkway where she could practice on a smooth surface. It wasn't long before we were shooed off by a quartet of elderly men on their way to the Chess and Checkers House, judging by the cases they were carrying. They made sure to properly chastise us with wagging knobby fingers and low, overgrown eyebrows, unyielding, even when we explained our plight. So we hung our heads and tried not to smile at our shoes.

Before we checked the bike back in, Annie retrieved her instant camera from her backpack, kneeling next to the bike to snap a picture. I had her get on the bike, so I could take another. She kicked her legs out to the sides and opened her mouth in a blinding smile. And then we took a selfie. Well, I took it, since my arms were longer.

When it developed, I wished we'd taken two.

Back into the park we went with Annie's itinerary in hand, and as we talked and laughed, I found myself lost in the wonder of her.

It wasn't the statue of Alice in Wonderland that struck me; it was the smile on her face when she gazed on it, so completely in that moment that nothing seemed to exist before or after it. It wasn't the Bethesda Fountain; it was the way she dipped her fingers in the cold water like it would anoint her. It wasn't the beauty of the tiled terrace, shining like gold; it was the way she experienced it, eyes wide, lips parted, like she wanted to swallow the world.

I was right to be hesitant about spending the day with Annie. Before today, I could tell myself it was attraction, pheromones, science. I could tell myself she was too young, that we were too different. But the truth was that none of those things mattered. There were roots—I could feel them working their way through me. They weren't superficial, spreading out under the surface; they were the kind of roots you could never excavate, the kind that became a part of all they touched in the most permanent way.

We walked toward the Mall, a wide lane lined with elm trees so old and tall, their branches touched far above the heads of people below in an arch like a gothic chapel. And I listened to her, watched her, unable to deny the allure of her lust for life, the optimism of her soul, the lightness of her heart, a heart that had been broken from the start.

I was high from the contact, hungry for the feeling, desperate for more.

As we approached the entrance of the grand walkway lined with those dignified trees, Annie gasped.

"Greg, there's a piano."

We stopped in front of the the Naumburg Bandshell, a beautiful stage under a high arch, the ceiling domed and stamped with recessed stone plates for acoustics. They held concerts there in the summer, and a public piano stood in front, painted in waving colors like a melting rainbow.

Play me, it encouraged from the panel above the keys.

And so, she took a seat and did just that.

It was a classical song I recognized, though I didn't know the name. Her fingers brushed the keys with certainty, and a slow waltz that sounded both happy and sad. Her eyes were down, her head bowed, her body moving gently, as did her arms, as did her fingers. The movement of her body was in synchrony with the movement of the song, rising and falling, speeding and slowing, the notes echoing from the wooden chamber that held the strings and hammers.

Her fingers stilled when the song tapered off, disappearing like magic realized and gone too soon, and when she turned to me, when she met my eyes, hers were full of tears, of pain and joy and deliverance. And I knew with absolute certainty that I would never find another woman like her.

Not as long as I lived.

Alley-oop
ANNIE

The afternoon had slipped away before I even realized it; I'd been happily distracted by Greg and New York and the wonder of new experiences.

But sharing it with him was the best part of all.

It was late by the time we made it to the tattoo parlor, and when he opened the door and we stepped in, my eyes widened with excitement as I took it all in.

I'd heard about Tonic—the shop that was on the TV show of the same name—but nothing I'd seen did it justice. Stone Temple Pilots played on the overhead speakers in the open space, and a few people looked up from the Victorian-era furniture in the waiting room as I gawked.

Everything felt old and gothic with velvet and leather and swirling rococo details on all the furniture. Lining one wall were booths with antique desks and retro tattoo chairs, curio cabinets full of bottles, and paintings in elaborate gilded frames.

A girl with hair the color of purple cotton candy, pinned up in glory rolls, walked toward us smiling with cherry-red lips. Her high-waisted pants had sailor buttons in the front and straight legs, and her tight T-shirt that bore the phrase *But Really* was tucked into the slim waistband.

"Hey. Annie, right?" she said as she approached, her wedges drumming the hardwood floor.

My heart picking up in its uneven gait. "Yeah, hi." I took her extended hand, struck by her gravity. She was confident and cool in a way I'd never come across in real life.

She jerked her chin at Greg in greeting. "Hey, Greg. How's it hanging?"

"Can't complain, Penny," he said with a smile.

"Come on back." She turned, and we followed. "Did you bring the drawing we talked about?"

"I did." I dug around in my bag as we walked, handing it over once I sat in her chair.

She nodded with appreciation. "Man, I love this. Where do you want it?"

"I was thinking between my shoulder blades."

Another nod as she looked from my shoulders to the paper and back again thoughtfully. "Yeah, that would be perfect. About four inches, like this." She held up her hand, thumb and forefinger spread. "Let me get a transfer ready. Wanna take off your coat and sweater? Do you have a tank or anything underneath?"

"I do."

"Perfect. Be right back."

When she was out of earshot, I looked at Greg and squealed like a little girl. "I cannot believe you got me in here."

He shrugged, but he was smiling that crooked smile of his. "Rose's boyfriend works here, so it wasn't all that hard."

"Don't be modest," I teased, stripping off my jacket, which he hung on a hook on the wall.

I pulled off my favorite yellow sweater next, and when my head was clear of the neck, I found Greg's eyes on me for just a moment before he looked away.

They weren't eyes of a friend or a boss or a big brother or uncle; those eyes sent a spark of heat through my chest and cheeks and pinched the air from my lungs.

I wondered if he'd gotten a good look at my scar, and I had a rare moment of insecurity about it. Maybe it disgusted him, reminded him of how imperfect I was. Maybe he was just curious. Maybe he hadn't seen it at all.

Penny walked over before I could consider the moment further.

"Got it," she said as she held up the transfer, smiling. "Swing your legs around for me."

I did as she'd asked, and she moved behind me.

"I brought two sizes." She handed me a mirror, and I angled it to face the mirror behind her. "This one," she held it up to my back, "and this one." She swapped it with the other.

"The bigger one," Greg said.

"I think so too," Penny agreed. "What do you think, Annie?"

"I'm not sure. So...go big or go home."

She laughed. "My kinda girl."

We spent a little time getting the transfer where I wanted it before she directed me to lie down on my stomach.

Greg sat in the chair at my head, and my heart thumped and jittered with anticipation as Penny set up her tattoo gun.

He leaned forward, hanging his elbows on his thighs. "You okay?" he asked quietly.

I nodded and tried to smile.

"That was super convincing."

105

I chuckled at that. "I can't believe you had both your arms done. How long did that take?"

He inspected his forearms in thought. "I dunno. Probably a dozen sessions. And these aren't all I have. There's more on my back and chest."

Penny chimed in, "I did the Ganesh on his back. So fucking cool."

"I wanna see!" I lifted up onto my elbows.

He glanced around. "Right now?"

"Well, why not? I took my shirt off."

A puff of a laugh left him, but he stood and turned, putting his back to me. And, in what almost seemed like slow motion, he reached back over his shoulders to grab a fistful of his shirt, pulling it over his head with a whispering of fabric.

On his wide, muscular back, the elephant god sat, drawn in black and white inside an ornate frame. The lotus flower under him curled out from his feet, and he looked out at us sagely, each of his four hands in motion, each with a different purpose. The piece looked immeasurably masculine, the lines strong and powerful, the details unreal. The shading was done in tiny dots; I could barely see them with the few feet that separated us. And the artwork was as impeccable and stunning as the ripples and curves of muscles underneath.

"Wow," I breathed, only in part at the artwork. I had seen a grand total of zero backs that looked like *that*. "Why Ganesh?"

He pulled his shirt back on, and I mourned the loss of my view when he turned around.

"It was a few weeks after my mom died. I was on the subway on a mostly empty train, and at one of the stops, this Indian man came in and sat right beside me, asked me my name, told me his. We chatted for a little bit, I can't even remember what about now, but just before we reached his stop, he looked into my eyes—his were so brown, they were almost black—and said, *An end is just a beginning in disguise.* And he handed me a silver token with Ganesh on it, saying something in Hindi before he disappeared. I wish he'd told me what it meant."

He looked down at his hands. My throat squeezed so tight, I couldn't speak.

"Anyway, it was exactly what I needed to hear at exactly the right moment, you know? So I got this tattoo for my mom. Ganesh is the god of beginnings, the mover of obstacles. He's the god of the first chakra, the one that roots you to the earth, the one that governs your safety and stability, the foundation for all your other chakras."

"Did you know all that when he gave it to you?"

He shook his head. "When I started researching, it just felt right, you know?"

I nodded. "I do."

Penny's machine buzzed as she tested it out. "You ready, Annie?"

I took a deep breath and lay back down on the table. "Yep," I said more confidently than I felt.

"Okay, I'm gonna do a little bit just so you can see what it feels like. One, two, three."

The buzz hit my ears first, then my skin, through the muscle, into my ribs, and up and down my spine in a jolt.

She stopped within a second. "What do you think?"

I assessed myself. Mostly, I felt the adrenaline zipping through me and my heart's *da-dum* but not really any pain, just a little sting, not even as bad as a paper cut.

"I think I'm okay. That wasn't so bad! I feel lied to. Cheated."

They both laughed.

"Wait until you've had something done that takes a few hours, and *then* tell me how you feel," Penny said. "I'm gonna go for it. Shouldn't take more than twenty."

She started up again, and a few minutes in, I could see how it could maybe get uncomfortable. My lips pursed. I could feel the vibration behind my eyeballs, which was more distracting than anything.

"Hanging in there?" Greg asked, concerned.

"Mmhmm. Tell me a story."

"Okay," he said, thinking. "So, my mom used to have this psychotic Chihuahua."

A laugh bubbled out of me.

"His name was Jacques Poosteau, and I'm almost entirely certain he was part of the legion of hell. He hated everyone but my mother, and he'd sit on her lap like he was guarding the Crown Jewels. And if anyone got close—*anyone*—he would bark and snarl and bite and snort in a blast of noise like a hairy chainsaw. Look, I've still got scars."

He held up his fingers in display, pointing at a few dashed white marks on his skin.

"So, my sister, Sarah, was obsessed with trying to get Satan's Mouthpiece to love her. She would bribe him with hot dogs—he didn't give a shit about dog treats, only the best for the King of Hell—trying to lure him into her room. More than anything in the world, she wanted that dog to sleep with her, cuddle up and snuggle like a normal dog. She even tried to dress him up once. She had this little sailor suit with a hat and everything—one of her doll's, I think."

"What happened?" I asked raptly.

"She got it on him and even had enough time to get a photo with our old Polaroid. And she only needed two stitches."

Penny and I laughed as Greg went on, "Anyway, so Sarah was a nut about it, had convinced herself that he was coming around. And, one morning, she woke up, and what do you know? Jacques Poosteau was curled up in her bed, fast asleep. She started yelling and screaming, and we all ran in there. Sure enough, there he was, but Mom's face fell. Her eyes darted to my dad, and then she started making this big production about getting us all out of the room. But Sarah wasn't to be deterred. She moved to pick him up, and…"

My eyes were wide. "And what?"

Greg leaned in. "He was dead, gone back to hell where he belonged. But before he'd jumped into bed to terrorize that her one last and most permanent time, he'd ripped all the stuffing out of her favorite stuffed animal, Mr. Bigglesworth."

My face dropped, but I laughed. "Oh my God."

He chuckled. "He was nineteen by the time he finally took the long sleep. But Sarah made us all hold séances and burn sage and everything for years after that. She was convinced Jacques was still hanging around. She might not have been wrong; we got a cat after that, and I swear, she'd go in there and hiss at corners. The moral of the story is, never fuck with a sure thing. Just leave it alone and let it be what it is. Jacques, he was the surest of things."

I laughed again, the discomfort mostly forgotten as he told another tale—this time of his brother and a rollerblade incident gone horribly, comically wrong—and before long, she was finished.

When I sat up, I took the mirror from Penny again to look in the opposite mirror. The ink was deep and black, my skin red and hot around the edges, and it was absolutely perfect.

"I love it," I breathed. "Thank you. Thank you so much, Penny."

She smiled. "Hey, no problem at all. I'm just glad to be your first," she said with a wink.

And I found myself blushing, my mind on Greg.

He knew the extent of how many firsts I still had to cross off the list, and that knowledge made me feel vulnerable in the most decadent way; he knew my secrets, and he would handle them with care.

"All right, let me cover this up for you, and I'll get you some salve and instructions."

Greg stood. "I'm gonna use the restroom. Be right back."

I sat up as Penny gathered tape and an opaque sheet of plastic.

"So, how long have you and Greg been dating?"

My cheeks caught fire. "Oh! No, no—we're not…we aren't…"

She raised one brow at me in the mirror in front of me, but she was smiling. "Well, why not?"

I made some sort of airy noise and rolled my eyes. "Because he's, like, *way* older than me."

"So?"

"I mean, I'm only eighteen."

"I know. But I honestly don't think that really matters if you're into him."

Was I into him? I didn't know for sure, and the thought made me uncomfortable.

"Well, I think he's into you. I've known Greg for a while, and I've never been able to figure out why he hasn't been snapped up yet. He's hot, he's funny, he's got a great smile, that jaw…I mean, the guy's a catch."

"He's my boss."

It was her turn to make a noise like an air leak. "Please, Cam and Rose don't give a shit about that. But do you?"

"Do you what?" Greg asked innocently enough that I knew he hadn't heard us.

I said a little prayer to Ganesh in thanks.

"I asked if she needed to hear the instructions for tattoo care again," Penny said like the hero she was.

"Nope!" I cheered. "Got it all the first time. Locked in. Right here." I tapped my temple like an idiot.

She laughed. "I bet you do. Come on, let's get you checked out."

A few minutes later, we said goodbye to Penny and were standing on the sidewalk, the itinerary cleared—even the sushi dinner, which I had decided I should have left alone—and the day was done. My feet were sore, my heart was full, and I'd had one of the best days of my life.

But it was over. And that shouldn't have made me so sad, but it did.

Greg and I stood outside the tattoo parlor, watching each other for a moment, and when we spoke, it was at the same time, my, "Well, I should probably—" on top of his, "Can I give you a ride home?"

"A ride home?" My brows pulled together.

He smirked. "On my board."

I eyed it sticking out of his backpack. "Is that … how do you …"

"It's easy. I have a longboard. You stand on the tail; I stand on the deck. I skate; you just hang on."

"I don't want you to go to any trouble, Greg. You've already wasted your whole day on me."

"Trust me, it wasn't a waste, Annie. Not at all."

I looked up at the quality of his voice, dusky and rough, but he looked away, slipping off his backpack to unstrap his board as he kept talking.

"I bet you've never ridden a skateboard before."

I chuckled. "How'd you guess?"

He glanced up at me, smirking. "Just a hunch. Let's cross off another first. Come on, we'll take the traverse through the park."

"Is that safe at night?"

"Sure, on the bike paths and main roads. They're well lit. You get in trouble when you go wandering around in the park. And anyway, you're with me. I wouldn't put you in any danger."

I knew without a doubt that was true.

As he put one foot on his board, he looked up at me with truth in his deep blue eyes, backpack in one hand and the other extended, palm up. "Do you trust me?"

I slipped my hand in his and said, "I do."

He kept hold of it as we walked out to the street, only letting it go to dig around in his backpack.

When his hand reappeared, it was with a navy sweatshirt, which he pulled over his head, then a sweater cap, which I expected him to put on his head. But instead, he stepped into me and slipped it on mine, tugging it over my ears.

"It's gonna be cold," he said as he situated it, taking a moment longer than was necessary.

My heart stopped, my breath frozen. His face was so close to mine, I could see the tiny creases in his lips.

He stepped away, breaking the connection when he grabbed his pack and put it on backward.

He'd kept my breath, taking it with him. I wondered if I'd ever get it back.

I wondered if I even wanted it back.

"Okay, so stand back here on the tail, feet next to each other, parallel to the deck. You're gonna have to hang on to me, which will help our balance. Just lean with me; don't try to stand still."

"Got it."

"All right. Alley-oop."

The board was crowded with both of us on it, but I found my footing on the back and wrapped my arms around his waist, slipping them between his pack and his sweatshirt.

"Put your hands in my pockets—they're freezing."

"Thanks," I said, sliding them into his kangaroo pouch.

"Okay. Ready?"

I laughed. "I think I've been asked that question more today than I ever have in my life."

He turned his head. He was smiling, his nose strong and straight and masculine, his breath coming in warm puffs against the dark night. "Must mean you did something right."

And then, he kicked off.

I squeezed, squealing a little as I tried to hang on to his bobbing torso.

Greg laughed, turning his head again so I could hear him. "You okay?"

The sound hit my ears and my chest, reverberating through his body into mine as I hung on.

"Stop asking me that," I said with another laugh.

It was colder once we were moving, and I wished I'd had my mittens and my big coat. My hands really *were* cold. But we went on, the rough pavement under us sending tremors up my legs and numbing my feet. He leaned with a turn, and I leaned with him, the world tipping up just a little as we rounded a curve. His body bobbed again as he kept us going.

He was warm and sturdy in my arms, the comfort of him both surprising and befitting. It felt *right*—the comfortable ease of two people who were well suited.

In friendship. That's all he wants—to be your friend.

My heart ached at the thought, and I closed my eyes, touching on every sense. The vibrating of my feet and legs from the wheels on the pavement. The chill on my cheeks like an icy kiss. The feel of Greg—his narrow torso in my arms, my cheek in the valley of his wide back. And I burned every sensation into my memory to keep.

Once he built up some speed and seemed sure of my balance and his, he took my hands out of his pockets and put them on his shoulders, shooting me a wink before he knelt down.

The wind hit me in a gust. We were on top of a hill and picking up speed, the dark park on either side of us, trees rolling by as the street under the wheels blurred past. And I held on to his shoulders, my lips parted and smiling and heart thumping hard enough to almost hurt. But it was the best kind of hurt.

I felt *alive*.

When I let out a whoop, Greg smiled up at me, his nose red and a happy laugh on his lips. The wind whipped my face and hair, numbing my knuckles, but I didn't feel anything but joy.

Too soon, we slowed, and he had to stand again.

My hands were in his pockets the second they had the chance, and my smiling cheek pressed against his back once more. His own hands covered mine in the depth of his pocket, big and warm and strong and *good*. And for a long time we rode like that, time marked only by intervals of his foot against the pavement.

And then we were at my building, and the day really was over.

I stepped off his board, and he put his foot on the tail to tip it up and grab the nose. And we stood there in front of each other, both of us smiling, neither of us seeming to know how to say goodbye.

"So, what'd you think?" he finally asked.

A slow smile spread on my face. "It was the perfect way to end today. Thank you. For all of this, for everything."

"You're welcome, Annie."

Another long moment stretched out before he finally looked away, dropping his board back to the ground. "Well, I'll see you tomorrow."

And I grinned at him like a fool and said, "Goodnight."

I didn't go inside until he rode away.

When George saw me coming, he popped out to hold the door open. "Hello, Miss Annie. Have a good day?"

"The best, George," I said with a giggle and kissed him on the cheek before heading inside.

A few minutes later, I was walking into the still apartment. The only light was over the oven in the kitchen. I could hear a television going from Susan and John's side of the house, but the Daschle side was dark and quiet.

I walked past my room, depositing my coat and shoes and bag before hurrying to Elle's room where I knocked softly on her door.

No response. Her light was off, too.

So, of course, I opened the door. "*Elle,*" I whispered. "Are you still awake?"

Silence.

I walked over to her bed, noting the slow rise and fall of her chest. "Elle," I said only quietly. When she didn't speak, I gave her a shake.

"*Whahum*?" she mumbled, dragging a breath through her nose.

"Oh, good, you're up. Scoot over."

She shifted to give me room, blinking at me before rubbing her eyes. "How was your day?"

"It was *so good*! I had hot dogs and rode a bike and got a tattoo and walked around Central Park and rode a skateboard!" I rattled off. "I had sushi too, but that was mostly just weird."

She laughed sleepily. "I'm glad you had fun. You were with your friend...Greg, right?"

"Yeah, he's so great. I mean, he taught me how to ride a bike, Elle. The man has the patience of a saint. And he told me stories while I was getting my tattoo, and I even got to see one of his, on his back. And let me tell you, he has got a *nice* back."

One of her brows rose, and she rolled over to face me, smiling. "So, Greg is cute, huh?"

"Oh, man, so cute. His hair is this thick, gorgeous mess, and he's got this jaw that's covered in scruff, square without being Paleolithic. And— gah!—his smile is so pretty. And he's got the *best* laugh. Seriously, his laugh could make me smile through the end of *Old Yeller*."

"Does he like you, too?"

"What?" I said with flaming cheeks. "I don't like him. Not like that."

A little voice in my rib cage whispered, *Liar*.

Elle frowned. "Oh."

"We're just friends, you know?" My confidence wavered as I considered her question. "I mean, there were a couple of times he looked at me like...I don't even know how to explain it. Like he wanted to ask me a question, but he never did. And he held my hands in his hoodie, but they were ice-cold. He was just warming them up.

Right? Like, he wasn't trying to hold my hand or something, was he?"

She looked skeptical. "He spent all day showing you around the city, sitting with you at a tattoo parlor, riding you home on his skateboard. If I had to guess, I'd figure he probably likes you. I mean, if he's not gay. He's not gay, is he?"

I laughed. "No, I definitely don't think he's gay. But wouldn't I know if he didn't just want to be friends? He's never asked me out or anything. In fact, I had to *beg* him to take me around. There are a million reasons he wouldn't want me—the topmost being that, when *he* was eighteen, I was eight. What would a grown-ass man want with someone like me? He needs a grown-ass woman, one with a real job and goals and relationship history and references."

"Well, you definitely aren't eight now, so I don't really think your age difference matters." She paused, assessing me. "You *really* don't like him? Because it *sounds* like you like him."

"Of course I like him." A frown touched my lips as I really thought about it. "He's funny and kind and smart. And he's *super* hot, but…I don't know. I had fun with him today, and I like being around him. I'd totally run around with him again without hesitation."

"But?"

"But I guess I honestly don't *know* if I like him or if I don't, and I don't know if he likes me. Which leaves me certain that I am not interested in him in the romantic way." The statement was so decisive, I almost believed it myself.

A laugh shot out of Elle. "That is not the conclusion I would have come to."

I propped myself up onto my elbow. "If I really liked him, I wouldn't question it. There wouldn't be any wondering. You know that old saying, *If you have to ask yourself the question, the answer is probably no*? Well, I shouldn't wonder. I want to be with someone who I *have* to scream from the mountaintops that I need them."

"And you think that should be totally clear after one date?"

"It wasn't a date. And yes, it should. If two people are really vibing, isn't it totally obvious? There's no checking in with yourself to consider if you *might* have feelings for them. I've read about a trillion romance novels, and pretty much every one of them says so."

"Since when should you use romance novels to replace life experiences?"

"Since it's my only relationship experience at this point, and romance novels are gospel," I said, impassioned. "They're about overcoming, about learning what it means to love and to trust. They show us the very best we can expect from someone we love and sometimes the very worst. Every page, every word is powered entirely by love. How could I not have learned from them?"

"Well," she said, ignoring my argument, "*some* people expect to get to know someone before deciding we love them."

"Decide? There's no *deciding*. Either you love someone or you don't."

She frowned. "Don't you think people fall in love after a time? Surely you believe that not *everyone* falls in love at first sight, don't you?"

"Of course I do. Like people like you, people who weigh things out and make pros and cons lists and *wait*."

"So, sensible people."

"Yes, exactly."

She made a noise that sounded like a laugh and a scoff at the same time.

"But I am ruled by *sensibility*, by feeling. I trust my instinct, and my instinct has no clear opinion on Greg. So that's my answer."

Elle watched me with a sadness in her eyes, but she smiled. "Well, I'm glad you had such a wonderful day. I can't wait to hear more. Tomorrow."

I kissed her forehead. "I love you. Go back to sleep."

"Your wish is my command."

Wishes & Dreams

ANNIE

I woke the next morning after sleeping like I was dead, feeling refreshed, if not a little foot-sore and jelly-legged. Everyone was awake when I exited my room, and I found Elle, who helped me wash my tattoo and rub on a little salve. But as I dressed and got ready for work, I found myself musing over the day before.

It really had contained its own magic, something simple and subtle, something I hadn't even really noticed or acknowledged until it was almost over.

Greg was a good friend, the best kind of friend. The kind you could spend a whole day with and never lack for conversation. The kind you'd lose track of a whole stack of hours with.

I tried not to think about the notion that he liked me as more than a friend. I also tried not to consider that I might like him as more than a friend too.

Like I'd told my sister—when you know, you know. And I didn't, which could only mean that it was all wrong for the romantic kind of relationship. On top of the fact that he had become my real and true friend, a friend I didn't want to do without.

I could do without kissing Greg, I told myself, *but I couldn't do without his companionship.*

A little voice in my head pointed out that I hadn't ever kissed anyone, so *of course* I could keep doing without it.

True as that might be, I'd said my piece and counted to three. Which was to say that I'd decided, and once I decided something, I'd be hard pressed to change my mind. It was a stubborn streak that had run in my family for at least three generations.

I headed out of my room and into the kitchen that Sunday morning. The cook had set up a whole spread—eggs and bacon, pastries and oatmeal, breakfast potatoes and tortillas and salsa—and I loaded a plate as I greeted everyone.

They sat at the table, eating without any ceremony, so I took a seat and tucked in.

"I hope you had a nice time yesterday, Annie," Susan started, smiling. "It was about time you saw the city for yourself."

"Oh, it was great," I said between bites. "Did y'all have a good day yesterday?"

"It was lovely, thank you. Oh!" she sang. "John. John!" She whacked his arm when he hadn't looked up from his paper.

"Hmm?"

"Tell Annie about *lunch* yesterday," she said with great intention.

He shook his paper out and folded it closed, a smile brightening his face. "Ah, *lunch.*" He set the folded paper on the table and sat back in his chair, a little askew as he crossed his legs. "An old friend of mine, Kurt Dobson, and I had lunch yesterday. He's been the head of the board of trustees at Juilliard for… oh, what would you say, Susan? Ten years?"

"Twelve, I think."

He nodded. "Anyway, *Valentin Fabre* gives money to a large number of causes, including substantial annual donations to Juilliard. And while we were eating, I mentioned you to Kurt."

Numbness spread down my arms and across my palms, trickling down each finger. My fork hung suspended over my plate, loaded with a salsa-slathered bite of eggs.

"You did?" I breathed.

"I did. Your mother told me that by the time you graduated, you'd outgrown your piano teacher by a few years, that she was having a hard time finding music that challenged you, and it got me thinking. Kurt said the applications for next year were due December first, but he was interested in hearing what you could do and would make an exception, if you were interested."

Thank God he kept talking because I couldn't speak.

"He said for you to go to the website and take a look at the prescreening requirements. If you can get him everything he needs by Friday, he'll consider you for auditions."

"I...how..."

He waited for me to finish, but I couldn't, my thoughts moving too fast for my mouth to catch one and speak it.

Mama looked just as stunned as I did.

But it was Elle who spoke. "Uncle John, that is an incredible opportunity. But..." She paused, her cheeks flushing, back straight. "We...we don't really have the means to pay for Juilliard. Do they... do they offer scholarships?"

John chuckled at that. "If Annie is accepted, her tuition will be covered. Don't worry."

I dropped my fork and drew a startled breath.

Mama finally found her voice. "John, we can't accept that—it's too much. Too generous. You've already done so much for us."

"Em, listen," he said, his face soft but his voice was insistent. "The vast majority of my money is yours as much as it is mine. Please, let me help. I already donate to the school, why can't I sponsor a scholarship? I can't think of a more worthy cause."

"I…I just don't know," Mama said.

Juilliard, my mind whispered. Could I even do it? Could I even make it past the first round of auditions? I thought the chances were beyond slim. I wasn't *that* good.

Was I?

I *had* outgrown my tutor, and she *had* found difficulty to challenge me. I mean, there were things that were *hard*, believe me, but I mastered everything she threw at me, including Chopin's Études, a few that I even memorized. We made a game of it; she would bring me a piece and give me a week to master it, and if I did, she'd drop a quarter into a jar she kept on her mantel. When I filled it up, we would go out to dinner together.

I'd never missed a single week, and I'd earned dozens of dinners.

The bigger truth was that this was an opportunity I wanted. It was everything I'd ever wanted but never thought I could have.

There was nothing to do other than look my uncle in the eye and say, "I want to try."

He smiled broadly. "I thought you might—Emily, don't look at me like that. I can give this to her. I can give her something that could change her life. Won't you let me?"

After a long, tearful look, she conceded with a nod. "Of course I will," she said softly. "Thank you, John."

I pushed back from the table and stood, hurrying over to him to give him a hug swiftly enough to send a little *oof* out of him just ahead of a chuckle.

"Thank you isn't enough," I said quietly.

He patted my back. "Oh, it really is nothing. I only had lunch with a friend. The rest is up to you."

I straightened up and smiled. "Then I'll do my very best."

"And I'm quite sure that will be more than enough."

Everyone broke out in chatter, and Aunt Susan pulled up the prescreening requirements on her phone, reading them off with her reading glasses perched on the tip of her nose. I'd have to submit a résumé and write an essay, submit my transcripts as well as academic referrals, and record a video of myself performing three pieces by memory, using a provided list as a guideline.

My confidence wavered when I heard that list.

The two sections of required selections were at the highest level—I didn't know why I was surprised; it *was* Juilliard after all— chosen to show skill and speed, timing and movement, emotion and feeling. And the third was a piece of choice from a list of composers.

I mentally flipped through the pieces I already had in my toolbox; there wasn't time to learn anything new, not at that skill level. And, preoccupied with the task, I waved goodbye to my family and headed downstairs.

Aunt Susan had called the driver, who was waiting for me at the curb, but I sent him on. Armed with several bottles of water, my notebook, an hour to kill, and the good fortune of a beautiful day, I decided to walk, to think, to plan.

I set off up Fifth, turning into the park. I had plenty of time and decided to kill it by taking the long way around the top of the reservoir. Every ten minutes or so, I'd stop at a bench and open my notebook, my fingers tapping my leg as I thought through the pieces in my repertoire, my gaze roaming my surroundings and the chilly breeze cooling my skin, damp from exertion.

By the time I reached the reservoir, I'd chosen my first piece— Chopin's Études Op. 20, No. 6—and my sonata—Haydn, Hob 23—and I was trying to decide on my third piece as I stood at the rail, looking over the length of the lake at Midtown, the buildings in miniature at that distance.

It started as a squeezing in my chest so complete that there was no point of origin. My breath slipped away, and I glanced down at my hands. My nail beds looked as if they'd been smudged with ink. And I couldn't call out with empty lungs, couldn't do anything but reach for the rail as darkness crept into my vision like tendrils of smoke.

My knees gave out, and I sank to the ground, blinking out of consciousness.

White Knight

ANNIE

His voice came from what seemed like a long way away. An immeasurable amount of time had passed under me like a river. A moan crept up my throat. My lashes fluttered. And I opened my eyes to find *him*.

His hair was as dark as midnight, eyes blue and crystalline, his nose elegant and lips wide, dark brows drawn together with concern. I rested easily in his lap, surrounded by him, more shocked at the sight and smell and sensation of him than that I'd fainted in the middle of the park.

"Oh, thank God you're awake. Are you all right? We were about to call an ambulance."

"No, no. I'm okay." I would have sat up to prove it, but honestly, I didn't want the moment to end.

His eyes searched my face, stopping on my lips. He brushed the swell of my bottom lip with the pad of his thumb. "Your lips…"

"Yes?" I breathed.

"They're a little blue. Are you sure you're all right?"

I sighed and finally sat, running through an assessment of my body. Heart was beating steadier than usual and with no pressure or pain or tightness in my lungs. "Yes, I'm sure. Thank you."

A few people had gathered around, but they seemed satisfied and went on their way. But the boy still sat at my side, angling toward me.

"Man, that was scary. I've never seen somebody faint before," he said, dragging his fingers through what had to be the most luscious hair I'd ever seen in my life.

"I'm sorry. I…I have a heart condition that sometimes likes to make itself known."

He chuckled. "Does it always drop you like a bag of hammers?"

I found myself chuckling back. "No, not usually. Thank you. For stopping and all."

At that, he smiled, and it almost blinded me with its brilliance.

"I've never rescued anyone before. Not that I did much," he admitted a little sheepishly.

It was adorable.

"Well, I've never been rescued, so it was a first time for both of us."

I noticed then that we were still sitting in the walkway and moved to stand, but he reached for my hand, helping me up, and once we were standing, he didn't let my hand go.

"I'm Will," he said with his eyes locked on mine and his lips smiling in a way that made my insides feel effervescent.

"I'm Annie."

He bowed dramatically. "Pleasure to make your acquaintance, madam."

I giggled, offering a curtsy as he kissed my hand. "Why, thank you, good sir."

"Allow me to call on you tonight to inquire after your health.

Prithee, would you honor me with your phone number?"

I laughed, but a crackling fire burned in my chest, the cold in my hands and face dissipating to make way for a flush that I felt through my whole body like a fever. "That would be most agreeable."

He smiled and pulled my arm into the crook of his elbow. "Can I walk with you?"

"You don't even know where I'm going."

With a smirk, he said, "Doesn't matter. I think I'd follow you anywhere."

And my only thought was that I'd died and gone to heaven after all.

We'd taken two steps when I wobbled, and when he caught me, I was tipped in his arms, looking up at him with the cloudless blue sky stretching off in every direction.

"Hold on to my neck," he said with a smile.

And when I did, he scooped me up like a princess.

"Oh!" I breathed, cradled in his arms, the closeness of him overwhelming. "You don't have to do that. I can walk."

"I'm sure you can, but this is so much better, isn't it?"

And I had to admit that it absolutely was.

GREG

Annie was the last thing I'd thought about when I fell asleep last night and the first thing I'd thought of this morning when I woke. And all I wanted to do when I saw her was ask her on a date—a *real* date. No more ignoring my feelings, no more wondering if she felt the same.

I'd find out for sure.

Lying in bed, trying to sleep, that little photo of her on the steps of The Met sitting on my nightstand, I had wished that I'd told her how I felt. I almost had—the words were on the tip of my tongue—but the truth was that I wasn't sure how she felt, and the fear of rejection had stopped me.

But not today, I told myself as I kept busy, waiting for her to show up to work, nervous as all hell.

Because I knew how I felt and what I wanted, but what she wanted was a mystery to me. I'd dissected every moment, looking for signals. But Annie didn't know how to send or receive signals. She really might not consider me as anything but a friend, and if that were the case, things were about to get real weird between us.

The thought made me feel a little ill, but I bolstered myself with faith and hope.

But the second she walked through the door, my hope drained out of me like soggy leaves out of a rain gutter.

Her face was alight, flushed from either the cold or the proximity of the man whose arm she clung to. His eyes were on her face, his expression thick with wonder and maybe even a touch of adoration.

And if it had been anyone but him, I might have found a way to accept it.

Will Bailey was a version of the devil just as much as Jacques Poosteau, but the difference was that Will *appeared* harmless. No one would have questioned Jacques's desire to separate your face from the rest of you. And of the two, Will was easily the more dangerous.

When Annie approached the bar, the look of gladness and trust and complete joy on her face was a bucket of ice on the dying embers of my hope.

"Greg!" she called as she walked toward me where I gripped the edge of the bar hard enough to turn my fingers white.

Will met my eyes, his expression shifting to something colder, more calculated than he'd ever show Annie, not until he chewed her up and spit her out.

"Hey, Annie," I said, hoping I sounded casual and cool as my heart set fire in my ribs.

"Oh my God, you will not believe what happened."

She burst into the story, her face open as a daisy and lips smiling like a bubbling spring, and I listened, that flaming organ in my chest sinking with every word.

Because one thing was painfully clear: I had missed my chance.

Discomfort gripped me, squeezing tighter at hearing she'd fainted. She was fine, she insisted, and she'd tell her doctor, she swore. And Will had *saved* her, she said emphatically. She spoke about him as if he'd slain a dragon or saved her from pirates or Vikings or drug dealers, her eyes wide and full of emotion so sincere, it scared me.

Not because she felt it. But, because she believed it so fully, she would never see Will coming.

When her story was told, Will chuckled and stepped back, separating them. Thank God for that because I was thirty seconds from dislocating the arm her hand was hooked in.

"I've got to go," he said, "but I'll see you tonight, Annie."

She blushed so fabulously, I was surprised she didn't faint again. "I can't wait."

"Me either," he said with a smile, not sparing me a glance before he turned and walked away.

Annie sat on one of the barstools and unwound her scarf. "Oh, *and* my uncle might have gotten me an audition with *Juilliard*!"

My mouth opened and smiled and laughed all at once in disbelief. "Annie, that's…that's incredible."

"I can't even believe it!" she mused. "I'm sure the chances are almost nonexistent, but even having the opportunity is just…" She shook her head and laughed. "God, I have never been happier in my entire life. I have a shot at Juilliard, I just met my dream guy, I have a real job, and I live in New York City. All of my dreams are coming true."

I pushed my feelings aside, turned my back on the things I

wanted and gave her the best lie I had. "I'm happy for you, Annie."

Her smile slowly faded. "Are you okay, Greg?"

"Yeah. I just have some stuff in the back I need to do," I said, needing an escape, needing a minute to compose myself. "I'll see you in a little bit."

Now she was full-on frowning, the coup de grâce on her hangdog, hurt expression. "Oh."

In that moment, I understood something vital.

I wanted Annie's happiness more than anything, even my own. And she was happy—so blissfully happy that the thought of shattering that overrode my own desires.

So I did the only thing I could.

I leaned on the bar toward her and put on my best smile, saying, "You know what? It can wait. Tell me about Juilliard."

And when happiness lifted her up like a kite, I knew I'd do anything for her. Even if it meant the end of me.

That Motherfucker

ANNIE

The day flew by, in part because we were so busy and in part because I floated through it like Snoopy in the Macy's Parade—high and smiling and bobbing through the people with a fool smile on my face.

Every second of the encounter with Will played through my mind, starting with coming-to in his arms. It was something out of a dream or a fairy tale, and I couldn't believe it had happened to me.

Nothing like that had *ever* happened to me.

But it was the season of firsts. And Will was a brilliant first. He was so handsome, so charming, so absolutely *grand*, and beyond all reason, he wanted to see me again. In fact, he'd insisted on picking me up from work to see me home.

There hadn't been anyone like him in Boerne, that was for sure.

Wasted Words was packed that day, the line at the registers never quieting for more than a minute or two. Not long enough for me to talk to Greg again.

He'd listened to me talk about Juilliard, but something in him had closed off, shut down, pulled back. It was as if the magic from yesterday had been sucked right out of him.

I tried to tell myself I was imagining things. I was just being paranoid. He didn't purposely choose the far side of the bar where I couldn't see him. He wasn't making it a point to go to the back at every opportunity.

He wasn't mad at me.

But I itched to ask him flat-out anyway.

I heard my sister in my head saying, *He probably likes you*, and the thought jarred me so thoroughly that I almost dropped the change in my hand as I passed it to a customer's open palm.

If he liked me, he certainly wouldn't be happy about my showing up with Will. I considered for a moment how I would feel if he showed up with a girl on his arm, and I was subjected to an irrational burst of adrenaline that made my heart stutter.

Maybe Elle was right. Maybe I *did* like him.

My pulse picked up at the thought, but I dismissed the idea completely. If I liked him, my insides would be going ape. Like full-blown tree-shaking, banana-throwing, howler-monkey nutso, like they did about Will.

I sighed wistfully, smiling at my hands as I scanned a stack of books, thinking of Will, remembering the feeling of being cradled in his arms as he'd carried me to his car, the way he'd held my hand, walked me into the store to make sure I was safe. I'd finally found someone who made me *feel* and feel so intensely that it was nearly all I could think about.

I couldn't believe he was real. I couldn't believe he was interested in *me*.

Life was weird. A few weeks ago, I hadn't been sure how life could even keep going, and now I found that life running away from me in the best way, like rolling down a grassy hill in the summertime.

I didn't believe in heaven or hell, but I believed in finding meaning and comfort where I could. And I had to think that, somehow, I had manifested my destiny strictly through my desire to honor my father and live my life in a new way.

The universe had granted me a gift, and I didn't want to take it for granted.

When I glanced over at the bar, Greg was there, his enigmatic eyes on me, the irises the color of midnight. But when I smiled, he smiled back, sending a slow crawl of relief through my chest. We'd just been busy, that was all. I was just being dramatic, which was a common trap for me, right alongside jumping to conclusions and judging things based on what I could see and the narrow lens I could see them through.

Unfortunately, that knowledge never stopped me from repeating my mistakes.

Once it hit six, I finished up and passed the baton to Ruby before taking my drawer back to the office. And once I was all set, I grabbed my things, clocked out, and headed to the bar to ask Greg if everything was okay before Will came to pick me up.

Only I never got the chance.

Will and Greg were exchanging words across the bar, and their body language said those words were unpleasant. Greg's shoulders were square, his face tight, the muscles at the corners of his jaw bouncing like he was clenching and unclenching his teeth. Will didn't look much better, though a little less aggressive; his eyes were narrowed, and he stood tall and square, but there didn't seem to be any bite behind his posture. Greg, on the other hand, looked like he could separate Will's head from his body.

They both put on the controlled facade of neutrality when I

approached.

"Is everything okay?" I asked Will before glancing at Greg.

A thousand questions were poised on the tip of my tongue, and Greg's dark eyes held a thousand things he wanted to say.

"Fine," Will clipped, his presence between Greg and me tangible and impeding. "Are you ready?" he asked, offering me his arm.

"Yeah," I answered as I took it.

Greg's eyes were dark and stormy, but he found a way to smile. It was a taut, unfamiliar version of the smile I knew. "I'll see you later, Annie."

"Bye," I said stupidly, and we turned to leave. But as Will swept me out of the bookstore, I chanced a glance back.

Greg still watched me, in the exact spot I'd left him. I didn't think he'd even exhaled.

The second we cleared the doors, I asked the question that had been burning at the back of my throat.

"Do you know Greg?"

Will reached for the handle of the hired Mercedes and opened the door for me. "I dated his sister in high school," he answered to my utter shock, ushering me into the car.

I scooted over so he wouldn't have to walk around, and he slid in next to me. My mind turned the news over and over, imaginings of what could have happened commandeering my attention as he asked me my address, which I absently relayed to the driver.

Once the car pulled away, Will sat back with a sigh. "It was a long time ago. He never did like me, and neither did his brother."

Relief loosened the rubber band around my ribs at the implication that Greg wasn't upset with me at all. He didn't like Will. Of course he hadn't been thrilled about me walking in with someone he didn't approve of.

It explained everything, though niggling doubt still clung to my thoughts.

"Why not?" I asked with the utmost honesty and curiosity.

He shrugged. "They're overprotective of her, and they hated me because I was so different from them. I was just some rich asshole who was dating their sister."

My brow quirked. "Why would they think that?"

"We come from different worlds. Prejudice happens from all sides. Their dad was a plumber, and mine's a partner at the law firm established by my great-great-grandfather. Blue collars and blue bloods."

I found myself frowning. That didn't sound at all like the Greg I knew. "They didn't like you because you had money?"

"It was hard for Sarah. She came to our prep school as an outsider—not just because she was new in a school of old friends, but because there was a class divide. When we started dating, she became a part of my group of friends. And when we broke up, she wasn't welcome."

"That doesn't seem very fair," I said with a flash of defensive anger in my chest.

He took my hand, twining his fingers in mine. "It wasn't, but…" His eyes shifted to the seat-back in front of him with a faraway look on his face. "We had gone to this party the night we broke up. She drank way too much, and we ended up in this huge fight about her brothers. She went one way, I went another. I figured we just needed to cool off, but when I went looking for her, she was in one of the bedrooms with a guy."

The vision made me feel ill.

"Everyone found out. They ostracized her from our clique, spread the news in mass texts with photos. I haven't seen Greg since Sarah and I dated, but I have a feeling he blames the whole thing on me."

"That's…that's…"

"I know." A deep sigh left his lungs. "Anyway, I'm sorry about what happened back there. I didn't realize he worked there."

I nodded, curious about the other side of the story, about what Greg believed.

Will smiled, a soft, genuine smile that sent warmth blooming in my chest. "But it's in the past, and I'd rather look forward. Wouldn't you?"

I smiled back, putting my curiosity away to indulge in the moment with Will. "That's been my personal motto lately."

Will watched me, his smile never wavering. "When can I take you on a date, Annie?"

A flash of excitement shot through me, warming my cheeks. "I'm free tomorrow after work. I get off around three."

"I'll pick you up at work again. The weather is going to be great tomorrow, even warmer than today. I have an idea, but is it all right if I surprise you?"

My smile widened. "I love surprises."

"Good, because I'm full of them."

I swooned in my seat. "I'm sorry it couldn't be today."

"Don't be sorry. You need to work on your audition, and I have plans to make for tomorrow."

Sadly, the driver pulled up in front of my building, and George opened the door with a tip of his hat and a questioning look at me as Will got out behind me. We stood on the curb, and Will took my hands in his, looking down at me with something akin to worship in his eyes.

I was ninety percent sure I mirrored him.

"I'm so glad I was in the right place at exactly the right time today," he said softly.

"So am I."

I didn't want him to let go of my hands, and I didn't want to go inside. I just wanted to exist in that moment for as long as I could, memorizing everything so that I could call on it and repeat it on a loop.

But his fingers relaxed and fell away, and he stepped back. "See you tomorrow, Annie."

"I can't wait."

He ducked into the car and reappeared, reaching for the door. "Me either."

And then he closed the door, holding his hand up in parting as the car pulled away.

I watched him go before making a noise that was something like a giggle-sigh and skipadee-doo'd inside, minus the actual skipping.

I floated into the house, picking up Franco, the Maltese, when the dogs overwhelmed me. I tucked the furry little thing into my chest; he madly licked my chin as I blew past Susan, who informed me of dinner in an hour.

But I was looking for Elle.

I found her in her room, and even though it was Sunday, a day for leggings and big sweaters, she was fully dressed in slacks and a button-down, though her feet were clad in wooly socks. Her sketchbook sat in her lap, pencil poised elegantly on the page.

She looked up, smiling. "Well, don't you look happy?" she mused, bookmarking her page with the ribbon in the binding before closing the sketchbook and setting it on her nightstand.

"I think I'm in love," I said wistfully and flopped onto her bed with a dramatic flair.

She laughed. "Greg?"

I made a face at her. "No, *Will*."

One brow rose. "And who is Will?"

"Oh, just my knight in shining Mercedes."

"What in the world does that mean?"

I giggled and rolled over onto my stomach, propping myself up on my elbows. "So I was walking to work today—"

Her face exploded into a frown so fast, I almost got whiplash. "You what? Susan sent for the driver! Why did you walk? Did you tell

Mama? Why would you—"

"Oh my God, will you just listen?"

She snapped her mouth shut, but the look on her face told me it had better be good.

"So, I sent the driver away because I had plenty of time before I had to be at work, and I wanted to walk. I stopped at every park bench, I swear. I wanted to work on what pieces to use for my audition and think about everything, and I was being *perfectly* responsible."

Her face softened. "All right, I'm sorry."

My bottom lip found its way between my teeth. "But then I was standing at the edge of the lake and ... I sort of fainted."

Another volcanic face explosion, this one into a mix of anger, shock, and fear. "You *what*? Annie, this is *exactly* why you're not supposed to do things like this on your own. You didn't tell *any* of us. *None* of us knew. What if something worse had happened? Did they have to call an ambulance? God, why didn't you call me?"

When she finally took a breath, I cut in. "I'm fine. Everything was *fine*. It was a mistake to walk, and I'll never do it again—I swear it. I just ... it was such a beautiful day, and I was so *happy*. I thought I had it under control, that I was being smart. And you know why I didn't tell Mama; she would have said no, and I didn't tell you because you would have told Mama."

She folded her arms and gave me a look that told me I was right. "Go on."

"So, I fainted, and when I woke, I was in his arms. Will. He was so worried, so funny and nice. And *God*, he's so handsome. When we stood up, I was still a little weak and fell into him. And *get this*: he scooped me up like a princess and carried me to the road so his driver could pick us up and take me to work. Can you believe it?" I giggled again, grinned and giggled and flittered and fluttered. "He insisted on picking me up from work and getting me home tonight, and tomorrow, he's got a surprise date for me. And then we're going to fall in love and get married in some super-fancy rich-people hotel and live in a penthouse and have a zillion babies."

Elle laughed. "You are so ridiculous."

I sighed. "I know. Isn't it grand? Imagining is half the fun."

"And what if it doesn't happen like you imagine?"

"Then I guess I'll just shrivel up and die."

She snorted a laugh.

"Daydreaming is fun and free and makes me happy. And if reality isn't what I've imagined, I'll just dream up something new."

"Well then, by all means, daydream away."

I rested my chin on my hand, still grinning.

"So, what happened to Greg?"

My smile fell like a sack of bricks. "Were you still asleep when we talked last night?"

"No, I'm just wondering what happened. He worked with you today, right? Did you tell him about Will?"

I found myself nibbling my lip again and forced myself to stop. "Yeah."

"Was he okay?"

"He was a little weird," I admitted, feeling suddenly uncomfortable. "But he and Will aren't on the best of terms. But I'm not worried. Everything will be fine. Greg is my friend, and Will turns my insides to glittery, sparkly goop."

She gave me a look that I met with a defensive frown.

"I know I'm being silly, but I met my dream guy today. Can't you just be happy for me?"

Elle sighed, her face slipping to acceptance. "Of course I'm happy for you. I just don't want you to get hurt. You trust everyone—"

"And you trust no one," I volleyed.

She looked hurt but rested her hand over mine. "I'm sorry I upset you. Your happiness makes me happy, and I can't argue with a guy who makes your insides turn into unicorn goop."

"Thank you," I said a little curtly, though I was smiling. "I love you."

"I love you, too."

I rolled toward the edge of the bed and stood. "Well, I've got to start practicing. *Juilliard*!" I squealed, my happiness bubbling up again.

Elle laughed and waved me off. "Go. You're going to be great, Annie. I know it."

"I hope so."

"I don't have to hope. I know."

And her faith fueled my own.

GREG

I rattled up Tenth toward home on my board, the familiar sound of my wheels on the pavement offering me no comfort.

Of all the guys she could have walked in with, it had to be *him*.

It was one thing to watch her walk in with him and another thing entirely to watch her walk away on his arm. I'd spent the entire day consumed by what it meant, trying so hard to make sense of it. But I only succeeded in making myself angry, so angry that when Will came in to pick her up, I lost my ability to keep cool.

I had always hated that motherfucker. The first time his punk ass had walked into my house, I knew he was going to be a problem, and he was.

And I'd thought I was largely over it, but I was not. Not by a long shot.

I'd never trusted the smooth-talking teenager with the prep-school jacket and lying smile. As the leader of the douche pack, he was Sarah's gateway into the cool crowd, and she trusted that smile to be truth, trusted his words as if they were gospel.

Until she didn't.

It seemed to happen slowly, a seed of doubt in his intentions that sprouted and took root. They started fighting. And then she was ready to walk away, only she was afraid of the consequences. She didn't want to lose the thin foothold in the group of friends she'd found in that fancy school on the Upper East.

When she finally left him, he made it his mission to ruin her.

The rumors were fierce, her ejection from their social group brutal and final. It wasn't until she graduated and started college at Columbia that she finally moved on. Two years of hell by his hand, all because she'd had the audacity to break up with him.

And now…now, he had ahold of Annie who, in so many ways, was far more inexperienced than Sarah had ever been.

I hopped the curb in front of our building and came to a stop, heading upstairs and out of the cold, though the ice in my bones wasn't likely to thaw anytime soon.

The apartment was serene. Dad was sitting on the couch, working on a puzzle with his reading glasses perched on the tip of his nose and gnarled fingers holding a tiny piece in front of him for inspection. Sarah and our brother, Tim, sat at the table—Sarah studying and Tim on his laptop, probably working, considering he was still in his suit and it was tax season. He was barely up the first rung of the ladder at his accounting firm, which landed him the worst hours known to man.

They turned to me with smiles I didn't return.

"Bad day, son?" Dad asked with one gray brow on the rise.

"Coulda been better." I propped my board in its spot next to the door and kicked off my shoes before carrying my bag to the table. I tossed it in a chair and headed to the fridge for a beer.

Once the cool glass was against my lips, I felt better. For a second at least. I imagined Will with his arm around Annie, and my fist clenched around the bottle hard enough for my skin to creak against the glass from the pressure.

"What's the matter with you?" Sarah teased.

I didn't laugh. "I saw Will Bailey today at work."

She paled and stilled in one breath. "Oh?"

"Yeah." I took a long pull of my beer.

"That motherfucker," Tim sneered, which was almost comical with him in a tie and button-down.

Sarah watched me for a second. "What did you do?"

My jaw clenched. "*I* didn't do anything. But *he*…he…" I shook my head. "He showed up at work with a girl on his arm—*my* girl on his arm."

Sarah's eyes widened. "Annie? The girl you were with yesterday?"

"The very one." Another nod and another swig, almost finishing it.

"That *motherfucker*," Tim repeated, seemingly beyond his ability to compose complete sentences.

"I can't believe this. *Him*. I lost my chance to *him*," I said, just as dumbfounded and pissed as Tim, I guessed.

"What does that Bailey boy want with your girl?" Dad asked from the living room.

"Give you one guess."

Sarah sat there, looking stunned. "Are they…dating?"

"I don't know what they are. Annie fainted in the park today, and he was there. He even carried her to his hired car. Can you believe that asshole?"

"*That motherfucker,*" Tim said again as invisible smoke pumped out of his ears like twin tailpipes.

Dad snickered. "Yeah, a real jerk, helping a poor girl out like that. Somebody oughta call the authorities."

I turned to glare at him. "I can't believe you'd even joke about him after what he did." I shook my head and met Sarah's worried eyes. "It was already hard for you at that school with all those rich kids. There you were, stuck in the middle of a pond of piranhas with nothing but a boat full of holes and a busted oar to protect you. And that son of a bitch was the piranha king. He made up those rumors, ruined your reputation. And for what? Because he got dumped? All because his pride was bruised? Man, fuck that guy. Fuck him. And now he's got Annie."

My stomach turned at the thought, and I tipped my beer back to drain it before getting another from the fridge. I twisted the top off with a hiss but held on to the bottle cap, squeezing it until the tin bit into my palm.

"He hurt you, and now he's going to hurt her too. She still believes in everyday magic, still sees the world as a safe place. Annie is completely untouched by the world and its cruelties, and if he hurts her, so help me God …" I couldn't finish, not as angry as I was, but I was sure we were all imagining exactly what I'd do. I knew I was.

Sarah had the strangest look on her face and opened her mouth, as if to speak. But she closed it again and shook her head.

After a moment, she said, "You've got to get her away from him. What can you do?"

I had no answer for that. "I don't know if there's anything I can do, not now. He's single-handedly wrecked every plan I had just by showing up at the right place at exactly the right time."

Tim fumed. "You can't give up, man. You can't let that motherfucker win."

"Hey, look at that—he speaks," Dad joked, standing to make his way over to me. "He's right, you know."

I took a sip, avoiding answering.

"You shouldn't let this girl go, not if you feel this strongly about her."

I ran a hand over my face and took my seat at the table, sagging against the back of the chair. "I shouldn't even want anything to do with her. She's only eighteen."

Tim made a face. "Bro."

"I know, I know." I waved a hand in his direction. "And she works at the bookstore. I'm not technically her boss, but it makes things a little…complicated. And all that is on top of the fact that I can't even be sure she's interested in me. I mean, she told me today that all her dreams were coming true, in part because of *That Motherfucker*. Like, what the hell was I supposed to say? And what am I supposed to do? Tell her I hate him? Tell her he's an asshole? Warn her off and hope she doesn't slam the door on me for being jealous?"

I ran a hand through my hair, plagued by the futility of it all.

"I want her to be happy. She *deserves* to be happy. She deserves someone who sees *her*," I said half to myself. "Someone who appreciates the rareness of her—the righteous, uncorrupt girl who wants to live every breath like it's her last. But I don't believe *That Motherfucker* is going to honor her or cherish her. He's just going to tarnish her shine."

Sarah smiled, her face touched with emotion. "You should tell her that. I bet she'd dump him within three heartbeats of that speech."

I huffed a humorless laugh and shook my head.

"Seriously, there has to be something you can do," she said. "And if you can woo her yourself, then Will won't be an issue. Take her back from him."

When I didn't say anything, she leaned in eagerly. "Come on, there has to be something. What does she like? What's she interested in? Where can you take her?"

I thought for a second. "She's got this list of things she's never done, and I've been helping her cross stuff off of it. The other day, we were talking about a list of donut shops and I thought maybe I could take her to some."

Sarah lit up. "Oh, wait! Hang on!"

She bounded out of the room while Dad, Tim, and I blinked at each other. When she trotted back in, it was with a little booklet titled NYC Donut Map. On opening it, we saw that it was a map of Manhattan with donut shops listed with a key full of details about the stores. I noted a couple, including a little shop called Lekker near the bookstore, and I wondered if we could go there during our break someday.

Sarah hung her hands on her hips, looking proud of herself. "Take that to her and ask her if she wants to go exploring with you. That's one date."

"Doesn't she have to be into me for it to be considered a date?"

She shook her head. "Listen, you just need to keep being there. Be her friend. She'll come around."

Tim rolled his eyes. "Nobody makes it out of the friendzone, and you know it."

Sarah glared at him. "First, don't crush Greg's spirit. Second, he's only *temporarily* friendzoned. Right, Greg? You said you guys were vibing yesterday."

Dad shook his head. "It's *almost* like you're speaking English. What the hell is *vibing*?"

"You know," Sarah answered, "when you really like somebody and you feel that ... zing. Like electricity. The attraction."

"Ah," he said with a nod. "I'm caught up. Continue."

Tim and I chuckled.

"So, what else?" Sarah asked, her eyes sparkling with enthusiasm and purpose. "Do you think she might like the ballet? I mean, Rose got us tickets once. Do you think she'd do it again?"

Tim nodded. "Bitches love the ballet, man."

I shook my head at him. "How the hell are you the one with the responsible, grown-up suit-and-tie job?"

He shrugged.

"Yeah," I conceded. "Rose could probably get me tickets again, but I don't know. The ballet? That's like a fancy, serious *date*, isn't it? I don't want to scare her off. And if she's with Will, I don't know if she'll even agree to go with me."

"Play the friend card," Tim encouraged.

"Oh, *now* being friendzoned is useful?"

"Look, I'm just saying, use every card you *can*. Throw the whole deck at her. Fifty-Two Card Pickup of the heart."

Sarah nodded. "I'm with Tim. Take her to the ballet. You've got two shots to impress her, and I'm sure we can come up with more. Just start there, see how it goes."

I thought on it and felt something more dangerous than anything —hope. "You know, it might work."

Tim laughed, a big, bawdy sound, and clapped me on the upper arm. "Attaboy. Go get your girl, steal her back from That Motherfucker. And if he gets in the way, just punch him. Twice."

"Why twice?"

He smirked. "Once for me."

Practically Perfect

GREG

S leep was an effective reset. I woke the next morning with a sense of renewed purpose. I had a plan in my pocket and a goal in mind: get that girl.

My girl, I'd said last night without thinking. Because the second I'd seen Annie with Will, that was my first and only thought.

Mine.

It was stupid and archaic, savage even, but the instinct was deep and automatic. That single word sang unbidden from my heart at the mere thought of her with another man. Maybe it was because part of me was already hers. Any choice I had to the contrary had long since passed, if there ever *had* been a choice.

That realization had at least spawned a plan, and when I pulled open the door to Wasted Words on my day off, it was with a donut map in my pocket, a smile on my face, and hope in my heart.

I scanned the store looking for Annie, spotting her behind the register on a stool with her chin propped in her hand and her eyes on an open book on the counter, her face soft and lovely and content. With a spring in my step and my speech on a loop in my mind, I headed over to her.

She looked up, first with the polite reception she would give a customer, a stranger, but when she saw it was me, her eyes lit up like New Year's Eve.

"Hey," she said cheerily, closing her book. "I didn't expect to see you on your day off."

I smiled, ignoring the squirming nerves in my stomach and that damnable fluttering hope in my chest. "I wanted to bring you something."

"Ooh, a surprise? I love surprises."

My smile tilted into a smirk. "Remember the other day when you said you'd like to get your hands on a list of donut shops?"

She nodded, grinning.

"Well, look what I found." I pulled the map out of my back pocket and slid it across the counter, feeling like a king when her face shifted into sheer elation.

"Oh my God!" She unfurled the map and pored over it. "I'm gonna gain fifty pounds and probably have a heart attack, but it's gonna be so worth it," she said with a giggle.

"I was wondering if you wanted to hit a few when your shift is over."

When she looked up, that fluttering hope took a dive. Her face fell, her green eyes disappointed.

"I'd love to, but Will is picking me up from work to take me out."

"Ah," I said, trying to hang on to my smile and mask my own disappointment. "So, are you guys, like...dating?"

She smiled, a bright, hopeful expression on her small face. "I don't really know yet. But I'm sorry, can we do it another day?"

"Sure." My mouth felt like the inside of a shoe in the summertime. "Where's he taking you?"

The question almost sounded like an accusation, but Annie didn't seem to notice, just flung herself into her explanation with a love-struck smile on her face.

"It's a surprise. He wouldn't tell me anything specific, but when we were texting last night, I got the impression that it'd involve a meal at the very least. That was all I could guess though. He's got me completely in the dark."

She was beaming and shining, and I consequently had no idea what else to say, my plans chucked out the window and my speech lying uselessly in the back of my mind.

I swallowed the stone in my throat, anxious to get out of her space so I could sort through my tumbling thoughts.

"Well, I hope you guys have fun. I guess I'll see you tomorrow—"

"Wait," she said, her smile fading. "Are you okay?"

"Sure," I lied.

"Because yesterday—" Her eyes darted behind me. "Will!"

The change to her face was so complete, so crystal clear, there could be no denying her feelings. But the more painful realization was this: the way she looked at him was nothing like the way she looked at me. He was the center of the universe, and I was Pluto, spinning around in the freezing cold on the edge of the solar system.

Annie walked around the register counter, stopping when she reached him like she wasn't exactly sure how to greet him.

That Motherfucker had no problem showing her.

He stepped into her like the interloper that he was, a bouquet of flowers in one hand, the other winding around her waist as he bent to press a chaste kiss on her cheek, a cheek that flushed eagerly under his touch.

I wondered if that was a first, something she would check off her list, and the thought made me so angry, I worried I might crawl out of my skin right there in the middle of the bookstore. My breath was shallow, chest on fire, but somehow the rest of me was a well-maintained mask of calm.

Will glanced at me, his arm still around Annie. "Brandon," he said in lieu of a greeting.

"Bailey." The bite in the word was low, but it was there all the same.

His eyes told me he'd heard it, and he'd heard it loud and clear.

Annie was as oblivious as ever, her eyes on his face with adoration. "Let me just go clock out and grab my things, okay?" She swung by the counter and retrieved the map, folding it back up before extending it to me. "Here, don't forget this, Greg."

I waved her off. "Keep it."

She took the map back with her cheer fading. "All right. Thanks." Her gaze met Will's. "I'll be right back."

He offered her a winning smile. "I'll be right here."

She floated away, leaving us alone.

Will Bailey and I stared each other down for a solid count of five before I turned to leave, unwilling to give him any more of my energy than I had to. And by *energy*, I meant full and unadulterated rage.

"Do you like her?" he asked my back.

I stopped dead and turned around slow, flattening him with a heavy glare. "Looks like she's with you."

"That's not an answer."

"I don't owe you anything, especially not an answer. You didn't deserve my sister, and you don't deserve Annie either."

"What's your problem, Brandon?"

My teeth ground together so hard, my jaw ached. "Don't ask questions you know the answers to."

He shook his head. "It's been a long time since Sarah, and I'm not the same guy I was. Annie's different—I know you see it too. I'm not going to hurt her."

"Let me tell you something, Bailey." My hands fisted, quieting their trembling by force. "If you do, I will end you. Do you hear me?"

His eyes narrowed, but he nodded once.

"Good." I turned, storming away with thunder at my back.

"But don't get in my way," he said from behind me, bringing me to a halt. "If you think it hurts now, just remember—I can make it so much worse."

I didn't acknowledge his words with a response, but they sank into my veins with an icy chill that did little to cool the fire in my chest.

Annie was heading toward me, but I didn't slow down.

"Hey, Cam wanted to see you," she said as I approached, her coat hanging over her forearms and her brow curious.

"Thanks," I muttered.

I marched to the back of the store as she called *Bye* after me.

Once in the back and away from them, I felt better by a small degree. I was even able to stop considering all the ways I could murder Will and the places where I could dump his body. In the office, Rose was sitting in front of her laptop across from Cam, who was kicked back in her rolling chair with her Chucks on the surface of her desk and a lollipop in her mouth.

She smiled around it, the white stick hooked in the corner of her lips. "What's up, man?"

I relaxed my clamped jaw. "Nothing. You wanted to see me?"

Her smile faded, and Rose turned to look at me. Both of them wore discerning expressions.

"Well," Cam started, "I *was* going to ask you if you could send me the bar schedule for next week, but now I'm gonna insist you tell me what's the matter."

"Yes, I'll send you the schedule, and I really don't want to talk right now."

One eyebrow rose, and she nodded to a chair next to their desks with authority that brooked no argument.

I rolled my eyes and sighed, dropping into the chair. "I don't know what you want me to say."

Rose closed her laptop and rested her elbow on her desk. "Is this about Annie?" she asked plainly.

"Well, she's with that fucking douchebag!" I spouted, flinging a hand back in the direction I'd come from. "I mean, of all the guys in New York, she had to find *him*."

Cam moved her feet to the ground and reached into a jar on her desk, her hand reappearing with a purple lollipop, which she extended to me. "Here. You need this."

I took it, tugging at the cellophane wrapper before popping it into my mouth. It really did make me feel a little better. Or maybe my mouth just needed something to do so it would shut the fuck up already.

Either way, when I spoke again, it was with a little more control. "He's not a good guy. I know because he dated my sister."

I told them an abbreviated version of what had happened with Sarah, and their faces grew heavier with every word.

"Okay, I see the problem," Cam started. "And we all know you're into Annie."

"It's that obvious, huh?"

"Like a blinking neon sign, dude," Rose said, opening and closing her hands at me like they were in fact blinking lights.

I sighed and closed my lips around the sucker stick, working that candy like I might find answers in the middle. "I had this big, stupid plan to take her out today, but *he* was here to take her on a fucking date. A date! And now I feel like a fool and a creep and a loser while she's fawning over that asshole."

151

"Are they *together*?" Rose asked.

"I mean, they've known each other for, like, five minutes. They've never even been on a date—until today." I sulked.

Cam nodded. "Then there's still time. You just need a plan. I don't think you're wrong to want to get her away from him. And I've seen you two together at work. It's obvious you guys have chemistry."

"Cam," Rose warned.

"What?" she asked innocently. "You even said you saw it too, so don't act like I'm off base."

Rose rolled her eyes.

"I'm just saying," Cam said, turning back to me, "until it's, like, *official*, I feel like you've got some wiggle room. You could ask her to the historical costume mixer. I know she loves historicals, so I have a feeling she'd be way into it."

I rubbed the back of my neck. "Yeah, I guess, but we'll both be working."

"What other ideas do you have?" Cam asked. "You should have seen her talking about your day together. Based on that alone, I'd say you definitely have a shot."

The thought only made me feel more miserable. "I was thinking about asking Rose for tickets to the ballet. One of Annie's things on her list is to see a Broadway show."

Cam lit up. "Oh my God, do it. Take her to the Russian Tea Room and the ballet. Do it. Do it!" She bounced in her seat. "Rose, get him tickets!"

Rose laughed. "I can get you tickets, easy."

"Don't you think that's a little obvious?" I asked.

"Well, why be subtle? It's romantic, and she'll feel like a princess," Cam insisted. "If there's anything between you, she won't be able to avoid it after a night like that. Think of it like … like a litmus test."

I shook my head. "I don't even know if she'll agree."

At that, Cam smiled with mischief on her mind. "Well, you know I'll help however I can. Need me to create an elaborate ruse? No prob. Well-placed encouragement? Consider it done."

And just like that, my fluttering hope was back, and my sense of self-preservation was shot. "You think I can honestly make it happen?"

"I know so. Don't you worry."

And for a brief, blissful moment, I let myself believe.

A N N I E

I took Will's arm and let him usher me out of Wasted Words, but my mind was turned back to Greg.

He was upset, and I was the reason.

If I hadn't had plans with Will, I would have gone with Greg on the donut scavenger hunt in a heartbeat—not just because I enjoyed spending time with him so much, but because I really wanted to talk to him. I had a million questions for him but no opportunity to ask.

He'd remembered my mention of something in passing, found a way to see it through, and come to work on his day off to deliver it to me. The gesture was considerate and kind, and telling him no hurt—not just because I wanted to go, but because of the look of disappointment on his face.

I wanted to see Greg happy, wanted to make him happy, wanted to give him a million yeses. And I would have, if it hadn't been for Will. Who was, if I had to guess, the other reason Greg was so upset. He wouldn't even look me in the eye when I said goodbye.

Judging by the testosterone fumes left lingering in the air, I thought they'd had words again, and I wanted to know what they were. It was no surprise they didn't get along. I knew Greg was protective, and if Will had hurt his sister, Greg would have defended her with his last breath.

And I was itching to hear the story from Greg. Because what Will had said, especially about Greg hating him for having money, didn't sound like the Greg I knew at all.

I knew Greg well enough to know that he was solid and loyal and honorable. He wouldn't lie, and if he had a problem, there was probably just cause.

On really thinking about it, I realized I knew him better than I'd fully admitted. There was a strange connection between us, something latent and natural. It just *was*. We just *were*.

It was a reminder of how little control we had over chemistry. When you typically met someone, you found commonality, connections, topics for conversation, but it was some level of work, even if it was enjoyable work. It took effort. But sometimes, we met people we fell into stride with so naturally that the connection required no thought or cultivation; it threw all of your other relationships into shadow by the sheer brilliance of the light.

That was Greg and me—easy and uninhibited, a joining of two streams to make a river.

Which is why he's such a great friend, I told the part of myself that imagined it could be more than that.

"You okay?" Will asked as he opened the car door.

"I was just thinking about Greg," I said before climbing in.

Will stiffened, waiting for me to scoot all the way in before getting in behind me. "What about him?"

"Did you fight? He seemed upset."

Will rolled his shoulder in a shrug. "He doesn't like me, Annie, and he never will."

I frowned at the prospect that they'd never get along. "You can't be civil?"

"*I* can. I don't know if *he* can."

"I'll talk to him," I resolved, the conversation already working in my mind.

He let out a sigh. "I wouldn't get your hopes up."

"Psh, I run strictly on hopes."

That earned me a little bit of a smile.

I changed the subject in the interest of not ruining my first date. "So, where are we going?"

He reached for my hand. "You'll see. How was your day?"

"Largely uneventful until there at the end," I teased. "How about you?"

"The worst. I've been waiting all day for this." He smiled, a sweet, genuine curve of his lips.

"Where do you work?"

The smile faltered. "I'm in between things right now."

"Oh?"

"Yeah. College and adulthood," he said. "I graduated from Yale last year, but I'm not ready to lock into a career. Fortunately, I'm in the unique position to do absolutely nothing for as long as I want."

I chuckled. "Must be nice."

"It is. My parents even *approve*; can you believe that? My dad said he took a few years off to travel and said I should do the same."

"Well," I started, "if you'd lived a couple hundred years ago in England, you would have been a gentleman. Like, that would have been your job—to do nothing."

He shook his head with mock regret. "I always thought I was an old soul."

I laughed, and he pulled me a little closer until I was leaning into him.

"Speaking of gentlemen in historical England..."

"That's an unexpected segue."

"*Speaking* of," I continued, "there's a costume mixer at the bar later this week, and I was wondering what you were doing Friday night."

One corner of his lips rose. "Are you asking me on a date?"

"I guess I am. That is, unless you're dead inside and you hate costume parties."

"I love costume parties, *especially* costume parties I get to attend with a gorgeous girl on my arm. What's the theme?"

"Well, it's historical night—we're supposed to dress up as half of a fictional historical couple. Guys who wear cravats get five-dollar wells. Otherwise, they won't dress up."

A laugh burst out of him. "Yeah, I could see that. So, who do you want to go as? Lizzie and Darcy?"

My mouth popped open in surprise. "You know *Pride and Prejudice*?"

He shrugged, but he looked mighty proud of himself. "I was a lit major."

"You took a course on Jane Austen at Yale?"

"I took a class in romance in classical literature. *Pride and Prejudice* was at the top of the reading list, as was Byron, works from each Brontë sister, Shakespeare's sonnets—to name a few."

I stared at him, so blissfully stunned, I couldn't speak for a moment. "That might be the hottest thing I've ever heard a man say."

He pulled me a little closer. "Oh, but you haven't even heard the good stuff."

I laughed to stop myself from sighing and melting into him like warm butter on a biscuit.

"So, no," I said, trying to get a handle on my brain, "not Lizzie and Darcy—too predictable. I was actually thinking of doing a newer historical. My first thought was to pick one of Julia Quinn's couples. Have you heard of her?"

"No, I haven't, but I don't read much romance."

"That's fair, but these aren't just romances; these are *fairy tales*. They're the most satisfying, entertaining stories, books that touch your heart, make you *feel*, make you want to sing and dance and laugh and cry, all within a few pages," I said earnestly and with a little too much enthusiasm.

He smiled down at me. "Well then, I'll have to read one. Which one should I start with?"

"Would you really read one? Really?"

"Of course I will," he said on a laugh.

"Well," I said excitedly, "my favorite is Eloise's book, but—oh! Francesca's, ugh, it's so good, and there's this big, beautiful Scotsman. But maybe…" I thought for a second, assessing his face like I was going to determine what color he would wear best. "You know, I think you should read Anthony's book. Enemies to lovers," I said with a waggle of my brows. "I'll pick one up for you at Wasted Words. We have a billion copies or something."

"A billion? That's a lot of books. So, which couple should we go as?"

"Sophie and Benedict," I answered definitively. "It's a Cinderella story, and her gown is just *beautiful*…" I trailed off, my heart sinking. "I don't know where I might actually get a dress like that."

"I bet I can find one. My brother's on Broadway, and he has access to, like, *a billion* costumes."

I gaped, slack-jawed again. "He sings on *Broadway*? Like, *the* Broadway?"

"The one and only."

I couldn't even wrap my head around it. "What's he in?"

"Right now, he's in *Hamilton*."

"You're *kidding*."

He shook his head. "I'd never joke about something so serious as the theater."

I laughed.

"I can get tickets to pretty much anything too, if you want to go."

"That would actually blow my mind. I might not survive."

"As long as it doesn't blow your heart, I'll take you."

"No promises on that either."

The car pulled over in the park, and Will straightened up, smiling. "Ah, we're here."

He opened the door and slid out, extending his hand, which I took. A moment later, we were walking toward the reservoir.

"You took me by surprise, Annie," he said as we approached the place where we'd met.

"A fainting girl will do that, I've heard," I teased.

"But it's more than that. You're just … *different.*"

"Good different or bad different?"

He pulled me to a stop. "Good. Definitely good." And then he turned me around to face a grassy knoll where a gorgeous picnic lay, spread out over a massive plaid.

I sucked in a breath, swinging around to face him. "Will, it's *perfect!*"

And as I tugged him toward the blanket, he laughed, and it was the most beautiful sound.

A charcuterie board was stacked with freshly cut meats and cheeses, a basket stuffed with bread was at its side, and another little tray held tiny jars with sauces and spreads. Another board held crackers and more cheese—glorious cheese—and was broken up by bundles of grapes and stacks of apple slices. There were trays of tarts and chocolate-covered strawberries, blocks of white and dark chocolate. It was a bona fide feast, laid out on a navy-and-emerald tartan.

"How in the world did you manage all this?" I asked as I sat, wide-eyed, to one side of the spread.

Will sat opposite me, still looking absolutely delighted. And delight*ful.* "Well, would you think I was an asshole if I said my cook put together the picnic?"

I laughed, a little shocked. He had a cook. Of course he had a cook.

"And then I had my assistant come set it all up and wait for us so no one jacked it."

I raised my eyebrows, smirking as I stacked cheese and sausage on a cracker. "Your *assistant*?"

He flushed a little, rubbing the back of his neck, but he was smiling. "I know. It's ridiculous."

"Well, thank him for me. Or her?"

"Him."

I felt a petty measure of relief that it wasn't a woman. "It's perfect. Today is perfect. Yesterday was perfect. Everything's just…"

"Perfect?"

I laughed and popped the cracker in my mouth.

Perfect.

A few hours later, we were sitting in the back of a horse-drawn carriage, circling Central Park. The sun had set, and it had gotten colder, but I was warm, tucked into Will's side under the heavy blanket.

He'd been the best sport, not teasing me when I broke out my camera a dozen times to note the moments. But I hadn't told him about my list, which made it that much sweeter when he didn't lose his patience or seem bored while I fooled with the charcuterie board or when I asked him to take a selfie with me. In fact, he'd asked me to take two so he could have one too.

I sighed, feeling lazy and happy and a little like I was dreaming as we ambled around the park. Neither of us had spoken for a while, the silence between us content, the time marked by the clop of the horse's hooves and the gentle swaying of the carriage.

"You know," I started, "when my dad died, I made this list of things I'd never done before."

He pulled me a little closer but didn't interrupt.

"We lost so much. Not just him, which was devastating on its own. Mama lost her legs, and we lost our home, our lives. And I wondered, *How will we ever survive? How can we dust ourselves off and go on?*" I took a slow breath that left me in a puff of smoke. "So, I started writing down all the things I'd never done, things I wanted to do. Ways to fill up my life and my heart. Because I didn't want to live quietly anymore. I wanted to live *loudly*. I didn't want to wait for life to come to me. I didn't want to experience it through books and music alone; I wanted to do the things that inspired me."

"Has it worked?" he asked quietly.

"It has. It's given me hope when I thought hope was lost."

Will didn't say anything for a moment, and neither did I.

"So," he said, breaking the silence, "what kinds of things are on your list?"

"Oh, lots of things—most of them silly, some of them not. Like, I wanted to eat a hot dog out of a cart and traverse the Brooklyn Bridge. There are some books I've always wanted to read. I want to eat ice cream when it's snowing and dance on the beach in the moonlight. I want to live, and my list exists as a way to make that living tangible and achievable."

Will didn't speak for a moment, but when he did, his voice had a strange quality to it, velvety and wondrous.

Bright star, would I were stedfast as thou art—
Not in lone splendour hung aloft the night
And watching, with eternal lids apart,
Like nature's patient, sleepless Eremite,
The moving waters at their priestlike task
Of pure ablution round earth's human shores…

"I can never remember the—" he started.

And my throat tightened as I recited the rest.

Or gazing on the new soft-fallen mask

Of snow upon the mountains and the moors—

No—yet still stedfast, still unchangeable,

Pillow'd upon my fair love's ripening breast,

To feel for ever its soft fall and swell,

Awake for ever in a sweet unrest,

Still, still to hear her tender-taken breath,

And so live ever—or else swoon to death.

"Keats," I breathed. "I love that poem."

"It describes you exactly, I think. You're a wonder, Annie. I've never known anyone quite like you."

I turned in his arms and looked into his eyes, emboldened by our connection. "Did you know that this entire date was on my list?"

He smiled. "Is it?"

I nodded, feeling a rush of anticipation zip through me when his gaze dropped to my lips.

"What else is on this list that I should know about?"

"I've never been kissed." It was a permission wrapped up in a request, and I held my breath as I waited for his answer.

His eyes caught mine and held them. "How is that even possible?"

I shrugged and looked down, my confidence faltering.

But he touched my chin and lifted it until our eyes met. "Well," he said softly, "I think I'd like to be the one who crosses that off, too."

He leaned in, our breath mingling, and then…he kissed me.

For something I'd thought so much about, something I'd anticipated for so many years, I found myself stiff and still and unsure. His lips pressed mine—not too hard, not too soft, wet but not too wet.

Perfectly adequate by all scales I had at my disposal—which, admittedly, weren't vast.

The kiss was *fine*, sweet even, if not a little sterile. But the admission in my sinking heart was that there were no fireworks, no marching band, no parting of the heavens or a hallelujah chorus. And, by more normal expectations, there was no spark, no instinctive recognition or undeniable bond between us.

Maybe I'd read too many romance novels to expect anything less than to have my breath stolen and my heart singing promises of forever.

When he pulled away, he smiled that indulgent smile of his, and I smiled back, hoping I looked reassuring as I nestled into his side.

I'd expected magic, and I'd gotten mediocre.

I shouldn't have been disappointed, but I was.

It had to be due to my complete lack of experience. I had probably been the worst kiss of his life. That was the only explanation because the date was perfect. The company and conversation was perfect. If the kiss really *had* been lackluster—I was already trying to rewrite history in my mind—it had to be on me and my lack of practice.

I smiled to myself, hoping practice would make that perfect, too.

"So, if you've never been kissed, is it safe to assume you've never had a boyfriend either?" he asked, his thumb shifting back and forth on my arm.

"I haven't," I admitted. "No one's caught my attention before."

"I'm the first for that too? It's dangerous how good that makes me feel."

I nestled a little closer, smiling up at the stars.

"Think you might want a boyfriend?" The words were cautious, maybe even a little nervous.

"Are you asking me to go steady?" I teased.

A little chuckle escaped him. "I know it's corny, but the truth is, I really like you, Annie. I don't want to see anyone else, and I hope you don't either. On top of the possibility that I could get addicted to checking off your firsts."

When I leaned away and looked into his eyes, his smile dazzling and his warm hand finding my cheek, there was nothing I could say but yes. And he kissed the word away until it was gone.

Take What You Can Get

GREG

Two tickets to the ballet were in the process of burning a hole in my pocket.

Rose had handed them over with a smug smile this morning, and into my back pocket they went along with a healthy helping of that trap that called itself hope.

I'd convinced myself that Will was temporary—a traffic cone, not a cement barrier. He'd declared himself before I was able to, but it was still early enough that I could take another shot.

I tried not to think about what would happen if she committed. Because as much as I hated Will, if he was who she wanted, I wouldn't stand in her way. He was a punk and an asshole, but if I tried to prove it to Annie, it would be *me* who was the asshole, not him.

My greatest hope was that it wouldn't be an issue. I'd take her out, show her what we could be together, and hope she would choose me.

When Annie walked into work with that smile on her face and her arms filled with a giant pink pastry box, that hope multiplied in size by at least five.

"Hey," she said cheerily as she approached, setting the box on the surface of the bar. "Gotcha something."

"And it's not even my birthday."

She laughed and hopped up onto a stool where she began pulling off her yellow coat and pink gloves. "Go on; open it."

I spun the box around and flipped the lid open. Inside were two-dozen donuts, stacked at an angle in matching pairs so they could all fit. Little flags on toothpicks noted the names of a dozen donut shops in Annie's handwriting.

She giggled, bouncing in her seat. "I hated that I couldn't go with you yesterday, and I thought, *What better way to thank you for such a thoughtful gift?* So I forced my poor driver to haul me all over Manhattan this morning, and I got two donuts from each place, one for each of us." She held up her hands and shook them like tambourines. "Ta-da!"

I couldn't help but laugh—not only at the sheer joy on her face, but at the jazz hands and kindness and sweetness that only Annie could possess.

"This is…" I said as I assessed the spread, my confidence flying. "This is pretty great, Annie. Thank you."

"No, thank *you* for bringing me the map." She leaned on the bar and looked into the box, wetting her lips. "Where should we start? I have to say, Lekker smelled the best. I got these blueberry-lemon things with cream-cheese frosting. These." She pointed. "We've got to go back there. It's just right around the corner."

My smile wouldn't quit. "Funny, that was the first thing I thought when I noticed it on the map."

"Did you? Well, it must be fate. We've gotta start there." Annie picked them both up, extending one to me. "Cheers!"

She tapped hers to mine, and we each took a bite.

It melted in my mouth, and a moan rumbled up my throat. "Oh God."

Annie's eyes closed. "Is this what heaven is like?"

"It has to be close." I took another bite and shook my head. "I can't believe you did this."

"I really wanted to surprise you, and I felt like scum when I left here yesterday."

Guilt washed over me. "I'm sorry, Annie. I should have texted you to make plans instead of showing up here and putting you on the spot."

"Oh, it's okay. Really. I've never had a social calendar before, so having overlapping plans is a new thing for me." She beamed as she took a bite.

I grabbed a couple of glasses and set them on the bar, filling them with ice and water as I asked a question I didn't want to know the answer to, "So, how'd it go yesterday?"

Annie was so happy, it looked like sunshine was shooting out of her eyeballs. "Oh, he took me on a picnic in the park. It was gorgeous; there was this big, pretty plaid and a basket and tiny cakes and everything, and he had all these fancy cheeses I'd never even heard of. And then he hired a carriage to drive us around the park. I crossed so many things off my list and went through two packs of film! Check it out." She reached into her bag and rummaged.

I tried to smile, setting her glass in front of her. "Well, you named two firsts—picnic and carriage ride. What else?"

Her cheeks flushed prettily, and she smiled with her lips together, her eyes on her hands as she arranged tiny Polaroids on the bar next to the donut box. "First kiss, and he asked me to be his girlfriend, can you believe it?"

My heart seized painfully in my chest, and almost every muscle in my body involuntarily flinched.

My first thought: *That Motherfucker.*

And then: *Going steady? What is he? In junior high?*

With the grand finale of: *I'm going to fucking kill him.*

Annie finally looked up, her face shifting, watching me like I might erupt like a volcano. She wasn't far off.

"I…I'm sorry," she said quietly. "I shouldn't have brought it up. I know you don't like him."

"That's a massive understatement, Annie." The low rumbling in my throat was almost a growl.

"But tell me there's a way for you to be civil. I don't need for you to be friends, but you're my friend, Greg. I don't want to lose you because I'm with him. And I don't want to lose him because I care about you. Please, don't be mad."

"I'm not mad at you," I snapped. "It's just that I…" *Wish you were mine.*

Confusion passed across her face, then some recognition, followed by a succession of stunned blinks. "Greg…do you…do you *like* me? Like, more than friends?"

If only I could tell her the truth. But nothing would come from that admission other than me losing Annie for good. And with her looking at me like she was, there was no way to dodge her. I had to answer, and it had to be clear.

So, I huffed with a shake of my head and lied to salvage whatever I could from the wreckage.

"Of course not, Annie. I'm just worried about you. I care about you."

The relief on her face was accompanied by a hot twist of pain in my chest. "I care about you too, Greg. You're my friend. And the thought of upsetting you upsets me." She shook her head and glanced down at her hands.

I had no idea what to say.

In a handful of minutes, the game had changed on me once again, sparked by that word.

Boyfriend.

Which meant she considered herself his *girlfriend.*

Which meant she had made a commitment, one I couldn't question. Because questioning that would put her in the most unfair of positions. I wouldn't only be forcing her to make a decision that could jeopardize our friendship, but I'd be asking her to betray a promise she'd made to another man.

Will Fucking Bailey.

My anger fired up like a goddamn steam engine at the thought of him. I hated to lose her, but to lose her to someone like Will was unbearable. He'd taken her on an idyllic, cheeseball Hollywood date, and he'd kissed her—her *first* kiss. Of course he'd kissed her. I would have kissed her too, if I'd had a real chance.

But she didn't want me.

She wanted him. She'd promised him. And there was nothing I could do about it.

So I reached into my back pocket and pulled out the ballet tickets, my plan singed to ashes under the smoldering remains of my hope.

"Annie, let me tell you something." I waited until she looked up and met my eyes before continuing, "All I want is for you to be happy, and you are. I saw it on your face when you walked in, and I see it when you talk about him. And if you're happy, I'm happy." I handed the tickets over. "I have these tickets to the ballet…you should go with Will."

Annie took the tickets with eyes as bright as Christmas morning, running the pad of her finger over the title. "*Romeo and Juliet?*"

I offered another weak smile. "Rose's best friend is with the New York City Ballet."

She looked confused. "Well, thank you. But…why do you have them? Were they for you and me?"

"You said you'd never been to a Broadway show, and this isn't a musical, but it's actually *on* Broadway."

"You didn't answer me."

I watched her for a moment. "Yeah, but you should go with your boyfriend."

Her face shifted; the corners of her lips slipped down as her brows gently came together, and her eyes, which were already so big and shining, somehow grew in both size and depth. "What do you mean? Do you not want to go with me anymore? Are you…are you mad at me?"

"No," I said as sick sadness wound through my guts and up into my chest, squeezing my heart until it stung. "No, I'm not mad at you, Annie." The words were soft and serious.

"Tell me what happened with Will." She searched my face, her sadness blooming. "He…he told me about your sister, and I—"

My jaw clamped shut. "What did he tell you?" I asked through my teeth. "Because he's a liar, Annie."

"Only his side. I've wanted to talk to you for days, but I've barely seen you to ask to hear yours. Please, tell me."

I drew a long breath and chose my words very carefully. "He dated my sister in high school."

She nodded, encouraging me to continue. I didn't want to. But I did.

"He's the master of saying all the right things at exactly the right time, and the longer it went on, the clearer it became that he didn't care about her at all. He's selfish and entitled, they fought constantly. And she accepted that behavior because she loved him. She broke up with him at a party, and there were rumors, rumors that had started with Will, all because he didn't get his way."

Her eyes widened, but she didn't speak.

"I know you don't know my sister, but I do. She loved him desperately, and he ruined her, made her life hell until she left for college. And I know this is just high school drama, but people like Will don't change. Someone who would treat another with so little respect or regard doesn't just grow up. It's a dark part of them that doesn't go away." I sighed. "There are two versions of him—the one who wants something and the one who didn't get what he wants. So, please—just promise me you'll be careful."

"I promise." Her eyes shone with understanding. "If one of my sisters were hurt in any way, in any context, I would be unforgiving."

"I know. And that's why he and I can't ever be friends."

She reached for my hand, her fingers warm and soft around mine, her face wholeheartedly sincere. "Thank you for telling me how you feel and the other side of what happened. I...I hate that this happened between you, and I hate that I'm caught in the middle. I don't know what I'm supposed to do, but I feel like I'm supposed to choose."

Do it. Choose me. But I couldn't do that to her. I couldn't do it to myself.

My throat clicked when I swallowed. "I won't make you choose, Annie."

Annie looked down at our fingers. "You're my friend, and I care about you. I don't want to give you up any more than I want to give him up; your friendship is just as important to me as being with Will is. But I want to see this ballet with you."

When she met my eyes again, her face was so ardent, so open, so absolutely beautiful in its honesty that I only gazed at her with my heart aching.

"Will you come with me?"

The word *no* had no place in my heart, not when it came to her. "Are you sure Will will be okay with it?"

"If he's not, then we'll have a bigger problem."

The possibility of *bigger problems* with Will had its own appeal.

Could I do it? Could I be her friend? Could I put my feelings aside and take what I could get?

If the alternative was no Annie at all, there was only one thing to say.

"Anything you want, Annie."

She brightened up again, eyes full of sunshine and spring grass, and I sighed, knowing what a magnificent mistake the whole thing was.

But with her happy, it was hard to care.

I didn't see Annie much of the rest of the day, although we *did* eat enough of those donuts to almost make ourselves sick. There were only three left by the time her shift was ending, which was impressive by anyone's standards.

As the time approached for her to leave, I found myself dreading it, wishing I had an excuse to get her to stay or get her to leave with me. It was relief I felt, a respite from the wanting, from the words that had hung between us since she'd walked through the door on Will's arm. For an afternoon, things were like they used to be. Before him.

Just before Annie was off, a girl walked in and headed to the bar. She almost made it onto the stool when Annie pounced on her with a hug.

The girl laughed and hugged her back, and when Annie pulled away, she turned to me with her cheeks high and smiling.

"Greg, this is my big sister, Elle."

"Nice to finally meet you," she said with a smile and extended her hand, which I took.

"You too. I've heard a lot about you."

She blushed, and I saw the resemblance. Elle was a little darker than Annie, but her skin was colored like peaches and cream, like Annie's, though Elle's had more color. Their lips were shaped the same, but Elle's eyes were hazel, colored with bursts of green and brown and gold.

"I'll just be a few minutes, okay?" Annie assured her. "Have a drink. Greg makes *excellent* drinks."

She laughed. "How would you know? I know you haven't crossed that one off the list."

Annie shrugged. "People talk. Be right back!" she said before bounding off.

I smirked and set a coaster in front of her. "So, what'll it be? Alabama Slammer? Jägerbomb? Shot of tequila?"

Elle chuckled. "How about a cup of coffee?"

"Coming right up." I turned my back to pour her one.

"I'm glad to finally meet you," she said from behind me. "Annie's told me so much about you. She's had more fun with you over the last few weeks than she has in years."

When I turned to face her, she was smiling sweetly, hands folded on the bar in front of her.

"It's been my pleasure. Really. She's something else," I said as I set her coffee mug in front of her and reached under the bar for a sugar caddie. "Need cream?"

"No, thanks." She pulled a couple of sugar packets out and shook them. "I know she's told you about Daddy and everything. And I want you to know that your friendship really does mean everything to her. Getting her this job, helping her with her list—it's brought her back in a way that's made all of our lives better. So, thank you."

It was that word again, the one that hung over me in big block letters—*friend*.

"Like I said, the pleasure's mine. She has a way of changing the people around her without even trying, doesn't she?"

"She does. It's something we can always count on. The sky is blue, the grass is green, and Annie will make you feel every possible emotion, sometimes in the span of an hour."

A gentle laugh burst out of me at the truth of it. "It's maddening and wonderful," I said, too honest for my own good. "So, Annie said you work at *Nouvelle* magazine?"

Elle nodded, a spark of excitement in her eyes. "Very recently, and just as a secretary, but yes."

"It's got to be crazy, working at a magazine of that size."

"It is, but I love it. The phone is always ringing, and the calendar is always pulled up and blocked off by the hour, sometimes by the quarter hour. Ward has to schedule lunch, the gym, even calls to his mother," she said on a laugh. "Maybe because she forces me to put them on his calendar. I don't know that he'd call her otherwise."

"None of that sounds as exciting as you make it sound," I teased.

"Trust me, I know. I love when things are orderly and neat and organized. Annie says I'm OCD, but it's not like I have to flip the light off and on thirteen times or wash my hands seven times in a row. I just like order. And even numbers."

I chuckled. "So, Ward is your boss?"

Another flush, this one deeper. "I really should call him Mr. Ferrars, but…well, we're friends. He's a friend of the family, which is how I even got the job. God knows I'm not qualified."

"Well, anybody who loves organizing schedules and answering phones sounds like a natural. Crowd control just comes with practice. Not that it's the same, but I came from being a barista at a coffee shop to running a bar. I honestly didn't think I could do it, but here I am." I spread my arms to display my domain. "Growing pains are normal. But I still have the worst anxiety dreams."

"Do you?" she asked, bringing her coffee to her lips.

"Oh, bad. People keep walking in the door and coming to the bar, but I'm the only bartender. At first, I have it under control, but the busier it gets, the angrier people get until they're yelling and climbing over the bar for me. I usually wake up right around the time I realize I'm naked."

Elle laughed. "I had one the other night where I had all the appointments on the wrong days, and the phone wouldn't stop ringing. And every person who called yelled at me. And, when Ward came in, he was so…*disappointed.*" She sounded so sad but shook it off. "It's awful."

"Goes with the territory of a high-octane job. There's a rush about it though. It's what keeps us adrenaline junkies coming back for more."

That earned me another laugh. She took a sip of her coffee, leaving us in silence for a moment, which was all the time my brain needed to say something I probably shouldn't.

"I…listen, I know it's not my place to say anything, but I guess I'm going to anyway."

She put all of her attention on me and set her mug down with a gentle nod of permission.

I took a breath. "I know Annie likes Will, but he hurt someone I love very much, and even though it was a long time ago, I don't trust him, not with her."

Elle's own worry creased her brow. "I understand. How worried should I be?"

I gave my head a shake. "I don't know. I'm too close to the situation to be reasonable about him. So just look out for her, okay?"

"I promise I will. Thank you, Greg, for telling me. Would it… would it be all right if we exchanged numbers? I don't want to conspire, but if the time comes that I might need more information, can I call?"

"Of course," I answered as I reached into my pocket for my phone, relieved to have an ally, someone to be there when I wasn't, to be aware.

I only hoped I was wrong about the whole thing, that we'd never need to talk about it again. But deep down, I knew that wish was nothing but fool's gold.

Bigger Problems

ANNIE

Cam looked up when I walked into the office to clock out. "Hey, Annie."

"Hey!" I reached for my coat. "I'm all set out front. Need anything else?"

"Nope, you're good to go." She watched me as I clocked out using the little machine in the back. "Excited about the mixer?"

"I cannot *wait*. I'm bringing my new *boyfriend*," I sang, waggling my eyebrows, feeling that zing of excitement and unfamiliarity of the word in my mouth.

"Boyfriend?" she asked, though I thought there was a little bit of shock in the question.

I nodded, smiling. "Will, the guy I met in the park the other day."

"Ah."

Disappointment? Was that what I'd heard? I shook off the notion.

"We're going as Sophie and Benedict from *An Offer from a*

Gentleman."

Cam nodded her appreciation. "Ooh, Julia Quinn. I like it. God, I wish I could be there. I was *this close* to convincing Tyler to come with me as Jondalar and Ayla from *The Valley of Horses*. He was pretty staunchly opposed to dressing up like a big, beautiful caveman." She shrugged. "Anyway, I'm not tall enough, and he's not blond or bearded enough. But man, what I would do to see him in a loincloth in public."

I laughed. "After that pitch, I can't believe he wasn't jumping at the chance. Also, that's definitely taking *historical* to new levels. I didn't realize we could go back thirty thousand years."

"I like to test boundaries."

"No…you?" I pulled on my coat.

"Shocking, I know." She smiled at me for a beat. "So, you and Will jumped right in, didn't you?"

I sighed. "He's just so…*romantic*, you know? Every word that comes out of his mouth is just…right."

"You know, I had my own Will once."

"Did you? A total dreamboat?"

"Oh, yeah," she said, leaning back in her chair. "Football player, total babe. Smart, funny, into me. But he didn't end up being who I'd thought he was."

The smile that had been on my face most of the day faded, and Greg's recount of Will's story crossed my mind.

"I'm sorry."

"It's okay. I learned a lot about what's real and what isn't, who to trust with my heart and who to keep out. But it wasn't an easy lesson to learn; it took me years to sort it out."

Apprehension snaked through my stomach, but I waved away the sense of foreboding. "Well, hopefully my Will doesn't do me like that."

"I'm sure you'll fare better than me, but it wouldn't hurt you to keep your eyes open," she said, the words holding more weight than I'd been prepared to shoulder. But then she smiled, and the moment passed. "I'm so bummed I won't get to meet him at the party. I *hate* missing it, especially historical night. All those cravats." A sigh slipped out of her. "But Tyler and I ended up having this last-minute dinner with one of his sports agency's clients."

I gave her a look. "You're missing a costume party for a work dinner?"

"Uh, yeah, but only because it's Julian Edelman. I hate the Patriots, but God, if I don't love me some Edelman." She paused. "Is Greg doing okay? I caught wind of some gossip about him and Will."

I sighed. "I think so, yeah. We talked about it earlier, and I think it's all right. We're going to the ballet in a couple of days. God, I'm so excited. My week is going to be the absolute best."

She smiled enigmatically. "I hope you guys have fun."

"Thanks. Me too. I'd better run; my sister's waiting."

"See you tomorrow, Annie."

I waved and left the office, hurrying to the front where Elle and Greg were still talking. They stopped before I made it to them, and Elle was off her stool and pulling on her coat in a second flat. And then we exchanged goodbyes and headed out into the chill, arm in arm.

"How was work?" I asked as we headed toward the burrito joint down the street that everyone always talked about.

"Fine. How was your day?"

"Good. How's Ward?"

Her cheeks flushed. "He's fine."

"Still handsome?"

She bumped me with her hip. "No. He came to work today, and his face was all wrong. Nose where an eye should be, ear where his mouth should be. It was like Picasso took a solid swing and landed him in the Cubist period."

"Ha, ha."

"Ward is fine. Everything is fine."

"I mean, with a word like *fine*, how could I not be assured?"

She laughed but otherwise ignored me, swiftly changing the subject. "Tell me about your day."

I sighed and gave up. "It was great. Greg asked me to the ballet to see *Romeo and Juliet*. Isn't that incredible?"

Elle didn't say anything right away. "What did Will say when you told him?"

I frowned—mostly at her, but partly at myself. "I haven't told him yet, but I'm sure he'll be fine." The second I said it, I thought of at least four reasons he absolutely would not be fine. Dread slithered through me.

She gave me a look.

"Well, he *has* to be fine with it. Greg's my friend, and I'm going."

"And if he's not fine?"

"Then I'll have the same talk with him that I just had with Greg. I don't want either relationship to interfere with the other."

"I know you don't, but they might despite the fact."

That dread took a hard left, looking for attention. "It's so stupid. Greg doesn't like me. I even *asked* him, and he said no."

She fixed another disputing look on me.

"Honestly, Elle, he had a chance right then to tell me if he did. I believe him. I trust him. He wouldn't lie to me."

She sighed but didn't argue.

"Why can't things be easy?"

"Because," she said gently, "easy is for fairy tales. Life is too fluid and unpredictable and nothing short of complicated. But the good news is that they say nothing worth having is easy."

"How's *that* the good news?" I chuckled, not feeling like it was at all funny.

She tightened her arm, bringing me a little closer. "I just mean that there's a payoff, if you can get through the hard part."

I blew out a noisy sigh. "If you say so."

"I say so."

"Then I have to believe it's true." I laid my head on her shoulder.

My mind turned in on itself, admitting first that I'd been relieved at Greg's answer. Because if the answer had been yes, could I have kept hanging out with him? Was I allowed to be friends with someone I knew had feelings for me? I didn't know the rules, wasn't sure of the protocol. And his answer saved me from having to consider it in detail.

But he'd said he cared about me, and I understood that. I cared about him too—a lot in fact. I wanted to tell him the details of my day and hear about his. I wanted to spend my time with him, craved his company. But most importantly, I didn't want to lose him.

But didn't all friends feel that way? Because we were just friends, right?

I drew in a breath full of resolve, filling my lungs up with decision. If I had to ask myself whether or not I felt more for him than just friends, the answer was no.

"So," I said, breaking the silence, "you're coming to the costume party with me, right?"

"Annie…" she sighed my name like she was exhausted.

I pouted. "Come on. It's gonna be so fun. Just think, there will be loads of guys there, and they'll be largely wearing cravats. *Cravats, Elle.*" I raised my head to give her a look so salacious, I could have been talking about porn.

She laughed. "Ugh, I don't know."

"*Come on,*" I full-on whined this time. "Please?"

Elle looked over my face for a second and sighed, rolling her eyes, and I knew I had her. "Oh, all right."

I cheered a *Woohoo!* imagining us at the party together—Will on one arm and Elle on the other—just as my phone rang. My heart skipped faster when I saw it was Will.

"Hey," I said with a smile. "I was just thinking about you."

"I like the sound of that." I could hear him smiling on the line. "Busy?"

"I'm just on my way to dinner with my sister. Why? What's up?"

"Ah," he said, disappointed. "I was hoping we could grab a bite. I knew I should have texted earlier. I just didn't want to bother you at work."

"Oh. I wish you had." I glanced at Elle and got an idea. "Hang on." I pressed my phone to my chest. "Think Will could meet up with us?"

Elle nodded. "Of course."

I pressed my phone to my ear, grinning. "Want to come meet us for burritos at Besos?"

"You sure your sister doesn't mind?"

"Not at all. You in?"

"Be there in ten," he said, sounding as giddy as I was.

We said goodbye, and I hung up, sighing like a fool while Elle chuckled at me.

"I know," I admitted. "I know. He's just...*perfect*, Elle."

"No one is perfect."

"Well, he checks all the boxes."

"I'm only saying that maybe you should get to know him a little better before you call him your boyfriend. You don't even really know if you like each other."

I gave her a flat look. "Elle, he's gorgeous, went to Yale, recites poetry, and took me on a dream date. What's not to like?"

"The dream date wasn't exactly original."

"Ugh, killjoy."

Amused, she shook her head and pulled open the door to Besos. By the time we sorted out what we wanted, Will was strolling through the door, looking like a movie star—tall and dark and dressed in clothes that looked both casual and rich, his hair disheveled in all the right places. And then there was that smile.

He pressed a kiss to my cheek in greeting, and I introduced him to Elle, who was as amiable as always. And a few minutes later, Will bought our burritos, and we were taking seats in a booth by the window.

"So, guess who I convinced to come to the mixer?" I asked, displaying my arms to Elle in a *ta-da!* gesture.

He chuckled. "You too?"

Elle nodded, pretending to look defeated. "There's no standing up to her when she gets like this."

"Well, I'll see if I can't find a dress for you too. Annie will tell me what kind of costume to get," he said before taking a bite of his burrito.

I leaned toward her. "His brother performs on *Broadway*," I said, as if that explained everything.

She looked confused. "Is he also a seamstress?"

"No," Will said with a smirk, "but he has access to costumes. I'll let the hair and makeup artists know they'll have two."

I frowned, confused. "Wait, what?"

"You're so cute, you know that?" He kissed my nose. "If you've got an authentic dress, your hair should match. Really, it's nothing. My brother set it all up."

I turned to Elle, still gaping. "Oh my God, we're going to be like actual princesses."

"All this for a mixer?" she asked Will.

"I don't do anything halfway," he answered with a wink.

"I guess not." Elle took a bite of her burrito, but oddly, I couldn't tell if she was impressed or not.

"How does it work, Annie, with you being eighteen in the bar?" he asked.

"Oh, it's no big deal. They wristband everyone at the door, and since it's a coffee shop too, the rules are a little different. But technically, I'll be working."

"Do you serve? Or…" he started.

"I'll be working the door. They do this thing where everyone gets name tags, and they all pick out their favorite books along with their favorite drinks and list them with us. So if you see someone you like, you can buy them a drink and their favorite book for a discount."

"That is genius," Elle said.

"Cam's brilliant. Anyway, I'll be ringing people up." Elle looked like she wanted to back out, and an idea struck me, one that put a wide smile on my face. "Don't worry; I'll make sure you're entertained. Promise."

She didn't seem persuaded but didn't press it.

"So, what do you do, Will?" Elle asked.

"Right now, I'm between things."

It was the same answer he'd given me, but she seemed less amused than I had been. "And what did you do before you were between things?"

"Yale."

That seemed to finally impress her. "What did you study?"

"Literature. Just trying to sort out what I'd like to do from here, you know? I want to be sure before I commit to anything."

Elle laughed softly. "Look before you leap? However did you end up with Annie?"

He offered a laugh of his own. "She sort of fell in my lap."

"What can I say? You've got a great lap."

"Thank you by the way," Elle said, setting down her burrito. "I'm glad you were there to help her."

"So am I," he said with a glance at me.

I would have died happy if there weren't so many things left on my list.

We tucked into our dinner, chatting all the while. And when we were through and pulling on coats and hats, he asked if I wanted to come over and watch a movie.

To which I answered with an emphatic, "*Yes!*"

We said goodbye on the sidewalk, and a few minutes later, I was nestled into Will as we drove through the park toward his apartment.

Will had a doorman, though he wasn't nearly as friendly as George, and his building was just as high-end as Susan and John's. I didn't think I'd ever get used to the splendor of the kind of luxury they lived in. I always felt a little like a fraud, as if someone would point right at me and announce to the room that I didn't belong there.

Passing the threshold of his apartment didn't make me feel any more like I fit in. How a twenty-two-year-old man had access to a place like this was beyond me. It was beautiful and open—no park views, but there was a great view of Madison Avenue, which felt ludicrous to even *consider*, never mind gaze upon with my own two eyes. The furniture was all sleek and simple, modern but with a mid-century nod.

"God, Will, how beautiful," I said, drinking in the view.

He laughed gently as he closed the door. "I'm glad you like it. And I'm glad you're here."

He moved to stand behind me, his hands finding my upper arms, his nose trailing against the curve of my ear, sending a sweet chill down my back.

"Me too," I managed to say.

"Oh," he said, his lips almost in my hair, "I got us tickets to *Hamilton* on Thursday. What do you say?"

I turned around to face him, slipping my arms around his neck, though I wondered if he was asking me if I wanted to go or if he wanted me to thank him. I couldn't do either.

Trepidation hung over me like a dark, heavy cloud. "Please tell me we can get tickets for another night?"

His pleased smile slipped into a frown. "You have plans?"

I nodded, not wanting to say with *whom* I had plans.

"You can't get out of it?"

"Well, I could, but I made those plans first. Can you really not get tickets for another night, Will?" I asked gently.

He brushed my hair from my face. "I can get tickets for almost any night, sure. Where are you going?"

I almost lied. I probably should, but alas, I was the worst liar in history and knew it. "To *Romeo and Juliet* at the Lincoln Center. Greg got us tickets."

Everything about his face hardened, even his eyes. Maybe his eyes most of all. "You're kidding, Annie. Please, tell me you're kidding."

I shook my head.

"You know he likes you, don't you?"

I huffed. "Not you too."

He stepped away from me and raked a hand through his hair. "I don't know what I'm supposed to do here. You don't take a friend to the ballet."

"And why not?" I asked, folding my arms across my chest.

"Because you just *don't*. He likes you, and you're going on a date with him."

"It's not a date, Will."

"It's a date, and I thought we were exclusive."

"Hang on just a second," I shot. "Because this isn't about me going to the ballet; it's about me going with *Greg*. I won't ask you to like him. I won't even ask you to be around him. But Greg is my *friend*. He was my friend before I ever met you, and he'll continue to *be* my friend. Just as much as I don't want my seeing you to be a problem for him, I don't want my friendship with him to be a problem for you. And if it's a problem for you, then we really *do* have bigger issues."

He watched me for a second, the muscle in his tight jaw bouncing.

"So, is it going to be a problem?"

Will let out an audible breath and unlocked his jaw. "No," he said as he stepped back into me, winding his arms around my waist.

"Good," I sang sweetly, trying to defuse the tension, my arms taking their previous spot around his neck.

"I just don't like him."

"I know."

"And I don't want him to interfere."

"He won't."

Will almost smiled. "He'd better not." He sighed, his anger dissipating. "I'm sorry, Annie. Sometimes when I get mad, get ... *jealous*," he admitted, "I say things I don't mean. Will you bear with me?"

My heart softened. "Of course," I said on a breath.

And then he kissed me.

I was so preoccupied with where my hands were or if he was enjoying the kiss or if I was any good at it; there was really no way I could even stop to enjoy it.

He pulled back with a crooked smile on his face. "Wanna make out?"

A giggle bubbled out of me, and I nodded, feeling like I was in junior high. Except in junior high, I had been too busy reading books and playing piano to kiss boys.

Will scooped me up and carried me to the couch, laying me down. My heart almost stopped when he started climbing on top of me, and I shifted, smiling nervously, putting him on his side with his back to the couch.

And thus began my very first make-out session.

We kissed in the same emotionless way I'd felt on our date, but we persevered until our lips were swollen, and a very alarming, very hard boner was pressed against my hip. I tried to mimic what he did with his lips, tried to match him motion for motion, tried to understand what to do with my tongue, tried not to wonder how humans had figured out that shoving your tongue in someone else's mouth felt good.

I spent at least two full minutes just puzzling through that particular discovery of mankind, but I couldn't quite sort it out.

A couple of times, he tried to roll on top of me, but I found ways to keep myself at his side, hoping he would remain content with our scissored legs, hips pressed together. I started sweating a little and spent a few minutes obsessing about whether or not I'd put on deodorant, which I thought might have made me sweat more.

I was in the dead center of that thought—*Did I put it on after my shower or when I brushed my teeth?*—when his hand roamed from my hip up to my ribs, and his broad palm cupped my breast.

I involuntarily pulled back—not out of surprise that he had done it, but out of shock from the contact. No one had ever touched me like that before.

We separated with a pop of our lips.

"Oh," I breathed.

His hand didn't move. Well, it didn't move *away*. He buried his face in my neck, his lips against my skin, his thumb brushing the peak of my nipple through the thin fabric of my bra, sending a jolt of heat down my stomach, between my legs.

"Oh!" I gasped and leaned back. "*Whoa!*" was all I managed before hitting the ground between the coffee table and couch with a thump.

He laughed without mocking me, and I looked up at him, blushing furiously as I wished I would just die already.

"You okay?"

I nodded and tried to smile. "I, um…"

"Come here," he said in an honest-to-God *come-hither* voice.

I fought the urge to run. *You are a grown woman, Annie Daschle. Now, get up and get on that couch with that boy.*

To which another part of my brain said, *Nuh-uh, no way.*

"I…I don't think I'm…it's just that…"

One of his brows rose. He was still smiling.

God, he's going to make me say it. "I don't know if I'm…ready for that."

His smile fell at that. "Oh. Right."

"Can we…do you want to maybe watch a movie?"

He cleared his throat and sat up, his face unreadable as he discreetly rearranged the steel pipe in his pants. "Yeah, sure." The words were level and distant.

Shame crept over me, and I climbed back up onto the couch. "I…I'm sorry," I said, wondering why the hell I was apologizing.

Will offered a smile I didn't believe, but he didn't absolve me. "What do you want to watch?"

He turned to the television and started talking about movies, but I only gave cursory answers as I tried to sort through how I felt.

Why did I feel so guilty? Should I have just gone along with it? Was he frustrated? Annoyed? Why did I feel like I'd let him down?

I agreed to a movie he said he'd wanted to see, some action flick I couldn't remember the name of and wouldn't remember the plot of the next morning. We didn't speak, but he pulled me into his side, throwing a blanket over us.

As close as our bodies were, he seemed a million miles away. But once it was playing, he finally looked at me and saw me.

"Hey," he started gently, and I looked over at him, trying for reassuring. "It's really fine, Annie. Okay?"

"Yeah. Okay."

He seemed appeased, turning his attention to the screen as I mercilessly lectured myself.

Because had he done anything wrong? Other than seeming put out, no. He wanted what most people wanted, and if that thing in his pants was any indication, he wanted it pretty bad. All he'd done was grab my boob. Most people did that their freshman year. It was *me* who was different, not him.

Maybe that was why I felt so bad, I told myself.

Because I was weird, and in that moment, he had known it. And for that moment, he hadn't been happy about it.

It was me who had the problem, and really, he didn't have to put up with it. He could tire of me at any time. I could almost guarantee he hadn't been with a virgin at any point in recent history, especially not one who had *zero* experience, not even with something so rudimentary as kissing.

I wondered how long he'd be patient. And I wondered if I could force myself to be ready for something I wasn't prepared for. Was it like jumping off the high-dive—you just needed to go for it—or was it like learning to do skateboard tricks—something that required instinct and practice and familiarity?

I told myself again that he hadn't done anything wrong. He'd stopped when I said to. And I was only imagining that he was unhappy with me.

By the time he took me home, I'd even convinced myself that was the truth.

Some Magic

ANNIE

I held up the quilt my nana had made for me before I was born, remembering a hundred moments in the span of a second, sparked just by holding that stitched, worn fabric.

"It feels like a lifetime ago," Elle said quietly.

In her hand was the painting she'd done of the rolling hills, dotted with trees and spring grass that lay behind our house—our old house, the house I'd never wander through again. The painting had hung over our mantel for years and had traveled thousands of miles in a moving pod, a little window into our old lives.

It was almost as hard to bear as it was a homecoming.

Boxes were stacked around the music room where there was plenty of room to spread out and sort through them. There were nonessential clothes and boxes of filed papers. Some were filled with photo albums and some with old schoolwork. And the rest were our own keepsakes.

Elle had arranged for the furniture Daddy had made to be put in a storage unit in Texas in the hopes that someday we would be able to bring it to wherever we were. And everything else had been sold, donated, or packed up in a big wooden box to travel here.

My boxes contained mostly books with some clothes, scrapbooks, and sheet music. I pulled the old Polaroid camera he'd given me when I was little and dozens of albums I'd accumulated over the years. But I had another full box devoted to things Daddy had made.

That box I put in my room to go through another time when there were less eyes to witness.

Susan cleared an entire bookshelf for me; it went all the way up to the ceiling, and I was more than a little excited to get on the ladder to add books to that topmost shelf. They were my old friends—my hardback set of Outlander and Harry Potter, stacks of Harlequin romances, piles of indie romances, the entire collection of Neil Gaiman books, which included one limited edition illustrated copy of *Neverwhere*, signed. In marker.

Mama came in when I was deep in the organizational throes, Mozart playing from my phone speaker and entire mind turned to the best way to order my books.

"You're making progress," she said as she wheeled herself over, stopping when she made it as close as she could with the maze of boxes.

I sighed happily. "It's so good to have our things. I don't know why, but it is. I don't think I could ever be a minimalist. I forget things if I don't have a touchstone to remind me."

She chuckled. "Meg's happy as a lark. She's got Daddy's old atlas split open on her bed, and she's poring over the pages like she's never seen them before."

I walked over and sat in an armchair next to her. "And how about you, Mama?"

She took a breath, her fingers winding together in her lap. "I'm not quite sure how I feel. My worlds have collided—the one from before I met your Daddy and the other one, the one from before he died. The third one, I'm not sure about yet. It's just as alien to me as it was when I woke up in that hospital bed."

I nodded, knowing there was nothing to say.

Mama glanced at the window. "When I left here, I didn't think I'd ever come back. And having the remainder of my life with your father here in boxes is comforting and sickening, all at the same time."

For a moment, she sat, unmoving and quiet.

"You know," she started softly, "when I met him, I knew. There was something about him, some magic, something in his smile and his eyes and the way his hand fit with mine, like they'd been cast together and split apart, and when they found each other again, there was a note plucked in both of us. And, after that moment, I marked my existence by the moments before and after him. So when my parents didn't approve, it didn't matter. There was only one thing I could do; I had to go with him. I had to be with him because I couldn't see my life without him in it. But I don't have a choice now either. He's gone."

"Mama," I breathed, emotion pinching my lungs and heart.

Tears slid down her cheeks, but her voice was steady and sure. "What I mean to say is that I chose love, and I'd choose it again. I chose him over everything—family, money, career—because it was the only way for me to be happy, *truly* happy. Someday, you'll find a love like that. You'll find someone you love beyond anything in this world, and when you do, you have to choose that love and let it guide you. It's all I wish for you girls—to love someone that much and be loved in equal measure."

"But what about now? Now that it's gone?"

She smiled, her breath hitching with a silent sob. "Oh, it's not gone, baby. It lives here." She touched her chest. "I'll miss him until

I draw my last breath, but his love made my life rich and full and meaningful. His love gave me three beautiful daughters, each who remind me every day of him—your smile and your eyes and your love for beauty in ordinary things, Elle's quiet nature and care for others above herself, Meg's laugh and uncanny ability to retain facts."

A small laugh escaped me, and I brushed tears from my face.

"Anyway," she said with a sigh that brought her composure, picking up a stack of books on the small table next to her, "I'm glad you have your things. Where are you going to put Lisa Kleypas?"

"Next to Eloisa James and Julia Quinn. Where else?"

She laughed and handed them over, and over the next hour, she helped me sort through it all until the massive shelf was packed ceiling to floor. And all the while, I thought over her admissions, sifting through my feelings and hers.

Deep down, I knew Will wasn't the kind of man my father was, and I knew that Will and I didn't have that magic, that awakening or devotion between us. I did have a lot of feelings though, feelings that hung in my mind like a fog, too vague to pinpoint without them disappearing.

I had a lot of feelings, but I didn't know how I felt.

Part of me wanted to hunt down an answer, but the rest of me said I should take the gift of a beautiful man who went so far out of his way to make me happy.

Greg's face flashed through my thoughts, my heart skipping a hard beat with a jolt. Because he fit that description just as much as Will did.

The difference was that I didn't question Greg at all, not once. I trusted him implicitly.

But did I trust Will?

It was a question I couldn't answer as easily as I would like, especially not after last night. I wondered how Greg would have handled it, handled *me*, but I only imagined he would have treated me with care and respect and quiet joy.

And I let myself wish for a moment that it could have been him instead.

Do vs. Feel

GREG

The fabric of my tie zipped as I tugged the knot apart for what had to be the tenth time.

I hissed a swear and lined up the tails, my eyes on my hands reflected in my bedroom mirror.

"Having trouble?"

I glanced behind me to find Sarah leaning against the doorframe, smiling. I grumbled a nonresponse.

This time, I'd pulled too tight. I huffed and pulled the knot out again.

"Nervous?" she asked.

"Does it show?"

"Not at all," she joked. "I haven't gotten the Annie update in a couple of days. Is she still... are they still together?"

My teeth clenched. "As far as I know. We have a sort of unspoken rule not to discuss him. But the last couple of days, she's been under house arrest working on her Juilliard application."

"That's good. She probably hasn't seen him either. And tonight, you're going out, and you're wearing *that* suit. There's no way she'll be able to resist you."

A dry laugh huffed out of me. "Well, suit or not, we're just *friends*, so I couldn't say. In fact, I'm not sure how I got myself into this. *Goddamn it*," I mumbled, the knot ruined again.

Sarah chuckled and pushed off the doorframe, walking around me to take the tie tails from me. "Here, let me." Her hands went to work. "I think I know how you got yourself into this; you care about her."

"And she isn't available."

She frowned, her head tilting as she worked on the knot. "You can't give up. Greg, you've got to get her away from Will."

"I know, but Sarah…I don't know what to say to change her mind."

"You told her what Will did, right? You told her he's not a good guy?"

I sighed. "I can't warn her off just because I don't like him. I can't do that to her. I can't put her in that position. And telling her the details of the rumors your ex-boyfriend told about you in high school, as much of a nightmare as that was for you, wasn't enough to warn her off from him for good. And if I push it, I'd look like a crazy person. I can't force her to choose me. I can't force her to leave him. She has to make her own decision, and I have to let her. And as hard as it is, all I can do is be her friend. All I can do is take what I can get and be there for her as best I can."

Her eyes were on her fingers as she smoothed my perfect tie, her face tight, throat working as she swallowed. "I just…I'm so afraid she's going to get hurt."

My chest ached, my voice softening. "Hey, don't worry, okay? Annie's going to be all right."

"It's just…Greg, I've been wanting to talk to you—"

Dad knocked on the doorframe. "Thought you might want to know you're about to miss your date."

I glanced at my watch with a whirl of anxiety and swore. "Sorry, let's talk later, okay?" I planted a kiss on her cheek and reached for my suit coat. "See you guys tomorrow," I called as I left the room, then the apartment with my strides long and my heart thumping.

The cab ride across the park was quiet but for my thoughts, which wouldn't quiet, wouldn't slow down. My wonder over what Sarah had wanted to talk about was quickly washed away by the force of anticipation of Annie, worrying over what the night would hold as much as I was eager to live every moment. And my nerves just wouldn't stop, not when I stepped out onto the sidewalk and not as I rode the elevator up to her uncle's penthouse.

Especially not when the door opened to a cacophony of barking dogs.

I couldn't help but laugh and pet them as an older woman did her best to wrangle while attempting to greet me over the pack of happy dogs. Elle made her way in and hugged me hello, introducing me to Susan before we fought our way past the dogs and inside.

"Sorry for the noise," Susan said, her cheeks pink from exertion. "I love the beasts, but they have no manners."

"It's no trouble."

Elle took my arm and ushered me in a little further. "Greg, I'd like to introduce you to our mother, Emily."

A beautiful woman with Nice to meet you. We've heard so much about you," she said.

Her hand was warm in mine. "Likewise. It's a pleasure."

"And this is Meg, our younger sister." Elle gestured to a bright-eyed, smiling little girl who thrust her hand out for a shake.

When I took it, she squeezed with surprising strength and pumped it like a pro.

I just stepped back when I saw Annie.

She entered the room with the lightness I'd come to associate only with her. Her hair was shining and golden, smoothed and pinned into a twist. The dress she wore was a shade of navy so dark, it was nearly black, the neck high and sleeves capped, tailored at her small waist, but the skirt was flared and shifted against her thighs with every step.

I found myself unable to breathe; all the air had been drawn from the room the moment she walked in.

Annie smiled and made her way over. "Sorry I'm a little late. Are you ready?"

I managed to swallow and nod.

She kissed her mother on the cheek as Meg grabbed her around the waist and squeezed. And with another kiss for Elle, we were saying our goodbyes and waving our way out the door.

When the elevator doors closed, she sighed. "Your suit is gorgeous, Greg."

Amusement and pride lifted one corner of my lips. "Not nearly as gorgeous as your dress."

She smoothed her skirt, blushing. "Thank you. I have on heels and everything! I just hope I don't break an ankle."

I offered my elbow. "Guess you'll just have to hang on to me."

And she slipped her hand into the crook of my arm, smiling up at me. "Guess I will."

"Mmm," Annie hummed an hour later, her eyes closing for a brief moment. "You have to try this."

She sliced off a piece of her chicken Kiev and spun her plate to put it in front of me.

I speared it, making sure it was well acquainted with the mushroom sauce before bringing it to my lips. "Mmm," I echoed when it hit my tongue.

Annie forked another bite of my Stroganoff, watching me eat with cheerful pleasure. "I know."

As I helped myself to another piece of her chicken, her eyes wandered from my face to our surroundings. We were secluded in a wraparound booth in the back corner of the Russian Tea Room. I'd been here a couple of times before, and when Cam had suggested it, I had known Annie would understand the magic and mood of the place and not only embrace it but amplify it.

The room was brilliant and rich and a little over the top—from the gold-leaf ceiling to the deep emeralds and blood reds of the walls and booths and carpet. Antique samovars shone from perches all over the restaurant—from the walls to the ledges between booths, their curved spouts proud and beautiful, their wide bellies waiting for tea. The walls were adorned with an eclectic mix of paintings in gilded frames; the one above our booth couldn't have been more appropriate.

I'd noticed it the second we walked up, inspecting it while Annie shrugged out of her coat and slipped into the booth. It was quirky and imperfect; a dark man in a dark suit stood in the foreground, patchwork hills stretching off behind him, and his hand held that of a lady who floated up and away, her face turned to him and her feet closer to the sun than the earth, her red dress caught in the wind.

It was Annie, light and floating away, and I was hanging on to her with blind devotion.

"So," she said with a secretive smile on her face, "I have something to tell you."

I smiled, ignoring a jolt of wishful thinking that her admission could be the words I longed to hear. "Oh?"

She nodded. "I sent my audition to Juilliard today."

"Oh my God, did you?"

"Mmhmm!" she hummed proudly, her back straight as an arrow and smile sweet and pretty. "Thank God I knew so much of the material already. All I've done the last few days is practice and do trial recordings, but I finally got it all put together, and *man*, I only hope I've got a real shot."

"Well, you did your best, right?"

"I did," she answered.

"Do you think it's good enough?"

"I do," she said with her shining eyes on mine.

"Then you did what you came to do. And now, you wait."

She groaned, the brief seriousness broken. "I hate waiting."

I chuckled and scooped a bite of Stroganoff up with my fork. "No…you? Impatient? I never would have guessed."

"I know; I'm the picture of restraint."

We both laughed, and Annie picked up her fork and knife again, her eyes on her hands as she spoke.

"I told you about how my parents scrimped and saved to put me through lessons, making deals with Mrs. Schlitzer, although I think she was glad to teach me. Maybe because we both loved it so much, more than anyone else we knew. Don't get me wrong. People tried to understand, but I don't know that anyone without a passion could understand true passion. It's easier to describe obsession, which is, I guess, almost the same thing. Like saying you're particular instead of picky."

I took another bite, content to listen to her talk as she was content to speak.

"But what a wonderful way to repay them all for what they've done for me. *Juilliard*," she said with a wondrous shake of her head. "I wonder what Daddy would have thought."

"Well, I didn't know him, but I can't imagine he wouldn't have been proud."

"I wish…" She shook her head. "You already know what I wish for. I'm sure you'd wish the same."

"Yes, I would."

"Wish in one hand, shit in the other. See which fills up first."

A brief, unexpected laugh burst out of me.

She shrugged, but she was smiling. "Something my pops used to say. A little nugget of grandfatherly wisdom he left me with."

"Do you have any other family? Besides your mom and sisters?"

"Daddy's parents died before I started junior high, and my dad was an only child. My mom's parents are alive, but I've never met them."

"Where do they live?"

"Here in New York."

I must have looked surprised because she explained, "They didn't approve of Daddy, wanted her to marry someone they knew, someone with breeding and a family name, not a woodworker from Nowhere, Texas, who hadn't even gone to college. When she made her choice, they cut her off."

"Jesus," I breathed. "I will never understand what would bring someone to put that much of their own expectations on their child."

"Me either. We didn't talk about them at all, growing up. My uncle—the one we're staying with—wanted to help, but Mama's as proud and stubborn as her own parents. My parents tried to make things work, even with all my medical bills and lessons and…well, with everything. It was why they didn't have much when Daddy died."

I nodded, swallowing hard. "When my mom died, the medical bills were—*are* a small fortune. With Dad unable to work, there was nothing we could do but move in with him and help him pay the debt down. There was no money saved. Everything had gone to keeping her alive after her diagnosis."

"It's so crazy to me that we have insurance for exactly these reasons, but what we're left with after insurance pays is enough to rob a family of everything they have. My first open-heart surgery was at three weeks old. Can you imagine? To have a baby so sick that you have to rely on science to save them and then have to pay for their life for the duration of yours?" Her hands moved into her lap, and she met my eyes with her entire heart shining in hers. "My parents sacrificed so much for me. I wish they'd accepted help from my uncle, so they wouldn't have had to suffer like they did. So they could have enjoyed their lives before…before…"

I reached into her lap for her hands, slipping my fingers through hers as my throat locked up.

She sighed and met my eyes with a smile that spoke to me of optimism and strength. "Even when we can't go on, we go on. Because the world keeps turning and the clock keeps ticking and our hearts keep beating even if we sometimes wish they would just stop. And so what else can we do with that inevitable time but honor the ones we lost by finding joy again? I've come to find that it's the only way I've been able to stitch what's left of me back together."

I drew a breath from deep in my lungs and let it slip out of me. "Where in the world did you come from, Annie?"

She smiled. "Out in the sticks and rivers."

"Must have been a good place to hide."

"Oh, it was. But I was never one for hiding."

"No," I said softly, "I don't suppose you were."

She turned back to her dinner, and the conversation drifted to easier things, things with less rust and pain. But mostly I just listened to her, watched her. Heard her. Saw her.

It wasn't her eyes, as wide and vibrant as they were, and it wasn't the swell or bow of her lips, as soft and lovely as they were. It wasn't the shine in her golden hair, and it wasn't her long, elegant fingers. It was Annie herself. Her beauty burned in her chest, in a heart that beat without rhythm.

And for a moment, everything was perfect.

The girl sitting at my elbow. The smile on her face. The way her bright eyes drank in the twinkling opulence and undemanding charm of the restaurant. The way her creamy skin looked against the crimson of the booth.

Perfect, except for one thing.

I'd tried to convince myself I could be her friend and nothing more. I'd considered the earnestness of her feelings, the depths I knew to be true; she cared for me and wanted me, just not in the way I wanted her.

I'd told myself I would take her any way I could get her. But the moment I'd first seen her tonight, I'd caught a glimpse of the truth; the task would not be simple or easy. And with every passing minute, that truth became more apparent, more invasive.

I couldn't be Annie's friend.

All things had a line that, once crossed, could not be stepped back over. And I had reached that line, passed it without realizing until I looked down. But instead of finding myself in her arms, I was pressed against the glass, the separation between us as thin as it was impenetrable.

And despite that knowledge, I didn't want to be anywhere else but exactly where I was.

Before we left the restaurant, I took her upstairs to the Bear Lounge. But I didn't see the bear aquarium or the perch swimming around in his vast belly; I saw her face bright with wonder as she peered inside, holding her breath. I didn't see the glass ceiling; I saw the colored lights on her cheeks and bridge of her nose as she tipped her small chin up to look. I didn't see the tree laden with glass eggs; I saw Annie with her fingertips pressed to her parted lips as she stepped under the branches, reaching for my hand without looking to pull me under with her.

But she'd pulled me under long before that moment.

ANNIE

I watched behind a curtain of tears as the music crescendoed and Romeo ran to Juliet's stone pedestal where she lay dead. Blinking only cleared my vision for a moment at a time, and I fought the urge to close my eyes.

I didn't want to miss a single thing.

And so my tears spilled down my cheeks in hot streams as I reached for Greg's hand, needing something to tether me to the ground. Romeo tried to wake her, lifted her up, and Juliet was a rag doll but still graceful, poised and beautiful, even in death. And the poison slipped past his lips just as she woke. The vision of her hands on his face and hers bent in pain, shining with tears. His body, too heavy to lift. The dagger, too sharp for hesitation. And she crawled back to him, nestled in his chest, held his face once more, pressed a final kiss to his lips, and then she was gone.

Their parents entered to find them both dead, and I sagged into Greg, my eyes finally closing as I let the wash of emotion win, my hiccuping sobs drowned out by the orchestra. And the curtain closed as the applause rose. We were on our feet in a breath, clapping through the curtain call, clapping until our hands stung and cheeks ached from smiling.

People began to exit, standing to pack the aisles, but rather than follow them, Greg sat.

I eyed him curiously. "Don't like waiting in lines?"

At that, he smiled. "No, it's just that I know how you love surprises."

My eyes widened with my smile. "What did you do?"

"You'll see. Come here and sit for a minute."

I did as I'd been told and leaned on the armrest between us. He was beautiful beyond the strong features of his face, beyond the lines of his body, defined brilliantly by the architecture of his suit. His beauty lay in the depths of his eyes where his heart and soul lived, in the joy of his laughter and the way he cared. Because he did care; he cared deeply.

There had been a moment under the egg tree in the restaurant when I turned my gaze from the wonders of our surroundings and met his eyes. I didn't know if it was the magic of the moment or something more, something in the air between us, something in his heart or mine. But for that long moment, we stood under the branches and breathed, our eyes connected. *We* connected. And I thought—wished—he might kiss me.

But he'd stepped away with a friendly smile, and I was reminded again exactly what he felt and where the boundaries of our relationship lay.

I reached for his hand and squeezed. "How can I ever thank you for tonight? It's been a dream. I wouldn't have wanted to experience it with anyone but you." *Not even Will*, I thought to myself, brushing the words away.

"You don't have to thank me, Annie."

"But I want to, and someday, I'll make it up to you."

Something in his face shifted, a flash of emotion in his eyes I couldn't catch before it was gone. "Annie, I…"

He didn't—couldn't?—finish, searching my face, as if the words were written on my cheeks and nose and lips.

"What?" I asked. The word was barely above a whisper. "You can tell me."

Greg took a breath, opening his lips as if to speak, but his eyes shifted to look behind me, and in a second's time, the moment passed.

"Ah, here we go," he said as he stood, his eyes behind me. "Come on."

He took my hand, and I followed breathlessly as Juliet herself stood at the side entrance of the stage, waving us up.

"Oh my God, Greg. *Oh my God!*" I giggled as he towed me up the stairs and to the stage, not stopping until we were standing right in front of her.

She was even more beautiful up close. Her blonde hair hung down her back in princess waves, her eyes big and blue, her legs ten miles long in her pink chiffon costume.

"Annie," he said with the most marvelous smile on his face, "I'd like you to meet Lily Thomas."

She extended her hand, her smile wide and friendly. "I'm so glad to finally meet you. Rose told me all about you."

A shocked laugh bubbled out of me. "You're kidding."

But she laughed sweetly. "She tells me pretty much everything, and I know enough about Wasted Words that it's a wonder I don't work there myself." She moved to press her cheek to Greg's. "It's good to see you."

"You too."

"I have to say," I started with a shaky voice, completely starstruck, "that was incredible. I've never…I mean, I've been to a few shows, but I've *never* seen anything like that. You were incredible. God," I touched my warm cheek. "That sounds so corny. I'm just speechless."

Lily laughed, her cheeks rosy, too. "Thank you, Annie. Really, it's all music and lights and production. I'm just lucky to be a part of it all. Can I show you guys around?"

And to my utter and complete joy, she did.

We followed her backstage. There was a line of mirrors with lights for the dancers, and props and people were scattered around backstage. She walked us to the sewing station, a special spot littered with supplies to sew their shoes. She even showed me how to do it. I got to hold a real-life ballerina shoe with satin ribbons backstage at a theater in the Lincoln Center.

I was checking off firsts I hadn't even known I had.

By the time we were finished, the stage was mostly empty, and the theater had cleared out other than a few people who seemed to belong there.

Lily left us to speak to a stern man who glanced at me and back at her with a disapproving arch of his brow and a conceding nod.

My hand was still in Greg's. I didn't even notice until he bent and brought his lips to my ear.

"I have one more surprise for you."

When he reappeared in my line of vision, his smile could have powered the sun.

"Come with me," Lily said, waving us behind her.

Down a set of stairs we went and to a doorway, passing through to bring us into the orchestra pit.

It was a place I'd dreamed of, a place I'd only imagined until tonight. And the vision left me breathless.

Greg let me go so I could wander around the cluster of chairs arranged in radiating half-circles, my tentative fingers brushing the tops of the chairs and trays of the music stands. I stepped around the director's podium and looked up to see the stage and theater from this angle. We were surrounded by the building itself, the sunken space the very heart of the theater, the place where the music lived and breathed.

I turned back to Greg, tears stinging my eyes again, but it was Lily who said, "Keep going."

When I looked back, my gaze found the piano.

I slowly approached it, touched the ebony and ivory, imagined the sound echoing against the balconies, wondering if, someday, I would be so lucky as to play in a place like this.

Greg was at my elbow. "Go ahead. Have a seat."

I whipped my head around to gape at him. "I can't."

Lily nodded around Greg, grinning. "Yes, you sure can."

"Are you...are you sure? I don't want to get you in trouble."

"It's no trouble. I have full and complete permission," she said with a sweep of her hand.

"I know it's not technically *on*stage," Greg said gently, "but I thought you might still be able to cross it off your list."

"I can't...I can't believe..." I muttered and took a wobbly step toward the bench.

Greg had ahold of me from behind before my foot hit the ground, one hand cupping my elbow and the other on my waist.

"Annie, are you all right?" The worry in his voice almost broke me into a million pieces.

"I'm fine. I'm better than fine," I answered with thanks I couldn't possibly verbalize.

My heart threatened to fight its way out of my chest, and I sat, partly to catch my breath. But once I was at those keys, I looked to Lily once more for permission, which she gave in the form of an encouraging nod.

And so, I played.

It was Mendelssohn, slow and haunting, crescendo and decrescendo, the sound floating up and into the space above me until each note disappeared, though my fingers kept going, kept making notes to fill the vast expanse of the room. And all of the feeling I had in me, every ounce of hope and love and joy and pain moving through me, through my hands, to the keys and hammers, to the strings and away.

When my fingers stilled, my cheeks wet with tears, I knew that there in that theater, on that bench, I had found the thing I wished for above all.

To play.

Lily swiped tears from her face and sighed, a deep and cleansing sound. "That was...God, Annie. That was lovely. Thank you."

I shook my head, brushing my cheeks. "Oh, please don't thank me. Not after the way you danced and not after arranging for me to play here. I should be thanking you."

"Consider us even then," she said ardently. "And I'd do anything for Greg's girl."

I froze. Greg was still as stone.

Lily kept talking. "When Greg told us he'd finally found someone, we all scrambled to help out. You know," she said with a laugh, "we'd been trying to find him a worthy girlfriend for years, and it was just never a good match. But you two just *look* right together, does that make sense? I guess he just needed us to butt out once and for all." She chuckled, sniffling, and ran her fingers under her eyes again. "God, I'm a mess. Between your playing and tonight's suicide, I'm all tapped out."

She laughed, and we mad a sad attempt to join her to as we followed her out of the pit, but the sound was tight and distracted. Both our minds whirred; I could feel his spinning just as well as I could feel my own.

My first thought was that it had to be a misunderstanding. She'd misconstrued what he'd said, jumped to conclusions, read into something that wasn't there.

My second thought was that Greg had exaggerated the situation so he could secure the surprise for me.

But when I chanced a look at him, when I saw his face, unmasked and open and full of the truth of his heart, I knew.

All the times I'd denied it came tumbling through my mind. All the moments between us fell under a spotlight—my hands in his hoodie pocket, the look on his face when I'd played in the park, the pain behind his eyes when he'd told me he didn't want me, not like that. I'd experienced them all completely in the dark.

I was stupid, a naive child who felt every bit my age.

Greg hadn't said a word.

We said our thank-yous and good-byes, and we walked out of the theater in silence as thick and heavy as midnight.

Greg didn't hate Will just for his sister's sake; he wanted me for his own.

He hadn't tried to give me the tickets to the ballet just to be a friend; he had done it because he couldn't stand to be with me if he couldn't have me.

When I'd thought he wanted to kiss me under the egg tree, it hadn't been my imagination.

But despite all that, he'd put his feelings aside, kept them secondary to what I wanted, what I felt, what I needed. He'd indulged every whim, every request, and not because of his regard for my friendship.

And I didn't know where that left me.

After tonight, after the magic and easy joy that always sparked between us, I asked myself the question, *Do I have feelings for him?*

And I found the answer was a resounding *yes*.

But I had a boyfriend, a boyfriend whom I had feelings for, too.

My heart was split, the lines of friendship and love too blurred to define. The two men were complete opposites. Will was cavalier and forward with his feelings while Greg stepped back and kept his heart hidden from me. Where one was loud and obvious, the other was quiet and subtle. Where Will seemed to care for my feelings equally to his own, Greg put mine above his.

But Will was my boyfriend, and Greg was my friend. And I found myself feeling foolish and blind and without direction. Because the truth of the matter was that I'd *wanted* Greg to kiss me. I *wanted* Greg to want me. Because I wanted him.

But I wanted Will too, and I couldn't comprehend how that was possible.

It wasn't until the cab pulled away from the curb that I mustered the courage to speak, not knowing what I'd say. But I had to say something.

He stared out the window, the strong angles of his face casting shadows on the planes.

"Greg—"

"Does Will make you happy?" It was as if he'd been waiting for me to speak, the question on his lips waiting eagerly to escape. Maybe he had been waiting on me to garner courage of his own.

Either that or he didn't want to hear what I'd been about to say.

"I…" I started, my composure teetering. I couldn't finish because I didn't know how to answer him honestly. Did he make me happy? Sometimes. Was I happy? No, in that moment, I wasn't at all.

But what I did know was the answer I was *supposed* to give when someone asked me if my boyfriend made me happy. So, I defaulted.

"Yes, of course."

"What about him makes you happy?"

"Well…" I thought about it for a set of irregular heartbeats, feeling myself unravel like a ball of yarn. "He… he's… well, he knows poetry and literature. He brings me flowers, knew to take me places he couldn't have possibly known I wanted to go—"

"Those are things that he *does*," Greg interrupted, his voice short and tight. "What about *him*? About the man himself? Tell me, Annie, for the love of God, because I need to hear that you're happy so I can let you go."

My heart lurched in my chest, my lungs tightening as a slow ache filled my rib cage.

But I had no answer to give. Because the man Will was—I realized it in that moment, far too late—was unknown to me. He was a stranger, and it wasn't *him* who had made me so happy but the *idea* of him, the prospect of happiness so much more than the man himself.

Greg, on the other hand, wasn't a stranger at all.

I reached to lay my hand on his forearm, but when he turned, when he pinned me with his gaze, so hurt and heavy with longing, the little bit of air left in my lungs disappeared.

Those emotions had been there all night, since before that, since always perhaps. But the smooth mask had fractured and crumbled and fallen away like dust, and the truth of his feelings were written in every curve and line of his face.

"Every day, it's gotten harder, every day since you met him. I've wanted to tell you how I feel, how you make every day brighter, better. How you're what I look forward to each time I walk through the doors, how you've changed the way I see the world. But you want him, and I couldn't interfere. So, I tried. I tried to stand aside, tried to be your friend. I've done everything you asked because it makes me happy to see you happy, but it hurts me, too. Coming here tonight was a mistake. I tried … I tried to give you the ticket. I tried …" Weariness cracked his voice, his Adam's apple bobbing in the column of his throat. "I thought I could do it, but I can't. It hurts too much."

He looked out the window again, and I stared at his profile.

"I'm sorry," I whispered, not knowing what else to say. Because I couldn't tell him what I didn't know. I couldn't give him answers I didn't have. I couldn't tell him I wanted him, and I couldn't tell him I wanted Will.

I couldn't bridle my racing heart.

He didn't speak for a long moment, a moment so heavy and thick, I felt like I might drown in it.

But he finally said, "Don't be sorry, Annie. You've done nothing wrong. I wish you every happiness, and I hope he endeavors to be the man you deserve." He turned the weight of his gaze on me, stopping my heart for a breath. "But I can't do this. I can't torture myself with your company, knowing you think of me like a brother or a friend. I can't bear it."

"We … we can't be friends?" I said, my voice trembling.

His throat worked, his jaw tight and eyes deep and dark. "Not now." He looked away. "I'm sorry. I shouldn't have come."

I wanted to argue. I wanted to tell him no, that the night was perfect, that he was the person I'd wanted to share that night with, who I wanted to share a hundred more nights with. I wanted to tell him I was sorry. I wanted to beg him to change his mind.

But shock left me speechless.

The cab pulled up to the curb, and we sat in silence for a second, then another, and another until it was too much. So, I opened the door and slipped out of the car, standing in the open mouth of the doorway.

"I'll see you around, Annie."

And then I closed the door, not knowing if I'd responded or what I'd said if I did, not knowing what I wanted or needed, what was right or wrong, what was true or false, as I watched the taxi drive away.

Welcome to Hell

ANNIE

My alarm beeped piously to wake me, but its efforts were lost. I'd been awake for at least an hour, lying in the dimness of the stormy daylight.

The colorless morning matched my heart.

Sleep had eluded me through most of the night; my mind had been consumed with all the things I should have said, should have done, should have known. Crying had given me no relief, no shed of emotion, no fresh perspective.

The night before resurfaced, the rush of happiness, the familiar comfort of Greg's company, the feeling of his arm under my palm, the look on his face when I'd played.

And the moment it'd fallen apart brought that joy down like a wrecking ball.

I'd lost him. I'd hurt him.

It didn't matter that I hadn't known how he felt; I should have.

I should have seen what his kindness meant. I should have seen the truth of his feelings. I should have told him I felt the same.

But I hadn't. Mostly because I'd had the obvious truth brought out from under my nose. And partly because I'd felt so much shame in the shadow of my inexperience. I was a fraud, a pretender, a little girl playing dress-up in her mama's heels, trying to be a grown-up.

My phone was still in my hand, the alarm turned off without any memory of quieting it. When it buzzed, I glanced at it, surprised. My heart jumped off a bridge when I saw it was Will, hitting the ground with an anxious thud when I read his message.

Hope your date was nice.

Nice. One couldn't ever say *nice* like that and it mean anything other than a lie.

I unlocked my phone and opened my messages to answer, wishing I could say nothing at all.

It was fun—I deleted *fun*—*eventful.* I deleted the whole thing and stared at my screen for a second.

I finally settled on, *The ballet was beautiful. What did you do last night?*

Within seconds of sending the message, he was typing. I waited, watching those little dots.

Sat around here, thinking about how much I hated that you were with him.

My stomach turned over. *I'm sorry.*

Just not sorry enough to have stayed home in the first place?

Tears blurred my vision. *It doesn't matter anyway. You were right. Greg has feelings for me, and we can't be friends anymore.*

For a second, nothing happened, and I imagined Will was stunned, reading the message over and over again. *Did he make a pass at you?*

No. He knows I'm with you, I answered painfully.

Dammit, Annie. You should have listened when I told you he liked you.

I know, I typed, not feeling like I knew much of anything. *Are you angry?*

Greg is an asshole, and he always has been. I don't want you anywhere near him.

I wondered briefly how much of that had to do with the wild differences in their stories about Greg's sister. And the following realization was that I believed Greg more.

Well, that's going to be hard to do since we work together.

Do you really think you should be working there anyway? It's not like you have to work, and with your heart and your surgery, it's not good for you.

You sound like my mother, I typed, which was poised like a joke, but it wasn't. At all.

I'm just saying. What about if you get into Juilliard?

Then I guess I'll deal with it then. I fumed, my thumbs flying with as much anger as thumbs could muster. *That job is the best thing in my life right now.*

Not me?

I frowned, my fingers tapping with enough force to make noise as I answered him. *Of course you too, and my sisters and Juilliard.* And Greg, I wanted to add. Except he wasn't going to be in my life anymore. *I can't believe you suggested that I quit.*

I can't believe you went on a date with another guy, but here we are.

It wasn't a date, and you know it.

Tell Greg that.

A frustrated tear charged down my cheek as I tossed my phone onto the empty side of the bed.

It was unfair, *so* unfair of him to treat me this way. He was petty and jealous, accusing and demanding.

Really, he was even more of a child than I was.

Greg never would have spoken to you like that, I thought, calling fresh tears to my eyes.

215

I climbed out of bed, reaching for my bathrobe on my way out of my room, still tugging it on when I knocked on Elle's door.

A sleepy *Come in* had me doing just that.

Elle propped herself up in bed with a smile that immediately fell when she saw me. "Annie? What's the matter?"

I closed the door, my chin flexing and cheeks tingling with a surge of anger and shame and hurt simply because she'd asked the question.

I didn't speak until I was in bed with her.

"Greg and I had a fight," I managed just before a sob escaped.

"Oh, Annie. What happened?"

"He…he…" I stammered, trying to catch my breath. "He said we couldn't be friends anymore because he had feelings for me."

Elle nodded and reached for my hand.

"I didn't know. I really didn't. How is that possible? How could I possibly be so s-s-stupid?" For a second, I couldn't say more. "I hurt him without meaning to, and now…now…"

I broke down again, and she smoothed my hair.

"*Shh*, it's all right."

"But it's not. It's not all right; *nothing* is all right. Will is angry that I went last night even though I *told* him I was going to be friends with Greg whether he wanted me to or not and even though he'd *agreed* not to give me flak. He was still mad after I told him Greg and I were through." Fresh pain twisted in my chest. "He even suggested I quit the bookstore just to keep me away from Greg. How ludicrous is that?"

"He's jealous. He and Greg don't get along, but you told him no and Greg yes."

"Yeah, but Will is my *boyfriend*. I thought that meant he understood he had some…precedence."

Her brows drew together in something close to pity. "You barely know him, and he barely knows you. It takes time to build trust."

"So, what—because he's my boyfriend, I should just do whatever he wants? Let him tell me who I can and can't spend my time with?" I shot.

"Of course not. I'm not saying he's right. But he had a feeling Greg liked you, and so did I. Do you really mean to say you didn't have *any* idea about Greg?"

"How could I have known? He never came on to me, never told me of his feelings. Will is an open book—he says what he feels and what he wants. From the first second I met him, he pursued me. And Greg did nothing to signal that he wanted to be with me. He was my friend. How could I have known he felt otherwise?"

That look was still on her face, and even though I knew it was compassion, it stung. "Not all love is loud and assuming. Sometimes it's silent, especially when it puts someone else's happiness above its own."

"My happiness," I mused. Fresh tears fell as my heart galloped in my ribs. "I don't know what makes me happy. I'm just a girl, a stupid, foolish girl with a silly list of meaningless things. I'm a skinny, sickly, naive child who couldn't see what was right in front of her, and now, I've lost it. I've lost him."

"Oh, Annie," she whispered and pulled me into her.

I tucked myself into her chest and cried until my breath was even, and she held me, stroking my hair and letting me be.

"Just because something is obvious doesn't mean it's right or honest. Sometimes it's how people hide things, behind shine and flash. Sometimes, that flash is meant to blind you."

I pulled back to look at her, suspicious. "What do you mean?"

She seemed to choose her words very carefully. "Only that I've met both of them, and I find myself trusting one over the other."

"And you deduced this in the few minutes you talked to them both?" And then I had a thought that set my mouth opening in surprise. "What did Greg tell you? At the bar?"

Her cheeks flushed. "Nothing specific, only that Will hurt someone he loves. Greg cares about you, Annie. But I'm not convinced Will does."

"How could you possibly know that?" I asked as I climbed out of her bed.

"It only took those few minutes with Greg to know that he cares for you and that he wants to protect you. Would you say the same for Will? Would you say, right now, with him wanting you to leave your job that he's trying to protect *you* or himself? Greg has done nothing but prove that he's worthy of your trust. He's been everything you want, even at the cost of his own happiness. Has Will?"

It was as close to a scolding that I'd maybe ever gotten from her, and I found myself speechless for a moment as I looked her over where she sat in her bed, her face angry and flushed.

"Annie, I know Will is handsome and charming. He says all the right things and makes all the right moves. But that doesn't mean he's right for you. That's all I'm saying."

"Maybe things could have been different," I said with a shaky voice, "but they're not. We're exactly where we are, and the train only goes one way. So, I appreciate your *concern*, but you don't know either one of them." I turned for the door, whipping it open with a whoosh.

"No, but I know you, and I don't want you to get hurt."

"Too late," I said, slamming the door behind me.

I got dressed in a rush, swiping miserable, mad tears from my face, which was swollen and splotchy. But my irises were electric, sharp with the multitude of feelings they held.

The apartment hummed with activity as everyone got ready for their workdays, but I made no unnecessary chatter and avoided contact with Elle entirely. She stood quietly in the kitchen watching me, not with anger or blame, only understanding and forgiveness, which somehow upset me even more.

The car was silent as I rode across town to work, the sky heavy with low gray clouds ready to drop their payload. And once at work, I stood outside the locked store as the first raindrops fell like a sigh.

Greg stepped out from behind the bar, and with every footfall, my breath thinned. His hard jaw was tight and square, his brows heavy and the emotion in his midnight eyes locked down like a jail cell.

The door swung open.

I walked past him.

He said nothing.

I carried the weight of that moment as I hurried to the back and he moved back to the bar and whatever task he'd been occupied with. And I tried to tell myself it was fine, everything was *fine*, today would be *fine*.

As it turned out, my day was anything but fine.

My heart was in especially rare form, skipping and fluttering like moth wings, erratic and unsteady, which landed me on a stool behind the counter.

A particularly aggressive customer argued with me for a solid five minutes about the price of a book. Ruby finally intervened after the lady yelled, *You dumb hick* at me.

The bright spot was the Monte Cristo I ordered for lunch, but as I sat in the bar with Greg so close, I found I couldn't eat.

His presence was a dark void in my periphery, sucking away all the light, all my will, all my composure.

What hurt worse than anything was the knowledge that he wasn't angry; he was hurt, so hurt that he couldn't even glance in my direction. He couldn't bear my company, and I couldn't blame him.

Greg had bared his heart, and I had given him nothing in return. I hadn't said *anything*; I'd been too confused and shocked to answer him. Even now, I didn't know how to answer him, not exactly.

What I did know was that Will wasn't all I'd imagined him to be, and Greg was more than I could have possibly bargained for.

The day wore on in a never-ending grind mill of minuscule injuries to my heart, one after another. Even when I thought the day was finally over and went to check out, my drawer was short six dollars and forty-two cents.

Rose didn't ask questions (past, *Are you okay?* To which I replied, *Just a bad day*). I started to cry a little, but she didn't press me for more, just offered me a lollipop from Cam's candy jar, which I took graciously. I paid the difference out of my pocket money, courtesy of Susan.

I kept my puffy, bloodshot eyes forward and my chin up as I walked past the bar. He watched me; I could feel the heat of his gaze and the pain it carried, as if he were whispering them in my ear. And through the doors I went, waiting in the cold for the driver. But the cold didn't bother me. In truth, I barely felt it. I was already numb.

When I made it home, I gave cursory answers and excused myself to my room, but before I could reach its comforting confines, Elle appeared in her doorway.

"Hey," she said gently.

"Hey," I echoed as my nose began burning again.

"I'm sorry for this morning, Annie. I didn't mean to hurt you or upset you."

"I know. And I'm sorry, too."

She stepped into the hall and embraced me. "No, don't be sorry. I shouldn't have pushed you."

"Sometimes, I need a good shove."

Elle chuckled and pulled away. "Rough day?"

I sighed. "It's that obvious?"

"You look like you dropped your favorite earrings down the drain."

"Not far off, I guess." I opened my bedroom door, and she followed me in.

We both sat on the bed. Well, she sat. I sagged.

"Was Greg there today?" she asked after a moment.

I nodded. "Although I might as well not have been. He wouldn't even look at me, Elle. I might as well have been a ghost." I stared at my wardrobe and through the branches and bird painted on its doors. "I want to believe it will get easier. It has to, right? *Time heals all wounds*, and all that."

"I think it will. And maybe, after some time and space, Greg will come around. In life, all things are temporary."

"That's both futile and comforting."

She smiled, lips together.

"Will hasn't texted me all day," I admitted with another flash of pain. "I thought he might apologize. But … I really screwed up, didn't I?"

"No, that's the thing. You didn't do anything to hurt anyone on purpose."

"But does my intention really matter?"

"I have to believe it does. To someone who loves you, intentions are everything." She toyed with my hair. "Are you going to message him?"

"What else can I even say? He hurt me, kept hurting me, even after I apologized. And I get that he's angry, but I don't know how to change that. I don't know what to offer him."

She watched me for a moment, her fingers still fiddling with one of my curls. "Annie, I really am sorry about Will and Greg."

"Me too," I said on a sigh that carried too many regrets to count.

The doorbell rang, the sound followed by a clamor of barking at multiple octaves, and a moment later, I heard Aunt Susan excitedly calling my name.

She swept into my room with her arms full of long boxes. "These just came for you. Whatever could they be?"

I moved out of the way as she set them on the bed. An envelope was fixed to the top, the paper thick and soft, and my heart skittered as I opened it and read the letter inside.

Annie,

I'm sorry for my jealousy and for the harshness of my words this morning. I was wrong. I never have liked to share, and I'm not always as patient as I wish to be, but those are faults of mine, and I'm sorry I punished you for them.

The dresses I promised are here for you. I hope you'll forgive me. I'd do just about anything to see you in it. And, if not, I'll only wish I could have been so lucky.

Yours,
Will

I passed the note to Elle and reached for the box on top.

"Well, what does it *say*?" Susan said from behind me, and Elle began to read it.

But I didn't hear them.

I lifted the top of the sturdy red box and gasped.

The empire-waisted dress was made of cream satin and silk chiffon, embroidered with beads that shimmered in the light, the neckline low and square, the back, I could see, dropped into a V. When I picked it up and saw it in full, I could have died from the sheer brilliance.

Elle gasped.

The skirts were made of the same delicate chiffon, the heavy hem scalloped and lined with more beads. It pooled on the ground, and the gathered silk in back spilled down to the floor in the slightest, most elegant train.

"Oh my God," I breathed. "How could I possibly wear this to a bar?"

Susan laughed. "Easy. You put it on and go. Don't you dare waste a dress like this."

Elle reached into the box. "Look, there are matching gloves and a fascinator. Annie, this is…"

"I know," I breathed. "Let's look at yours."

I laid my dress down in its box and moved it out of the way. Pulling off the lid of the other box elicited gasps from all three of us at once.

The gown was taffeta, the iridescent blue-green like that of a peacock feather. The empire waist was lined with delicate gold fringe, and a large, sweeping floral pattern was embroidered in shimmering gold down the front of the skirts and around the hem.

"Well," Susan said as we all gaped at the spoils Will had sent, "I think he's maybe earned another chance. Don't you think?"

I picked up the note and read it again, touched the strong, square letters.

At my fingertips was an apology from a man I cared about. I'd lost Greg, but Will was still here, still eager and willing. And if he could prove himself, maybe we could find our way back to the magic of the beginning.

And so I decided to defer to my list, to my newfound outlook on life, my cure to move forward when life got hard. I would live in the moment and survive on my hopes.

So with a smile, I said, "I believe he does, too."

GREG

The second Annie walked out the doors and slipped into the black Mercedes, I threw my towel in the dish well with shaking hands and stormed to the back.

All day, I had felt her there, so close and a world away. Her face was drawn, her nose red and eyes brilliant from crying.

And those tears were because of me.

A war had raged in my ribs between the desire to wipe those tears away and the knowledge that to do that, I'd only inflict more pain on myself. I'd almost been tempted despite the fact.

Don't be so fucking dramatic, I told myself, raking a hand through my hair. *She's just a girl.*

But that was a lie, and I knew it in my marrow. She wasn't just any girl, and I couldn't pretend like she was.

"Uh, you okay?" Rose asked when she saw me wearing a track in the cement, her brows knit together in concern.

"No, I'm not fucking okay," I muttered and paced away from her like I had somewhere to go.

"What happened?"

"I took her to the ballet," I answered, like that explained everything.

She didn't say anything, and when I turned to pace back toward her, her arms were folded as she waited for me to elaborate.

"Lily didn't realize Annie had a boyfriend who *isn't me.*"

"Oh God." Her eyes widened. "Oh *God.* Cam!" she called over her shoulder.

I turned again to stalk away. "After that, we got in the cab and I…I just couldn't pretend anymore. I spilled it all, and I told her I couldn't do it anymore."

When I turned again, Cam was at Rose's side, and they wore matching expressions of shock and dismay.

"Well, what did she say?" Cam asked.

"Nothing. She said nothing."

I stopped in the middle of the room, hands hanging on my hips, my eyes searching the walls, then the ceiling for answers.

"Greg, I'm so sorry." Cam's words were soft and sad and did absolutely nothing to ease my aching heart.

"I can't even fucking look at her."

"You're mad?" Rose asked, surprised.

A tight laugh fought its way out of my narrowing throat. "I'm not mad. I'm *gutted*." I ran a hand over my mouth. "I don't even know what happened to me, how I got here, how I came to care so much, so fast. But here I am." I spread my arms in display. "Welcome to hell."

"Greg…" Cam started, concerned.

I took a breath. Let it out. Straightened my face.

My heart did what it wanted.

"I'm fine. Really. I'll be fine," I insisted, pushing the line we all knew was bullshit. "Seriously, stop looking at me like that. I just… I just need a minute after spending an entire day thinking about how upset she is and how much I hurt her."

They didn't look like they were buying it, but Cam sighed. "All right. We're around, if you want to talk about it."

"Thanks, Cam, but there's nothing left to say. And Rose, thanks for the tickets and for helping to get Annie behind the piano. You should have seen her face." My voice cracked, and I cleared my throat. "I'll be in the cage if you need me. We got that whiskey shipment in today."

"Sure, okay," she answered, touching Rose's arm.

And then I was alone once again with nothing but my regrets to keep me company.

All That Glitters

ANNIE

"Okay, open your eyes."

I did as I'd been told, drawing in a breath of surprise when I saw myself in my bedroom mirror.

The makeup artist stood at my side, smiling as she watched my reaction, my eyes roaming my face and hair in wonder.

"I can't believe that's me."

I turned my head side to side, inspecting my hair, which was piled in romantic curls on my head. A gold velvet ribbon wound around my crown twice at intervals, weaving in and out of my hair in a Grecian fashion. The fascinator was pinned just above my ear, a beaded pair of leaves over a frame of creamy feather tips. And my makeup, though simple and natural, changed my face somehow, opened my eyes up, made them brighter, brought color to my cheeks and lips.

It was miraculous.

"Like it?" she asked eagerly.

"I love it," I breathed. My eyes moved lower to the angry, welted scar between my breasts, which were pinned and swelling from the confines of the bodice of my dress.

I ran my finger over the scar, wishing I had the porcelain décolletage of the movies.

"Did you want me to cover that up?" she asked. "I have some stage makeup that covers up tattoos and scars."

But I smiled. "No, that's all right. It's just as much a part of me as anything else."

The doorbell rang, sending the dogs on their tear through the house. I stood, gathering my skirts and hurrying out of the room as best I could, nearly falling over when I saw Will just inside the door.

He was utterly gorgeous—from top hat to riding boots and everywhere in between.

But my heart swung back when it remembered the pain he'd caused, swinging even further away when I wished for a fleeting moment that it were Greg standing in the entry in a cravat and tails, smiling at me like I was the center of the universe.

Will doffed his hat and bowed as I approached. "Why, Annie, you look lovely tonight and all nights."

I curtsied, lowering my eyes and composing my thoughts as Susan wrangled the dogs away.

He replaced his hat and took my gloved hands in his, pulling me close enough to speak in a hush, "I'm sorry, Annie. I…I am a jealous man, and that jealousy drives me to say things I shouldn't. I'm sorry I was harsh. I'm sorry I hurt you. Am I forgiven?"

I smiled, but the gesture was thin. I'd not yet healed from the lashing, but the bandage was a beautiful effort. With some time, I hoped we could put it behind us. But if his habit of flying off the handle was any indicator, it would only be a matter of time before we found ourselves there again.

For now, I would have faith.

"Of course I forgive you," I answered as his thumb stroked my hand through my satin glove.

And with that liberation, he brought my hand to his lips.

Mama was at my side, and Susan approached, red-faced and smiling as she brushed an errant hair from her face. "Will Bailey! How is your mother? Well, I hope."

"She is. Thank you, Mrs. Jennings. Though I've barely seen her; she's working on a charity ball for next month that has had all of her attention."

"Oh, I'm sure. It's stunning every year, and the amount of work— *oh*!" she breathed, glancing behind me.

I turned to find Elle entering the room, blushing prettily, her skin like a dish of cream against the deep teal of her dress.

Mama's eyes were teary. "Oh, Elle, you look radiant."

And she really did. Between the shine of her dress and the flush in her cheeks, she was practically glowing.

"Thank you," she said, looking down.

It almost made me feel bad for the surprise I was going to spring on her at the mixer.

Susan looked us all over proudly. "You all look *wonderful*. These costumes are simply amazing. Here, let me take your picture." She opened her hand for my camera, which was nearly the sole content of my small handbag.

We posed for a few photos before Will offered his arm. "We should be going."

"Yes, of course," Mama said.

I bent to kiss her cheek before taking Will's offering.

And then we were off.

The chatter in the car was excited and buzzing, the three of us laughing and happy and subject to the magic of the evening.

But when I walked in the door of the bar, that magic was sucked out of me in a whoosh and replaced with something far more real.

I saw Greg behind the bar the second I passed the threshold, my feet still moving as I walked at Will's side, my hand in the bend of his elbow.

But when my eyes met Greg's across the room, the room stilled, quieted, disappeared, the thread between us tightening with my lungs.

He stood tall, the overhead lights casting his eyes in shadows from the line of his gathered brows and highlighting the hard edge of his jaw. A cravat of crisp white linen was wrapped around the column of his neck and tied in a loose knot at the place where I knew I'd find the hollow of his throat, if I'd been able to slip my fingers into the tie and unfurl it. The dark coat over his vest was tailored to perfection, the shoulders straight and marking the broad expanse of his frame, the tapering to his waist with buttons that served, in my mind, only to accentuate that lovely angle of his body.

But it was his eyes, dark and shrouded, that held everything in me still, commanding me without the need for a single word.

A tug of my hand snapped the connection.

Will smiled at me as if he'd asked me something.

"What was that?" I muttered.

"Can I get you a drink?"

I smiled back. "Just water, thank you."

He patted my hand before letting it go. "I'll be back."

I chanced a look back at Greg. He hadn't moved, but somehow, everything about him was harder, more insistent, more desperate.

Elle took my arm. "Where do you have to be?"

I glanced around, finding the table a little in from the bar. "Right over here. I'm running the register on the Book and Booze special all night. Think you'll be all right?"

"I'm sure I can manage," she answered with a smile.

And when I scanned the crowd and saw Ward, I smiled back. "I bet you can. Look."

I nodded in his direction, and she gasped.

"Annie, oh my God." Her voice was low and frantic. "What did you do?"

I shrugged. "Oh, I didn't tell you I invited him? Hmm, I swear I mentioned it."

"No, you most certainly did *not* mention it."

"I just figured he's single too. I mean, technically, it *is* singles' night."

Her blush was so furiously pretty, I could barely stand it, and neither could Ward, it seemed. He waved and began making his way over.

Her arm tightened in mine, her voice low. "Oh my God, *oh my God.*"

"What is the matter with you? He's a friend, isn't he?"

She leveled me with her gaze. "He is my *boss.*"

I shrugged again. "You're not allowed to talk to your boss outside of work?"

"No, it's not that. I just—" She froze, her eyes darting away.

"Good evening, ladies." Ward's voice was deep and velvety, his smile a little crooked as he bowed. He wore a lovely Regency suit, perfectly accurate, even down to the cravat.

Really, it was the most brilliant dream realized—a room full of masculine necktie porn.

"That costume is perfect, Ward. Where did you get it?" I asked.

"My mother knows of a rental place she's used for parties before. Thanks for the invitation by the way. This is spectacular," he said, glancing around.

It really was. Cam had gone a little extra, stringing hanging lights covered by small paper lanterns across the open space. Candelabras dotted the room on available surfaces, lit with electric candles. She'd even had dance cards made, which were sitting on the table where I was supposed to already be.

"Well, I need to go clock in and get to work. Ward, will you keep my sister company for me? I'd hate for her to stand here in that dress all alone."

His smile widened. "Oh, I don't think such a thing could ever happen, *especially* not in a dress like this."

She blushed so hard, I thought she might faint from a rush of blood to her head.

I laughed. "I'll be back in a bit. Have fun!" I called as I headed to the back.

Greg's eyes were on me—I could feel them like a tether—but I kept my chin up and my feet moving, clocking in once in the office and collecting the iPad and credit card reader before making my way back out.

The table at the front was marked with little signs, dance cards, name tags, that sort of thing. Jett sat after, looking dapper as hell and as natural as an Austen hero. His hair was raven, his eyes the color of cornflower, rich and velvety blue, shoulders wide and nose elegant. He was checking IDs and issuing wristbands, taking down drink and book combinations for the Books and Booze deal. Ruby was in charge of pulling the books and drinks once they were purchased, and I was set to take orders from suitors and ladies alike.

Will was at my elbow a moment after I sat down, and he set a tall glass next to me.

"Thank you," I said and took a sip, nearly choking when it hit the back of my throat. I looked at the glass as if it contained poison. "This is not water."

He bent to bring his lips to my ear. "It's vodka and water."

Panic rose in my chest. "I can't drink this!" I hissed. "I've never—"

"I know," he soothed. "Another first. And here's to many more."

He clinked his own rocks glass to mine and took a sip. I didn't.

"Will, I'm working. This is wrong."

At that, he knelt next to my chair, putting him just below my eye-level, his gaze turned up to mine, handsome and persuasive. "It's just one drink, and it's a tall. No one will know, and you won't get drunk. Don't worry—I'll take care of you."

I didn't want to be a baby, and I didn't want to tell him no. I wanted to be the cool girl, the easygoing, anything-goes girl. And I didn't want to fight with Will anymore.

So I sighed and said something I would later come to regret very deeply.

"All right. Just one."

Anywhere But Here

GREG

For some reason, I kept expecting things to get easier.

I wasn't exactly sure why—they'd been on a steady decline for several days, longer, if I were being honest with myself. And over the course of three hours, they kept speeding downhill.

Seeing Annie walk through the door left me first breathless, then seething. The sight of her at the table in my line of vision was the sweetest torture; sweet because it was *her*, and she was dazzling in that dress, torture because the smile she wore had nothing to do with me. It was for the bastard at her elbow. And he didn't leave her side for any longer than he had to.

I wouldn't have either, had I been him.

The night moved on as time did, with no care for the ache in my chest or the anger buried in its center. It was nearing eleven, the bar packed to the seams with people in costumes. They had really shown up for the occasion, most of them dressed in stunning gowns and finery. Of course, Cam threw a couple of legendary regency costume parties—among a host of other costume parties and singles' nights—every year, so people committed to springing for the good stuff.

I'd bought my own costume, as had most everyone at the bookstore. Before the first historical party, Cam had even given cravat-tying lessons. I'd laughed about it at the time, but—no lie—once I had seen how the girls at the bar reacted to that strip of linen around my neck, I'd found myself fully on board.

Cam had only said *I told you so* once.

But that night, Annie was set apart from everyone else in the room. I could imagine her in a ballroom long ago, her face lit by candlelight, her gloved hand in the hook of my elbow.

I could imagine her anywhere but here, with him. That reality was the one thing I couldn't find a way to suffer.

Fortunately, we were busy, and keeping a wall of people between us seemed to be my only defense. I was flanked by Beau and Harrison, each in their own costumes, the three of us like veritable gentlemen, if it weren't for our filthy mouths. Though we always found ourselves speaking a little more eloquently in cravats and collars.

I tossed a coaster down, offering my bartender smile as one customer moved, and another stepped forward. But the smile spread genuinely when I saw that it was Elle.

"Good evening, Miss Daschle," I said. "Might I offer you something to drink?"

She laughed. "Thanks, but no. I was actually about to leave, but I wanted to swing by to see you first." Her face grew curious and sincere. "How are you?"

I drew in a breath and kept my smile fixed. "Fine."

"Because Annie isn't."

"Are you sure of that? She seems like she's doing just great."

"Well, looks can be deceiving. She told me what happened."

With nothing left to deny, I gave up the fight. "I don't know, Elle. I'm not sure what to do."

"You're angry with her, I know, but—"

"I'm not angry. Not with her. I'm hurt, but not by her. The entire thing is my own doing."

She frowned. "I don't understand."

"I don't much either." I sighed. "Annie didn't do anything wrong, and it's not her fault she's ended up in the position she's in. I knew better than to get close to her, but...well, I couldn't help myself. You know, I think I knew from the very first moment I saw her that it would all end in tears," I said with futility. "And now, she's with him, and that's what it is."

Elle's eyes were heavy with sadness that weighed down the corners of her lips in a frown. "You won't talk to her at all?"

I shook my head. "I can't trust I'll keep my feelings to myself anymore. Not now that she knows. I can't pretend anymore, Elle."

At that, she nodded with understanding behind her eyes and reached for my hand where it rested on the bar. "I suppose that's fair. And I hope it gets easier, Greg. For both of you."

"So do I."

We said our goodbyes, and with a parting squeeze of my hand, she turned and walked away.

I blew out a breath and took the next drink order, and within a couple of customers, I had compartmentalized as best I could.

Until I tossed a coaster that read *All is fair in love and war* and looked up to find Will in front of me.

He looked ridiculous in a fucking top hat, his smile smug and eyes cruel. And I wondered just how the hell he'd landed a girl like Annie.

I reminded myself that he was a spectacular liar—that was how—which didn't make me feel better.

"Tall Grey Goose and water," he instructed curtly.

I said nothing, just reached for a glass and scooped ice in.

He half-turned, looking back at Annie. "She's beautiful, isn't she?"

I set the glass on the bar and turned for the vodka.

"That dress was practically made for her. Maybe, if I'm lucky, I'll see it in a heap on my floor tonight."

Hot coals burned in my belly, the steam climbing up my throat. I poured the vodka. "Maybe, if you keep talking, I'll see you in a heap on the sidewalk."

Will laughed. "I told you not to get in my way. I told you not to give me a reason to twist the knife. But you didn't listen. Can't say I'm all that surprised." He picked up the coaster and held it up in display. "How appropriate."

I picked up the soda gun with a hand shaking with desire to grab him by the throat, unfulfilled with the task of topping the glass off with water.

Will Bailey was not worth losing my job over.

"She made her choice," he said when I didn't respond.

"Yes, she did." I set the drink in front of him.

"Put it on my tab." He picked up the drink before stepping back, that horrible smile of his hitting me like a spear in the breastbone.

He disappeared, and the next person moved into his place to order a drink, so I accommodated them, all while attempting to calm myself down with little luck.

What I needed was to leave, but there was nowhere to go. I was caught in a cage of mahogany and overhead lights, a spotlight on my discomfort, lighting me up for the whole world to see.

A moment later, the crowd opened up, and I saw Annie sitting at the table, her lips smiling at Will and her gloved hand around her drink.

The drink I'd just poured.

The nuclear explosion that went off between my ears was deafening.

I turned on my heel and flew out from behind the bar, weaving through the crowd toward her, stopping only once I reached the table.

Shock registered on her face when I snatched the drink from her hands and smelled it.

I turned on Will. "Are you fucking kidding me?" I growled, slamming the drink back on the table as I stepped around it and toward him.

He took a step back, the superior look on his face washed out, leaving him stupefied.

"Get out," I said through my teeth. "Get the fuck out of my bar."

Annie hooked her arms in one of mine and pulled, "Greg, stop!"

I whirled around, arching over her.

She shrank under the weight.

"Don't," I ground out from behind clenched teeth. "Do not."

"Listen—" Will started.

I whirled back on him. "You gave a drink to an underage girl in my bar. I don't have to listen to a goddamn word you have to say. *Get the fuck out. Now!*"

He jumped at the impact of the last word and glanced at Annie, reaching for her hand.

When she moved to step around me, I moved with her, keeping my body between them.

"She is not going with you."

"That's not for you to decide," she shot.

I turned, pinning her with a glare I felt into the depths of my chest. "You are on the clock. And if you leave with him, you're fired."

Color rose in her cheeks, her eyes shining with angry tears. "Oh, so *now* you want to be my boss?"

I didn't respond, only held her still with my glare.

"Goddamn it, Greg," she whispered but didn't move to follow.

"Let her go," Will said, his shoulders square.

"No."

His eyes darted to her. "Come on, Annie." He extended his hand.

"I'll call you later," she said miserably.

Fury flashed across his face. "If you stay here with *him*, we're through. You don't need this fucking bullshit minimum-wage job anyway."

"Watch it, asshole," I warned.

"You're *both* assholes!" she shouted, tears clinging to her lashes. "Screw both of you, and screw your ultimatums."

"Annie—" he started, but she cut him off.

"If that's how you feel, then go. I'm through with this, through with you. Through with your jealousy and through with the arguing. I'm *through*."

She took a furious breath that shuddered in her chest, a sob fueled by betrayal and hurt, a sob that sent a flash of rage through me, tightening my fists at my sides.

"Get out of here, Bailey. Because if I put my hands on you to make you, I swear to God, I won't be able to stop."

Will stood very still, his eyes on her, then me, then her again, as if weighing his options. When he came to his senses, it was with a tug on the hem of his vest and the straightening of his back.

"Your loss," he said, his cold eyes on Annie.

"Do not show your face here again. If you walk through those doors, I will have you thrown out. Do you hear me?"

After a long, strained stare, he nodded once and turned.

The only people who had heard were those adjacent to us, and the party went on undisturbed but for our little island of blame.

When I turned to her, tears spilled from her accusing eyes.

"I cannot believe that just happened," she spat. "I cannot believe you just did that."

Every muscle in my body was flexed and furious. "*You* can't believe? Do you realize we could lose our liquor license? Did you happen to forget you were on the clock and working? I should fire you on the spot."

"Well then, why don't you?" she cried, her voice full of contempt.

"You and I both know why."

I turned to walk away, and she didn't say a word more.

The rest of the night was a blur. Somehow, I managed to get back behind the bar and spent the next few hours in a haze marked by automatic movements—*smile, pour, nod*. And then it was last call, and the night wound down.

The crowd thinned, then emptied, leaving only the employees. Ruby bussed her tables while Jett and Annie cleaned up their things, running the box of name tags and dance cards and tablecloths back. We were breaking down the bar when Annie appeared in front of me, the bartop between us.

"I'm finished," she said quietly but not gently.

I didn't look at her. "Good. Clock out and sit down."

She took a breath through her nose, the sound frustrated. "I would like to leave, please."

"You will sit and wait for me to finish. We have things to discuss, and when that's done, I'll put you in a cab."

"I am *not* a child!"

"Then stop acting like one."

I looked up when she made another sound, this one somewhere between a gasp and a sob. The hurt on her face was nearly the end of me. Because that hurt written in the soft curves of her cheeks, the brackets on either side of her lips and the furrow between her brows told me she felt every bit the child I'd accused her of being.

I couldn't take it anymore.

I stormed out from behind the bar with Beau and Harrison watching me, exchanging glances when I rounded the corner. The second Annie was in grabbing distance, I did just that, hooking her upper arm with my hand to drag her into the back.

What I had to say didn't need an audience.

I let her go once we were in the depths of the store, my chest heaving as I looked down at her. "I cannot fucking believe you did that. I cannot believe you put me in that position."

"It was just a drink!"

"Jesus Christ, Annie. One drink could cost Rose tens of thousands of dollars in fines and the store's license. And you don't even drink! This was *his* doing, not yours. And don't you dare lie and tell me that was your idea."

More tears. So many tears.

"I'm sorry. I'm so sorry. I…I just didn't think it would be a big deal. He said no one would know, and I'd never had a drink, and—"

"This isn't you. None of this is you. It reeks of that son of a bitch."

"Greg, you banned him from the bar, and you kept me here, held me hostage when you should have let me go. It wasn't right, how you handled things. It wasn't," she said, angry sobs hiccuping in her chest.

And my own anger won over, bursting out of me in waves. "This is *my* bar, and I don't want him here, not after tonight. You'll do what I say because you are *my* employee. You'll follow *my* rules because I am your boss."

Her sadness shifted to furious accusation. "That's bullshit, and you know it. Because I don't think this is about *him* so much as it's about *you*."

My breath kicked out of my lungs. "That is not what this is about."

"You're a goddamn liar. You would have found any excuse to kick him out and keep me here. You would have found any reason to keep me away from him. Well, it's over now. Are you happy? Are you fucking happy?" Her voice broke, her face bent and shining with tears.

I rushed her, grabbing her arms, pulling her into me, desperate and overcome and frustrated beyond measure. "You don't understand, not what you want, not what he wants from you, and not how I feel."

My breath trembled, my eyes searching the depths of her emerald irises, the ring of gold flashing. "You don't see that he was hurting you, chipping away at you sliver by sliver. You don't see that I"—*need, desire, love*—"want you. You can't see it, even when it's right in front of you."

Her face softened with understanding and surprise, her lips parted, as if a thousand words waited somewhere just beyond her tongue, her hands on my chest and chin tipped up. And I felt myself leaning, felt her weight in my arms, felt her breath on my lips.

And I let her go. God knew how, but I let her go.

One step back wasn't enough, and it was too much.

I turned and rushed out of the back and into the store, empty of everyone but Beau. When he looked up, I tossed my keys to him.

"Lock it up."

He frowned as he caught them. "Shit, man, I have a date."

"It'll have to wait."

"Where are you going?" he called after me.

"Anywhere but here."

I pulled open the door, welcoming the chill, hoping it would cool my anger.

With every step, I knew I was just as wrong as I was right. With every footfall, I pictured her face, etched with pain by my own hand. I'd left her there alone. I'd treated her unfairly.

It only took a block before I came to a stop in the middle of the sidewalk.

It wasn't that I hadn't been justified, but I'd been harder, crueler than I had to be. I could have let her go. I could have dealt with the whole thing tomorrow. And she was right; if it had been anyone but her, I would have handled it differently.

But it was Annie, and where she was concerned, I found I couldn't be rational.

I turned around with a sigh and headed back to the store, my anger ebbed to expose the shores of guilt. When I reached the door, I found it still unlocked, though the store was abandoned, everyone gone except Beau. I didn't see him, but I could hear him whistling.

My goal was singular.

Past the bar I went, past the hall where the office was and into the back of the building.

I found her in nearly the same spot as I'd left her, sitting on a stack of empty crates with her face buried in her hands and her soft sobs echoing off the concrete walls.

Annie looked up at the noise of my footfalls, almost immediately looking away, like she'd just been readying herself to leave. She swiped at her tears and sniffled, her eyes down.

And with a bruised and bloodied heart, I dropped to my knees in front of her and took her hands in mine, meeting her eyes with remorse and repentance.

"Annie, I'm sorry."

Her chin quivered, the weakly tamped tears springing from her eyes again. "No, Greg, I—"

"Please, let me apologize," I said gently.

She nodded once.

"You're right—I can't be reasonable when it comes to you. And even though I had to act, I didn't have to act like that. I have a hundred excuses, but you know them all, and none of them matter. So I'll only beg for your forgiveness. I never wanted to hurt you; I only want your happiness. I just haven't been able to sort out how to balance your happiness and my own."

"Of course I forgive you," she said, though she still cried, an unending stream that pained me to no end.

"God, please don't cry anymore. I don't want to make you cry anymore," I begged, reaching for her face, tipping it so she would meet my eyes. "I'm sorry."

She nodded again. "So am I. I…I was wrong, and I screwed up b-b-bad. I'm so sorry."

A sob broke out of her, and I rose enough to pull her into my chest, slipping my fingers into her curls.

"*Shh*, it's okay. It's okay."

"No, it's not," she said against my lapel. "I've ruined everything. Your friendship. My reputation." She sniffled and pulled back. "Your coat."

I chuckled and looked down. "It'll survive. And so will you. And so will I."

She tried to smile, her brows still together, but her tears were dry for the moment.

I stood. "Come on, let's get you home. It's almost three."

She sighed and stood too, looking as weary and worn as I felt. "All right."

We walked out of the back in silence, and when I stepped into the store, I stopped dead.

All the lights were off, and the metal gate in front of the door was down.

"*No, no, no, no. NO*," I muttered as I hurried to the door to make sure that, against all odds, I wasn't seeing what I was seeing.

Once confirmed, I turned to Annie with numb hands.

"We're locked in."

Did He?

ANNIE

A half an hour later, I was sitting behind Rose's desk, gently spinning the chair from side to side.

The night felt like it had been a decade long; too much had happened and too much had changed for it to have only been a few hours.

As I watched Greg dial the phone again, his dark brows drawn with a frustrated furrow between them, I marked the swing of emotions I'd felt. Wonder when I put on the dress, the thrill when I took that cursed drink from Will, the fear when Greg stepped in, the guilt at the knowledge of his rightness. The betrayal by Will of my wants and wishes. The feeling I had as I watched him walk away.

The truth of that emotion was that it wasn't remorse but *relief*. Because Will had demonstrated once more that he wasn't the man I'd believed him to be, and he'd had enough chances to prove otherwise.

Will had wanted his way solely for the sake of having his way. Greg had intervened because he was trying to protect me, in his heavy-handed, ill-conceived way.

And when it all shook down, I found myself glad that Will and I were through.

I watched Greg, his face tight, phone pressed to his ear as he mashed another set of numbers and waited for it to ring.

He'd been so angry, so disappointed. So right. About everything.

When he kicked Will out, I was livid. I steamed through the rest of the night feeling stupid and confused and hurt. Angry because I'd been manipulated by them, backed into the corner I found myself in.

But when Greg took me to the back and tore me down like I deserved, when he reached for me, held me close, his dark eyes fevered and tortured, I only felt ashamed and sorry. I wanted to wipe his pain away, wash away what I'd done, tell him the truth of my feelings.

Greg slammed the phone back on the receiver. "Goddamn it," he hissed and dragged a hand through his dark hair. "No one is answering their phone, and the extra key's not in the safe where it's supposed to be."

He pinched the bridge of his nose, his eyes closed as a noisy breath left him.

"What about the fire exit? In the back?"

He shook his head and sat back in Cam's chair, looking exhausted. "It'll open without a key and put us in the alley, but the fire alarm will go off, and *that*, you can only turn off with a manager's key, which Beau has."

"And Cam and Rose."

"And if they picked up their fucking phones, we'd be all set." He scrubbed his hand over his face.

"What time will someone be here in the morning?"

"Cam will be here at eight. Did you text your sister?"

I nodded. "She won't get it until the morning, but at least no one will freak out that I didn't come home. They all knew I'd be working late—just not *all-night* late—so the good news is, they're not waiting up and worrying."

"Maybe I should try Cooper, the other owner. He's mostly just an investor though. I'm not sure it's even in his jurisdiction, if I could even get ahold of him."

I drew a heavy sigh. "Don't bother him. We can sleep here for a few hours until Cam gets here. At least there are couches."

Greg groaned. "I am so sorry. I cannot believe that fucking bonehead locked us in."

"Thank God you came back. Otherwise, I'd be locked in here by myself."

He looked a little sick at the thought.

But I smiled. "If we're stuck here, might as well make the most of it. Come on," I said as I stood.

We made our way back into the store, and I turned on the candelabras again, so we had a little bit of light; it was too creepy when it was totally dark. I grabbed one, and Greg did the same as we headed to the romance side of the bookstore. A good-sized seating area sat in the middle; two velvet sofas faced each other, and oversized armchairs flanked them.

"Seems as good a place as any to rest," I said, setting my candelabra on the coffee table in the middle.

"I'm sorry about Will," he said from behind me.

"Are you?" I asked, doing a poor job of hiding the hope in those two words. "I'm not sure I am."

"I'm sorry he hurt you. I'm sorry he didn't treat you with the care you deserve."

I turned to face him. "I'm sorry I didn't see him for who he really was. I didn't see a lot of things, things I should have noticed and reached for. But I'm not sorry it's over. The truth is, deep down, I've known for a little while that he wasn't who I wanted."

"You did?" he asked, narrowly winning the battle of keeping his emotion from his face and voice.

I nodded, looking into his eyes with my heart fluttering. "I kept comparing him to you, and he always fell short."

I couldn't wait for him to speak; I was too afraid of what he'd say. So, I made for the bookshelves, anxious for something to do with my hands. My eyes scanned the shelves until I found one of my favorite books and picked it up, smiling.

"You're going to read?" he asked from behind me, his voice rough, but I could hear a smile on his lips.

I shrugged as I made my way back toward him, still avoiding his eyes. "I always read before bed. Plus, I love this book. She writes the best first kisses," I said dreamily.

His smile fell but not into a frown. Something in him changed, the air between us changing with it. "Does it measure up?" he asked.

My face quirked in confusion. "Does what measure up?"

"First kisses in fiction to first kisses in reality."

"Oh," I breathed.

He took a step closer to me. "So... does it?"

"It... it was..." I paused, searching for a word that didn't exist. "It was fine." That tepid, cursed word left me before I could catch it and reel it back in.

"*Fine*," he mused, taking another step, putting him so close to me that every molecule was full of him, of the smell of him, the feel of him, though he hadn't touched me.

My only thought was the deep, thrumming wish that he would.

"Tell me, Annie," he whispered as the candlelight danced across the strong line of his nose and the swells of his lips, "did he hold your face in his hands and understand what he had?" His fingers brushed my skin until they rested in the curve of my neck, his thumb in the hollow of my jaw, his palm soft and warm against my cheek.

He stole my breath along with my ability to move or think. All I could do was listen and feel, held captive by his hands, his breath, his words.

"Did he touch the softness of your skin and tell you how lucky he was?" His thumb shifted reverently against my fevered skin.

He didn't wait for an answer to his question, and I had none to offer as our bodies merged, my chin lifting so I wouldn't lose the connection of his gaze. "Did he look into the depths of your eyes," he breathed, the words brushing my lips as he peered into my very soul, "like the answers to his happiness were hidden there?"

My eyes closed with a flutter as he trailed the tip of his nose up the bridge of mine.

"Did he tell you how beautiful you are, Annie?" he asked.

When he pulled away only by the smallest degree, my eyes opened again, full of desperate desire I saw reflected in his.

"Because you are," he said. "You are so beautiful, I can't bear to look. You've left me blind and exposed, disarmed and defenseless."

The length of my body was flush against him, my hands on his chest, my eyes searching his and my lips tingling, my heart thumping its uneven beat.

"Did he worship you, Annie?" he asked, his dark eyes on my lips, his hand splayed across my back, holding me against him with insistence and quiet power. "Did he?" He whispered two words, two syllables that commanded my body and soul, commanded my lips to speak the truth.

"*No.*" It was a plea, a desperate request, permission and blessing.

His lips curved into a smile as he drew a breath that brought me closer, millimeter by blessed millimeter. And those lips, those beautiful, smiling lips brushed mine, striking all else from my mind.

The moment they touched, they became a seam, a hot, soft meld of lips coupled with a sharp intake of breath. It was demand met with demand, mine for his, his for mine, his body leaning into me and mine leaning back. My arms wound around his neck and flexed, pulling my chest against his, the soft command of his lips sweet and relieved and exalted.

And mine matched his without thought, without expectation, only the rightness of him and the sureness of me.

With a sweep of his tongue, my lips parted. The feeling of his tongue and mine passing each other drew a breath from deep within each of us, as if something in me had been taken and would be found in him.

All I could do was acquiesce, and I did so with more desire than I had known I possessed.

His lips slowed, then closed, and he kissed me once more, capturing my bottom lip gently in his.

I opened my heavy lids and looked into his eyes with the realization that was my first true kiss and that his lips belonged to me as truly as mine belonged to him.

"That was…" My breath trembled.

"I've never…" he whispered and kissed me again, as if to test a theory.

Our bodies wound together in answer, as if that was their natural state, the connection of our lips sparking the action without intention.

He broke away once more, that theory proven—there was magic between us, singular to us, latent and waiting to be let free. And now that it was out, we'd never be able to bottle it back up.

"I…I shouldn't have—" he started.

"Yes, oh yes, you should have. You should have a long time ago."

With a laugh heavy with emotion and light with relief, he kissed me again, his lips smiling against mine.

When he let my lips go, I was thankful his arms were around me. I didn't think I'd otherwise be able to stand.

He took a seat, his hand holding mine, his eyes on my gloved fingers as he toyed with them.

"What happens now?" he asked, not looking up.

It was my turn to kneel at his feet and look into his face, colored with worry and hope. "Well, I'd like to kiss you some more. Maybe until I die."

Greg chuckled, but the sound was tight.

"And tomorrow, I'd like to spend the day with you, if you'd like."

He watched me, his face unchanged. "What about Will?"

I frowned. "We're through. After tonight, I hope I never see him again." When his worry didn't leave, I reached for his face, peering into his eyes. "Do you believe me?"

He turned his head to press a kiss into my palm. "It's just been a lot of change in one night. I want to know that you're sure before I let go of the leash on my hope."

"Can I tell you something?"

He nodded.

"It wasn't until you that I learned to see things for what they were. All I had to do was listen to your actions, and I could see what you wanted, what you felt. I could see what was important so I could reach out and grab it. And now that I have a hold, I don't want to let go."

The fear written in the lines of his face smoothed.

"I'm just sorry I didn't understand sooner. I didn't think there was any way you could want me, and you were so quiet about how you felt. Will, on the other hand, is about as quiet as a tuba."

A small laugh bobbed his shoulders, but his lips came back together. "So all this time, all I had to do was kiss you for you to know how I felt?"

I shrugged. "Guess so."

"I almost did after the day we spent together. I should have. Did you know when you came to work the next day, I was going to ask you out on a proper date?"

My heart ached. "But I showed up with Will."

Greg nodded and looked back down at my hand in his. "And

then… God, Annie. What was I supposed to do? You were happy, and you wanted him. What was I supposed to do?" he repeated, this time to himself.

"There wasn't much you could have done. I had to see Will through to the bitter end."

He frowned.

"The more he acted out, the less interested I became. Every time we fought about you, he only underscored your differences and tipped the scales in your direction. Really, you should thank him," I joked.

His lips flattened into a line. "Never in a million years. You fought about me?"

"The morning after the ballet, he was so jealous and angry, and we got into an argument before I left for work."

A dark, guilty shadow passed behind his eyes. "That day was unbearable."

"It was. But it's behind us. We're here now, together. And I really want to kiss you some more. Can I please kiss you some more?"

He laughed and nodded again, and into his arms I went. And kissing we did. We kissed until we were breathless and our bodies were twisted together so completely, we were left a tangle of arms and legs. I untied his cravat with a whisper of linen and kissed the soft skin of his neck. He ran his fingers across the neckline of my dress, sending a shudder of pleasure down my body. He pulled off my gloves, loosening them finger by finger, sliding them from my arms so I could touch the hot skin of his chest in the slight opening his shirt made.

But there was no more than that and no expectation, no urgency. Only moments that we lived in fully, without thought or care for more, content in exactly what we had.

And when the hour was late, he took off his wool coat and slipped it over my shoulders, and I lay on his chest, my head tucked in the curve of his neck, and fell asleep.

Old Lies

GREG

I woke, creeping from dreams so seamlessly that, for a moment, I believed Annie in my arms was a fantasy created by my sleeping mind.

But she wasn't. She was warm and small, curled into my chest. I could feel the rise and fall of her ribs as she breathed the long, slow rhythm of sleep. And for a long while, I just lay there, committing every detail to memory.

She stirred, nestling into me, nuzzling her face in my chest, her arms folded between us.

I kissed her hair and tightened my arms.

She stilled, and I thought she'd gone back to sleep, which was perfectly fine with me. I could hold her like that forever.

"Am I dreaming?" she asked, her voice raspy.

"I hope not."

She chuckled and pressed a kiss to the bare skin under the

hollow of my throat. "You know, crossing this off my list was the best unexpected surprise of my life."

"Crossing what off?"

"Waking up with a man, for starters."

"For starters?"

Annie leaned back to gaze upon my face, and I gazed upon hers with wonder and a sense of belonging.

"First breakup."

I scoffed.

"First kiss."

"I wasn't your first." The statement wasn't in any way light or without regret.

"As far as I'm concerned, it was. Will never kissed me like that. Not once."

"Tell me how horrible it was. I need more reasons to hate him."

She laughed softly, her cheeks high and rosy. "It was like kissing the back of my hand. I felt nothing other than anxiety that I was doing it wrong, probably *because* I felt nothing. I knew I should have felt *something*. But," she shrugged, "nada."

"And kissing me?"

"A religious experience."

I tightened my arms and leaned into her, pinning her against the back of the couch with a kiss that left her legs tangled in mine and her fingers in my hair.

She sighed when I released her, her heavy-lidded eyes meeting mine with a smile. "Will was all pyrotechnics and no substance. You, Greg Brandon, are both and a hundred other brilliant things."

"Will is the king of flashy paint jobs. You aren't the first girl he's dazzled."

"No, I'm not, and I doubt I'll be the last."

I held her for a moment, staring up at the rafters and air ducts of the exposed ceiling. "Is it really over?" I asked, plagued by uncertainty.

"Of course it's over," she said. "All I want is you." The sincerity in her voice quieted my fears without another word.

The ache in my chest was back, but where it used to be broken with longing, it was now tight with joy.

"Oh! Can we take a picture?"

I smiled. "Absolutely."

She sat, reaching for her little bag that had hung from her wrist all night, and a few minutes later, we had taken five pictures of the two of us, one of us kissing, her hands on my face and my arm extended as far as I could reach. I only hoped I caught it.

We set them on the table and waited for them to develop.

"I have a confession to make," I said, reaching for my wallet on the table.

"Oh?"

"Mhmm." I unfolded it, opening the long pocket and pulling out the little photo I'd taken of her on the steps of The Met. There was so much joy in that picture, in her tipped chin and high cheeks, her closed eyes and the flash of her smile, wide and open as she laughed.

She took it from my fingers, her face soft and awed. "You kept it?"

"It's been with me ever since I took it." *You've been in my heart ever since I met you.*

Her eyes told me she'd heard the silent admission, and when she reached for me, when she kissed me, she answered me with yes after yes until we were stretched out on the couch again, Annie across my chest.

When she broke the kiss, it was to nestle under my chin. She sighed. I sighed. We lay in the quiet.

My phone rang from the table next to the couch, and I remembered our predicament, reaching for it. Cam's name was on the screen.

"Hey," I answered.

"Oh my God, Greg. I am so sorry."

I moved to sit, and Annie moved too, situating herself next to me, yawning.

"It's all right. But what the hell happened?"

She sighed, and I heard her shuffling around on the other end of the line. "I didn't realize my ringer was turned all the way down. I can't believe Beau locked you in. Rose not answering, I can understand—she sleeps like she's actually dead."

I humphed a laugh. "Beau I can believe, which is exactly why I will never be nominating him for a promotion. Are you heading this way?"

"As fast as I can. And don't think you're going to get out of there without telling me what happened with Annie."

I glanced at her, smirking. "Then I'll start working on my story."

We said goodbye and hung up. Annie was checking her phone with her face drawn.

"Everything okay?" I asked, not sure I wanted to know the answer.

"Will messaged me—he's trying to apologize. He wants to see me."

A warning shot fired down my spine.

She sighed heavily. "I think I've got to meet him. Hear him out and let him say his piece, and then I'll tell him again it's through."

"You can't text him?"

Annie made a face. "Last night, we were all shouting at each other and throwing around demands. I think I owe it to him to tell him face-to-face that it's over, don't you?"

"I don't think you owe him a goddamn thing."

Annie nodded, her long fingers moving to my vest to smooth it. "That's fair, but…would you think worse of me if I said I wanted to? I'd like to break it off clean. I'd like to treat him like I'd want to be treated."

It was my turn to sigh, and I angled toward her to press a kiss to her temple. "No, I wouldn't think worse of you at all."

She leaned into me. "I just have to figure out where to meet him."

"Here," I said without hesitation.

"I thought he was permabanned."

"I'll make this one-time exception. As much as I want to be here when it happens, I don't think I can be in the same building with him without doing something I shouldn't. And if I'm not going to be present, at least there will be people here I trust."

"What do you think he's going to do? Throw me over his shoulder and carry me back to his cave?" she asked on a laugh.

I didn't even crack a smile. "Just humor me, Annie."

"All right," she conceded with trust behind her eyes, behind the words.

"Message him. Meet up as soon as you can. Because the second it's through, I want to see you. I want every minute, every second I can get." My voice trailed off to a whisper.

"Then you'll have it."

And I cradled her small face in my hands and kissed her.

A half an hour later, Cam had liberated us, and our tale had been recounted in broad strokes that seemed to satisfy her, if her dreamy smile was any indicator. We ran the plan to have Will come to the store by Cam, and Annie set up a time. And once that was all done, it was time to go.

She donned her yellow peacoat and pink hat and mittens, and we hopped on my board at her insistence. I didn't think either of us wanted to say goodbye, and even though it was cold, a cab ride just seemed too fast. So we rode through Central Park on my skateboard in historical costumes, my tails flapping and cravat keeping my neck warm, the train of her gorgeous ballgown bustled and her gloved hands around my waist.

Everything had changed in one night with a few words and a kiss.

When we reached her building, I kissed her on the sidewalk, kissed her like my life depended on it, kissed her like I'd never see her again, like I needed to brand my name on her heart so she wouldn't forget me. And as we kissed, the snow began to fall.

The wonderment on her face when she saw her first snow was perhaps the loveliest thing I'd ever seen in my life.

We took a picture with her little camera, kissing goodbye once more before she finally went inside. I stood on the sidewalk with my hands in my coat pockets as I watched her walk into the building, waving back when she looked over her shoulder before passing through the doors.

Only then did I ride away.

By the time I made it home, I was exhausted and freezing and happy beyond measure. The house was asleep, and the shower was long and hot. And once I lay down in bed, there was no keeping me awake.

I woke a few hours later, feeling groggy and hungry for more sleep, but the second Annie touched my thoughts, I was fully alert. I reached for my phone, finding a text from her that was only a few minutes old.

Heading to Wasted Words. Text me when you're up. <3

I smiled, but the expression faded as I thought about her meeting Will. Everything had happened so fast, and part of me still wondered if she might change her mind. Will talked a good game, and Annie took everything at face value.

It was a quality I loved about her just as much as I found it dangerous.

I texted her back to wish her luck before I sighed and climbed out of bed.

Sarah was sitting in the quiet living room, surrounded by textbooks. A spiral notebook lay on her thighs, and she looked up from jotting in it. "Hey. You slept late."

"Long night." I sat in the armchair next to the couch. "Where is everybody?"

"Tim's sawing logs, and Dad ran to the store. Well, maybe not *ran*, but you know."

I smiled, imagining Dad running to do anything.

"So was it a good long night or a bad one?"

"Started off bad, ended good. Very good."

Her brows rose. "Oh?"

"Me and Annie."

A smile broke out on her face. "Oh my God, are you serious?"

I nodded, feeling like a million bucks. "It's a long story, but yeah. She's dumping Will now."

Sarah's face paled. "Is she?"

"Yeah, at the bookstore. He wanted to apologize for being a dick and getting kicked out of the bar last night, and she thought she should break up with him in person."

The color kept draining from her face.

I frowned. "You okay?"

She cleared her throat and looked at her notebook like she might find a suitable response there. "Yeah. For sure."

"That was real convincing."

She tried to smile. "Just feels familiar, that's all. Will doesn't always take no for an answer."

My heart jolted. "What do you mean?"

"Just that…he's used to getting his way. And when he wants something, he's not one to let it go."

"Do you think he's going to push her? Fight for her?"

"He won't fight for anything but himself and what he thinks is owed to him."

I ran a hand over my mouth, worried and filled with dread. But, the more I thought about it, the surer I was of one thing. "Annie won't go back to him."

She didn't say anything; her bottom lip was busy, pinned between her teeth.

"I mean, what's the worst he could do? They're in public—our friends are there."

She took a breath that skipped in her chest, the sound dangerously close to a sob, a sound that sent a cold shot of fear through me.

"Sarah, what are you not telling me?"

Her throat worked, fingers pressed to her lips. She shook her head. "It's ... I wanted to tell you before. I should have told you before, but I didn't know if it would change anything."

"Told me what?" I asked, the words as quiet as the eye of a storm.

Sarah moved her notebook and leaned over. "It's just that I've never told anyone. And when you said Annie was with him..." She shook her head. "If we had been alone, I probably would have said it, but then ... then it felt too late."

"*Said what?*"

"I never told you what really happened that night, the night of the party."

A tingling numbness climbed down my arms to my fingers, up my neck to my face as she spoke.

"You know that before that night, I'd been planning to break up with him, but the time was never right. I never knew what to say. I was afraid I'd lose so much more than him. I had a thousand excuses, and none of them mattered in the end." She wouldn't meet my eyes. "We went to that party and ended up in a huge fight. And I was so mad, so over it, I just blurted out that I was through. I was through fighting, through being controlled by him, fed up beyond the point of caring about the repercussions.

"We were in the middle of arguing about it when he finally realized I was serious, and he just ... changed. I thought at the time that he was calm, resigned, *accepting* even. He told me we could be friends and that we should enjoy the party. And I was so relieved that I took the drink he'd offered and the one after without a second thought."

She took a long breath, and when she spoke again, her voice was unsteady, her eyes on her trembling fingers as they twisted each other, seeking comfort.

"I only remember bits and pieces. Dancing in the living room. Laughing on the balcony. Feeling slow and tired and clumsy. Will taking me to a dark bedroom. Wondering if he'd drugged me as he laid me down in the bed. And I thought…I thought he was going to…" She shook her head. "But he didn't. He left me there, and I remember how relieved I was. Until someone else came in."

A heavy tear dropped from her lashes and to the floor. "I don't know who he was—a boy from another school, I think. He was everywhere, and there was nothing I could do; I couldn't move, couldn't fight, couldn't scream. And then he left me there in that room, just like Will had, but he'd taken everything from me before he'd gone."

The words broke, her hand moving to press her lips, as if she could keep the sobs held down, and within a breath, I was at her side, pushing the textbooks away and pulling her into me, thinking only thoughts of agony and murder.

"Why didn't you tell us?" Tears pricked my eyes, flooded my vision, my fingers in her hair and her face against my chest.

"Because there was nothing I could do. I had no proof, couldn't remember what he even looked like. And I know I shouldn't have been ashamed, but I was. I *am*. Pictures of…of me started floating around school in group texts. And Will didn't do a goddamn thing about it but use it as ammunition to ostracize me from everyone I knew. And I was afraid that if I said something, if I accused him, no one would believe me. It was easier to be labeled a whore than branded a liar."

"And all this time…"

She pulled away, though my shirt was still fisted in her hands. "Those rumors I told you he spread were true. It happened, just not the way everyone said. I asked him once, begged him to tell me why he'd left me there, and he said that I shouldn't have fucked with him. And when I asked him if he'd meant for me to get raped, he looked at me with dead eyes and said he stopped caring the second he walked out the door."

My vision dimmed, my pulse driving my heart to the point of pain.

"Ever since he came back into your life, it's been weighing on me. I didn't know if it would help or hurt or make any difference at all. And I tried to tell you so many times, but I couldn't speak the words. I'm sorry. I'm so sorry."

I pulled her back into me, pressing her to my body, wishing I could undo what had been done to her. "Don't apologize. Don't you say you're sorry, not for this," I breathed. "But Annie's with him right now. I have to go—I need to get her."

She nodded, still crying.

I cupped my sister's cheek and looked into her eyes. "Everything's going to be fine," I said, hoping it was true. "Don't add this guilt to your heart."

She nodded, but I knew the agreement was empty. Her heart would carry that guilt forever.

But I had to go, wouldn't wait. I only hoped that son of a bitch was still there when I got to Annie.

Because I had so much to say.

Heartbeats

ANNIE

"So, let me see if I've got this straight," Will said coolly from the other side of the booth. "You stayed here. Last night. With Greg. In the dress I gave you. And now you're breaking up with me for him?"

My fingers were restless in my lap. "Will, I'm sorry."

I didn't even know what I was apologizing for. His hurt feelings? Mine?

"Listen," he said, his face softening with his voice, "last night I said things I didn't mean. I care about you, Annie, and I want to be with you. What do I have to do to prove that to you?"

"Nothing," I said simply. "It just happened this way. It wasn't your fault."

It was another lie, and I couldn't understand why I kept making excuses for him. But more than anything, I wanted this business done and over with. If placating him got me there, so be it.

"But we're great together, Annie. I'm sorry for what I said last night. I just can't keep suffering interventions from *Brandon*." He spat the name like a curse.

Anger blew through me in a gust. "Stop it, Will. I'm sorry I even brought him into this. It's about you and me. And last night wasn't the first time you failed to take my feelings into account."

He laughed, a cold, bitter sound. "*Your* feelings? Not once did you listen when I told you he was trying to get between us. Not once did you seem to care what I wanted, what I'd asked for. But I'm the one who's insensitive? That's rich, Annie. Real rich."

My cheeks prickled with heat. "I cannot believe you. Are you so blinded by jealousy that you can't see you've been acting like a child?"

"A child?" he said, his eyes narrowed and voice on the rise. "You hadn't even been kissed when I met you. You have no fucking clue what the world is about, not *one*." He slapped the table, and I jolted at the sound. "God, even now you have that look on your face like a lost little girl."

Tears sprang in my eyes, and I felt just as inexperienced as he suggested. *I should have listened to Greg—I never should have agreed to this.*

But my gaze was steady and hot as the sun. "Thank you for making this so easy for me. Have a nice life, Will. And I wouldn't come back here if I were you."

I scooted to the edge of the booth to get the hell away from him, but before I could get all the way out, he sighed and dragged a hand through his hair, reaching for my hand.

"Wait."

I met his eyes, pulling my hand away before he could touch me.

Another sigh. His face was touched with resignation, but his eyes were dark and stormy. "Annie, I'm sorry. I'm…I'm just surprised, that's all. I don't like being caught off guard, and I thought I was coming here today to get you back. I know I can be a dick. Please, forgive me."

I softened. "Thank you. And I'm sorry to do this to you. I'm sorry for hurting you."

His lips twitched in a sad smile. "*All is fair in love and war*, right?"

I offered an apologetic smile of my own. "I should go."

"You're not working today?" he asked.

"No, I'm off. I just came here to meet you."

"Well, let me give you a ride home." His face was turned down as he pulled on his coat.

"Oh no, that's okay. I'll catch a cab," I said without hesitation.

He straightened his collar. "I insist. My car's right outside. It's the least I can do after my little outburst."

I eyed him, looking for any sign of danger, but I found none. "All right. Thanks, Will."

"Don't mention it."

Cam was sitting at the bar, pretending to work on her laptop, but I knew it was a charade. Her eyes met mine in question.

"Let me go say bye to Cam real quick, okay?"

He nodded once, reaching for the dress boxes I'd brought. "The car's just out front."

I said my thanks, and we parted ways.

"What happened?" Cam said quietly when I approached, as if someone might overhear.

"It's done. He's going to give me a ride home."

Her brows knit together. "You sure that's okay?"

"It's a ten-minute drive, and it'll save me cab fare. It'll be okay."

"Okay," she said, not sounding at all convinced. "Text me when you get home, okay? I worry."

I laughed and made my promise.

A minute later, I slid into the Mercedes with Will, who leaned toward his door, face propped on his hand, staring out the window.

The driver pulled away from the curb.

The car was silent, and with every tick of the clock, the quiet screwed tighter until it was thrumming between us.

"I can't believe you chose him over me," he said, almost to himself, the words touched with disbelief and disapproval.

I'd naively thought it was over. Stupid me. Discomfort slid over me. "Will, I thought—"

"What could he possibly give you that I can't? How could you possibly choose him over me? Didn't I do everything you wanted?"

He turned to look at me, and for the first time, I saw Will as he truly was. The angles of his face sharpened, his eyes glinting with superiority.

"Didn't I give you the things you wanted, like that day in Central Park? Didn't I tell you we could take it slow even though it was the last thing I wanted? Didn't I put up with your bullshit with Brandon? I cared about you. I thought... I thought you could be a fresh start, a second chance, one I didn't even deserve. I would never hurt you, no matter what that asshole says about me."

I watched him rant with my lips parted, my eyes skimming his hard, angry body.

"I can't believe I lost to *him*."

I didn't realize I'd been shifting to the door, the instinct to get out of the car hijacking my body, sending a cold chill up my back and to the hairs on my neck.

His face shifted, flashing with anger, his hand darting out to grab my wrist. His fingers closed around the small circumference and yanked, pulling me across the leather bench and into him. I yelped in surprise.

"You should be mine."

"Let me go, Will," I said through my teeth, twisting my flaming wrist, but it was locked in his fist.

"Sir?" The driver eyed us in the rearview mirror.

"You're hurting me," I bit out, tears filling my eyes.

"You're supposed to be *mine*," he said, holding me still as he pressed a rigid kiss to my lips.

I fought against him, uselessly pushing his stony chest with my free hand and turning my head to escape his unyielding mouth, but he pulled me closer. My heart jackhammered, dimming my vision in pulses.

"*Sir!*"

Will's face turned to the driver as the car came to a stop.

I pulled my free hand back and slapped him hard enough to send the sting up to my elbow. And in his shock, he relaxed his grip enough for me to reclaim my wrist. I flew across the car and opened the door, scrambling out just before his fingers closed on the back of my jacket.

And the moment my feet hit the pavement, I ran.

He shouted a string of insults out the open door, but they didn't reach me. I barely registered the honking cars or the Mercedes pulling away. All I could hear was the erratic thump of my pulse in my ears. All I could feel was the cold ground beneath my feet. All I knew was that I had to escape.

When I came to a stop, I dropped to my knees, my vision vibrating with my heartbeat, my heart fluttering so fast, too fast, the muscle spasming frantically. I fumbled for my phone with shaking hands, unable to draw enough breath, my lungs empty and scraping against my ribs. —I couldn't call I couldn't speak.

I pulled up my sister's last message and fired off a text.

Need help. I'm in the park, sending you my location.

There wasn't enough air, my limbs moving laboriously as a creeping blackness in my vision pulled me to the ground. And then I felt it—the jerk in my heart, like a string had been pulled. It was on fire, my heart in my chest beating so fast, so hard, so bruised, that I pressed my palms to my sternum in disbelief of the deep measure of pain, a hot slice of a knife through the very center of me.

And with a final gasp of air from the very depths of my lungs, I slipped away, onto the cold, icy ground, into darkness.

GREG

I hopped off my board and ran to the door of the bookstore, whipping it open, rushing inside, scanning the bar for Annie. I found Cam instead.

"Where is she?"

Alarm commandeered her, arresting her face and planting her feet on the ground. "She left with Will, not five minutes ago. He was giving her a ride home."

I swore, pulling my phone out of my back pocket to text her again. She hadn't answered my text from before, and my mind jumped from one conclusion to the next without taking a breath.

My phone buzzed in my hand with a text from Elle.

Have you seen Annie? Something happened. She's in the park, but I don't know where.

My fingers flew as I sent back three words.

I'll find her.

I turned and ran back out without a word, throwing my board onto the pavement in front of me and jumping on without thinking about what I was doing or the cold or what would happen.

Every thought I had was focused on her.

My mind raced with my wheels, tracking the path he would have used to take her home, not certain why it was urgent, but knowing it was all the same. The temperature had dropped, my breath leaving me in bursts of burning cold, my eyes scanning the park around me, not knowing what exactly I was looking for.

And then I saw it—the flash of yellow between trees, the same sunshiny color of her coat.

I hopped the curb and jumped off my board, leaving it where it was, running full tilt for the heap in the frosted grass. And with every footfall, my hope slipped away, replaced by cold awareness.

I fell to my knees at her side and rolled her into my lap, my heart stopping when I saw her lifeless face.

Her skin was an unnatural shade of gray, her lips a deep shade of purple, the blue veins in her closed lids visible.

"Annie," I whispered, my throat locking.

Her body was limp, dead weight in my arms, her head lolling. I held her cheek; it was cold as ice.

"Annie, can you hear me?" I pressed my fingers to her neck and found her pulse easily; it was beating double the time it should have been.

"Jesus Christ," I breathed, pulling her into me, my face turning to the expanse of gray sky. "Please. God, please."

She stirred in my arms, the smallest moan escaping her lips, and I held her, looking into her face as her lids fluttered open.

Her lips parted as if to speak, but only a soft *Ah* made it through before her eyes closed again.

"*No*," I whispered, fumbling for my phone. "*Don't leave me*," I begged as the line rang. "*Hurry*," I demanded after I gave the dispatcher everything I could.

And then it was just her and me, the birds in the park and my fingers on her careening pulse, the sirens in the distance and her life on a thread. And I prayed to every god I knew.

Waiting

GREG

The only sound in the waiting room was the soft, unintelligible conversation from the nurses' station. A television was playing *Planet of the Apes* with the captions on, an empty gesture made commonplace by some psychologist somewhere who had determined that people waiting for bad news needed something to mark time in the room besides a clock.

Not that anyone ever watched it beyond a cursory glance or an empty gaze; in that circumstance, it wasn't possible to offer anything more.

My eyes weren't following Charlton Heston through his mysterious adventure—they were on my hands, clasped and hanging between my knees, the carpet beyond them blurred.

The deep, staggered lines in my knuckles caught the attention of my subconscious. They were surrounded by skin covered in infinitesimal cracks, barely visible, rarely noticed. But I saw each tiny one, thousands of them connecting to make a web spread across every inch of me.

I was reminded of a time that seemed to be a hundred years ago, most of that distance traveled in the last eight hours, when a thirteen-year-old version of my sister had become obsessed with reading palms. She'd sat with me on the rug in her room as I moaned and groaned and rolled my eyes, poring over the lines in the meat of my hand as she flipped through a book that would help her decipher them.

I turned my hand over and opened it, trying to remember what she'd told me, which line was which. I only remembered two—the love line and the life line.

The one meant for love was deep, running in a clear path from well off the side of my hand, curving up all the way to the point where my forefinger and middle finger met. It was supposed to mean that I would find true love, my soul mate, and that love would be as deep and true as that unassuming crease in my hand. Sarah had been starry-eyed and sighing at my luck. I'd thought it was nonsense.

The line for my life was also deep and long, stretching in a gentle arch from an inch from my thumb and down to curve around the heel of my palm. I'd live until I was a hundred, as far as that line was concerned.

I felt a longing so irrationally deep in that moment, a frantic regret that I hadn't looked into Annie's palm, that I hadn't traced the lines with my fingers. I wanted to see that crease travel across her hand and never end. I wanted to know that she would live until she was a hundred too, and that line would be some proof to carry me through the waiting, the unending waiting in a warp of time marked by a lost space man and infomercials for Brett Favre's copper brace.

A shuffling caught my attention. Elle was transferring Meg's sleeping torso to her aunt's lap, who brushed the little girl's hair from her face with reverence. Their mother sat in her wheelchair, staring at the television without seeing, with exhaustion on her face so deep, it seemed to reach all the way through to her bones. Her uncle's elbow was propped on a hard plastic armrest, his face propped wearily in his hand and legs kicked out in front of him, his body sagging in the seat.

No one had spoken in a long time, long enough that Elle only spoke in a whisper, which they each answered with a nod.

She came to me last, taking the empty seat next to me, with her hazel eyes tired and kind and worried. "I'm going to get coffee. Can I get you a cup?"

"Yeah, sure," I answered with a dry, creaky voice.

"I hope it's not much longer. I don't know if I can stand it."

"Me either."

She stared at a spot on the ground, her eyes unfocused. "I can't stop wondering what happened, how she ended up alone. You said she left the bookstore with Will, but what *possibly* could have happened between there and where you found her? How did she end up running through Central Park alone?"

"I don't know, but whatever it was, it was his fault. There's no other explanation."

She shook her head and looked down at her hands, just as I had. "I wish I hadn't texted him. I only saw her for a second when she came home. She was so tired, and we agreed to talk later. I didn't see her again. I didn't … I didn't know they'd broken up."

"I don't fault you for texting him, nor am I surprised that he hasn't answered you."

Elle sat silently for a moment. "What did he do, Greg? What did he do to hurt you?"

I ran a hand over my lips, looking to her family. We were speaking quietly, and they were distracted enough that they didn't seem to be paying us much mind.

"He used to date my sister. I wish it were as simple as him breaking her heart, but he took it so much further than that, so beyond what I

271

could have even imagined. She told me he'd started rumors about her, which effectively ruined her reputation, and that was true. But she didn't tell me the truth of the matter until today, before … before …"

I swallowed hard, clamping my jaw before speaking again.

"He drugged her and left her at a party, and she was assaulted by a stranger."

Her hand moved to her mouth.

"I didn't know. If I had, I never … I'd never have …" The words piled up in my throat. I swallowed them down again and started over. "I don't know what he did to Annie, but the second I know she's all right, the moment I see it with my own eyes, I intend to find out."

Another stretch of silence passed, mine laden with determination, hers busy processing what I'd confessed.

She reached for my hand, which my eyes had found once more without my realizing.

"You didn't know, Greg. You couldn't have known."

"Then why does this feel like it's my fault?"

"If it wasn't for you, she might not still be with us. If you hadn't found her, she might have been lost to us forever. We owe you a great debt."

I shook my head. "You don't owe me anything. All I want is Annie whole and well."

"I believe we will have our wish, and you have to believe too."

"I do. Because if I lose my faith, I'm afraid of what will happen to me."

Elle squeezed my hand and let it go, and I turned my attention back to my empty hands.

A little while later, those hands held a cup of bitter coffee that I drank without tasting. And I didn't look up.

Not until I heard a gasp from Elle.

Will stood across the room, his hair disheveled and eyes glassy and bloodshot. At the unexpected sight of him, the whistling emotion

I'd so carefully tamped down came unsnapped, letting loose in a hot wind of fury that propelled me out of my seat and to him.

My hands didn't care about the liquor on his breath or the repentance in his eyes as they reached for the lapels of his coat where the cold still hung.

I pulled him into me like a rag doll and arched over him. "What did you do to her, you son of a bitch? *What did you do?*"

His eyes, momentarily alert and wide with fear, bounced between mine. "I…I…"

I shook him once, hard. "*What the fuck did you do?*"

Commotion erupted around us, and hands pulled me away. I let him go and stepped back, my composure a breath away from shattering completely.

"Is she all right?" he asked.

"She will be, no thanks to you." Elle stepped forward, her face drawn. "Are you…drunk?"

"I…" he started, his eyes on the ground and shoulders sagging. "I didn't know what else to do. When I knew…when I heard…" He ran a hand through his dark hair. "It's my fault."

I took a step, but Elle stayed me with a hand on my arm. "Tell us what happened."

With one hand, he clamped his forehead, his thumb and fingers pressing his temples. He swayed when his eyes closed. "We fought. I…I said things I shouldn't have. She left me for *you*."

I spoke the question again, for the last time, "*What did you do?*"

"I…I told her she should be mine, kissed her to prove it, but I wouldn't let her go, not until the driver stopped, and she ran—"

I heard nothing more; I was flying toward him, cocking my fist, letting it go. I didn't register the smack, didn't feel the crunch of bones in my hand or the jolt it sent up my arm when it connected with his jaw, didn't stop as he fell, and I descended with him.

But I was lifted away, struggling against unseen hands, thrashing and gnashing and desperate to hit him again.

"*You left her!*" I screamed over everyone else, the cords of my neck taut and burning. "You fucking left her there, just like you left Sarah. *They* paid for your fucking pride. She could have *died. Do you understand that?* I told you I'd fucking end you if you hurt her. *I fucking told you!*"

Will propped himself on his elbow, and when he looked up, I knew he'd heard every word.

"You don't deserve her—you never deserved either of them. After what you did, you have no right to be here. You're *lucky* you're not in jail. You're *lucky* I don't fucking show you just how sorry you should be." I tried to shake off the hands that bound me, but they tightened, holding me back.

It was for the best; I didn't know if I'd be able to stop myself.

He stood, making no motion to straighten his coat or wipe the spill of blood from his lip, meeting my eyes. His words were thick, slow, and slurring. "I've never been a good guy; we both know that. But I never meant for this to happen. I never meant for any of it to happen, not Sarah, not Annie, and now…now…" He sagged, but his eyes met mine, bright with pain. "I'm sorry—"

"*No!*" I screamed, straining to get free. "I will *not* feel sorry for you, and *nobody* believes you're sorry. Don't ask for forgiveness because there is none to give. Not for this, not for *anything.*"

His eyes hardened, but he nodded once. Two police officers ran into the room. Those bodiless hands disappeared from my arms and chest, and somehow, I didn't reach for him again.

With the stern authority that only cops could manage, a brief questioning took place, and the general details of what had happened were given. They asked Will if he wanted to press charges. He shook his head, thumbing his lip when he met my eyes.

In fact, Will watched me until the police were gone—though they stayed near the elevators—and he looked at me with sincerity that I had no taste for.

"Tell Annie I'm sorry," he finally said.

Before I could tell him to go to hell, he turned and walked away.

My hands trembled as I turned to face Annie's shocked family.

"I…I'm sorry," I stammered. "I shouldn't have—"

"Don't be sorry," her uncle said with dark eyes, his hand hooking my shoulder. "I only wish I'd taken the initiative to pull off a shot of my own."

We moved to sit again, each of us stunned silent—Meg with her wide eyes, curled into Susan's lap, and Annie's mother, her hand cupped over her lips and eyes locked on a spot on the wall.

Elle rested her hand on my arm.

But I looked back at my hands, now scuffed up and stinging, red and shaking.

And I waited.

An hour passed before the surgeon appeared, looking tired but smiling.

The relief of that smile was instant and complete.

He told us the details of the surgery. Her shunt that kept oxygenated blood flowing through her had collapsed, which caused the immediate danger, but rather than replace the shunt, they'd performed the surgery Annie had planned. They'd repaired the valve and closed the hole in her heart. She was stable, and we'd be able to see her soon.

A few minutes afterward, a nurse came to take Elle and her mother to see Annie. And for another half hour, I waited some more.

So much waiting, I almost lost my mind from it.

When Elle returned, her face was swollen and red from crying. Meg began to cry at the sight of her.

Elle took the seat next to her, pulling her youngest sister into her arms, gently rocking her, soothing her as best she could.

"She's okay," Elle assured her. "She's all right."

"I want to see her," Meg pleaded.

"Not tonight," Elle answered with a shaky voice. "Susan, will you take her home?"

"I don't want to go!" Meg wailed.

"I know, I know, but Annie's still asleep, and she'll be that way for a while. Tomorrow, you'll come back first thing, all right? And then you can see her once she's awake."

Meg sobbed miserably into Elle's chest.

Elle looked to her aunt for help, and Susan drew the little girl into her arms, speaking in a gentle, light cadence that made it feel like everything would be all right, listing off what they would do until the time when they came back.

Everyone stood, and goodbyes were said, coats donned. And then they were gone.

Elle collapsed into a chair, her composure gone the minute the elevator doors closed behind her sister.

I sat next to her and pulled her into me, rocked her as she cried into my shoulder, her hands clutching my shirtfront over the spot where my aching heart hammered my ribs. And I was somehow certain that she hadn't let herself go all the way, not until that moment.

It was a little while before she caught her breath and pulled away, blotting at her nose with a tissue balled in the shape of her fist, swiping her tears away with her fingers. And then she reached for my hand, meeting my eyes with weight that scared me more deeply than anything I'd seen that day.

"Greg, I need you to prepare yourself."

"Tell me," I croaked, my mouth dry as ash.

"She's okay. I want you to know that. Like the doctor said, the surgery was successful, and she should be fine. But it's not going to be easy. And what you're going to see is hard, harder than I can explain or you can imagine."

I listened mutely as she told me of Annie's physical state, what I would find down the hall and in the ICU room. But she was right in that there was no way to prepare myself, not even after living with my mother's lupus.

The room was dim but not dark, the bed in the center of the room so big and Annie so small. The low light made the dozens of tubes look sinister, like a beast behind her bed had slipped its tentacles around to feed. A white tube was taped to her chin and cheeks, disappearing into her partly open mouth, and a thick line wound around from a machine and into the artery in her neck. The entry point was exposed, the bulge the needle made in her neck disturbing and shocking, the tube into it the deepest shade of crimson.

Blood, I realized distantly.

There were tubes running into her chest, into both wrists. So many tubes, so many wires, even more beyond what I could see, carrying things into her and out of her.

Soft stays rested on either side of her, nestling her in the center, holding her there like an embrace. It was the only thing in the room that seemed to be there as much for her comfort as her safety.

My throat caught fire and burned, squeezing until tears pricked my eyes and fell. I wanted to touch her, wanted to feel her warm fingers in mine, but I didn't move, afraid I would somehow hurt her, that the moment I touched her, alarms would sound, her heart would stop, that all the things I feared would come true.

And so I stood just inside her room, out of the way of the nurses next to Elle, who took my hand and cried with me.

Nurses came in and out with businesslike purpose, talking to each other in soft voices as they prepared the room for her to wake, which should be at any time, they told us.

I saw the moment it happened, though no one else did. It was the rise and fall of her chest that changed, picked up speed. I took a step without thinking, then another, and I was at her side, her mother and sister next to me. Her hand lay delicately by her thigh, and I took it in my own.

She squeezed, just a flicker of pressure.

A laugh that was a sob passed my lips and her sister's and mother's. The nurses were on the other side of the bed, one of them watching the heart monitor, smiling.

"Hi, Annie," she said with that light nurse's tone. "Welcome back. Can you open your eyes for me?"

It took a second, but her lids opened for a brief, shining moment before disappearing again.

"Good job."

She stirred.

"Try to stay still, okay? We're going to take the breathing tube out in a few minutes, but until then, just try to be still."

She nodded almost imperceptibly, her eyes opening, then closing again.

"It's all right," I whispered.

Her eyes snapped open, the beeping of her heart monitor ticking up. She met my eyes; a tear fell from the corner and down her temple.

I leaned over, brushed it away, kissed her forehead.

"I'm here," I whispered again.

Another slight nod.

I let her go, moved out of the way to exchange places with Elle. Her mother watched on with longing, unable to stand or get close enough with her chair for the wires coming from every direction.

It was probably fifteen minutes of her awake and speechless, still and barely conscious before they removed her breathing tube. I'd been prepared for a gruesome exit from her throat, but it was out so fast, I'd almost missed it. She coughed, her face bent in pain, the nurse on one side of her applying pressure to a pillow she'd been instructed to hold against her split chest.

"Can you tell me your name?" one of the nurses asked.

Her pale, dry lips parted to speak, but no sound came out. Her eyes were hardly open.

"I know it's hard, but I need you to say your name and make a sound."

She seemed to summon the power, taking a shallow breath, whispering, "*Annie.*"

The nurse smiled. "Perfect. Okay, in fifteen minutes, we'll get you some ice chips, and if you keep that down, we'll get you something solid."

She nodded, but the nurse had already busied herself with another task.

Annie turned her head, her eyes glassy and struggling to stay open. Her lips moved, but no sound came. She swallowed and took a more purposeful breath. "*Greg…*"

My heart skipped a beat, and I stepped to her side. Her hand lifted. I took it.

With my other hand, I cupped her cheek, now free of tape but still tethered by an oxygen line. "Hey, Annie."

She smiled, just the smallest curve of her lips. "*You…found… me…*" The laborious words were almost inaudible, a shallow breath needed to power each one.

"I found you," I echoed.

"*Don't…go.*"

To that, I smiled, my eyes teeming with tears. "Don't worry—I'm not going anywhere."

Yours
ANNIE

"That's *disgusting*," Meg whispered in wonder two days later, hunched over the photos of my exposed heart during surgery. "There's your superior vena cava," she said, pointing at a thick blue vein, "and that's your aorta. I can't believe they cut through your sternum, Annie. Do you know how much power it takes to crack that bone?"

I flinched against the visual and the following wave of nausea. "No"—I took a breath to power the rest of the sentence—"and I'd rather not know."

Mama laughed. "Come on, let's put these away."

Elle swept the photos into a stack, separating them from the little instant photos I'd taken over the last couple of days, and put them back in the folder I hoped never to see open again. Meg watched them disappear before lighting up again.

"Please, can we watch the video of your surgery? *Pleeease*?" she whined.

I laughed, the sound quiet and rough, my throat still shredded from being intubated. "Never in a million years."

"Can I see your scar again?" The hope on her face was almost comical.

I waved her over, and she climbed up the bed, mindful of the tubes. I pulled the neck of my robe down and lifted away the top of the taped bandage, already loose from showing her twice that morning.

"*Cool,*" she breathed, eyes wide. "There are actual staples in you. You're a badass, Annie."

"Meg!" Mama scolded, shocked.

But the rest of us laughed, and after a second, Mama was laughing too.

The last two days had been a blur of pain and commotion. I'd been moved out of ICU and into a regular recovery room where I got no rest, in part because nurses made their rounds about one REM cycle apart and otherwise because the crushing pain was so immense, it was impossible to ignore, pain meds aside.

The first day was the hardest. I barely remember waking, only flashes of fuzzy memories like a disjointed dream. I drifted in and out once I finished with all the *doing*; I had to stand, move around, speak, prove that I wasn't in distress, regardless of the fact that the movements themselves put me in their *own* form of distress.

The pain was indescribable, white-hot and blinding, requiring all thought, all energy to endure. And when it was through and I was left to rest, I slipped away into a dreamless sleep.

When I woke, it was to tears.

I'd thought it couldn't hurt any worse, but it did. People joked about feeling like they'd been hit by a bus, but that was honestly the closest I could come to explaining it. It was like I'd been crushed, shattered, and sewn back together, my bones stinging and burning and rubbing against each other like sandpaper. I couldn't breathe past the most shallow of breaths, my throat a wasteland, dry and lined with glass. I wanted to drink, but the water hurt, the force of my muscles working my throat hurt. *Everything* hurt. So I lay there, parched and obsessively considering each pain, wondering how I could possibly survive this, wondering how long it would be until I felt better, *if* I would ever feel better.

Somehow I'd made it through that night. And the next morning, it was better. Not very much better, but enough to give me the first glimmer of hope.

And this morning, I'd woken to improvement, leaps and bounds ahead of where I'd been.

It felt like nothing short of a miracle.

Greg had been there through it all. I remembered flashes of moments—lying in his arms in the park as I'd said goodbye, the vision of his face in the ambulance with the humid oxygen mask on my face, wondering if I was going to die, holding his hand when I'd woken, knowing he'd been there all along, knowing he'd stay.

And so, I was in good spirits, good enough to let Meg pull out those gruesome photos of my open chest and bleeding heart, which, in hindsight, I regretted. What little food I'd been able to keep down churned in my guts, even after they were packed away.

Meg chattered on, relaying medical facts about the heart, and I looked over my family—my mother in her wheelchair laughing, the sun shining in her blonde hair; my elder sister smiling, her cheeks rosy and high and happy; and my youngest sister with shining eyes, everything about her vibrant and alive. And my heart beat a sweet, solid rhythm for the first time in my life. My hands were warm and full of color. My body, as broken as it was, was already healing, and my heart itself had already healed.

The hole was gone, all patched up, and not a bit of happiness would be lost again.

A knock sounded on the door, and Meg bounded off my bed to open it, my heart picking up pace when I saw Greg standing in the threshold with a bouquet in his hand.

Meg jumped into his arms, and he made his way around the room, saying hellos. But he saved his most brilliant smile for me.

As he sat on the edge of my bed, I took the flowers, bringing them to my nose. The bouquet was made of cream roses touched with the gentlest shade of pink and miniature lilies, dotted with sprigs of lavender, and the smell was incredible. Meg hadn't stopped talking, and Greg kept her going with attentiveness, though his hand found mine, his thumb shifting against my skin all the while.

"Well," Mama said the second Meg finally took a breath, "I am starving. Elle, Meg, you must be hungry too. Annie had her lunch an hour ago."

Meg frowned. "I'm not hungry."

"Yes, you are. Come push my chair."

She groaned but did as she'd been asked. And without much more than a clandestine wink from Elle, they left Greg and me alone for the very first time since I'd been admitted.

"Oh, thank God," I breathed, reaching for him.

He laughed and cupped my cheek. He kissed me with tenderness and longing, too gentle, as if I were fragile, as if he might break me. I wanted to wind my arms around his neck, but with the tubes and my cracked breastbone, I had to settle for my hands on his chest, slipped in the warm space between his shirt and jacket.

I was breathless too soon; with my deepest disappointment, he noticed and broke away.

"Well, hello," he said, smiling. "God, you look good."

I chuckled. "It's my new hospital gown, isn't it?" I took a breath. "This color of green complements my eyes, I thought."

"That must be it." He smirked. "How much better are you feeling?"

"About a million times. I even ate pudding today and didn't immediately want to ralph. Next stop, Ironman."

"You look brand-new. Must be the pudding."

I snorted a laugh. "Brand-new. That's funny, Greg."

He took my hand, toying with my fingers, a smile on his glorious lips. "I'm sorry it took me so long to get here."

"Don't be sorry. How was work?"

"Fine. I was anxious to get out of there, and they knew it. But they wanted me to bring you this."

He reached for his backpack and rummaged around, coming back with a card printed on cream paper.

Watercolor flowers framed the words, *Obstinate, headstrong girl. —Jane Austen.* Inside, it said, *We would wish you to get well, but a girl like you needs no wishes, for she eats wishes for breakfast and dreams for lunch. Come back to us soon.* And everyone in the bookstore had signed it.

Grateful tears nipped at the corners of my eyes. When I looked up at Greg, he was smiling at me.

He reached for my face, thumbing my cheek. "Your skin is pink, your eyes brighter…you really do look so good."

"Upsides to a working heart," I joked.

But he didn't laugh.

"I mean it. I can't imagine how hard this has really been for you, but watching it has been the most terrifying, life-altering event I've ever experienced. But you're going to be able to live now, Annie, in a way you never could before. You can run. Ride roller coasters. Go skydiving."

I laughed. "Maybe let's start a little smaller. Like getting me home."

"Soon. Soon, you'll be well, and all of this will be a distant memory."

"I'm ready. I need to get home so I can practice." I watched his face for a reaction, smiling.

First was confusion. "Practice? Practice wha—" His eyes shot open. "Juilliard?" he breathed. "You got the audition?"

I nodded, my smile breaking into a grin as he whooped, leaning into me to kiss me again, his hands on my face, fingers in my hair.

He tried to pull me into him, but I was attached to too many damned machines. He settled for an arm under my shoulders and my head in the crook of his neck, forcing him to bend at the most awkward angle, but he didn't seem to mind, and neither did I.

"You did it. I knew you would." He kissed my temple and pulled away, reaching for my hand. He played with my fingers as he spoke, "I've never felt so helpless as I have the last few days. Seeing you in this bed, finding you in the park…" He took a breath. "I'm just so happy to see you like you are today. For a minute, I wondered if you'd ever come around again."

"So did I." I watched him watching my hands, asking the question I would have asked a hundred times if there hadn't been a forever multiplying number of people around. "What happened that day?"

"I…" His lips came together, his Adam's apple bobbing. "When Elle texted me, I took off from Wasted Words and rode into the park. It was your jacket; that was how I found you. I saw this streak of sunshine in the grass, and I just ran. I…I've never been so scared in my life as I was when I rolled you into my lap and saw your face, waxy and gray. You were barely breathing, but your heart was going crazy."

"I remember but just a flash—your arm around me, the look on your face…" I paused, collecting myself as emotion rose through me, starting in my stomach, ending at the corners of my eyes. "I don't think I'll ever forget that look."

"I thought you were gone. I thought I'd lost you." His voice broke, his eyes cast down to our hands.

"I'm here," I soothed, my heart aching beyond the sutures and cuts. "I'm here."

"Will came to the hospital, did they tell you?"

I nodded, swallowed, ached at the thought of what had happened, thankful I hadn't been there.

"I knew he would hurt you, but I never imagined this. If I'd had any idea, I never…"

"I know."

He shook his head. "No, there's more you don't know."

"What?" My brows quirked.

"That day, when you were with him, my sister told me the truth. Annie, he didn't just start rumors. He…" He said nothing for a long stretch, then straightened up, meeting my eyes. "He drugged her and left her at a party. Someone assaulted her."

I sat, stunned, in the hospital bed, my hands tingling. "What?" I whispered.

He nodded, the weight of the confession heavy on his brow.

My mind raced, pieces clicking together, disgust and shock when I thought about what he'd done to Sarah. "I am so sorry."

"Don't be—it's him who should be sorry. And what's really fucked up is that I believed him when he said he was."

I squeezed his hand.

"I'm sorry I couldn't save you from him."

"But you did save me. I don't want to even think about what would have happened if you hadn't."

"I've already thought about it, obsessed over it, dreamed of it. The vision of you lying in that grass will haunt me until I die, Annie." And he looked tortured and tired, dark smudges under his eyes, cheeks hollow, the change in him so slight, I hadn't noticed it until that very moment.

There was nothing to do but reach for him, and though I couldn't rise to meet him, he knew what I wanted and filled my arms, filled my lungs, filled my heart, kissing me with gratitude and adoration that was met with my own.

I didn't realize I was crying until he pulled away and thumbed a tear on my cheek.

"Don't cry," he whispered.

"I can't help it," I said. "I should have seen you from the beginning."

"I should have told you from the beginning. But I don't want to look back. I want to start now, right now. I want you, Annie, and I've wanted you since the first time I laid eyes on you. And now, you're mine."

"Now, I'm yours," I echoed.

Beholden

GREG

A week later, George greeted me at the door and buzzed me up to the Jennings' apartment, and I was grateful for his help with the doors, as my hands were full of gifts for Annie.

Elle greeted me with the pack of dogs at her feet, but when I got a good look at her, her face was drawn. My optimism slipped out of me like air from an untied balloon.

"How is she?" I asked, already knowing the answer.

"It's a bad day," she answered simply.

"Okay. Well, let me see what I can do."

"She's just in her room."

I nodded. "Thanks, Elle."

Past the kitchen and living room, beyond the music room and study I went, down the hallway to her room. I placed my haul just outside the door and rapped softly.

"Come in," she said, her voice muffled by more than the door between us.

I opened it with a quiet creak. The room was dark even though it was the middle of the day, the shades drawn and lights off. And Annie was lying in bed on her side, only the very top of her blonde crown visible under the fluff of her blankets.

"Heya, sunshine," I said jovially, making my way to the empty side of the bed.

She didn't move, just uttered a *hello* that sounded like a sigh.

I kicked off my shoes and climbed in, scooting toward her until her back was nestled into my chest and my knees rested in the bend of hers.

For a minute, I didn't say anything, and neither did she. And I gladly let her be, let her breathe.

"I'm sorry," she said after a bit.

I frowned. "What for?"

A sigh was her answer.

"Tell me, Annie," I said gently, a command in name only.

She drew another breath and shifted to roll over in my arms, and I moved to allow her room.

She didn't speak until we were settled in, her voice small and quavering. "I'm helpless. I'm helpless and hurting, and I just can't. I can't keep lying in this bed. I can't keep letting everyone fuss over me, but I need their help, too. I'm a burden." She was crying, her breath shuddering, ribs shuddering with it in the cage of my arms. "I'm a mess. And my audition is happening whether I'm well enough for it or not. I can't practice, can't work, can't do *anything*, and I think I'm going crazy."

She stopped there and tried to calm herself, succeeding at least in schooling her breath. And I waited for her before speaking.

"I know it doesn't change anything," I said, my hand tracking a slow path up her back, then down again, "but we're all here because we want to be. You're not a burden. In fact, the highlight of my day is coming here and taking you for our walks."

She chuckled sadly, her nose stuffy when she said, "Our shuffles, you mean."

"Yes, our nursing-home shuffles up Fifth Avenue. And I have a feeling you'll be able to practice again soon. It's just a bad day, Annie. A fresh one's around the corner."

"It doesn't feel like it."

"It never does, but that's just how life works. Ups and downs, good days and bad, sunshine after the rain."

She didn't speak for a second. "I don't know why you put up with me."

I kissed her forehead. "Oh, I think you do."

Annie leaned back to look at me, her eyes so green, the honey-gold burst warm and luminescent. "I mean it, Greg. If it wasn't for you, I wouldn't even get out of bed. I just want to give up." The words broke, but she kept going, "It's too tempting to just slip into the sadness and let it take me away."

"I know it is. And you know what? I'll even cosign some constructive wallowing. Whatever you want to do. *Carte blanche*. Want to curl up here in the dark and sleep all day? I'm in. Want to watch Nicholas Sparks movies and eat ice cream all day? I'm down."

Her smile was soft and amused.

"But then we're going to get out of bed and go for a walk. Or open the curtains and let the sun in. I'm going to remind you that things will get better, even if it's inch by inch. You're allowed to feel just how you feel for as long as you feel it. But I'm here to remind you that there's hope, and I'll be with you every day, every step of the way."

"I don't deserve you," she whispered, resting her hand on my jaw.

"The feeling's mutual," I whispered back.

And I kissed her so she knew it was true.

I broke away, smiling. "I brought you something."

She brightened. "You did?"

"I did." I kissed her nose and climbed out of bed, opening her door to bring in the gifts as she brought herself up to sit.

"First, this." I handed her the big one.

She smiled, her long fingers making quick work of the paper. And when she saw what it was, she gasped, her big green eyes meeting mine.

"Greg!"

I smirked. "Now you can practice. I mean, sorta."

Annie looked over the small piano. "You bought me a Casio!"

"I really just wanted to hear Mendelssohn in a sweet '80s synth. I swear, my intentions were selfish."

She laughed. "Seriously, this is amazing. I can play with it in my lap."

"I know it only has half of the keys you need, but I figured it would give you something to do."

She flung herself at me as best she could from half under her covers and with a piano between us. "God, you're amazing."

"Please, hold your applause until the end." I handed her a flat, floppy package.

Her eyes were curious as she unwrapped it, and when she breathed my name, I felt like a king.

I'd do anything to make her happy. Anything.

She ran her fingers over the top page of the Victorian sheet music, the heading of Mendelssohn's *Songs Without Words* illustrated with a beautiful scene around the title.

"Where did you find this?"

"The internet. I found a lady in California who collects vintage sheet music. She didn't have the entire thing—I guess some weren't printed until later—but I took everything she had."

She was still looking through the pages, each song illustrated with a new image. "They're beautiful. I can't believe you did this."

"Really?"

With a laugh, she said, "No."

"Feel a little better?"

She sighed again, but this time, the sound was light and airy. "Much. How do you do that?"

I twiddled my fingers in the air. "Magic."

As she giggled, I reached for the book I'd brought, holding it up.

"If you want to be sad for a little longer, I brought Byron."

She brightened up and made to pick up the piano box. "Oh, will you read to me?"

"Of course." I took the box from her before she had the chance to lift it. "And then I think we should fool around a little."

"Hmm," she buzzed, her face sparking with devilry. "I think I could be persuaded."

"And then we'll go on our walk."

"Shuffle," she corrected.

I chuckled, climbing back under the covers. "Shuffle. And then the world is our oyster—"

"Shuck it!"

She nestled into my side, and I opened up Lord Byron, turned to *The Giaour*, and read her the long tale of the infidel who fell in love with a girl in a harem, drowned by her master when the affair was discovered. When the infidel professed his regret in the end of the poem—once exacting revenge, of course—Annie cried silent tears, tears from the girl who felt everything, those feelings vibrating through her like a tuning fork.

It was a wonder to behold.

I hoped I would behold it forever.

I kissed the cool track of tears, kissed the sweetness of her lips. Those lips opened up just as her heart had, granting me passage. Her body molded to mine, our legs twined and hips flush, breaths heavy and hands eager.

But I practiced restraint without second thought. I let Annie lead, gave her what I could without working her up even more than she already was. Hidden away in her bedroom with her heart still mending was the last place I wanted to take her, the last way I wanted her to experience the thing we both wanted so desperately.

I wanted every sigh. I wanted my skin against hers. I wanted to touch her.

Eventually, that time would come, and I'd wait for it patiently and gladly. Because the truth was that I loved her. I loved her, and someday, I would say those words written on my heart.

And in the meantime, I would show her with every action, every kiss, every touch that I was hers.

First & Last

ANNIE

A river of sound spilled from the piano at my fingertips as the Rachmaninoff sonata came to a close, echoing from the walls, filling the room with its ebb and flow until it drifted away, note by precious note.

I smiled and stood, bowed to the audition committee with wobbly knees as they thanked me for the hour-long performance, their faces unreadable though pleasant. I made my way down the line of them and shook their hands through a fog of adrenaline. And, having nothing to gather but myself, I left the audition room.

Greg jumped to his feet and swept me into his arms, spinning me around in the hallway. "God, Annie, that was beautiful."

I laughed and kissed him. When I pulled away, I gazed up into his adoring face. "Thank you."

"I couldn't tell if you messed up. It went too fast."

"I did but nothing major. I don't think it will crush my chances.

At least, I hope not. Anyone who could perform for that long and not mess up would have to be superhuman, and if they've got mutants at Juilliard, I'm probably better off elsewhere."

Greg hadn't let me go yet, and I stood there in the halls of Juilliard with his arms around me and mine around him.

"You did it."

I smiled. "I did it."

"You tired?"

"A little bit. But I've done nothing for the last week but practice the whole run-through. It's like training for a marathon but for my fingers."

"Are you still up for today?" There was trepidation in his voice, behind his eyes. He was giving me an out.

I smirked. "Why? Trying to back out on me?"

A little laugh puffed out of him. "Never in a million years. I just want to make sure you're ready," he added with sincerity.

"I'm ready," I answered without hesitation.

His hands moved from my waist to my cheeks, which he held with reverence as he kissed me gently, sweetly. "Then let's go."

He took my hand, and I followed him out. I'd follow him anywhere.

The sky was blue and cloudless and as high as my hope as we walked toward the park. My chin lifted, eyes up, admiring the shade of blue, and when I sighed, Greg pulled me closer.

"I'm trying to decide just what color the sky is," I said, slipping my arm around his waist with my gaze still up. "It's like Caribbean ocean on white sand or the color of rock candy. Or spun sugar, soft but ... *electric*, layers and layers of color so deep that it almost seems endless."

"I don't know how you do that, Annie."

"Do what?" I asked, meeting his eyes.

"Make the ordinary extraordinary."

My heart sang, my face angling for his. He took the signal, pressing a swift kiss to my lips.

"You live out loud," he said when we settled back into our pace. "It's just like your list says. Just like your dad would have wanted."

"I wish you could have met him."

"So do I," he said quietly.

"You would have been friends. He would have approved of you. He might have tried to scare the shit out of you first, but once you understood murder was on the table in exchange for my virtue and honor, you would have been thick as thieves."

Greg chuckled.

"Anyway, I think I'm going to retire my list."

"Oh?" The single-syllabled question was laden with curiosity.

"I started the list as a girl who wanted to start over, move on, live a life that was full of intention, and I am. Its purpose is fulfilled. In fact, I think its purpose was to lead me to you."

He pulled me to a stop on the sidewalk, his eyes bright with love and adoration, his heart shining behind them as he held my face as he so often did, as if I were precious and fragile and priceless. And when he kissed me, I knew he loved me. The words had never been uttered, but I knew it all the same.

Once I was safely tucked under his arm again, we headed into the park. I didn't have to stop once to rest, never had to catch my breath, didn't break out into a sweat or need to down a gallon of water. That was still a marvelous thing in itself.

Over the last week, I'd felt so good that Greg and I had even gone for a jog just to see if I could.

I could. I also discovered that running was the actual worst and vowed never to do it again unless someone was after me with a weapon.

But through it all, through good days and bad, Greg was there with warm hands and deep eyes and lips that I needed and wanted and dreamed of.

Today was a day to celebrate, and we had big plans.

A wild, late season flurry had dropped nearly two inches of snow the day before, blanketing the city in a colorless layer of magic. Of course, today it was a sooty, filthy shade of slate, pushed off to the gutters and clinging to the feet of the buildings. But the park was untouched by a thousand boots and tires and exhaust pipes.

In the park, that sparkling magic remained, so in we went, looking for a knoll where we could build a snowman. Greg had even brought charcoal briquettes, a moth-eaten old scarf for his neck, and a carrot for his nose. It didn't even matter that he was a little lopsided and his middle briquette button wouldn't stay on. He was one of the most perfect things I'd ever seen.

We took two selfies with my little camera, our snowman, Kevin, photobombing us like the joker he was, and the second our pictures were safely stowed, Greg chased me, pelting me with snowballs while I squealed, scrambling for handfuls of snow that I threw blindly behind me, my feet slipping around like a baby deer until I fell.

I rolled over onto my back, laughing so hard, I could barely breathe. When Greg tried to help me up, I pulled with all my weight, and he tumbled down on top of me, the two of us laughing until we were kissing, kissing until we didn't feel the cold at all. And all the while, my heart thumped like a ticking clock, steady and reliable and sound.

I'd already grown used to the normalcy even though I'd never known it. The affliction I'd known all my life had all but disappeared, and more than anything, I found myself awed by the real understanding of how everyone else lived.

To Greg's we went so he could change into his suit and get his bag, and by cab, we made it to the apartment where my family was waiting to hear the recount of the audition. And when I changed and packed a bag of my own for our vaguely named *overnight trip*, my family caravanned all the way down to Delmonico's for dinner.

The building was a striking brick wedge that filled the triangular space of a split street, the entrance to the restaurant at the juncture. The inside was just as incredible, rich and decadent, with dark wood–paneled walls and deep colors that gave it a very old-boys'-club feel. And though I was destined to a life of eating well for my heart's sake, I cheated and ate a filet mignon that melted in my mouth in a way that I'd had no idea meat was capable of.

My family was happy, I was happy, and Greg was at my side, smiling. Nothing could have been more perfect.

A few hours later, Greg and I were in a cab, headed into Midtown, snug and warm and quiet, my body curved into his, his hand on my thigh, my head resting in the crook of his neck. We never stopped touching, not in the cab, not through dinner, his hands and my hands twined together, fingers shifting, hearts thrumming the same note like they ran on their own frequency. And every time our eyes met, it was accompanied by a spark of anticipation.

Because tonight was another night of firsts.

When the car came to a stop at the curb of The Plaza, I was caught in a rush of sights that overcame all other thought.

Crimson carpet lined the steps under the wide awning, soft and plush under my heels as we entered the building. The lobby was lovely, the floor a mosaic laid to look like a Persian rug, with a magnificent chandelier hanging over the center of the room. Tourists snapped photos, milling around and gaping like I was, but Greg and I didn't stop for long.

We checked in at the front desk, our eyes meeting and agreeing silently that we didn't belong, sharing a note of worry that they'd figure it out and boot us back through those gleaming brass doors and onto the sidewalk. Instead, they handed him keys and offered a smile, directing us to the elevators, and away we went, smiling like we'd gotten away with something.

Every detail spoke of another era, another time, from the caged elevators to the frescos on the walls. And down the hall we walked, hand in hand, to our room.

It was as rich and lovely as the rest of the hotel, dominated by the bed, which was piled up with pillows and framed by an elegant gilded headboard.

Greg set our bags next to the dresser and turned to me, his eyes touching on my face with desire and restraint, with devotion and reticence. And for a moment, he didn't move other than the rise and fall of the broad expanse of his chest as he drank me in.

But the weight of his gaze didn't calm my mind, which was three steps ahead of where it should be. The stillness sent uncertainty trickling through me, the quiet moment before we began, the anticipation cold and heavy and distant, as it was consuming, waiting for the starting bell with every nerve on alert.

Knowing me as he did, he recognized the tightening of my nerves from across the room. My mind's train had run away, and the smile he offered pulled the brakes with the skill and ease only he possessed.

His long legs paced him into my space, where I always wanted him, and the moment he was close enough, he brought his fingers to my jaw, tracing it with a feather's touch.

"Are you afraid?" he asked simply, honestly.

"No," I answered with the same regard. "I just don't know what to do." The words slipped into a whisper.

His eyes, touched with protection and longing, looked into mine and saw all of me, to the depths of my soul. "Are you sure you're ready? Because I'm in no hurry. I'd wait forever for you, Annie."

I knew that to be an absolute truth.

Nerves flitted around the cage of my ribs, landing, then taking flight, then landing again as I took a breath and spoke the words I'd rehearsed for so long.

"I want this first to be ours, just as I want the rest of my firsts to be ours. I know…I know that I'm young, and even though I don't know much about love, I know what it *is* at its very center. Love gives itself without condition or expectation simply because it must. Love is devotion, and I find myself devoted to you, body and soul. I love you. As little as I know, that is the thing I am most certain of."

Exaltation shone from him like the sun. "I've loved you since the start," he whispered. "I've almost told you a thousand times."

"And a thousand times, you did without speaking. So know that I'm not afraid, and I am exactly where I want to be. Is it too much to hope that you'll be my very last first?"

"No, Annie." His voice was soft and rough. "No, it's not."

He brought his lips to mine, the absolute rightness of him overwhelming me, drawing me into him.

He collected me in his arms, holding my body against his own as he kissed me deep, deeper still. And with every shared breath, every sweep of his tongue against mine, with every beat of my heart against his, the bond that twisted through us wound tighter until one was indistinguishable from the other.

I broke away, my heart drumming madly astride his as our eyes closed and foreheads bowed until they touched. And after a moment of reverie, I took an unwavering step back and turned, collecting my hair with trembling hands to expose my zipper.

His fingers—they trembled too, a sweet tremor of awe and affection—touched the fastener and pulled, the sound sending a jolt of heat through me, the feel of his breath between my shoulder blades and his lips against my skin settling that heat deep and low in my belly. His hands brushed my shoulders, pushing the dress over the curves and down to the ground in a whisper.

I stepped out of my heels and dress at once, left in nothing but a small swath of black lace around my hips. A single moment of fear tripped my heart with a lurch. But I drew myself tall, stretching the length of my spine until it was straight and sure, felt the fear disappear as faith took its place. And then I turned to face him.

What I found when I looked upon him was a bottomless expression of ardent worship, the expression of a man who saw the sun breaking the horizon after a lifetime of blindness. His hand seemed to move of its own accord to capture the ends of my hair in his fingers, rolling the strands between his fingertips, as if they were fine silk.

Those same fingertips moved to the welted scar between my breasts, reverential and possessive, sparking memories and wishes and desires in the wake of his blazing touch. And, when he reached the bottom of that puckered red line, he brushed the curve of my breast with the backs of his fingers so delicately, a chill rushed across my hot skin, peaking my nipple with anticipation.

He spoke, a gravelly rumble. "I will never know greater fortune than having you for my own. Not as long as I live."

And as if to seal that vow, he brought his lips to mine with deep emotion, with a hundred things said and unsaid passing between truthful lips.

My blind hands removed his jacket, my fingers working the knot at his neck, then the buttons of his shirt, then slipping into the warm space between his shirt and his skin, relishing in the heat of his solid chest against my palms, the feel of his heart beating as wildly as mine.

He backed me toward the bed, pulling off his shirt when I sat on the edge with my lips waiting, my arms open. His pants were gone in a second along with his shoes and socks, leaving him in nothing but a sheath of black jersey that brought my eyes first to the span of his narrow waist, then to the rigid column of his length, then to the tops of his thighs where the tight fabric clung to the thick cords of muscles.

But my eyes wanted more, wanted him exposed as I wanted to be exposed. I wanted to give him every soft, vulnerable part of me. And he saw the offering and filled my arms to claim it, laying me down, pressing me into the luxurious bed with his body.

Of all the times we had kissed in my room, of all the times we had brushed the edge of desire, never had we erased the boundary so resolutely. He'd touched me before but never like this. I'd felt the length of him against me, but never had I been able to relish in the strength of it or the heat of my need, heat that pooled low in my belly. Heat that spawned tendrils of steam, curling down with slow fingers to lick at the aching tip of my desire.

My hips rolled, seeking connection, seeking pressure, seeking *him*.

He listened to the hum of my body, knowing what I wished for. And so, down my body his lips moved and across my jaw, down the length of my outstretched neck, brushing my collarbone in a soft, wet trail, climbing down me as he went, settling his torso between my thighs, opening them up to accommodate the breadth of his chest.

His lips took their time when they reached my breasts, and he took his pleasure there, the swell in his big palm, his hot mouth over my tight nipple. And with every sweep of his tongue, with every gentle graze of his teeth, with every quiet moan of appreciation, a shock of fire rushed to my core, fanning the flames he'd already built.

I had no idea what I wanted or needed, but my body knew, and Greg knew, and neither of them needed me to think, which was fortunate for all of us.

His mouth vanished, leaving my slick nipple pulling almost painfully taut, the warmth of his lips gone. But he had another purpose, one that called those lips over the curves of my stomach, one that had his fingers hooked in the band of lace at my waist to rid us both of its obstruction.

I lay in the bed, my chest heaving and lips swollen, my eyes on his hands as he slid the black lace down my thighs; my skin tingled in its wake, a ghost trail of his touch. His eyes met mine for a moment, as if asking permission again, and I whispered a plea that seemed to fill him with single-minded purpose, which he applied at the place where my thighs met.

Under my legs he went, his hands guiding my thighs to rest on the rippling muscles of his shoulders. I watched him with a thundering heart and an emptiness between my legs that I'd never felt before, but his eyes were on the warm, waiting juncture at his fingertips.

It was a slow exploration of a part of my body I barely knew; he touched it with unhesitating gentleness, spreading me open with his fingers, slicking them with my heat, touching the silky point of my body that every nerve ending reached for.

A gasp filled my lungs, sharp and burning, my hips flexing involuntarily.

But nothing could have prepared me for the moment he closed his velvety lips over me and sucked.

My back snapped off the bed, my neck stretched in an arch and my chin pointed at the ceiling, the contact so pervasive, so encompassing that I found myself lost completely. My body was no longer mine; it belonged to him, to his fingers buried in the flexing center of me, to his lips and his stroking tongue, to his heart that loved me and to his soul that whispered my name.

And I called his as the trembling heat thundered through me, uncontrolled and all-consuming. He gave me the pressure I craved with his glorious mouth, his face nestled between my legs, brows drawn with intent, with benediction and quiet worship.

The sight of him was too much to bear, every sense flaring at once, white-hot and blinding as my body found release, kneading his fingers, drawing him into me. My lungs pulled in a breath so deep, it singed my ribs, burned with my heart, burned with the pulsing center of me. I burned for him.

His lips slowed as I found my way back to my body, testing first my fingers as my breasts heaved, then my neck as I turned my face and tried to open my eyes. Up my languid torso he moved, kissing a trail toward my breasts. But rather than settling back on top of me—even now in my sated state, I wanted to feel the weight of him against me—he lay at my side, pulled me into his arms, and brought his lips to mine.

The tang of my body on his lips sent an echoing pulse of my waning orgasm through me. And when he pulled away, his lids were heavy, his eyes hot as coals, his smile warm with love.

"Are you all right?" he asked, cupping my cheek like he was checking me for injury.

My brow quirked with confusion. "Is that a real question?" I asked back, my voice smoky and satisfied and amused.

Greg chuckled, taking that for the yes that it was, and kissed me again.

"I don't know how I can top that," I said, curling into his chest, the self-consciousness of the next step, the *real* step, finding its way into my voice.

His smile immediately soothed me. "Right now, you don't need to know anything, except that I love you."

"I love you, too," I whispered before kissing him.

I kissed him with thanks and adoration, my hands on his chest and his on my bare hip. But down my fingers roamed, across the curves and ripples of his chest and abs, to the waistband and under, to the inflexible, unsatisfied length of him. My fingertips curiously marveled at the simultaneous stony hardness and decadent silkiness of him, relishing in the feel of him in my palm, the weight of him in my hand. I touched him gently, exploring the ridge underneath his crown and the wet slit at the tip, not knowing any other way, only thinking that, if it felt good to me, it would feel good to him too. His pumping hips told me I was right.

I tugged at the band, wanting to free him, wanting nothing left between us. The heat I thought I'd expended at the mercy of his mouth seemed to build again, starting in my heart and slipping down through me like a smoky fog.

He helped me slide his remaining clothes away, and our bodies came together—the heat of his chest against my breasts, the feel of his strong thigh slipping between mine, the length of him pressed to my flesh. And that need caught fire in both of us.

In a breath, I was under him, that glorious weight of him caging me, pinning me, leaving me unable to move and with no desire to. The kiss went unbroken as he spread my thighs with his legs, pressed his hips to mine, the length of his shaft shifting against my center, awake and tender and restless again. My body angled for him, my hips shifting and arching, the hollow in me aching to be filled by him. And he relinquished restraint, breaching me with only the very tip of his crown.

He broke the kiss, held my face, whispered my name, and I whispered his.

And when he flexed his hips, I was forever changed.

The pain was different than I could have possibly imagined, a breathtaking sting that drew on and on, a searing stretching of my body to make room for him. He edged into me, kissing my quivering lips, slowly gaining ground before pulling out again. His trembling arms bracketed my head, his fingers in my hair, but my mind was occupied solely with the point where our bodies connected.

He rolled his hips to press deeper, deeper still, and then he was fitted so completely inside of me, there was no space for anything but him. Not in my body, not in my heart.

For a moment, we breathed, a ragged drawing of air through parted lips, our eyes tethered together, using that thrumming line of connection to transmit all that we felt, those things for which there were no words.

Another flex of his hips, and the pain was less by miles, the utter bliss at the feeling of holding his length inside of me, of being filled by him so entirely, set my pulse hurtling. Again and again, first slow, cautious and gentle, but as my body relaxed under him, moved with him, opened up to him, his pace quickened. And with every thrust, each more demanding than before, his body tightened. His arms around me. His fingers in my hair. His sinewy neck and wide shoulders. His flexing ass. His straining cock in the sheath of my body. And I urged him with my hips and hands and lips to let go.

With a gasp and a grunt so deeply satisfying, my core flexed around him, he came, shuddering with exertion from holding back the urge to slam into me like I knew he wanted to, his fingers making deep divots in my hip.

He collapsed on top of me, burying his face in my neck, his breath fast and loud, the length of him still throbbing inside me.

I held him like that until our heartbeats matched, my fingers skating circles across his back, my cheek pressed against his ear.

He slipped his arms underneath me, and mine locked around his neck, bringing us as close together as two people could get. Twin tears slipped from my eyes.

Greg rolled us over, pulling out of me gently. The tears standing in his eyes as he touched my face shocked me in their rightness and truth.

"Tell me once more that you love me, Annie, and I'll never want for another thing in life."

"I love you," I whispered.

And the kiss he bestowed on me sealed the promise of those three little words.

Hours later, after a long, hot bath together, we lay awake in the dark, talking about nothing and everything, talking of the future and the past, of the moon and the stars and our place in the constellations. And I knew without a single doubt that we would have more perfect nights such as this, just as I knew that not all nights would be perfect.

But I had a feeling they'd be pretty close.

Epilogue

ANNIE

T he lights were turned down just enough in my uncle's penthouse, the hum of conversation hanging in the air of the room, punctuated by the occasional laughter.

Uncle John had decided to throw the cocktail party the minute I received my acceptance letter to Juilliard, and immediately following, Susan had thrown herself into planning.

I barely knew anyone on the guest list, but the invitation had also been extended to my friends at Wasted Words. They'd all shown up. Tyler and Cam stood near Rose and her boyfriend, Patrick. And Ruby, Harrison, Beau, Jett, and a few others were clustered near the windows overlooking Central Park.

It was overwhelming and humbling to have so many people had there to celebrate me, offering their congratulations and well wishes. Even Fanny had offered words of kindness, though nothing about her tone could have been considered warmhearted or affectionate.

My eyes wandered to Elle where she stood across from Ward, just outside of the crowd. The air between them was charged, but their faces betrayed little—until he said something that sent a flash of emotion through her, gone as soon as it had appeared.

She spoke again and walked away, leaving him watching after her.

I moved in her direction, reaching for her hand the moment I was able to. "Are you all right?"

She offered a smile that would have fooled anyone but me. "I'm fine."

Fine—the greatest lie ever told.

Before I could press her for more, Susan appeared at my elbow.

"Oh, Annie." She beamed, pulling me in for a hug. "I am just so *proud* of you. I hate that word, the implication that I did anything to earn the right to feel pride for your achievement, but it's the best I can do. I'm so happy for you, I could just fly away."

I leaned into her, breathed her in, letting the peace I'd found in my life settle into my heart. "Thank you, Susan."

She squeezed once and let me go, her eyes teeming with tears. "You're so very welcome. Are you girls having fun?"

"It's been incredible," I said with a smile I felt in my bones. "The food, the company—all of it. I can't thank you enough for putting this together for me."

"Well, we had to celebrate. Everyone wanted to come and wish you well." She leaned in, glancing around. "Even your grandparents."

A little shock shot down my back, and Elle and I exchanged a look.

"They didn't," I said.

"They did, but John refused. This isn't the time or place. I don't know when there ever *will* be a time or place."

Elle's face held worry. "I think we're going to have to deal with them at some point."

The three of us glanced at Mama, who was laughing at something

Meg had said.

"But how?" I asked, knowing there was no answer.

Movement caught my eye, and I looked toward the bar to find my uncle leaning in to speak to Greg. With a nod, Greg picked up a flute of champagne and turned to meet my eyes, smiling.

That smile lit me up like a campfire, warm and crackling and comforting.

Uncle John picked up a champagne flute of his own and pinged the glass to get everyone's attention.

When Greg reached me, he pressed a kiss to my flaming cheek, placing the champagne in my hand just as John began to speak.

"There are few things in this world so uplifting as art. Music, in particular, has been a joy of mine, even back to the days when my sister, Emily, and I made our loved ones suffer concerts wherein we butchered such greats as Joni Mitchell and Bob Dylan."

A chuckle rolled through the room.

"But Annie possesses a talent for music that her mother and I never did. And after hearing her play, as we did earlier tonight, I think we can all understand why Juilliard would have been mad not to want her."

A few people called, *Hear, hear!*

"And so, tonight, we celebrate Annie. Tonight, we wish her luck, though her talent stands on its own. We drink to her success, knowing it is at her fingertips. We raise our glasses and congratulate her with all of our encouragement behind her." He raised his glass and met my eyes. "Here's to you, Annie, and to the joy your music brings to the world. May it bring you the happiness that you bring to each and every one of us."

The sting of my nose and the tears in my eyes accompanied my smile as we all raised our glasses, and the room turned to me with cheers on their lips to precede the champagne.

Greg stayed by my side as a line of people made their way over to shake my hand and speak with me. And when the crowd ebbed, he took my hand and stole me away, pulling me into the music room.

The lights had been dimmed, the noise of the party far away. The moment we were in the room, he pulled me into him for a kiss.

His lips transcribed the words of his heart, telling me how much he loved me and how proud he was of my success, of my future. And I told him without speaking, through my own lips and the tips of my fingers on his face, that I wanted nothing more in the world than him.

When he broke away, I was breathless and smiling, caught happily in his arms.

He smiled back. "How do you feel?"

I didn't even have to consider my answer. "Like I could do anything. Like all possibilities are mine for the taking. Like my whole future is laid out in front of me, and I'm about to step into it."

"You can, and you will."

"And I'll step into it with you."

He looked into my eyes, his smile shifting, coloring his face with adoration and reverence. "I'll be here as long as you'll have me, as long as you love me."

"Forever, then?" I asked quietly.

He pulled me closer. "If I'm lucky."

"Oh," I said with a smile, "luck has nothing to do with it."

And the dizzying depth of his kiss served to secure his everlasting place at the very top of my list.

Acknowledgments

As always, I have so many people to thank.

Jeff — Once again, you have shown up to save the day in every small way and every big one. You silently take care of everything in our lives to ease the burden on me so I can do this thing I love so much. And it's just one of the many reasons I love you.

Kandi Steiner — Every day, you save me. Every day, you inspire me. Every day, you love me, and that love makes me stronger. Thank you for always being there. #MTT

Ace Gray — This book wouldn't be what it is without you. Your constant good cheer and positivity motivated me every single day, and your willingness and gladness in shouldering my incessant obsessing over the details of each scene deserves a medal. I can't tell you how much I appreciate you and how much you mean to me because there aren't words, so I'll just say thank you. Know it's from the very bottom of my heart.

Lori Riggs — My life twin, I am so happy to have you back. Thank you for your brain, your love, your advice, your time. Your photographic memory of the Austen works will never cease to amaze me. I love you.

Kyla Linde — Every single morning, I look forward to you. I am so honored to have a friend as giving and driven as you are, and I am so grateful to have found you. Our friendship means so much to me, and every time we speak, I find new purpose and hope. Thank you, thank you, thank you.

Tina Lynne — Your support has changed my life and my career for the better. Thank you for everything you do for me. Thank you for the hours spent at Onze plotting and obsessing and beating my story until it submitted. Thank you for your joy, your love, your giving nature, your smile—all those things make my life so much fuller.

Karla Sorensen — Even when you're "not helping", you always help me, because being friends with you makes me a better person just by influence alone. Thank you for your help, for reading for me, for putting up with me. You're a saint. An evil, whip-wielding saint. And I love you.

To Lauren Perry — Once again, you have outdone yourself. The photoshoot is brilliant and beautiful and perfect. Please never leave me!

To Jenn Watson, Sarah Ferguson, and the team at Social Butterfly PR — Thank you for your constant support with my releases, for organizing all the chaos, for guiding me through this and every release. Your help over the years has changed the path of my career, and I will forever be grateful.

To Megan Bandfield — Thank you for the time spent answering all of my medical questions! It was such a relief to have a resource who could help me pin down the details, and I can't thank you enough.

To the Ebstein's anomaly group, and to Crystal — Thank you for sharing your experiences with me, for letting me bother you with the millions of questions I had, for supporting me in writing a story about a girl afflicted by a condition that has brought so many of you pain and fear and worry. Your help was invaluable.

To my beta readers — You are all incredible. Thank you for the hours you spent reading, putting together notes, answering my questions, and even re-reading for me when I ripped it all down and put it back together again. Thank you, thank you, thank you.

To my readers — I wouldn't be here if it wasn't for you all. Thank you for your love and support—it's what keeps me going.

About Staci

Staci has been a lot of things up to this point in her life: a graphic designer, an entrepreneur, a seamstress, a clothing and handbag designer, a waitress. Can't forget that. She's also been a mom to three little girls who are sure to grow up to break a number of hearts. She's been a wife, even though she's certainly not the cleanest, or the best cook. She's also super, duper fun at a party, especially if she's been drinking whiskey, and her favorite word starts with f, ends with k.

From roots in Houston, to a seven year stint in Southern California, Staci and her family ended up settling somewhere in between and equally north, in Denver. They are new enough that snow is still magical. When she's not writing, she's gaming, cleaning, or designing graphics.

Made in the USA
Middletown, DE
16 August 2020